Author Chronologies

General Editor: **Norman Page**, Emeritus Professor of Modern English Literature, University of Nottingham, UK

Published titles include:

William Baker
A WILKIE COLLINS CHRONOLOGY
A HAROLD PINTER CHRONOLOGY

J. L. Bradley
A RUSKIN CHRONOLOGY

Michael G. Brennan and Noel J. Kinnamon
A SIDNEY CHRONOLOGY 1554–1654

Gordon Campbell
A MILTON CHRONOLOGY

Alison Chapman and Joanna Meacock
A ROSSETTI FAMILY CHRONOLOGY

Edward Chitham
A BRONTË FAMILY CHRONOLOGY

Martin Garrett
A BROWNING CHRONOLOGY
ELIZABETH BARRETT BROWNING AND ROBERT BROWNING
A MARY SHELLEY CHRONOLOGY

A. M. Gibbs
A BERNARD SHAW CHRONOLOGY

Graham Handley
AN ELIZABETH GASKELL CHRONOLOGY

J. R. Hammond
A ROBERT LOUIS STEVENSON CHRONOLOGY
AN EDGAR ALLAN POE CHRONOLOGY
AN H. G. WELLS CHRONOLOGY
A GEORGE ORWELL CHRONOLOGY

Edgar F. Harden
A WILLIAM MAKEPEACE THACKERAY CHRONOLOGY
A HENRY JAMES CHRONOLOGY
AN EDITH WHARTON CHRONOLOGY

Lisa Hopkins
A CHRISTOPHER MARLOWE CHRONOLOGY

John Kelly
A W. B. YEATS CHRONOLOGY

Owen Knowles
A CONRAD CHRONOLOGY, SECOND EDITION

Nicholas Maltzahn
AN ANDREW MARVELL CHRONOLOGY

John McDermott
A HOPKINS CHRONOLOGY

Roger Norburn
A JAMES JOYCE CHRONOLOGY
A KATHERINE MANSFIELD CHRONOLOGY

Norman Page
AN EVELYN WAUGH CHRONOLOGY
AN OSCAR WILDE CHRONOLOGY

John Pilling
A SAMUEL BECKETT CHRONOLOGY

Peter Preston
A D. H. LAWRENCE CHRONOLOGY

Author Chronologies
Series Standing Order ISBN 978–0–333–71484–3 hardback
(outside North America only)

You can receive future titles in this series as they are published by placing a standing order. Please contact your bookseller or, in case of difficulty, write to us at the address below with your name and address, the title of the series and the ISBN quoted above.

Customer Services Department, Macmillan Distribution Ltd, Houndmills, Basingstoke, Hampshire RG21 6XS, England, UK

A Romantics Chronology, 1780–1832

Martin Garrett

palgrave
macmillan

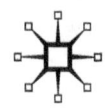

© Martin Garrett 2016

All rights reserved. No reproduction, copy or transmission of this publication may be made without written permission.

No portion of this publication may be reproduced, copied or transmitted save with written permission or in accordance with the provisions of the Copyright, Designs and Patents Act 1988, or under the terms of any licence permitting limited copying issued by the Copyright Licensing Agency, Saffron House, 6–10 Kirby Street, London EC1N 8TS.

Any person who does any unauthorized act in relation to this publication may be liable to criminal prosecution and civil claims for damages.

The author has asserted his right to be identified as the author of this work in accordance with the Copyright, Designs and Patents Act 1988.

First published 2016 by
PALGRAVE MACMILLAN

Palgrave Macmillan in the UK is an imprint of Macmillan Publishers Limited, registered in England, company number 785998, of Houndmills, Basingstoke, Hampshire RG21 6XS.

Palgrave Macmillan in the US is a division of St Martin's Press LLC, 175 Fifth Avenue, New York, NY 10010.

Palgrave Macmillan is the global academic imprint of the above companies and has companies and representatives throughout the world.

Palgrave® and Macmillan® are registered trademarks in the United States, the United Kingdom, Europe and other countries.

ISBN 978–1–137–27326–0

This book is printed on paper suitable for recycling and made from fully managed and sustained forest sources. Logging, pulping and manufacturing processes are expected to conform to the environmental regulations of the country of origin.

A catalogue record for this book is available from the British Library.

A catalog record for this book is available from the Library of Congress.

Typeset by MPS Limited, Chennai, India.

Contents

Preface	vi
General Editor's Preface	viii
Chronology	1
Sources	254
Author/Name Index	257
Title Index	278
Subject Index	314

Preface

Between 2 and 9 May 1814 the annual Royal Academy exhibition opened, Louis XVIII arrived in Paris and Napoleon on Elba, Mary Wollstonecraft Godwin met Percy Bysshe Shelley for either the first or the second time, Byron saw Kean as Iago at Drury Lane, and *Mansfield Park* was published. One of the main purposes of a chronology is to reveal juxtapositions, connections, possible links. It cannot, given the immense amount of material available for the years 1780–1832, be very detailed. But it should, I hope, provide readers with some leads to pursue.

The choice of opening and closing date is inevitably somewhat arbitrary, but in the early 1780s writers including Crabbe, Wollstonecraft and Burns are active, and in 1832 Scott and Goethe die and the Reform Act passes into law. At the beginning such representatives of an older generation as Samuel Johnson are still writing, and in the late 1820s and early 1830s many people usually thought of as Victorians are starting their careers. In 1832 Elizabeth Barrett is twenty-six, Alfred Tennyson twenty-three, Charles Dickens twenty.

The chronology focuses in particular detail on the life and works of Austen, Blake, Burns, Byron, Coleridge, Hazlitt, Hemans, Keats, Charles and Mary Lamb, Landon, Scott, Mary and Percy Bysshe Shelley, Turner, Wollstonecraft and William and Dorothy Wordsworth. Beyond this group there are varying levels of coverage of other writers, painters, dramatists, actors and composers of the period in Britain, and of relevant political, religious, military, scientific and industrial developments. Material from other countries is included either where it has special bearing on Britain or where it illustrates the more general climate of the time: what, sometimes surprisingly, coincides with what. For both these reasons there is a fair amount on the French Revolution, the Napoleonic wars, and German and French Romanticism. Perceived Romanticism is not a necessary qualification for inclusion. Different spheres and ideas overlap, integrate or collide, and figures traditionally seen as non- or anti-Romantic (Austen, for instance) may of course be influenced by or influence those who are normally considered Romantic.

The format is simple. Events that can be assigned to a particular day are followed, at the end of the month, by material datable only by month rather than day. Some events and publications are gathered, similarly, at the end of the relevant year. Sometimes a sequence of events or of responses – journeys, reactions to Waterloo and Peterloo – are collected together rather than listed strictly chronologically.

People's full names and dates are given when they are first mentioned. Usually first name or initials as well as surname continue in use where there are two or more people with the same surname, for instance Sir Joshua and John Hamilton Reynolds, John Constable the painter and Archibald Constable the publisher. There are occasional exceptions to this rule: for example it seems unnecessary, in the light of just a few occurrences of John Scott of *The London Magazine*, always to use Sir Walter Scott's full name.

MARTIN GARRETT

General Editor's Preface

Most biographies are ill-adapted to serve as works of reference – not surprisingly so, since the biographer is likely to regard his function as the devising of a continuous and readable narrative, with excursions into interpretation and speculation, rather than a bald recital of facts. There are times, however, when anyone reading for business or pleasure needs to check a point quickly or to obtain a rapid overview of part of an author's life or career; and at such moments turning over the pages of a biography can be a time-consuming and frustrating occupation. The present series of volumes aims at providing a means whereby the chronological facts of an author's life and career, rather than needing to be prised out of the narrative in which they are (if they appear at all) securely embedded, can be seen at a glance. Moreover, whereas biographies are often, and quite understandably, vague over matters of fact (since it makes for tediousness to be forever enumerating details of dates and places), a chronology can be precise whenever it is possible to be precise.

Thanks to the survival, sometimes in very large quantities, of letters, diaries, notebooks and other documents, as well as to thoroughly researched biographies and bibliographies, this material now exists in abundance for many major authors. In the case of, for example, Dickens, we can often ascertain what he was doing in each month and week, and almost on each day, of his prodigiously active working life; and the student of, say, *David Copperfield* is likely to find it fascinating as well as useful to know just when Dickens was at work on each part of that novel, what other literary enterprises he was engaged in at the same time, whom he was meeting, what places he was visiting, and what were the relevant circumstances of his personal and professional life. Such a chronology is not, of course, a substitute for a biography; but its arrangement, in combination with its index, makes it a much more convenient tool for this kind of purpose; and it may be acceptable as a form of 'alternative' biography, with its own distinctive advantages as well as its obvious limitations.

Information not readily assignable to a specific month or day is given as a general note under the relevant year or month. Each volume also contains a bibliography of the principal sources of information. In the chronology itself, the sources of many of the more specific items, including quotations, are identified in order that the reader who wishes to do so may consult the original contexts.

NORMAN PAGE

Chronology

1780

January
22 Antonio Canova (1757–1822) sets off to see Naples, Pompeii, Herculaneum and Paestum. In December he returns to Rome, where he spends much of his career.

February
22 *The Belle's Stratagem* by Hannah Cowley (1743–1809) opens at the Theatre Royal, Covent Garden.

April
Late this month George Crabbe (1754–1832) comes to London, moving into lodgings on 24.

27 Marie-Joseph du Motier, Marquis de Lafayette (1757–1834), arrives in Boston as part of the French expedition to aid the rebels in the American War of Independence or Revolution, which began in 1775. He leaves for France on 23 December 1781.
Foundation, by John Cartwright (1740–1824) and others, of the Society for Constitutional Information. This year Cartwright publishes *The Legislative Rights*, expanding *Take Your Choice!* (1778).

May
12 British forces capture Charleston. They hold it until 13 December 1782.
31 Last performance at the Theatre Royal, Drury Lane, by Mary Robinson (1758–1800), famous as 'Perdita' since playing this role in *The Winter's Tale* in 1779. Between June and December she is the lover of George, Prince of Wales (1762–1830; later George IV); on 5 September 1781 she accepts £5,000 and a pension for returning the Prince's letters. At the height of fashion and notoriety, she is painted in 1781–2 by Sir Joshua Reynolds (1723–92), Thomas Gainsborough (1727–88) and George Romney (1734–1802).

June
2 Lord George Gordon (1751–93) presents a petition, with 45,000 signatures, against the Catholic Relief Act of 1778. An immense

crowd accompanies him to the House of Commons; the anti-Catholic 'Gordon riots' continue until 8. About 700 people are killed and much damage is done to property. About thirty rioters are executed and many more are transported or sent as soldiers to Africa. According to Alexander Gilchrist's 1863 *Life of William Blake*, William Blake (1757–1827) is among the rioters. Crabbe witnesses the burning of Newgate on 7. *A Plain and Succinct Narrative* ... by Thomas Holcroft (1745–1809) is published soon after the events. Gordon is charged with treason and acquitted in February 1781.

19 William Beckford (1760–1844) sets off on his Grand Tour, travelling via the Netherlands and Germany to Venice, which he reaches in August. He proceeds to Lucca (16 September), Florence (October), Rome (29 October) and Naples, where he stays in November and early December with his cousin Sir William Hamilton (1731–1803), British Envoy Extraordinary since 1764. Beckford returns to Venice in December and stays in Paris before arriving in England on 14 April 1781.

July
John Nichols publishes, at the author's expense, Crabbe's *The Candidate: a Poetical Epistle to the Authors of the Monthly Review*.

August
5   *The Chapter of Accidents* by Sophia Lee (1750–1824) opens at the Haymarket Theatre.
29 Birth of Jean-Auguste-Dominique Ingres (1780–1867) at Montauban.

September
About now William Blake, Thomas Stothard (1755–1834) and several fellow artists, sketching by the River Medway, are detained for some time as suspected spies.
11 William Wilberforce (1759–1833) is elected MP for Hull.
12 Richard Brinsley Sheridan (1751–1816) is elected MP for Stafford.
25 Birth in Dublin of Charles Robert Maturin (1780–1824).

November

11   First meeting of Tarbolton Bachelors' Club, established by Robert Burns (1759–96) and his brother Gilbert (1760–1827).
29   Empress Maria Theresia of Austria dies. Her son Joseph II, Holy Roman Emperor since 1765, now becomes ruler of the Habsburg lands until his death in 1790.

December

14   Death in London of Charles Ignatius Sancho (1729?–80). *Letters of the Late Ignatius Sancho, an African* is published in 1782.
26   Mary Fairfax, later Mary Somerville (1780–1872) is born in Jedburgh.
29   First performance of the pantomime *Harlequin Freemason*, by Charles Dibdin (1745–1814), at Covent Garden. It plays 52 times this season.

Sophia Lee and her sisters Charlotte (c.1748–?) and Harriet (1757/8–1851) found their school in Bath, which continues until 1803.

Joseph Priestley (1733–1804), who moved to Birmingham a few months ago, agrees to become senior minister of the Unitarian New Meeting.

1781

January

1   Official opening of the Iron Bridge, built by Abraham Darby III (1750–91), near Coalbrookdale in Shropshire. Ironbridge develops by the bridge.
29   First performance of Wolfgang Amadeus Mozart's (1756–91) opera *Idomeneo, re di Creta*, in Munich.

Early in the year Nourse publishes the sixth and seventh volumes of *The History of England* by Catharine Macaulay (1731–91). The eighth and final volume comes out early in 1783.

February

13   Philippe Jacques de Loutherbourg (1740–1812) is elected to the Royal Academy. On 26 his spectacular 'Eidophusikon, or Representation of Nature', opens at his house off Leicester

Square. The first season runs until May, the second from December this year to May 1782. It re-opens at Exeter Change at the end of January 1786.
15 Death of Gotthold Ephraim Lessing (1729–81).
28 Foundation of the Literary and Philosophical Society of Manchester.

Thomas Paine (1737–1809), who has lived in America since 1774 and been actively engaged in the Revolution, is a member of a fundraising mission to Paris, returning to America in August. His *Letter to the Abbé Raynal, on the Affairs of North America*, appears in 1782.

March
1 Publication, by Strahan and by Cadell, of volumes two and three of Edward Gibbon's (1737–94) *History of the Decline and Fall of the Roman Empire*.
6 Erasmus Darwin (1731–1802) marries his second wife, Elizabeth Chandos Pole (1747–1832). Following a visit to London they settle, in May, at Radburn Hall near Derby. Darwin practises medicine in the city, as in Lichfield since 1756. In 1783 the family moves into Derby. Darwin remains in contact with other members of the Lunar Society of Birmingham (established in about 1765, particularly flourishing in the 1780s); they include Matthew Boulton (1728–1809) and his business partner James Watt (1736–1819), Priestley, Richard Lovell Edgeworth (1744–1817), Thomas Day (1748–89) and Josiah Wedgwood (1730–95).
13 William Herschel (1738–1822) discovers the planet later called Uranus. From August 1782, at Datchet, he and his sister Caroline (1750–1848) survey the sky, discovering comets and over two thousand nebulae.

Edmund Burke (1729/30–97) becomes Crabbe's patron in response to his appeal in a letter sent in February or March. As a result James Dodsley publishes Crabbe's *The Library* on 24 July.

April
This spring the third volume of a projected four in *The History of English Poetry*, by Thomas Warton (1728–90) is published by Dodsley and others.

June
The four-volume edition of *The Lives of the Most Eminent English Poets; with Critical Observations on Their Works* by Samuel Johnson (1709–84) is published early this month by a consortium including Thomas Davies and Rivington and Sons.

July
4 Burns is initiated as a freemason at St David's Lodge, Tarbolton.

August
23 Death of John Eccles, fiancé of Mary Hays (1759–1843). Their parents long opposed the match. She compiles a manuscript 'Love Letters Book' from her correspondence with Eccles.

September
Joseph Johnson's (1738–1809) first edition of *Hymns in Prose for Children* by Anna Laetitia Barbauld (1743–1825). She and her husband run a school for boys at Palgrave in Suffolk between 1774 and 1785.

October
5 Sudden death of Rev. John Coleridge (1719–81), father of Samuel Taylor Coleridge (1772–1834).
13 Holcroft's *Duplicity* is performed at the Theatre Royal, Covent Garden.
19 British forces surrender to American and French at Yorktown after the last major battle of the war.
Mary Robinson visits Paris, where she meets Queen Marie-Antoinette. This autumn Mary Wollstonecraft (1759–97) comes back to London from her post as a companion in Bath to be with her sick mother, who dies in April 1782.

November
c.29–30 The crew of the British ship *Zong*, under sail in the Caribbean, kills about 140 slaves by throwing them overboard. The owners are able to claim insurance on them, although the insurers challenge this in court in 1783. The incident later informs the growing abolitionist movement.

December

21 Crabbe is ordained deacon. He is ordained priest on 4 August 1782. He serves briefly as curate at Aldeburgh in 1782.

Late in the month Beckford gives a party at Fonthill Splendens house, with scenery and illuminations by Loutherbourg – an influence on *Vathek*.

This year *Kritik der reinen Vernunft*, by Immanuel Kant (1724–1804) is published in Riga.

Canova works on *Theseus and the Minotaur* between 1781 and 1783.

1782

January

1 Death in Paddington of Johann Christian Bach (1735–82), 'the London Bach'.

13 First performance, in Mannheim, of *Die Räuber* by Friedrich Schiller (1759–1805). The first English version, based on Friedel and de Bonneville's *Les Voleurs* (1785), is by Alexander Tytler (G.G. and J. Robinson, 1792 and later editions). The play is translated and adapted for private performance in August 1798 at Brandenburg House, Fulham, by Elizabeth (Berkeley Craven), Markgräfin of Brandenburg-Ansbach (1750–1828); the first public performance in England is of Joseph Holman's version, *The Red-Cross Knights*, at the Haymarket on 21 August 1799.

February

5 Edmond Malone (1741–1812) is elected to Samuel Johnson's Literary Club. The members already include Sir Joshua Reynolds, Thomas Percy (1729–1811), Burke, Sheridan, James Boswell (1740–95), Charles James Fox (1749–1806), Gibbon, Joseph Warton (1722–1800) and Sir Joseph Banks (1743–1820).

March

20 Lord North (Frederick North, 1732–92) resigns as Prime Minister in the political aftermath of the defeat at Yorktown. The new ministry, led by Charles Watson-Wentworth, Marquess of Rockingham (1730–82), includes Fox as Secretary of State for the Northern Department and Sheridan as his Under-Secretary.

23 John Cartwright dates his pamphlet *Give Us Our Rights!*

23   Anonymous publication in Paris of *Les Liaisons dangereuses* by Pierre Choderlos de Laclos (1741–1803).
Poems by William Cowper [1731–1800], *of the Inner Temple, Esq.* is published by Joseph Johnson.

April
29   The annual Royal Academy exhibition opens. It includes *The Nightmare* (1781) by Henry Fuseli (Heinrich Füssli, 1741–1825). Fuseli returned to London in 1779 having studied and worked in Rome since 1770. He becomes associated in the 1780s with the circle of the publisher Joseph Johnson. John Wolcot (1738–1819), as 'Peter Pindar', responds to the exhibition in *Lyric Odes to the Royal Academicians, for MDCCLXXXII* (published by Kearsley & Forster). He produces sequels in 1783 and 1785 and *Farewell Odes, for the Year 1786*. Among his other popular works is *The Lousiad* (1786).
Romney paints Emma Hart (1765–1815; born Emma Lyon) – the first of his series of portraits of her between now and 1791.

May
In the House of Commons William Pitt (1759–1806) proposes parliamentary reform including the abolition of rotten boroughs. The motion is defeated, as is his similar one of 7 May 1783.
12   Crabbe is appointed domestic chaplain to the Duke of Rutland. From 1783 he also holds livings at Frome St Quintin and Evershot, which are exchanged for West Allington in Lincolnshire and Muston in Leicestershire in January 1789. In addition he is curate at Stathern from May 1785.
16   Birth of John Sell Cotman (1782–1842) in Norwich. He spends much of his life in Norfolk but lives in London in 1798–1806; his *Specimens of Norman and Gothic Architecture, in the County of Norfolk* is published in 1817 and *A Series of Etchings Illustrative of the Architectural Antiquities of Norfolk* in 1818.
Beckford sets off again for Italy, reaching Padua on about 11 June. He is in Naples between 8 July and 10 September and returns to England in November.

June
12   Publication of Fanny Burney's (1752–1840) *Cecilia, or Memoirs of an Heiress*, in five volumes. 2,000 copies are issued and she

is given £250 for the copyright. Her sales potential has been established by several editions of *Evelina* (1778); there are twelve more between 1783 and 1829.

July
1   Rockingham dies. He is succeeded on 4 by William Petty, Earl of Shelburne (1737–1805), with Pitt, from 10, as Chancellor of the Exchequer.
16 First performance of Mozart's *Die Entführung aus dem Serail* at Theater an der Burg in Vienna.

August
18 Blake marries Catherine Boucher (1762–1831) at St Mary's Church, Battersea. Later she works with him on the production of his illuminated books. Probably they move at once into lodgings at 23 Green Street, Soho; from there they go to 27 Broad Street in late 1784 and to 28 Poland Street in autumn 1785. At Broad Street Blake works briefly in a printing partnership with James Parker.

September
15 First performance, at the Hermitage in St Petersburg, of *Il barbiere di Siviglia, ovvero La precauzione inutile*, after Beaumarchais, by Giovanni Paisiello (1740–1816).
22 Schiller deserts from the army of the Duke of Württemberg, who has ordered him to end his literary activities. He goes into hiding and exile for a time, living in Thuringia between late 1782 and summer 1783, but the Duke does not, in the event, proceed against him.

Coleridge starts as a pupil at Christ's Hospital (until 7 September 1790). Charles Lamb (1775–1834) begins there on 9 October 1782 and leaves in 1791. Subsequently Leigh Hunt will also be a pupil here between 24 November 1791 and 1799. Memories of and references to the school feature in works including Coleridge's 'Frost at Midnight' (1798), Lamb's essays 'Recollections of Christ's Hospital' (1813) and 'Christ's Hospital Five-and-Thirty Years Ago' (1820), and Hunt's poem 'Christ's Hospital' in his *Juvenilia; or, a Collection of Poems* (1801).

October

10   Sarah Siddons (1755–1831), after a period acting in Bath, appears at Drury Lane in the title role of Thomas Southerne's *Isabella; or, The Fatal Marriage*. Her fame is established during the 1782–3 season. In 1783 she is appointed 'reading preceptress' to the daughters of King George III and Queen Charlotte.

November

14   Cowper's 'The Diverting History of John Gilpin' appears, anonymously, in *The Public Advertiser*. It is reprinted with *The Task* in 1785.

30   Preliminary Articles of Peace are signed by Britain and the United States.

December

1   William Jones (1746–94) issues his translation of *The Moallakát, or Seven Arabian Poems Which were suspended on the Temple at Mecca*.

Priestley's *Essay on the Corruptions of Christianity* is published in two volumes by Joseph Johnson.

Confessions, by Jean-Jacques Rousseau (1712–78) is published in Geneva in 1782 and (the second part) 1788. An English translation of the first part is published by Bew in 1783 and of the second by Bew and G.G. and J. Robinson in 1790.

Richmond Blamire publishes William Gilpin's (1724–1804) *Observations on the River Wye, and Several Parts of South Wales, &c. Relative Chiefly to Picturesque Beauty*. Gilpin produces further volumes of *Observations* on Cumberland and Westmorland (1786), the Scottish Highlands (1789), western England and the Isle of Wight (1798), Hampshire, Sussex and Kent (1804) and eastern England and North Wales (1809), and *Remarks* on the New Forest (1791).

This year the second volume *of A General History of Music from the Earliest Ages to the Present Period*, by Dr Charles Burney (1726–1814), is published. The first came out in 1776 and the third and fourth follow in 1789.

Dodsley publishes Thomas Warton's *An Inquiry into the Authenticity of the Poems Attributed to Thomas Rowley* – part of the debate over the work of Thomas Chatterton. Dodsley also brings out the second volume of *An Essay on the Writings and Genius of Pope* by Joseph Warton;

the first appeared in 1756. Warton's edition of Pope is published by a consortium including Joseph Johnson and G.G. and J. Robinson in 1797.

In about 1782–3 Joseph Wright of Derby (1734–97) paints *Arkwright's Cotton Mills by Night*.

1783

January
17   Henry Cort (1740–1800) patents his grooved rolling process. In February 1784 he patents another important development in the manufacture of iron, the puddling furnace.
23   Henri Beyle (1783–1842), who writes most of his work as Stendhal from 1817, is born in Grenoble. He leaves for Paris in October 1799.

February
6   Lancelot 'Capability' Brown (1716–83) dies at Hampton Court.
24   Shelburne resigns. Fox and North form a coalition, with William Cavendish Bentinck, Duke of Portland (1738–1809) as Prime Minister from 2 April. Sheridan is joint Under-Secretary to the Treasury.
25   Cowley's *A Bold Stroke for a Husband* is at Covent Garden.

March
By early March Erasmus Darwin has founded the Derby Philosophical Society.
29   Foundation of the Royal Society of Edinburgh, replacing the earlier Philosophical Society of Edinburgh.

April
3   Birth of Washington Irving (1783–1859) in New York.
15   Beckford decides, under family pressure, not to go ahead with publication of *Dreams, Waking Thoughts and Incidents*. Most of the five hundred copies printed by Joseph Johnson are destroyed.
Burns makes the first entry in the commonplace book which he keeps until October 1785. It includes versions of 'Green grow the

rashes' (c. August 1784) and 'Death and Dying Words of Poor Mailie' (June 1785; first written 1782).

This spring Jane Austen (1775–1817) and her sister Cassandra (1773–1845) attend Mrs Ann Cawley's boarding school in Oxford. In the summer the school moves to Southampton. Having fallen ill during a typhus outbreak in September the Austens are taken home to Steventon in Hampshire.

May
23 Dodsley publishes Crabbe's *The Village*. It includes six lines by Samuel Johnson, whom Crabbe met in 1782 through Sir Joshua Reynolds and Burke.

June
7 In London, Strahan, Cadell & Creech publish *Lectures on Rhetoric and Belles Lettres*, in two volumes, by Hugh Blair (1718–1800). Publication in Edinburgh follows on 5 July. Blair first lectured in Edinburgh in 1759 and became Regius Professor of Rhetoric and Belles Lettres in 1762.

July
20 First performance of Schiller's *Die Verschwörung des Fiesko zu Genua* in Bonn. A translation by George Noehden and Sir John Stoddart, *Fiesco; or the Genoese Conspiracy*, is published by Joseph Johnson in 1796.

This month Hannah More (1745–1833) begins circulating her poem *The Bas Bleu, or, Conversation* (published 1786), among her friends. She is one of the younger members of the 'Bluestocking' circle which flourishes from the 1750s to the 1790s, prominent in which are Elizabeth Montagu (1718–1800), Frances Boscawen (1719–1805), Elizabeth Vesey (c.1715–91) and Elizabeth Carter (1717–1806).

August
More visits Horace Walpole (1717–97) at Strawberry Hill.

September
3 Peace of Versailles, by which Britain recognizes American independence. Benjamin Franklin (1706–90), American minister in France since 1778, is one of the signatories.

7   George, Prince of Wales visits Brighthelmstone (Brighton) for the first time. Here he rents a farmhouse in 1786, expanded from 1787 into the Marine Pavilion.
25 Sir William Jones (knighted on 20 March this year) arrives in Calcutta to take up his post as a judge in the Supreme Court of Bengal.
30 Drury Lane debut of John Philip Kemble (1757-1823), Siddons's brother, as Hamlet.

November
17 Blair is elected as a fellow of the Royal Society of Edinburgh.
21 First manned flight, in a Montgolfier hot-air balloon, at Versailles.
Walter Scott (1771-1832) enters Edinburgh University (until 1786). His schooling was at Edinburgh High School (1779-83) and Kelso Grammar School (1783), where his fellow pupil was James Ballantyne (1772-1833), later his printer, editor and close adviser. Scott spends a second period at the university in 1789-92.

December
15 Crabbe marries Sarah Elmy (1751-1813).
17 Fox's East India Bill is defeated in the House of Lords. On 18 the King dismisses the Fox-North coalition and on 19 Pitt takes office as Prime Minister, serving until 14 March 1801.
23 George Washington (1732-99) resigns as commander-in-chief of the American or Continental army.
Probably this month Sir William Jones starts work on 'A Hymn to Camdeo', published in London in *A Discourse on the Institution of a Society* in 1784. This is the first of nine such hymns written between now and 1788.

Blake's *Poetical Sketches* ('By W.B.') is printed. The poems were written mainly in the 1770s. Some he sings at the salon of Harriet Mathew, which he attends in about 1782-4; her husband Rev. A.S. Mathew pays for the printing with John Flaxman (1755-1826).

Publication in Riga of Kant's *Prolegomena zu einer jeden künftigen Metaphysik*. John Richardson's translation *Prolegomena to Every Future Metaphysic* is published in London by Simpkin & Marshall in 1819.

Sophia Lee's *The Recess, or, A Tale of Other Times* is published in three parts by Cadell in 1783–5.
Day's *The History of Sandford and Merton* is published by J. Stockdale in three parts (1783, 1786, 1789).
The *Tragedie* of Vittorio Alfieri (1749–1803) are published in five volumes between 1783 and 1789.

1784

January
Early this month Wollstonecraft rescues her sister Eliza Bishop, who she feels will never recover from post-natal depression while she continues to live with her husband. For a time they go into hiding in Hackney. Later in the year, with Wollstonecraft's friend Fanny Blood and her other sister Everina Wollstonecraft, they attempt to set up a school in Islington. They go on to start one successfully in Newington Green.

11 Schiller's *Kabale und Liebe: Ein bürgerliches Trauerspiel* opens in Mannheim. It is translated by Matthew Gregory Lewis (1775–1818) as *The Minister: a Tragedy in Five Acts* (Bell, 1797). Lewis's version opens at Covent Garden on 4 May 1803 as *The Harper's Daughter; or, Love and Ambition*.

23 More, Walpole, Sir Joshua Reynolds, Carter, Fanny Burney and Charles Burney are together.

February
28 John Wesley (1703–91), while maintaining continued membership of the Church of England, formalizes 'the Conference of the People called Methodists' by deed of declaration in Chancery. His followers establish a more fully separate church in 1795.

March
11 Treaty of Mangalore between Tipu Sultan (1750–99) of Mysore and the East India Company, ending the war of 1780–4.

Following the death of his father on 13 February, Burns moves with his brother Gilbert and mother to Mossgiel farm, near Mauchline. He meets Jean Armour (1765–1834), with whom in March or April 1786 he contracts a form of marriage.

April

7   Wilberforce is elected as MP for Yorkshire, serving until 1812.
26 *Les Danaïdes*, by Antonio Salieri (1750–1825) is given at the Paris Opéra.
28 Watt patents parallel motion and several other mechanisms.

May

15 Publication of *Elegiac Sonnets, and Other Essays* by Charlotte Smith (1749–1806).
22 Siddons plays in Edinburgh for the first time, as Belvidera in Otway's *Venice Preserved*. This season the Royal Academy exhibition includes Sir Joshua Reynolds's portrait of Siddons as 'The Tragic Muse'. In 1786 the Academy will show 'Mrs Jordan in the Character of the Comic Muse' by John Hoppner (1758–1810). (Hoppner first exhibited here in 1780.)

June

30 Boswell and Samuel Johnson meet for the last time.

July

6   *The Mogul Tale*, a farce by Elizabeth Inchbald (1753–1821), is at the Haymarket.
23 Hester Thrale (1741–1821) marries, as her second husband, Gabriel Mario Piozzi (1740–1809). They land at Calais on 7 September and travel extensively in Europe, returning to London on 10 March 1787; her *Observations and Reflections made in the Course of a Journey through France, Italy, and Germany* appears in June 1789.
31 Death in Paris of Denis Diderot (1713–84).
Late this month Gainsborough, after disputes with the Royal Academy about the hanging of his paintings, opens his frst exhibition at Schomberg House, Pall Mall.

August

2–3 A mail coach, financed by John Palmer (1742–1818), reaches London from Bristol in sixteen hours. Pitt agrees to the use of Palmer's efficient new system on other routes.
13 Pitt's East India Act is passed. The Board of Control gains in authority over the East India Company.

More stays with Montagu at Sandleford Priory, Berkshire.
Lafayette visits the United States between August and December.

October
19 Birth of (James Henry) Leigh Hunt (1784–1859).
Charlotte Smith meets William Hayley (1745–1820).
Jacques-Louis David (1748–1825) goes to Rome, where he completes and displays *The Oath of the Horatii* (1785).

December
13 Death of Samuel Johnson at 8 Bolt Court in London. He is buried in Westminster Abbey on 20. Malone's obituary of Johnson is in *The Gentleman's Magazine* for December. A monument in St Paul's Cathedral is put up in 1796.

14 Premiere at the Haymarket of *The Follies of a Day*, Holcroft's adaptation of Beaumarchais' *La Folle journée, ou Le Mariage de Figaro*, which was first performed in Paris on 27 April. (Holcroft repeatedly attended performances at the Théâtre de l'Odéon in order to memorize it.) There are 28 performances of *The Follies* this season and many subsequently. Holcroft plays Figaro on the opening night.

Rumours circulate about Beckford's homosexual relationship with William Courtenay, eight years his junior and from a powerful family. Social ostracism results; Beckford and his wife Lady Margaret (Gordon) (c.1760–86) retreat to Switzerland in July 1785. She dies there and he returns to England in January 1787.

Blake writes the work later known as *An Island in the Moon* probably in 1784–5.

Burns writes 'Address to the Unco Guid, or the Rigidly Righteous' in about 1784–6.

Ideen zur Philosophie der Geschichte der Menschheit, by Johann Gottfried Herder (1744–1803), is published in Riga and Hamburg between 1784 and 1791. A translation by T. Churchill, *Outlines of a Philosophy of the History of Man*, is published by Joseph Johnson in 1800.

Joanna Baillie (1762–1851) comes from Scotland to live with her brother at Windmill Street, London, until 1791. She lives in Colchester before moving to Hampstead in 1798.

1785

January

1   *The Daily Universal Register* starts publication. On 1 January 1788 it becomes *The Times*.
7   Jean-Pierre Blanchard (1753–1809) and John Jeffries (1745–1819) cross the English Channel by hydrogen balloon.

By early this year Sir William Jones has written 'The Enchanted Fruit; or, The Hindu Wife'. It is published in the *Asiatick Miscellany* in 1786.
Early this year Burns writes 'Holy Willie's Prayer'.

February

2   Siddons's London debut at Drury Lane as Lady Macbeth, one of her most popular roles.
5   First number of *The Lounger*, edited and mostly written by Henry Mackenzie (1745–1831). The last number appears on 5 January 1787.
8   Charles Dibdin's *Liberty Hall; or, The Test of Good Fellowship* opens at Drury Lane.

March

7   Birth in Milan of Alessandro Manzoni (1785–1873).
24 Sir William Jones delivers 'On the Gods of Greece, Italy, and India' to the Asiatick Society of Bengal, which he founded on 15 January 1784. It is published in *Asiatick Researches* in 1788.

April

2   *La finta principessa* by Luigi Cherubini (1760–1842) is performed at the King's Theatre. Cherubini works in London between 1784 and 1786, when his *Giulio Sabino* opens at the same theatre.
11 An exhibition of 25 paintings by Wright of Derby opens at Robins's Rooms, Covent Garden, continuing until June.
14 William Whitehead (1715–85), Poet Laureate since 1757, dies. His successor from 1785 to 1790 is Thomas Warton, who this year also becomes Camden Professor of ancient history at Oxford and publishes his edition of Milton's *Poems upon Several Occasions* (Dodsley; revised edition 1791).

18 Another of Pitt's parliamentary reform bills is defeated in the House of Commons.
28 Blake's 'The Bard from Gray' is one of his four drawings in this year's Royal Academy exhibition. Two others were in the 1784 show.

Rev. Edmund Cartwright (1743–1823) patents his power loom.
Schiller lives in Leipzig until July 1787. Here he writes 'An die Freude' in 1786.

June

Poems, on Several Occasions by Ann Yearsley (1753–1806), known sometimes as 'the Bristol Milkwoman', is published by a subscription organized by More. Yearsley and More quarrel over how the profits should be handled: More and Elizabeth Montagu set up a trust for Yearsley but she insists on being given the whole sum immediately. With some help from other patrons she publishes *Poems, on Various Subjects* in 1787.

July

24 Franklin arrives in Southampton on his way back to America from France. He reaches Philadelphia on 14 September. During the voyage he works on the Maritime Observations included in his *Philosophical and Miscellaneous Papers* of 1787. His successor in Paris, until October 1789, is Thomas Jefferson (1743–1826).

By this month, in Colchester, William Keymer publishes Reeve's *The Progress of Romance Through Times, Countries, and Manners*.
Jane and Cassandra Austen start at Mrs Latourelle's Ladies' Boarding School, Reading. They are pupils here until December 1786.

August

Early this month Cowper's *The Task: a Poem in Six Books* is published by Joseph Johnson.
4 Inchbald's *I'll Tell You What* opens at the Haymarket.
5 Thomas De Quincey (1785–1859) is born in Manchester.

September

Publication in Florence of *The Florence Miscellany*, with a preface by Piozzi and poems by her, Robert Merry and other 'Della Cruscans'.

The group is satirized by William Gifford (1756–1826) in *The Baviad* (1791) and *The Maeviad* (1795).

October

1   Charles Dilly publishes Boswell's *The Journal of a Tour to the Hebrides, with Samuel Johnson*. A second edition follows on 22 December.

18 Debut at Drury Lane of Dorothy Jordan (1761–1816) as Peggy in Garrick's *The Country Girl*. She plays many roles here in seasons between 1785–6 and 1808–9. Scandal is generated from 1790 by her relationship with the Duke of Clarence (later William IV, 1765–1837), with whom she has ten children between 1794 and 1807.

18 Franklin becomes President of the Supreme Executive Council of Pennsylvania until 14 October 1788.

18 Thomas Love Peacock (1785–1866) is born in Dorset.

November

10 First performance at Covent Garden of Holcroft's *The Choleric Fathers*.

13 Birth, as Caroline Ponsonby, of Lady Caroline Lamb (1785–1828). Wollstonecraft goes to Lisbon to join Fanny Blood, who dies in childbirth.

Burns writes 'To a Mouse, On turning her up in her Nest, with the Plough, November, 1785'. It is published in his 1786 *Poems*. Probably also this autumn he writes 'Love and Liberty – A Cantata', which is published in 1799 as 'The Jolly Beggars; or Tatterdemallions. A Cantata'.

December

15 George, Prince of Wales secretly marries Maria Fitzherbert (1756–1837).

In late 1785 Burns writes 'To a Louse, On seeing one on a Lady's Bonnet', and in late 1785 or early 1786 'The Cotter's Saturday Night'. Both pieces are published in his 1786 *Poems*.

This year R. Faulder publishes William Paley's (1743–1805) *The Principles of Moral and Political Philosophy*. It is a prescribed part of the Cambridge University syllabus from 1787.

1786

January
In January or February Wollstonecraft closes the school at Newington Green.

February
2   Sir William Jones gives 'The Third Anniversary Discourse, on the Hindus', to the Asiatick Society of Bengal. He identifies the 'affinity' of Sanskrit with Greek and Latin and posits the existence of 'some common source'. The lecture is published in the first volume of *Asiatick Researches* (1788).

Paine's *Dissertation on Government; the Affairs of the Bank; and Paper Money* defends the Bank of North America.

March
25 Piozzi's *Anecdotes of the Late Samuel Johnson* is published by Cadell. Her *Letters to and from the Late Samuel Johnson* comes out on 8 March 1788.

April
26 Hart arrives in Naples to live with Hamilton. Her 'Attitudes' – performances suggestive of classical scenes and figures – are much celebrated and depicted, most famously in Goethe's *Reise* (see September). Hart and Hamilton marry in London on 6 September 1791.

'Haymakers and Reapers' by George Stubbs (1724–1806) is at the Royal Academy.

Hays's 'The Hermit: An Oriental Tale' is in *The Universal Magazine* for April and May.

May
1   Opening performance of Mozart's *Le nozze di Figaro* at the Theater an der Burg in Vienna.

Cadell publishes Charlotte Smith's anonymous two-volume translation *Manon Lescaut, or the Fatal Attachment*, from the 1753 text of the Abbé Prévost's novel.

June
4   George III's birthday is celebrated in Thomas Warton's ode 'When Freedom nursed her native fire'. Burns's outspoken response, 'A Dream', is written soon afterwards and included in his *Poems* in July.
7   Beckford's *Vathek: an Arabian Tale* is published with Joseph Johnson, without the author's permission and anonymously, by its translator Samuel Henley; Beckford wrote it in French between January and May 1782 and has the French text published at Lausanne in December 1786. He works on the separate 'Episodes' for *Vathek* intermittently from 1785.
25 Burns appears before Mauchline Kirk Session, as three more times in July and August. He acknowledges paternity of the twins who will be born to Jean Armour in September, and is granted a certificate to say that he is not married.

Cadell publishes *Poems*, in two volumes, by Helen Maria Williams (1759–1827). This month Cadell also publishes, with J. Phillips, *An Essay on the Slavery and Commerce of the Human Species* by Thomas Clarkson (1760–1846). The essay translates the Latin dissertation for which Clarkson won a Members' Prize at Cambridge in June 1785.

July
9   Boswell starts writing his *Life of Johnson*. He is encouraged and assisted by Malone.
17 Fanny Burney becomes Second Keeper of the Robes to Queen Charlotte (until 7 July 1791).
31 John Wilson of Kilmarnock prints Burns's first collection *Poems, Chiefly in the Scottish Dialect*. Its success dissuades Burns from emigrating to Jamaica. The first Edinburgh edition is published by William Creech on 17 April 1787, followed by a first London edition (Strahan, Cadell & Creech) on 5 July. The work is published also in Dublin in 1787 and in Philadelphia and New York in 1788. There are enlarged editions in February 1793 and in 1801.

August
12 Death of Frederick the Great (1712–86) of Prussia.

September

10   Johann Wolfgang von Goethe (1749–1832) arrives in Italy. He spends two long periods in Rome (29 October 1786–22 February 1787 and 7 June 1787–23 April 1788), between which he visits Naples and Sicily. He returns to Weimar on 18 June 1788. Goethe's account of his travels, *Die Italienische Reise*, is published between 1816 and 1829.

26   Trade treaty between Britain and France.

Wollstonecraft goes to Ireland as governess to the daughters of Lord and Lady Kingsborough at Mitchelstown Castle, County Cork, and in Dublin from February 1787. She is with the family in Bristol in the summer but is dismissed in August 1787. In January or February that year her *Thoughts on the Education of Daughters* is published by Joseph Johnson and that summer she writes *Mary, a Fiction* and 'The Cave of Fancy'.

This autumn Burns writes 'The Brigs of Ayr, a Poem', which is included in his 1787 *Poems*.

November

c.19   Birth of Carl Maria von Weber (1786–1826) in Eutin.

27   Burns arrives in Edinburgh. He lodges at Baxter's Close, Lawnmarket and in 1786–7 enjoys some celebrity in Edinburgh society. James Cunningham, Earl of Glencairn (1749–91), becomes his patron and he meets Blair and Mackenzie, who in *The Lounger* on 9 December salutes him as 'this Heaven-taught ploughman'. In 1787 Burns also meets the fifteen- or sixteen-year-old Walter Scott.

At a dinner in Hampstead the idea of Alderman John Boydell's Shakespeare Gallery is launched. (Boydell [1720–1804] becomes Lord Mayor of London in 1790–1.) Other guests at the dinner include Fuseli, West, Romney and Hayley. The gallery opens at 52 Pall Mall on 4 May 1789.

December

6   In Vienna Mozart completes his Symphony no.38, the 'Prague'.

19   Burns's 'To a Haggis' is in *The Caledonian Mercury*. It reappears in *The Scots Magazine* in January 1787 and in the 1787 *Poems*. By 27 – probably earlier in the month – he has written 'Address to Edinburgh', also published in the 1787 *Poems*.

This year Joseph Johnson publishes *Epea Pteroenta, or The Diversions of Purley*, by Rev. John Horne Tooke (1736–1812). There is a revised version in 1798 and a continuation in 1805.

1787

January
11   Opening of the Assembly Rooms in Edinburgh New Town.

February
7   In the House of Commons, Sheridan speaks for over five hours on the seizure or attempted seizure of the treasure of the Begums of Oudh by Warren Hastings (1732–1818) in 1781. Hastings resigned as Governor-General of Bengal in 1785 and Burke first called for his impeachment for corruption and mismanagement in April 1786.
10   Inchbald's *Such Things Are* opens at Covent Garden.
11   Death of Blake's brother, Robert (1767–87). Blake believes that he instructs him, in a vision, in the technique of relief engraving.

March
12   First performance of Holcroft's *Seduction: a Comedy* at Drury Lane.

Beckford goes to Portugal, where he remains until December and to which he returns between November 1793 and June 1796 and again between October 1798 and July 1799. He lives mainly in or near Sintra.

The Life of Samuel Johnson by Sir John Hawkins (1719–89) is brought out by a consortium of booksellers.

April
9   Burns makes his first entry in a second commonplace book, used mainly between 14 June 1788 and summer 1790. Among the poems included is 'Elegy on Captain Matthew Henderson'. Burns meets Henderson (1737–88) in 1787.
17   The pugilist Daniel Mendoza (1764/5–1836) defeats Sam Martin the 'Bath Butcher' in a prize fight at Barnet.

May

5 Burns sets off from Edinburgh to tour the Borders and parts of northern England. From Berrywell near Duns he goes to Coldstream (7), where he sees Patrick Brydone (1736–1818), Kelso (8 and 11), Jedburgh (8–11), and Innerleithen (14) via Melrose, Dryburgh and Selkirk. He is at Berwick-on-Tweed on 18 and then goes to Eyemouth (19), Dunbar (21), Newcastle (30) via Alnwick and Warkworth, Hexham (30), Carlisle (31) and Annan (1 June). In early June he renews his affair with Armour; she gives birth to twins who die on 10 and 22 March 1788.

10 Formal impeachment of Hastings.

22 Establishment in London of the Committee for the Abolition of the Slave Trade. In June Clarkson goes to Bristol to investigate on its behalf.

26 Paine lands in France, having left America in April. In Paris he sees Jefferson. He leaves for England at the end of August and returns to Paris in December.

Publication of the first volume of James Johnson's *The Scots Musical Museum*, containing three songs by Burns. He contributes much more extensively to the subsequent volumes published in February 1788, February 1790 and August 1792. Further songs are included posthumously in the volumes of December 1796 and 1803.

Arthur Young (1741–1820) embarks on the first of three extensive tours of France (May to November 1787, August to October 1788 and June 1789 to January 1790; he is in Italy in September to December 1789). His *Travels during the years 1787, 1788 and 1789: undertaken ... with a view of ascertaining the cultivation, wealth, resources and national prosperity ... of France* is published by W. Richardson in 1792.

June

1 George III issues a proclamation for the discouragement of vice. Partly in response, More writes *Thoughts on the Importance of the Manners of the Great to General Society*, published anonymously in March 1788.

c.24 Burns embarks on his West Highland tour. He goes to Inveraray, Arrochar (28), Loch Lomond, Dumbarton (29) and home to Mossgiel via Paisley.

27 Gibbon, in Lausanne, finishes the last volume of his *Decline and Fall*.

July
20 Schiller moves to Weimar, where he spends much of the rest of his life.

August
2 Burns writes his 'Autobiographical Letter', with details of his early life, to Dr John Moore (1729–1809). He sends him a second memoir on 4 January 1789.
4 First performance, at the Haymarket, of *Inkle and Yarico*, by George Colman the Younger (1762–1836). It runs for nineteen more nights between now and 15 September.
25 Burns begins his tour to the eastern Highlands. He is at Bannockburn on 26. In Stirling, on 27, he inscribes on the window of his inn the anti-Hanoverian 'Here Stewarts once in triumph reign'd'; the poem circulates and causes some scandal. Burns smashes the window when he comes back in October but the lines are printed in James Maxwell's *Animadversions on Some Poets* ... in 1788 and in *The Edinburgh Evening Courant* on 2 July 1792. The tour continues to places including Crieff (28), Dunkeld (30), Aberfeldy where Burns writes 'The birks of Aberfeldey' [sic] on 31, Blair Atholl and Blair Castle where he stays with the Duke and Duchess of Atholl on 31 August–1 September. On 2 September he begins 'The Humble Petition of Bruar Water to the Noble Duke of Athole' (published in *The Edinburgh Magazine* in November 1789) and goes on to Aviemore, Inverness (4 September), Culloden (6), Forres, Elgin and the Duke and Duchess of Gordon at Gight (7), Aberdeen (9), Stonehaven (10), Montrose (12), Dundee (13), Perth (14) and Kinross (15). He returns to Edinburgh on 16 September.
29 First performance of Schiller's *Dom Karlos, Infant von Spanien*, in Hamburg. *Don Carlos, Infant of Spain*, translated by Noehden and Stoddart, is published by Miller in 1798.

September
17 United States constitution signed. It is eventually ratified in 1789–90. Amendments are contained in the Bill of Rights ratified on 15 December 1791.

24 John Flaxman and his wife Ann Flaxman (1760–1820) set off for Italy. They travel to Navarre, Paris, Milan and Florence, which they leave for Rome on 28 November. From Rome they go on to Naples, setting out to return to Rome on 24 February 1788. Ann Flaxman keeps a manuscript 'Journey to Rome'. They remain in Italy until autumn 1794. John Flaxman's friends in Rome include Canova.
Wollstonecraft visits her sisters, Everina in Henley and Eliza in Market Harborough.

October

c.4–20 Burns travels again, revisiting Stirling and spending about a week at Harvieston, where he proposes marriage to Margaret (Peggy) Chalmers (1763–1843) and is refused. He sends her 'My Peggy's face' and 'Where braving angry Winter's storms'.
29 Mozart's *Il dissoluto punito, ossia Il Don Giovanni* is performed for the first time at the National Theatre, Prague.
30 William Wordsworth (1770–1850) is entered at St John's College, Cambridge. (He takes his final examinations in January 1791.) He was at Hawkshead Grammar School from 1779.

November

4 Edmund Kean (1787–1833) is born in London.

December

4 Burns meets Agnes McLehose (1759–1841) in Edinburgh. They exchange letters as Sylvander and Clarinda and he addresses several poems to her.
16 Birth of Mary Russell Mitford (1787–1855) at Alresford in Hampshire.

The highly popular *Paul et Virginie*, by Jacques-Henri Bernardin de Saint-Pierre (1737–1814) is published this year in the third edition of his *Études de la Nature*. *Paul and Mary* is an English translation of 1789; Helen Maria Williams's better known *Paul and Virginia* appears in 1796. Between 1787 and 1793 Austen writes her 'Juvenilia' (copied later into 'Volume the First', 'Volume the Second' and 'Volume the Third'). Beginning of the friendship between Fuseli and Blake. They may be introduced by Joseph Johnson.
Canova works on *Cupid and Psyche* between 1787 and 1793.

1788

January
11   Boswell becomes Recorder of Carlisle (until 12 July 1790).
22   Birth of George Gordon Byron in Holles Street, London. He lives with his mother, Catherine Gordon Byron (1765–1811) in Aberdeen between 1789 and 1798, attending the Grammar School in 1794–8.
26   Establishment of the penal settlement at Sydney Cove.
30   Death in Rome of Charles Edward Stuart (1720–88), the 'Young Pretender'.
31   Cowley's *The Fate of Sparta; or, the Rival Kings* is performed at Drury Lane.

Between this month and June 1789 Sarah Trimmer (1741–1810) edits *The Family Magazine*.

February
8   Publication by Cadell of More's *Slavery: A Poem*.
13   Beginning of Hastings' trial at Westmister Hall. Proceedings continue until April 1795. The prosecution is led by Burke, with Fox and Sheridan also prominently involved.
23   Burns arrives in Mauchline. In early March he marries Jean Armour. Mauchline Kirk Session confirms this marriage, more acceptable than the earlier contract, on 5 August.
24   Mozart completes his Piano Concerto no.26, in D, the 'Coronation'.

Salieri is appointed imperial Hofkapellmeister in Vienna (until 1824).

March
c.13–20   Burns is in Edinburgh.
21   Olaudah Equiano (c.1745–97), a former slave, petitions Queen Charlotte against the slave trade. His *The Interesting Narrative of the Life of Olaudah Equiano, or Gustavus Vassa, the African* is 'printed for and sold by the author' in 1789. In 1791–2 he tours to address abolitionist meetings in Ireland, Scotland and northern England.

April
Charlotte Smith's *Emmeline, the Orphan of the Castle* is published by Cadell at about mid-month.

Joseph Johnson publishes Wollstonecraft's *Original Stories from Real Life: with Conversations, Calculated to Regulate the Affections, and Form the Mind to Truth and Goodness*. Late this year Johnson also publishes her *Of the Importance of Religious Opinions*, translated from the French of Jacques Necker.

May
3   *The Star* newspaper begins publication. (It becomes part of *The Albion* in 1831.)
8   Publication, by Strahan and by Cadell, of volumes four, five and six of Gibbon's *Decline and Fall*.
Joseph Johnson and Thomas Christie launch *The Analytical Review*, which is issued until June 1799. Contributors include Wollstonecraft, Cowper, Fuseli and Hays. This month Johnson also publishes Wollstonecraft's *Mary, a Fiction*.

June
11 Burns moves to the farm he has leased at Ellisland, near Dumfries. He gives up the lease on 10 September 1791 and leaves for Dumfries that November.
In mid-June Paine comes from Paris to London. During his visit he and Burke become friends.

July
25 In Vienna Mozart completes his Symphony no.40. No.41, the 'Jupiter', follows by 10 August.

August
2   Gainsborough dies in London.
This month Humphry Repton (1752–1818) embarks on his career as a landscape gardener. His first commission is for Catton, near Norwich, where he works in September. He compiles his first Red Books for Brandesbury (or Brondesbury) and Holkham in 1789. His *Sketches and Hints on Landscape Gardening* (1795) responds to *Essay on the Picturesque* (1794) by Uvedale Price.

September
7   First meeting of Goethe and Schiller. Their friendship proper begins in 1794.

This autumn Mary Robinson, as 'Laura', begins publishing Della Cruscan poems in *The World*. She writes more often as 'Laura Maria'.

November

1   Publication by Benjamin White, dated 1789, of *The Natural History and Antiquities of Selborne, in the County of Southampton*, by Gilbert White (1720–93).

George III's attack of insanity prompts Pitt to propose that the Prince of Wales become Regent but subject to conditions which are opposed by Fox, Burke and their allies.

December

17   Burns sends 'Auld Lang Syne', combining his own and earlier words, in a letter to Frances Dunlop (1730–1815). A revised version is in Johnson's *Scots Musical Museum* in 1796.

Blake produces *There is No Natural Religion* and *All Religions are One*, his first illuminated books.

Publication in Riga of Kant's *Kritik der praktischen Vernunft*.

First edition of *Bibliotheca classica, or; A classical dictionary containing a full account of all the proper names mentioned in antient authors* by John Lemprière (c.1765–1824). An enlarged edition appears in 1797.

1789

January

Early this year Richard Cruttwell of Bath prints, anonymously, *Fourteen Sonnets, Elegiac and Descriptive. Written during a Tour* by William Lisle Bowles (1762–1850).

February

12   Franklin presents his remonstrance against slavery to Congress.

George III recovers his sanity. Burns, as 'Agricola', writes 'Ode to the Departed Regency-Bill', published in *The Star* on 17 April. Between about 16 and 27 February he is in Edinburgh.

March

Lavoisier's *Traité Elémentaire de Chimie* is published in Paris. G.G. and J. Robinson bring out Robert Kerr's translation, *Elements of Chemistry*, in 1790.

April

Early this month Erasmus Darwin's *The Loves of the Plants*, the second part of *The Botanic Garden*, is published anonymously by Joseph Johnson. The second part precedes the first, *The Economy of Vegetation*, which follows in June 1792 (dated 1791).

13 William and Catherine Blake sign the resolutions of the Swedenborgian New Jerusalem Church. He soon becomes disenchanted with Swedenborg however, attacking him particularly in The *Marriage of Heaven and Hell* (1790).

28 Fletcher Christian (1764–93?) leads a mutiny on the *Bounty*, several weeks after it leaves Tahiti. The captain, William Bligh (1754–1817), and eighteen crew members are cast off in a small boat which eventually reaches Timor.

30 Washington is sworn in as first President of the United States. He is re-elected in 1792 and holds office until 4 March 1797.

May

5 The Estates General meet, for the first time since 1614, at Versailles.

12 Wilberforce's first major speech, in the House of Commons, on the slave trade, drawing on the Privy Council report of 25 April. From January 1790 he is a member of the select committee on the trade.

June

17 At Versailles the Third Estate or 'commons' and some clergy, supporters of individual rather than block voting in the Estates General, form the National Assembly. After their meeting hall is closed they assemble at a tennis court on 20 and swear the 'Tennis Court Oath'. (David's painting of the scene is shown from 21 August 1791 at the Salon for that year.) The National Assembly becomes the National Constituent Assembly on 9 July.

25 First performance, at Caserta, of Paisiello's *Nina, o sia La pazza per amore*.

July

14 Storming of the Bastille, following days of unrest in Paris. (There are insurrections in many other parts of France this summer.) Thelwall writes 'Ode on the Destruction of the

Bastille', published in *The Biographical and Imperial Magazine*. Astley's company stages the storming from 30 at the Royal Amphitheatre. A rival production, John Dent's *The Triumph of Liberty, or The Destruction of the Bastille*, opens on 5 August at the Royal Circus and runs for 79 nights. And *Gallic Freedom; or, Vive la Liberté* opens at Sadler's Wells on 31 August. (See Burwick, Goslee and Hoeveler [2012], p. 1487.)

August

4   The French National Constituent Assembly abolishes feudal rights. The Declaration of the Rights of Man and of the Citizen follows on 26.

21 Wilberforce visits More at Cowslip Green, her home near Wrington in Somerset between 1785 and 1801. They first met in summer 1787. She goes with him to Bristol on 24 and on to tour the Wye Valley, returning in mid-September.

September

1   Burns takes up a post as exciseman in the Dumfries jurisdiction.

1   Birth, near Clonmel, of Margaret Power (1789–1849), later Countess of Blessington.

15 Birth of James Fenimore Cooper (1789–1851) at Burlington, New Jersey. He adds the 'Fenimore' in 1826.

October

1   Constitutional monarchy is established in France. On 5–6 protesters, helped by Lafayette and the National Guard, effectively force King Louis XVI to ratify the abolition of feudalism and the Declaration of the Rights of Man and to move the court from Versailles to the Tuileries palace in Paris.

25 The first of the Mendip schools set up by More and her sisters opens at Cheddar. Poor children are taught Bible reading and the Catechism. The scheme is financed by Wilberforce, Montagu and others.

Anonymous publication, by Joseph Cooper in Calcutta, of Sir William Jones's translation *Sacontalá, or, the fatal ring; An Indian drama by Cálidás*.

November

2 Church property in France is nationalized; land of the royal domain follows on 9 May 1790.
c.20 Publication by Cadell, in five volumes, of Charlotte Smith's *Ethelinde, or the Recluse of the Lake*.
26 Formal opening of the Thames-Severn Canal, begun in June 1783.
29 The Society for Constitutional Information sends congratulations to the French National Constituent Assembly.

Paine is in Paris between this month and late March 1790. He is there again from October 1790, returning to London on 7 March 1791.

December

7 Charles Dibdin's *The Oddities, or, Dame Nature in a Frolic*, opens at the Lyceum. (Also this year Dibdin writes a number of his best-known songs including 'Tom Bowling', 'Push the Grog About' and 'Every Inch a Sailor'.)
11 Joseph Mallord William Turner (1775–1851) is admitted as a student at the Royal Academy Schools.

Late in the year Blake produces his *The Book of Thel*. He also produces *Songs of Innocence* this year and works on *Tiriel*.

Boulton's steam-powered mint at the Soho Manufactory in Handsworth begins producing coins. New machinery is installed in 1798 and remains active until 1813; a new mint opens in 1824.

T. Payne publishes *An Introduction to the Principles of Morals and Legislation*, by Jeremy Bentham (1748–1832).

1790

January

1 Opening of the Oxford Canal, linking Oxford and Coventry.
26 First performance of Mozart's *Così fan tutte, ossia La scuola degli amanti* in Vienna at the Theater an der Burg.

Publication (dated '1787') of the second volume of *The Antiquities of Athens measured and delineated* by James 'Athenian' Stuart (1713–88) and Nicholas Revett (1720–1804). The first volume came out in 1762.

There are further parts in 1794 and 1816 and in 1830 *The Antiquities of Athens and other places of Greece, Sicily etc.*

February
4   Louis XVI attends the National Constituent Assembly.
10 Fuseli is elected to the Royal Academy, where he has been an Associate since 1788. He embarks on his own 'Milton Gallery' to follow Boydell's Shakespeare Gallery. Mainly during the next decade he will produce over thirty works illustrating *Paradise Lost* and some of the shorter poems.

March
3   Barbauld dates *An Address to the Opposers of the Repeal of the Corporation and Test Acts*. She is reacting to a parliamentary debate on 2 carried by the opposers.
25 Franklin, as 'Historicus', publishes his satirical defence of slavery in *The Federal Gazette*.
Goethe's second Italian journey begins. He is in Venice between 31 March and 22 May.

April
Lewis matriculates at Christ Church College, Oxford. (He graduates in 1794.) He was at Westminster School from 1783.
16 Stephen Storace's (1762–96) *No Song, No Supper* opens as an afterpiece at Drury Lane.
17 Franklin dies in Philadelphia. The first part of his autobiography is published in 1791 in Paris, by Buisson, as *Mémoires de la Vie Privée de Benjamin Franklin*. Two English translations appear in 1793; *Memoirs of the Life and Writings of Benjamin Franklin* (three volumes, Colburn, 1817–18) adds the second and third parts of the four Franklin wrote.
26 The Royal Academy exhibition includes twelve portraits by Thomas Lawrence (1769–1830). Turner exhibits for the first time – a watercolour of Lambeth Palace. In the 1790s he travels and sketches extensively in England and Wales and exhibits regularly at the Academy
In April–May Josiah Wedgwood displays jasper ware copies of the Portland Vase at a private exhibition in Greek Street, Soho. Wedgwood and his employees and collaborators worked from

June 1786 to October 1789 to perfect the process. It is referred to in Erasmus Darwin's *The Botanic Garden* (1791), with an illustration by Blake.

May
21 Thomas Warton dies at Trinity College, Oxford, where he has spent most of his career.

June
6   Burns finishes 'Lament of Mary Queen of Scots'. It is published in the 1793 edition of his *Poems, Chiefly in the Scottish Dialect*.
13 Austen finishes 'Love and Freindship' (sic).

July
13 William Wordsworth and his friend Robert Jones arrive in Calais on their way to tour the Alps. They are at the Grande Chartreuse on 4–5 August and reach Chamonix on 12 and the Simplon Pass on 17. They spend late August and much of September in the Swiss Alps and return to England, via Basle, Cologne (28–29 September) and Ostend, in October. The journey informs elements of *Descriptive Sketches* and features in Book VI of *The Prelude*.
14 On the anniversary of the fall of the Bastille the first Fête de la Fédération, on the Champ de Mars in Paris, is attended by about 400,000 people. There is much spectacle and oaths are sworn both to and by the king and queen. Lafayette is prominently involved, as is Charles-Maurice de Talleyrand-Périgord (1754–1838), Bishop of Autun until January 1791.
17 Death of Adam Smith (1723–90) in Edinburgh. His final revision of *The Theory of Moral Sentiments* (1759) came out this summer; that of *An Inquiry into The Nature and Causes of the Wealth of Nations* (1776) in 1785.

September
About now Radcliffe's *A Sicilian Romance* is published anonymously, in two volumes, by Hookham.
By this month Catharine Macaulay's *Letters on Education with Observations on Religious and Metaphysical Subjects* is published by C. Dilly.

October

21 Alphonse de Lamartine (1790–1869) is born in Mâcon.

This autumn the Blakes move to 13 Hercules Buildings, Lambeth (until September 1800).

November

1 Edmund Burke's *Reflections on the Revolution in France* is published. He is reacting to a sermon given by Richard Price on 4 November 1789 and published in 1790 as *A Discourse on the Love of Our Country*.

29 Wollstonecraft replies, anonymously, in *A Vindication of the Rights of Men, in a Letter to the Right Honourable Edmund Burke*, published by Joseph Johnson. Her name is given in the second edition in December.

29 Publication of Malone's ten-volume edition of *The Plays and Poems of William Shakespeare*.

Minerva Press publishes *Dangers of Coquetry*, by Amelia Alderson (later Opie, 1769–1853), in two volumes.

Faust: Ein Fragment appears in the seventh volume of *Goethes Schriften* (Leipzig: Göschen, 1787–90). *Iphigenie auf Tauris: Ein Schauspiel* is in volume three (1787) and is translated by William Taylor (1765–1836) as *Iphigenia: a Tragedy* (Joseph Johnson, 1793); *Egmont: ein Trauerspiel* is in volume five (1788); *Torquato Tasso: Ein Schauspiel* is in volume six (1790).

Joseph Johnson brings out Priestley's *Experiments and Observations on Different Kinds of Air, and Other Branches of Natural Philosophy, Connected with the Subject*. It gathers and revises six earlier volumes of *Experiments and Observations*. Priestley's work on oxygen or 'dephlogisticated air' began in 1774.

In Rome John Flaxman works on his sculptural group *The Fury of Athamas* between 1790 and 1793.

1791

January

2 Haydn arrives in London. He is in England until late June or early July 1792. In 1791–2 he writes the 'London' Symphonies 93–98.

4 and 6 Alderson acts in private performances in Norwich of her tragedy *Adelaide* (written in 1786).

19   Burke dates *A Letter to a Member of the National Assembly*, published in Paris in April and in London in May.
     Wordsworth is in London until May. He then stays, until September, with Robert Jones at Plas-yn-Llan, Llangynhafal, Denbighshire.

February

2   Death of Honoré Gabriel Riqueti, comte de Mirabeau (1749–91). On 4 he is the first to be buried in the new national Panthéon. On 21 September 1794 his body is replaced by Marat's.
     G.G. and J. Robinson publish Inchbald's *A Simple Story* in four volumes. A second edition comes out in March.

March

2   Wesley dies in London, at his house next to the chapel in City Road. He is buried nearby on 9. He preached his last sermon on 23 February at Leatherhead in Surrey.
16 Paine's *The Rights of Man* (Part One) is published by J.S. Jordan. Joseph Johnson, fearing prosecution, withdrew from publishing the work in February. In April another response to Burke, Sir James Mackintosh of Kyllachy's (1765–1832) *Vindiciae Gallicae: A Defence of the French Revolution and its English Admirers*, is published by G.G. and J. Robinson.
18 Burns's 'Tam o' Shanter: a Tale' is in *The Edinburgh Herald*. It also appears in *The Edinburgh Magazine* for March and, in April, in Francis Grose's *Antiquities of Scotland*, volume two; Burns sent the poem to Grose on 1 December 1790 and probably wrote most of it that November.
30 A bill to incorporate the Sierra Leone Company is passed. The first settlers, mostly former American slaves, found Freetown on 11 March 1792. (An earlier attempt to establish a free black colony failed in 1787–9.)

April

16 *Wild Oats* by John O'Keeffe (1747–1833) opens at Covent Garden.
20 Wilberforce's motion for an Abolition of Slavery bill is defeated in the Commons; Joseph Johnson publishes Barbauld's *An Epistle to William Wilberforce, esq. …* on the subject. At his next

attempt, on 3 April 1792, a motion for 'gradual' abolition is passed instead. Further motions are defeated each year between 1796 and 1799 and, at second reading, in 1805. Following the defeat of the 1791 bill abolitionists call for a boycott on sugar from the West Indies.

27 Date on which Burns may have completed the first volume of the Glenriddell Manuscript for presentation to his friend Robert Riddell of Glenriddell (1755–94). Possibly, however, the date should be 1793: see Burns (2014), volume 1, p.173. The second volume, mainly consisting of letters, is not handed over: Riddell breaks off relations with Burns in late December 1793 after an incident involving his sister-in-law, Maria Riddell (1772–1808). (She and Burns are reconciled in spring 1795.) Following Robert Riddell's death in April 1794, Burns asks his widow to return the first volume.

Paine, now an increasingly radical republican, is in Paris until early July.

May

16 Publication by Dilly of Boswell's *The Life of Samuel Johnson* in two volumes.

26 Publication by Hookham and Miller of Clara Reeve's *The School for Widows* in three volumes.

June

12 Publication in Paris of *Justine ou les Malheurs de la vertu*, by Donatien-Alphonse-François, marquis de Sade (1740–1814). *La Nouvelle Justine* follows in 1797.

20 The 'Flight to Varennes': Louis XVI and his family attempt unsuccessfully to reach their supporters' forces.

July

1 Publication by Joseph Johnson of Cowper's *The Iliad and Odyssey of Homer translated into English blank verse*.

6–8 Haydn is in Oxford to receive a doctorate of music from the University. He performs his Symphony no. 92, which becomes known as 'the Oxford'.

11 Voltaire's ashes are reinterred in the Panthéon in Paris.

14   A Bastille Day dinner organized by the Constitutional Society of Birmingham is the occasion, or excuse, for several days of rioting. Damage includes the destruction of the Unitarian Old and New Meeting Houses and of Priestley's house and laboratory. The authorities are slow to restore order.

August
2   Byron's father John Byron (1756–91) dies at Valenciennes.
22   Beginning of a slave-revolt against French rule in Saint-Domingue. François-Dominique Toussaint-l'Ouverture (1743–1803), a former slave, emerges as one of the rebel leaders in 1793. From May 1794 he serves the French Republic but becomes, by the late 1790s, effectively an independent ruler.

In late summer Burns and his family move to Dumfries, living in Wee Vennel (now Bank Street) until 19 May 1793, when they transfer to Mill Hole Brae (now Burns Street).

Scott visits Northumberland and the Borders. His tours of the Borders continue roughly once a year until 1799.

September
1   Blake designs and engraves pictures for a new edition of Wollstonecraft's *Original Stories from Real Life*. He engraves drawings (December) for Erasmus Darwin's *Botanic Garden* (1791) and in 1792–3 for a third work published by Joseph Johnson, John Gabriel Stedman's *Narrative, of ... the Revolted Natives of Surinam* (1796). Johnson agrees to publish Blake's 'The French Revolution' but only the first Book reaches proof stage.
6   First performance of Mozart's *La clemenza di Tito* at the National Theatre, Prague.
13   Louis XVI accepts the new French constitution.

In mid-September *Les Ruines, ou Méditations sur les révolutions des empires*, by Constantin-François de Chasseboeuf, comte de Volney (1757–1820) is published in Paris. The first English translation, by James Marshall, is brought out by Joseph Johnson in 1792.
22   Birth of Michael Faraday (1791–1867) at Newington Butts in Surrey.
26   Birth of Théodore Géricault (1791–1824) in Rouen.
27   Slavery is abolished in France (but not in its colonies).

30 First performance of Mozart's *Die Zauberflöte* at the Theater auf der Wieden, Vienna.

Helen Maria Williams settles in France. (She first visited in summer 1790.) Her *Letters from France* (1790–6) is an important commentary on the revolutionary period.

This autumn Burns works on 'Lament for James, Earl of Glencairn', published in his 1793 *Poems*.

October
1 First meeting of the Legislative Assembly in Paris.
14 Foundation of the Society of United Irishmen of Belfast. The Dublin equivalent is founded on 9 November. (Theobald) Wolfe Tone (1763–98) is closely involved on both occasions.
16 Coleridge begins residence at Jesus College, Cambridge.
26 William Wordsworth visits Charlotte Smith in Brighton.

November
10 Thomas Lawrence is elected Associate Member of the Royal Academy. He becomes a full Academician on 10 February 1794.
13 Wollstonecraft and Godwin meet for the first time at Joseph Johnson's. Paine is also present.
26 Austen finishes 'The History of England'.
29 Burns is in Edinburgh until 11 December.
30 Wordsworth arrives in Paris, leaving for Orléans on 5 December. Here he and Annette Vallon (1766–1841) meet and fall in love.

December
3 Cowley's *A Day in Turkey, or the Russian Slave* is at Covent Garden.
4 Foundation of the Sunday newspaper *The Observer*.
5 Death of Mozart in Vienna. His last compositions include the unfinished *Requiem*.
8 Sir William Jones reads 'On the Mystical Poetry of the Persians and Indians' to the Asiatick Society of Bengal. It is published in 1792 with his translation of Jayadéva's *Gītagovinda*.
27 Burns sends McLehose 'Ae fond kiss', published in *The Scots Musical Museum* in 1792. They saw each other for the last time in Edinburgh on 6.

Towards the end of the year Radcliffe's *The Romance of the Forest, Interspersed With Some Pieces of Poetry* (Hookham and Carpenter) comes out in three volumes, anonymously. Her name is supplied in the second edition in spring 1792.

The first volume of Mary Robinson's *Poems* is published by J.Bell, followed by the second (Evans and Becket) in January 1794.

The first edition of Isaac D'Israeli's (1766–1848) *Curiosities of Literature* is published by Murray. Seven further editions between now and 1823 include much addition and omission of material.

1792

January

25 First meeting of the London Corresponding Society at the Bell tavern, Exeter Street, London. The founding secretary is Thomas Hardy (1752–1832). Horne Tooke, though not a member, is partly responsible for drafting the society's constitution. The subscription is 1d. a week; the membership is dominated by artisans but includes people from a wider range of social backgrounds.

Wollstonecraft's *A Vindication of the Rights of Woman: with Strictures on Political and Moral Subjects* is published by Joseph Johnson.

In January and February food shortages in Paris lead to protests and violence, as in other parts of France in February and March.

February

2 Mary Robinson's novel *Vancenza; or, The Dangers of Credulity* is published by Joseph Bell in two volumes. It reaches a fifth edition in 1794.

16 Publication of *The Rights of Man; Part the Second, Combining Principle and Practice*. Paine is named as the publisher in order to make less likely the prosecution of J.S. Jordan for printing it.

18 Holcroft's *The Road to Ruin* is at Covent Garden, the first of 37 performances this season.

23 Death of Sir Joshua Reynolds at 47 Leicester Square, London. He has been President of the Royal Academy (the first) since 1768. The last of his Discourses was delivered in 1790. His successor as President is Benjamin West (1738–1820).

29 Gioachino Rossini (1792–1868) is born in Pesaro.

In London Wollstonecraft meets Talleyrand, the dedicatee of *A Vindication of the Rights of Woman*.

Wordsworth moves from Orléans to Blois, Vallon's home town. Here his friendship with the republican soldier Michel de Beaupuy (1755–96) develops.

March
1   The Holy Roman Emperor Leopold II dies and is succeeded by Franz II.
16 Gustav III of Sweden is fatally wounded in Stockholm, the victim of an aristocratic conspiracy. He dies on 29.
24 In Dublin John Field (1782–1837) gives his first public recital.

April
15 Charles Lamb starts work as a clerk at the East India Company (until 1825).
16 William Frend (1757–1841) writes to Hays, expressing approval of her *Cursory Remarks on an Enquiry into the Expediency and Propriety of Public or Social Worship* (as 'Eusebia', 1791). They meet in May and form a close relationship between now and 1796. He either does not return her love or chooses not to take it further. Hays draws on their situation in *Memoirs of Emma Courtney* (1796).
20 France declares war on Austria. The German states support Austria.

Mary Blachford, later Tighe (1772–1810) composes 'Verses Written in Solitude, April 1792'.

Robert Southey (1774–1843) is expelled from Westminster School (where he started in 1788) having written an essay against flogging as the devil's work. He matriculates at Balliol College, Oxford, in November, takes up residence in January 1793, and leaves without a degree in July 1794.

May
21 A royal proclamation against seditious writings is issued.
24 The London Corresponding Society issues an address *To the nation at large*. A thousand copies are distributed.

The Pleasures of Memory, a Poem by Samuel Rogers (1763–1855) is published, anonymously, by Cadell. Rogers is first named as author in the fifth edition in August 1793. 22,000 copies sell by 1806, when the fifteenth edition appears.

Holcroft's *Anna St Ives: a Novel* is published in seven volumes by Shepperson & Reynolds.

June

Charlotte Smith's *Desmond* is published by Robinson at the end of June or beginning of July.

Heinrich von Kleist (1777–1811) serves in the Prussian army from now until 4 April 1799.

July

11   Scott is admitted as an advocate. Earlier (indentured 31 March 1786) he trained as a solicitor.

27   Lewis begins his stay in Weimar. Here he meets Goethe and Christoph Martin Wieland (1733–1813) and starts translating some of their work. He returns to Oxford to finish his degree in May 1793.

August

4   Birth of Percy Bysshe Shelley at Field House, near Horsham in Sussex. His father, Timothy Shelley (1753–1844) is a landowner who succeeds as baronet in 1815 and is MP for New Shoreham 1802–18.

10   The French monarchy is deprived of its remaining powers. The royal family are taken to the Temple prison in Paris on 12.

26   Paine is made a French citizen by the Legislative Assembly and is elected deputy for the Pas-de-Calais in the Convention.

Cowper, Charlotte Smith and Romney (who sketches Cowper and Smith) are together at Hayley's home at Eartham in Sussex. Here Smith works on her four-volume *The Old Manor House: a Novel* (published by Joseph Bell in spring 1793).

September

2–6   September massacres in Paris: at least a thousand prisoners are murdered.

17   David is elected to the National Convention (which first meets on 20). In mid-October he becomes a member of the Committee of Public Instruction and organizes such revolutionary festivals as the Ceremony of the Supreme Being of 8 June 1793.

20   Divorce becomes legal in France.

20   French defeat of the Prussians at Valmy.

21   The National Convention votes to abolish the French monarchy. On 22 the Republic is proclaimed.

Hays's letter to Wollstonecraft in response to *A Vindication of the Rights of Woman* begins their friendship.
Probably this month Wordsworth and Vallon go back to Orléans.
This autumn, or possibly in 1793, Scott makes his first journey to the Highlands.

October
2   In Paris the Committee of General Security is formed; in March 1793 it becomes the Committee of Public Safety.
2   Foundation in Kettering of the Particular Baptist Society for the Propagation of the Gospel Among the Heathen (Baptist Missionary Society).
28   Crabbe and his family settle at Parham in Suffolk. He becomes curate at Sweffling in 1794 and at Great Glemham in 1797.
29   Wordsworth goes to Paris. At the end of November he returns to England.
29   Godwin and Inchbald meet.

November
7   A joint message of support from the London Corresponding Society and organizations including the Manchester Constitutional Society is read to the French National Convention. The address, signed by Maurice Margarot (1745–1815) and Hardy, is published in Paris and London.
20   John Reeves (1752–1829) founds the Association for the Preservation of Liberty and Property against Republicans and Levellers.
Holcroft joins the Society for Constitutional Information.

December
8   Wollstonecraft sets off alone for Paris. She hoped to go with a group including Fuseli, with whom she has been unrequitedly in love; she met him through Joseph Johnson in 1788. In Paris, early in 1793, she meets Gilbert Imlay (1754–1828) and they become lovers. Registering as his wife, since he is American, gives her some protection during this troubled period in France. In summer 1793 she moves to Neuilly-sur-Seine and in January 1794 to Le Havre.
15   Birth in Orléans of Anne-Caroline Wordsworth.

18 Paine is convicted (in his absence) of seditious libel in *The Rights of Man*. He returned to France on 14 September.

Burns's political sympathies are investigated by his superiors in the Excise. By 5 January 1793 they are apparently satisfied.

The 'Clapham Sect', known at the time as 'the Saints', begins to come together this year. Wilberforce is its most notable member.

Publication by Blamire of Gilpin's *Three Essays: On Picturesque Beauty; On Picturesque Travel; and On Sketching Landscape*.

1793

January
21 Execution of Louis XVI. Yearsley prints her 'Reflections on the Death of Louis XVI' soon afterwards in Bristol.
26 Thelwall delivers a lecture on 'Animal Vitality' to the Physical Society of Guy's Hospital (published this year as *An Essay Towards a Definition of Animal Vitality*).
29 Publication by Joseph Johnson of Wordsworth's *An Evening Walk* and *Descriptive Sketches*.

February
1 France declares war on Britain (and Britain on France on 11). A state of war between the two nations will continue until the Peace of Amiens in 1802. France is also at war with the Netherlands from 1 February and with Spain from 7 March.
7 Foundation of the Literary and Philosophical Society of Newcastle upon Tyne.
14 William Godwin's *An Enquiry Concerning the Nature of Political Justice, and its Influence on General Virtue and Happiness* is published in two volumes by G.G. and J. Robinson.

John Flaxman's illustrations of *The Odyssey* are distributed between now and April, and those of *The Iliad* and Dante in July. A further series for Aeschylus follows in January 1795.

March
3 William Charles Macready (1793–1873) is born in London.
10 The Revolutionary Tribunal is formed in Paris. It is abolished on 31 May 1795.

April
Publication of Thelwall's *The Peripatetic; or, Sketches of the Heart, of Nature and Society; In a Series of Politico-Sentimental Journals ... of the Eccentric Excursions of Sylvanus Theophrastus. Supposed to Be Written by Himself.*

May
17 François-René de Chateaubriand (1768–1848), having served with royalist forces, arrives at Southampton to begin seven years' exile in England.

Frend is tried for sedition in Cambridge University Senate House following the publication of his *Peace and Union Recommended*, which criticizes the Anglican liturgy. He is banished from the university. Coleridge is among his keenest supporters and knows him later in London.

Publication of George Thomson's *A Select Collection of Original Scottish Airs for the Voice*. Burns contributes songs; further work is included in the later volumes published between 1798 and 1818.

In late May or early June Cadell publishes Charlotte Smith's *The Emigrants, A Poem*.

June
2–3 Austen writes the last of her 'Juvenilia'.

Having lived in London since December 1792, Wordsworth visits the Isle of Wight in June–July. Soon afterwards, having crossed the Plain, he probably composes *Salisbury Plain*.

July
10 Georges Danton (1759–94) is voted off the Committee of Public Safety; on 27 Maximilien Robespierre (1758–94) is voted on.
13 Murder of Jean-Paul Marat (1743–93) by Charlotte Corday (1768–93). Her execution on 17 launches the Terror. David's painting of the murdered Marat is finished in October.
13 Birth of John Clare (1793–1864) at Helpston in Northamptonshire.
c.27 Burns tours in Galloway, returning to Dumfries on 2 August. He visits Galloway again in June 1794.

28   Fanny Burney marries Alexandre d'Arblay (1754–1818) at Mickleham in Surrey.

Pitt visits Bentham at Queen Square Place to see a model of his plan for a prison, the Panopticon. Its use is proposed in *Panopticon; or, the Inspection-House* (1791). The scheme eventually founders having encountered a series of political difficulties over the next twenty years.

Between July and September Southey works on *Joan of Arc*, making some additions in November and December. He revises the poem extensively between May and autumn 1795.

August

31   In Edinburgh the radical Thomas Muir (1765–99) is convicted of encouraging sedition and sentenced to fourteen years' transportation to Botany Bay; in Perth Thomas Fyshe Palmer (1747–1802) is sentenced to seven years' transportation on 13 September.

29   Toulon surrenders to the British. It is recaptured by the French on 19 December, with Napoleon Bonaparte (1769–1821) commanding the artillery. He is promoted *général de brigade* on 22 December and *général de division* on 16 October 1795.

Wordsworth reaches Tintern Abbey (to which he returns in 1798). By late August he is again with Robert Jones at Plas-yn-Llan.

September

4   Establishment of the Board of Agriculture. Arthur Young becomes Secretary and is himself responsible for reports including those on six counties between 1794 and 1809.

6–8   British and Dutch forces are defeated by the French at Hondschoote.

14   George Macartney, Viscount (later Earl) Macartney (1737–1806) is presented to Emperor Qianlong in Peking (Beijing). He was appointed ambassador in 1792. Dismissed by the imperial authorities in October 1793, he visits Canton (Guangzhou) before leaving.

14   David becomes a member of the Committee of Public Safety (until July 1794).

25   Birth in Liverpool of Felicia Dorothea Browne, later Hemans (1793–1835).

Nelson meets the Hamiltons in Naples.

October

5   Mary Blachford marries Henry Tighe. They live mainly in England, with frequent visits to Ireland, until 1801.
5   France introduces its new republican calendar, which is observed until the end of 1805.
7–8 Major defeat by French forces of the Vendéen rebels who have been fighting them since the spring.
9   France bans the import of British manufactured goods and orders the arrest of British citizens.
16 Execution of Queen Marie-Antoinette. David sketches her on the way to the scaffold. Mary Robinson's 'A Monody on the Death of the Late Queen of France' is in *The Oracle* on 18 December; her 'Marie Antoinette's Lamentation, in her Prison of the Temple' was in *The Oracle* on 8 March and her *Impartial Reflections on the Present Situation of the Queen of France* appeared in August 1791.
21 Thelwall joins the London Corresponding Society. It holds a major open-air meeting on 24.
Arrest of British citizens in Paris. Among them, for two months, is Helen Maria Williams.
31 Twenty Girondin leaders are guillotined in Paris, followed by (Louis) Philippe 'Égalité', Duke of Orléans (1747–93), on 6 November and Marie-Jeanne (Manon) Roland (1754–93) on 8 November.

November

7   Coleridge's first published poem, 'To Fortune', is in *The Morning Chronicle*.
10 The Festival of Liberty is held in Paris.
19 The British reform convention in Edinburgh, which met initially in October, re-opens. Margarot and Joseph Gerrald (1763–96) attend as delegates for the London Corresponding Society. They are arrested with William Skirving (c.1745/50–96), secretary of the Scottish Society of the Friends of the People, on 5 December and charged with sedition on 12.
Thelwall begins his political lectures at Compton Street, London.

December

2   Coleridge, in debt and unhappy in love, enlists in the 15th Light Dragoons. He uses the name Silas Tomkyn Comberbache. His discharge is purchased by his brothers on 7 April 1794 and he returns to Cambridge on 10.
26 By now Wordsworth is at Whitehaven. He is in the North-west much of the time until January 1795.
28 Paine is arrested in Paris. He is released from prison through the intercession of James Monroe (1758–1831), the new American ambassador, on 4 November 1794.

Blake completes *Visions of the Daughters of Albion* and *America a Prophecy*.

Austen works on 'Lady Susan' probably between 1793 and 1795.

1794

January

7   In Edinburgh Skirving is sentenced to fourteen years' transportation to Botany Bay, as are Margarot on 14 January and Gerrald on 13 March. They become known, with Muir, Thomas Palmer and other radicals, as the 'Scottish Martyrs'. Only Margarot lives to return, in 1810.
16 Death of Gibbon in London.

Beginning of Cowper's final period of depression.

Joseph Bell publishes Charlotte Smith's one-volume *The Wanderings of Warwick*.

Publication of *An Address to the People of Britain*, by Horne Tooke and John Martin.

February

4   Slavery is abolished in the French colonies. It is largely restored by the law of 20 May 1802.
5   Haydn returns to London. He leaves on 15 August 1795, having led performances of work including his Symphonies 101 ('The Clock') on 3 March 1794 and 104 ('London') on 4 May 1795.
5   Holcroft's *Love's Frailties, or, Precept Against Practice* (after Otto Heinrich von Gemmingen, *Der deutsche Hausvater*, 1779) is performed at Covent Garden.

13 Publication by Hookham and Carpenter of Mary Robinson's two-volume *The Widow, or A Picture of Modern Times. A Novel in a Series of Letters.*
22 Execution of Jean Capot de Feuillide, husband of Austen's cousin Eliza (Hancock) de Feuillide. The widow will marry Austen's brother Henry in 1797.
   This month William and Dorothy Wordsworth are together, for the first time in over three years, at Millbank, near Halifax. They travel to the Lakes in April, staying mainly at Windy Brow, a house near Keswick and then, between May and July or August, in Whitehaven.

March
1 Sir William Jones publishes *Institutes of Hindu Law; or, The Ordinances of Menu* in Calcutta.
12 The new Drury Lane Theatre, seating 3,611, opens with a Handel concert. The first dramatic production, on 21 April, is of *Macbeth*, with John Philip Kemble as Macbeth and Siddons as Lady Macbeth. The previous theatre was demolished in 1791.
28 Death in prison at Bourg-la-Reine of Nicolas de Caritat, marquis de Condorcet (1743–94). His *Esquisse d'un tableau historique des progrès de l'esprit humain* is published later this year. A translation, *Outlines of an Historical View of the Progress of the Human Mind*, is brought out by Joseph Johnson in 1795.

April
5 Execution of Danton, Camille Desmoulins (1760–94) and their associates.
7 Open-air reformist meeting on Castle Hill, Sheffield, convened by the Sheffield Constitutional Society. A similar meeting is held in Halifax on 24 by the Friends of Peace and Reform.
8 Priestley, who has decided to emigrate, sails for America. He arrives in New York on 4 June and goes on to Philadelphia later in the month and to Northumberland, Pennsylvania, in July. He becomes a friend and correspondent of Jefferson.

9   The Society for Constitutional Information and the London Corresponding Society plan to organize a reform convention similar to the one held in Edinburgh in 1793.
27 Sir William Jones dies in Calcutta.
Publication by Joseph Johnson of Erasmus Darwin's *Zoonomia; or, The Laws of Organic Life*, Part I. It reappears with Parts II and III in the edition of 1796.
Burns's 'O My Luve's Like a Red, Red Rose' is included in Pietro Urbani's *A Selection of Scots Songs*.

May

8   *The Jew*, by Richard Cumberland (1732–1811), is at Drury Lane.
8   Burns's 'Scots, wha hae' ('Robert Bruce's March to Bannockburn') is in *The Morning Chronicle*. It was written in its first form probably in late August 1793 and is later included in Thomson's *Select Collection* in 1799 and in Johnson's *Scots Musical Museum* in 1803.
c.9 G.G. and J. Robinson publish Radcliffe's *The Mysteries of Udolpho, a Romance; Interspersed With Some Pieces of Poetry*, in four volumes. The Robinsons pay her £500 for the copyright and there are six editions by 1806. Victorine de Chastenay's much reprinted French translation first appears in 1797. On 29 Radcliffe and her husband arrive in Holland to begin the tour described, with another to the Lake District this autumn, in *A Journey Made in the Summer of 1794, Through Holland and the Western Frontier of Germany ...* (Robinson, June 1795).
12   Hardy is arrested, followed by Thelwall on 13 and Horne Tooke on 16. Later in the month they are moved to the Tower of London. At this stage they are charged with sedition. The government has moved against them, and other radicals arrested at the same time, on the basis that the planned National Convention (see 9 April) may become an insurrection. During his time in prison Thelwall writes *Poems Written in Close Confinement* (1795).
14   Birth at Le Havre of Fanny Imlay (1794–1816), daughter of Wollstonecraft and Imlay. In late August Wollstonecraft follows Imlay to Paris but he leaves for London.
15   Lewis arrives at The Hague as attaché to the British ambassador. Here he works on *The Monk*, finishing it on 23 September.

19 Birth in Dublin, as Anna Brownell Murphy, of Anna Jameson (1794–1860). The family moves to England in 1798.
23 Habeas Corpus is suspended (until 1 July 1795).
26 Publication by Crosby, in three volumes, of Godwin's *Things as They Are; or The Adventures of Caleb Williams*. Robinson publishes second and third editions in 1796 and 1797.

Work starts on Marple aqueduct, Salford, by Benjamin Outram (1764–1805), continuing until 1800.

The Prince of Wales obtains George Brummell ('Beau' Brummell, 1778–1840) a commission in the 10th Hussars (the Prince's regiment). He becomes a close associate of the Prince and, particularly after he leaves the army in 1798, an arbiter of fashion.

June

1 British ships defeat French in the 'Battle of the Glorious First of June'. Crowds in London celebrate for several weeks. On 11 they wreck Hardy's house and shop, which may contribute to the death of his wife, Lydia Hardy, in childbirth on 27 August.
2 Robespierre is elected President of the Convention.
8 Festival of the Supreme Being in Paris. (The cult was established on 7 May.) Robespierre presides.
10 Beginning of the 'Great Terror' in France.
15 Coleridge and a fellow student, Joseph Hucks, set off on a walking tour. A few days later, in Oxford, Coleridge meets Southey. They are soon discussing a plan for 'Pantisocracy', an experiment in communal living to be carried out in Pennsylvania.
27 British ships land émigré forces in France from the Bay of Quiberon. Their expedition fails in July.
29 Godwin and Alderson are at a dinner given by her father in Godwin's honour in Norwich.

July

4 First issue of *The Sheffield Iris*, edited, and from 1795 to 1825 owned, by James Montgomery (1771–1854).
5 Coleridge continues his walking tour, first from Oxford to Gloucester. He goes on to Herefordshire and North Wales.
25 Execution of André Chénier (1762–94).
27 Robespierre is overthrown by his opponents and guillotined on 28. Many of his supporters are executed soon afterwards.

August

5   Coleridge arrives in Bristol, visiting Southey and Robert Lovell (1770–96), with both of whom on 22 he begins work on *The Fall of Robespierre: an Historic Drama*. It is published by W.H. Lunn and by J. and J. Merrill in September, without Lovell's contribution, under Coleridge's name.

5–10   Following the fall of Robespierre and the end of the 'Great Terror', large numbers of prisoners in Paris are released.

14   Southey and Coleridge set out on a visit to Somerset, where they see Thomas Poole (1765–1837) at Nether Stowey.

15–22 Riots are directed at 'crimp houses', the taverns where men are detained and press-ganged into the army and navy. There are similar attacks on 6–14 July 1795.

Charlotte Smith's *The Banished Man: a Novel* is published in four volumes by Cadell and Davies.

September

9   Birth of John Hamilton Reynolds (1794–1852) in Shrewsbury.

17   Coleridge, after a period in London, returns to Cambridge. He continues to try to persuade others of the virtues of Pantisocracy. He visits London again in November and then in December, this time leaving Cambridge permanently, without completing his degree. His friendship with the Lambs is established.

17   Godwin and William Hazlitt (1778–1830) meet.

The Cabinet, a radical periodical, starts publication in Norwich. Alderson contributes fifteen poems in 1794–5.

Joseph Johnson publishes the first (and only) volume of Wollstonecraft's *An Historical and Moral View of the Origin and Progress of the French Revolution; and the Effect it has produced in Europe*. She started work on the book by June 1793.

About now Southey writes *Wat Tyler*.

October

11   Rousseau's remains are installed in the Panthéon.

Thelwall, Horne Tooke and Hardy are moved from the Tower to Newgate prison. Holcroft is arrested and sent to Newgate. The charge against them is now to be high treason. Godwin campaigns on their behalf. His *Cursory Strictures on the Charge Delivered by Lord*

Chief Justice Eyre to the Grand Jury, 2 October 1794 comes out in *The Morning Chronicle* on 21 and also separately. The pamphlet war continues and Godwin's *Reply to an Answer to Cursory Strictures* appears on 31.

Hays and Godwin begin their correspondence.

November
5   Hardy is acquitted after trial at the Old Bailey. Horne Tooke is tried on 17–22 and Thelwall on 1–5 December. They too are acquitted and charges against other radicals, including Holcroft, are dropped. Thomas Erskine (1750–1823) appears for the defence in all three trials and Sir John Scott (1751–1838, later Earl of Eldon), the attorney-general, for the Crown. Godwin attends throughout. Alderson is also there. Thomas Lawrence sketches Godwin and Holcroft. Pitt is subpoenaed to appear as a witness for the defence in Tooke's trial: he admits attending earlier reformist meetings. Works reflecting on the trials include Holcroft's *A Narrative of Facts, Relating to a Prosecution for High Treason* (1795) and his *A Letter to the Right Honourable William Wyndham* (1795), and Thelwall's *The trial at large of John Thelwall. For high treason …* (1795).
29 Unsuccessful performance of Mary Robinson's satire *Nobody*, starring Jordan, at Drury Lane.

December
1   Between now and 29 January 1795 Coleridge's sonnets on 'Eminent Contemporaries' are published in *The Morning Chronicle*.
12 Coleridge and Godwin meet.
24 Date given by Coleridge to 'Religious Musings' (completed spring 1796).

This month, dated 1795, *Poems* by Lovell and Southey is published by Cruttwell in Bath.

Late this month Burns becomes acting supervisor of the Excise in Dumfries.

In France (mainly Lyon and the south) the 'White Terror' begins: counter-revolutionary massacres, continuing into summer 1795.

Paley's *A View of the Evidences of Christianity* is published. It becomes part of the Cambridge University syllabus in 1822.

Blake completes *Songs of Experience*. He combines it with the earlier volume as *Songs of Innocence and Experience: Shewing the Two Contrary States of the Human Soul*. Blake also produces *Europe* and *The First Book of Urizen*.
Thomas Dibdin (1771–1841) publishes *Comic Songs* this year, under the name T. Merchant.
Caspar David Friedrich (1774–1840) studies in Copenhagen at the Royal Danish Academy between 1794 and 1798.

1795

January
1   First performance at Covent Garden of *The Mysteries of the Castle*, by Miles Peter Andrews (1742–1814), derived from Radcliffe's *A Sicilian Romance* and *The Mysteries of Udolpho*.
3   Death of Josiah Wedgwood at Etruria Hall. His Etruria factory was established in 1768–9. He is buried on 6 in Stoke-on-Trent.
Death, in about the first week of the month, of Raisley Calvert (1773–95), with whom Wordsworth has often stayed since last September. He leaves him £900.
11 Southey comes to London, where Coleridge has been lingering, to bring him back to Bristol. There they live together at 25 College Green until September. In late January and February Coleridge gives three 'Moral and Political Lectures', the first two probably in the schoolroom of the Bristol Corn Market and the third in a vacant house near Castle Green (Coleridge [1969–2002], 1.22).
22 Montgomery is sentenced to three months in prison, served in York, for seditious libel in *The Sheffield Iris*.
31 Burns is involved in the formation of the Dumfries Volunteers. His song 'The Dumfries Volunteers' appears in *The Edinburgh Courant* (4 May), *The Dumfries Journal* (5 May) and *The Caledonian Mercury* (7 May).
This month Thomas Moore (1779–1852) starts at Trinity College, Dublin. His enrolment is made possible by the Catholic Relief Act of 1793. Among his Trinity friends is Robert Emmet (1778–1803).
Early this year Cadell and Davies publish, in two volumes, Charlotte Smith's *Rural Walks: in Dialogues. Intended for the Use of Young Persons*. The sequel, *Rambles Farther*, follows in two volumes in August 1796.

February
10 John Hoppner is elected as a Royal Academician. He was elected Associate on 4 November 1793.
28 Cumberland's *The Wheel of Fortune*, with John Philip Kemble as Penruddock, opens at Drury Lane.
Between this month and early August William Wordsworth is in London. He associates with radicals including Godwin (whom he meets on 27), Holcroft and Frend.

March
14 Southey gives twelve or thirteen 'Historical Lectures' in Bristol between now and c.24 April. Coleridge plays some part in the writing of the lectures.
21 Single performance at Drury Lane, with Siddons and John Philip Kemble, of Fanny Burney D'Arblay's *Edwy and Elgiva*.
Distribution of *Cheap Repository Tracts* begins. The scheme is organized, and many of the tracts written, by More and her sisters.

April
5 France makes peace with Prussia and then on 16 May with the Batavian Republic (proclaimed in Amsterdam in January) and on 22 June with Spain.
8 The Prince of Wales marries Princess Caroline of Brunswick (1768–1821). (He is already illegally 'married' to Maria Fitzherbert.) They separate in 1796.
12 Wollstonecraft, a few days after leaving France, arrives in London, hoping to be reunited with Imlay. In May, depressed at his infidelity, she attempts suicide.
15 John 'Gentleman' Jackson (1769–1845) beats Mendoza in a fight at Hornchurch. Soon afterwards Jackson opens his Pugilistic Club at 13 Bond Street, next to the fencing academy run by Henry Angelo (1756–1835) and then from 1817 by his son, also Henry (1780–1852).
23 Hastings is acquitted.
Tighe meets Seward and the 'Ladies of Llangollen', Lady Eleanor Butler (1739–1829) and Sarah Ponsonby (1755–1831).
Anonymous appearance of Eliza Fenwick's (1766?–1840) *Secresy; or, The Ruin on the Rock* in three volumes. It is published, at the author's expense, by William Lane and others.

May

2   Holcroft's *The Deserted Daughter* (a version of Cumberland's *The Fashionable Lover*) is at Covent Garden.
10 Re-formation, at a meeting in Belfast, of the United Irishmen (effectively suppressed in Dublin in May 1794) as a secret association. Lord Edward Fitzgerald (1763–98) becomes one of the main leaders.
16 Treaty of The Hague, bringing the Batavian Republic firmly into the French sphere of influence.
19 Coleridge gives the first of his 'Six Lectures on Revealed Religion' at the Asssembly Coffee House, the Quay, Bristol. The probable dates for the other lectures are 22 or 26 and 26 or 29 May and 2, 5 and 9 or 12 June. (See Coleridge [1969–2002], 1.xxxv–vi.)
19 Boswell dies in London. He is buried at Auchinleck on 8 June. Malone works on the third (1799) and several subsequent editions of his *Life of Johnson*.
22 Mungo Park (1771–1806) sets off on his first attempt to trace the course of the Niger, returning in December 1797 and publishing his *Travels in the Interior Districts of Africa* in 1799.

June

8   Death of Louis 'XVII' (1785–95), son of Louis XVI.
16 Coleridge lectures 'On the Slave Trade' at the Assembly Coffee House in Bristol.
16 Wollstonecraft, with her baby and a maid called Marguerite, sets off on a business mission to Scandinavia for Imlay. Unfavourable winds prevent the ship from leaving Hull until at least 21. She arrives in Gothenburg on 27 and Tønsberg by 18 July; here she begins work on *Letters Written During a Short Residence in Sweden, Norway and Denmark*, published by Joseph Johnson early in 1796. She returns to Gothenburg on 25 August. In September she travels via Copenhagen to Hamburg and reaches Dover by 4 October.
29 The London Corresponding Society leads a mass reformist meeting at St George's Fields, Southwark.

August

20 Date given by Coleridge to 'Effusion XXXV' (renamed in 1817 'The Eolian Harp'). The poem is finished by the end of the year.

Between mid-month and late September Wordsworth is in Bristol. He meets Southey and Coleridge.
This month Scott proposes marriage to Williamina Belsches (1776–1810). She is engaged to another man in October 1796.

September
21   Catholic agrarian 'Defenders' fight Protestants near Loughall in Armagh in what becomes known as 'the Battle of the Diamond'. Protestants found the Orange Society (later Orange Order) soon afterwards.
26–7 William and Dorothy Wordsworth move into Racedown Lodge, Dorset, with Basil, child of a widowed friend, Basil Montagu (1770–1851).
28   Russia enters an alliance with Britain and Austria against France.

Coleridge writes 'Lines written at Shurton Bars'.
Piozzi and her husband move into Brynbella, the house they have built near Bachygraig in North Wales. She moves to Bath in 1814, five years after his death.

October
1   Annexation of the Austrian Netherlands (Belgium) by France.
4   Marriage of Coleridge and Sara Fricker (1770–1845) at St Mary Redcliffe, Bristol. They live in Clevedon, where they are visited by Joseph Cottle (1770–1853) on 7. Coleridge met him in August 1794.
5   An attempted royalist rising in Paris is suppressed by Jean-Nicolas Barras (1755–1829) and Bonaparte, who becomes commander of the Armée de l'Intérieur on 26.
10   Wollstonecraft's second suicide attempt.
26   The London Corresponding Society organizes a mass meeting at Copenhagen Fields, Islington, and holds its general meeting at Copenhagen House on 12 November. There is another rally at Marylebone Fields in December. Thelwall speaks on all three occasions.
29   A crowd attacks George III's coach on its way to the opening of Parliament and again on the way back. This is one trigger for the government introduction of the 'Two Bills' – the

'gagging acts' which become law as the Treasonable Practices Act and the Seditious Meeings Act on 18 December. Criticism of the king, 'Government and Constitution of this Realm' becomes treason and unauthorized assemblies of over 50 people are banned.
31 Birth of John Keats (1795–1821) in London.

November
3   In France the Directory takes office (until November 1799), replacing the Convention.
14 Marriage of Southey and Edith Fricker (1774–1837). On 19 Southey sets off for Spain and Portugal, where he remains until May 1796; his *Letters Written During a Short Residence in Spain and Portugal* are published in January 1797 by Cottle in Bristol and by G.G. and J. Robinson and Cadell and Davies in London. Pantisocracy has been abandoned, causing a rift between Southey and Coleridge.
20 By now Wordsworth has substantially revised his Salisbury Plain poem as 'Adventures on Salisbury Plain'. Work continues in 1796 but the poem is not, as intended, published. (A later version appears as *Guilt and Sorrow* in 1842.)
21 Joseph Johnson prints an anonymous pamphlet by Godwin, *Considerations on Lord Grenville's and Mr Pitt's Bills, concerning Treasonable and Seditious Practices, and Unlawful Assemblies. By a Lover of Order.*
25 Hays and Godwin meet.
26 At the Pelican Inn in Bristol Coleridge delivers his Lecture on the Two Bills (see 29 October and 21 November). It is revised and published, probably c.10 December (Coleridge [1969–2002], 1.278) as *The Plot Discovered; or An Address to the People, Against Ministerial Treason*. Also in November Coleridge writes 'Reflections on Having Left a Place of Retirement' (see October 1796).

December
3   Publication in Bristol of Coleridge's *Conciones ad Populum. Or Addresses to the People*, derived from and expanding the lectures of January–February.

4 Thomas Carlyle (1795–1881) is born at Ecclefechan in Dumfriesshire.

24 Egerton and others publish (dated 1796) *Miscellaneous Papers and Legal Instruments Under the Hand and Seal of William Shakspeare* ... : forgeries by William Henry Ireland (1775–1835).

Publication by Cottle in Bristol, dated 1796, of Southey's *Joan of Arc, an Epic Poem*. A revised version is published at about the beginning of May 1798.

For six weeks in December 1795 and January 1796 Charles Lamb, during some kind of mental breakdown, is confined in the asylum at Hoxton.

A French fleet sails for Ireland but is beaten back by storms.

Austen probably writes 'Elinor and Marianne', the first version of *Sense and Sensibility*, this year.

Blake works on *The Song of Los*, *The Book of Los*, and *The Book of Ahania*.

Daniel Boileau's translation from Schiller, *The Ghost-Seer; or, The Apparitionist* is published by Vernor. The original, *Der Geisterseher*, was first published in 1787–9.

Between 1795 and 1798 David works on *The Sabine Women*. Ingres, his pupil from 1796, is among his assistants. The painting is privately displayed in Paris until 1805, making the artist considerable sums of money.

1796

January

1 Mary Robinson's *Angelina; a Novel* is published in three volumes by Hookham and Carpenter.

7 Birth of Princess Charlotte Augusta (1796–1817), daughter of the Prince and Princess of Wales, at Carlton House, London.

8 Hays reintroduces Wollstonecraft and Godwin.

9 Coleridge sets off on a tour of the Midlands and North to raise money for his proposed *Watchman*. In Derby on about 22 he meets Erasmus Darwin and Joseph Wright of Derby. He returns to Bristol on 13 February.

21 A year after his first sentence, Montgomery is fined £30 and sent to prison in York for six months. On 7 August 1795 *The Sheffield Iris* expressed support for soldiers involved in a protest

about pay and conditions. Montgomery's *Prison Amusements* (under the name 'Paul Positive') is published by Joseph Johnson in 1797.

30 Grand opening by Boulton of the Soho Foundry at Smethwick on the Birmingham Canal. The Boulton & Watt company produces engines here. Watt retires in 1800 but his son, the younger James Watt (1769–1848) remains a partner as does Boulton's son, Matthew Robinson Boulton (1770–1842).

This month G.G. and J. Robinson publish Inchbald's *Nature and Art* in two volumes. There is a revised edition in 1797.

Tom Lefroy (1776–1869) is briefly involved in a romantic relationship or flirtation with Austen.

Between January and April Thelwall lectures on classical history at Beaufort Buildings, where he gave his more overtly political lectures before the 'gagging acts'.

February

9–10 Mary Robinson sees Godwin. She also soon comes to know Wollstonecraft.
17 Death of James Macpherson (1736–96). He is buried in Westminster Abbey.

March

1 Coleridge's *The Watchman* begins. There are ten issues between now and 13 May.
2 Bonaparte is given command of the Army of Italy. His victories over the Austrians there include Lodi (10 May), Arcola (14–17 November) and Rivoli (14–15 January 1797).
9 Marriage of Bonaparte and Joséphine de Beauharnais (1763–1814).
12 Colman the Younger's *The Iron Chest*, after Godwin's *Caleb Williams*, is performed at Drury Lane with J.P. Kemble as Mortimer (the equivalent of Falkland) and with Godwin in the audience.
12 Lewis's *The Monk: A Romance* is published by Joseph Bell. Lewis's initials are replaced, in the second edition in October, by his name followed by 'M.P.' (He is MP for Hindon 1796–1802.) Attacks on the novel as obscene or blasphemous result

in alterations for the fourth edition in 1798, which is retitled *Ambrosio; or, The Monk*.

31 Malone's *An Inquiry into the Authenticity of Certain Miscellaneous Papers and Legal Instruments Attributed to Shakspeare* provides clear evidence that Ireland is a forger. On 2 April Ireland's *Vortigern*, which he earlier claimed to be by Shakespeare, has one unsuccessful performance at Drury Lane with J.P. Kemble in the title role. Ireland admits his fabrications in *An Authentic Account of the Shakspearian Manuscripts, &c.* (Debrett, 1796) and *Confessions of William Henry Ireland* (Goddard, 1805).

This month the Coleridges move to Oxford Street, Kingsdown, Bristol.

William Taylor's *Lenora: A Ballad from Bürger* is in *The Monthly Magazine* for March. 'Lenore', by Gottfried August Bürger (1747–94), first published in 1773, has been republished in London as *Lenore: Ein Gedicht*. Several other translations come out in 1796, among them Scott's *William and Helen* (see 1 November); John Thomas Stanley's (1766–1850) *Leonora. A Tale*, with illustrations by Blake; and William Robert Spencer's *Leonora*.

April

16 Coleridge's *Poems on Various Subjects* is published by Cottle. It includes four pieces by Charles Lamb.
20 Siddons stars in Sophia Lee's *Almeyda, Queen of Granada* at Drury Lane.
25 Turner shows an oil painting at the Royal Academy for the first time: *Fishermen at Sea*.

May

14 Edward Jenner (1749–1823) successfully vaccinates an eight-year-old boy against smallpox, inoculating him with cowpox matter. Results and conclusions based on this and further vaccinations are included in Jenner's privately printed *Inquiry into the Causes and Effects of the Variolae Vaccinae ...* (1798), supplemented by similar works of 1799 and 1800.

The Coleridges stay with Poole at Nether Stowey.

From this month until May 1797 Thelwall tours, giving classical history lectures – often disrupted – in places including Norfolk,

Derby and Stockport. In August he is attacked and nearly taken by a press-gang in Yarmouth, prompting his *An appeal to popular opinion, against kidnapping and murder* ...

June
This summer Wollstonecraft begins *The Wrongs of Woman*.
Wordsworth is in London in June and early July. He sees Godwin and may meet Charles Lamb for the first time.
Between now and June 1797 Blake engraves illustrations for Edward Young's *Night Thoughts* (one volume of the proposed four, 1797, with an anonymous introduction by Fuseli).

July
12 T. Payne, and Cadell & Davies, publish Fanny Burney d'Arblay's *Camilla: or, a Picture of Youth* (five volumes), as the work of 'the author of Evelina and Cecilia'.
21 Death of Burns in Dumfries. He is buried in St Michael's churchyard on 25. A new mausoleum is erected there in 1815–17.

August
Early this month Coleridge visits his mother and other family members in Devon. At mid-month he goes to the Peak District and to Moseley, where he meets Charles Lloyd (1775–1839). Lloyd joins Coleridge as his private pupil from October to December and returns to live with the Coleridges between February and April 1797.

September
19 Birth of (David) Hartley Coleridge (1796–1849) in Bristol. His childhood features in his father's 'The Nightingale' and 'Frost at Midnight' and William Wordsworth's 'To H.C. Six Years Old'.
22 Mary Lamb (1764–1847) stabs her mother to death at 7 Little Queen Street, Lincoln's Inn Fields, where the family has lived since 1792. It is accepted that she acted in temporary insanity and she is released into the care of her brother Charles.
In late summer and autumn work is under way on Fonthill Abbey, designed by James Wyatt (1746–1813) with much input from the owner, Beckford. Building continues for many years. The tower collapses in May 1800 and is replaced. The north range dates

from 1806–12. Beckford is finally able to move into the Abbey in summer 1809.

October

5   Spain, now an ally of France, declares war on Britain.
8   Charles Dibdin opens the New Sans Souci Theatre, Leicester Place, with his entertainment *The General Election*. His original Sans Souci opened at 411 The Strand on 31 October 1791.
16   Austen begins work on 'First Impressions' (finished in August 1797), later rewritten as *Pride and Prejudice*.
22   Mary Robinson's *Sappho and Phaon. In a Series of Legitimate Sonnets* appears.
24   Wordsworth has begun work on the play eventually published in revised form as *The Borderers* in 1842. A first version is finished probably by early June 1797, with revisions until the autumn.

Coleridge's 'Reflections on Entering into Active Life' (subsequently 'Reflections on Having Left a Place of Retirement') is published in *The Monthly Magazine*.

Poems by Coleridge, Southey, Lloyd and Charles Lamb are included in *Sonnets by Various Authors*.

Unsuccessful peace talks between Britain and France are held in Lille (October–December), continuing in late summer and autumn 1797.

Burke's *Two Letters on the Prospect of a Regicide Peace* is published by Rivington.

November

1   Scott's *The Chase and William and Helen: Two Ballads from the German of Gottfried Augustus Bürger* is published in Edinburgh by Manners and Miller.
17   Catherine II 'the Great' (1729–96) of Russia dies and is succeeded by her son Tsar Paul (1754–1801).

G.G. and J. Robinson publish Hays's *Memoirs of Emma Courtney*.

December

22–27 French forces fail to invade Ireland, defeated by gales.
26   Coleridge publishes *Ode on the Departing Year*; a shorter version comes out in *The Cambridge Intelligencer* on 31. He and his family move to Nether Stowey.

Publication of Radcliffe's, *The Italian, or the Confessional of the Black Penitents* in three volumes, dated 1797. The publishers, Cadell and Davies, buy the copyright for £800.

Cottle publishes Southey's *Poems*, dated 1797. More poems are added in later editions including those of 1799, 1800 and 1801.

Between late 1796 and June 1797 Wordsworth writes 'Old Man Travelling' (renamed 'Animal Tranquillity and Decay: a Sketch' in 1800).

Probably this year Blake begins work on 'Vala' or 'The Four Zoas', eventually abandoned in 1807.

Gibbon's *Miscellaneous Works*, including his Memoirs, are published in two volumes by Cadell and Davies.

William Lane publishes Robert Bage's *Hermsprong; or, Man as He is Not. A Novel ... By the Author of Man As He Is. Man As He Is* came out in 1792.

Publication in Lausanne of *De l'Influence des passions sur le bonheur des individus et des nations*, by Anne-Germaine (Necker), baronne de Staël-Holstein (1766–1817). The first English translation appears in 1798.

The Life of Lorenzo de' Medici by William Roscoe (1753–1831) is published by Cadell and Davies and others.

Probably between 1796 and 1800 Austen writes her 'Sir Charles Grandison', adapted from Samuel Richardson's novel.

1797

January
31 Franz Schubert (1797–1828) is born in Vienna.

February
Early this month Sheridan commissions Coleridge to write a play – *Osorio* – for Drury Lane.
2 Bonaparte captures Milan.
14 British naval victory off Cape St Vincent.
14 Scott and others meet in Edinburgh to discuss the formation of a volunteer cavalry unit. In April the Royal Edinburgh Volunteer Light Dragoons are constituted, with Scott as secretary and quartermaster.
26 A banking crisis leads the Bank of England temporarily to suspend cash payments.

27 The Robinsons publish Godwin's *The Enquirer, Reflections on Education, Manners and Literature. In a Series of Essays.*
Southey begins studying law at Gray's Inn. He eventually gives up his intention of becoming a lawyer in July 1801.

March
2 Walpole dies at his London home in Berkeley Square.
4 Inchbald's *Wives as they Were and Maids as they Are* is at Covent Garden.
4 John Adams (1735–1826) takes office as Pesident of the United States until 4 March 1801.
13 Premiere of *Médée*, by Luigi Cherubini (1760–1842), at the Théâtre Feydeau in Paris.
c.17 Wordsworth goes to Bristol and, about two weeks later, to see Coleridge at Nether Stowey. There he also meets Poole.
18 Publication in London of Chateaubriand's *Essai ... sur les révolutions anciennes et modernes considérées dans leurs rapports avec la Révolution française.* The first English translation is published by Colburn in 1815.
29 Marriage of Godwin and Wollstonecraft at (Old) St Pancras Church. Their sexual relationship began on 21 August 1796.
The first phase of Wordsworth's composition of *The Ruined Cottage* is between this month and March 1798. (From 1799 it evolves into *The Pedlar* and then into Book One of *The Excursion*, published in 1814.)

April
16–24 Naval mutiny at Spithead, as again on 7–14 May, followed by the Nore mutiny of 12 May–15 June.
23 The Royal Academy exhibition includes nine watercolours by Thomas Girtin (1775–1802), based on his tour of northern England and the Borders in 1796.
Wollstonecraft's 'On Poetry, and our Relish for the Beauties of Nature' is in *The Monthly Magazine* for April.
Publication by Cadell and Davies of Wilberforce's *A Practical View of the Prevailing Religious System of Professed Christians in the Higher and Middle Classes* ....

May

12   In response to ultimatums from Bonaparte, in Venice the Great Council meets and votes for the dissolution of the Venetian Republic. Bonaparte makes his entry to the city on 16. Wordsworth's 'On the Extinction of the Venetian Republic' is written either in May 1802 or early 1807.

June

4   Coleridge preaches in Bridgwater at the Unitarian chapel. Between about 6 and 28 he is with the Wordsworths at Racedown.

Charles Watkin Williams Wynn (1775–1850) begins paying Southey an annuity of £160; in April 1807 Wynn arranges instead for him to receive a state pension of £200 a year.

July

2   Between about now and c.13–16 the Wordsworths visit Coleridge in Nether Stowey. Charles Lamb joins them for a week on 7. Coleridge composes 'This Lime-Tree Bower my Prison' with reference to a walk taken by Lamb, the Wordsworths and Coleridge's wife, Sara, on 7. The first version of the poem is included in a letter to Southey on 17; publication, signed 'ESTEESI', is in *The Annual Anthology*, edited by Southey, in February 1800.

9   France forms the Cisalpine Republic, called the Republic of Italy from January 1802.

9   Death of Burke in Beaconsfield.

c.13–16   The Wordsworths move to Alfoxden (or Alfoxton) House, a few miles from Nether Stowey. Coleridge often stays or visits.

17   Thelwall comes to stay with Coleridge at Nether Stowey. He also sees William Wordsworth at Alfoxden. Association with the famously radical Thelwall is one reason (together with local gossip and misunderstanding) for the investigation of Wordsworth and Coleridge as possible French spies or subversives by James Walsh, a government agent, on 15–16 August.

Coleridge says in his 1816 preface that 'Kubla Khan: or A Vision in a Dream' was written this summer, but the date remains uncertain. In a manuscript note he gives 'the fall of the year, 1797'.
31 The general meeting of the London Corresponding Society at St Pancras is broken up by magistrates and soldiers.

August
20 Coleridge walks from Bristol to Stowey.
29 Wright of Derby dies in Derby.
30 Birth of Mary Wollstonecraft Godwin (1797–1851), daughter of Wollstonecraft and Godwin, at 29 The Polygon, Somers Town, near London.

September
6 Coleridge leaves for Shaftesbury to visit Bowles.
10 Wollstonecraft dies of puerperal fever. She is buried in Old St Pancras churchyard. Hays's anonymous obituary is in *The Monthly Magazine* for September; she writes and signs another for the *Annual Necrology, 1797–1798* (1800). Hays's friendship with Godwin founders, partly because she objects to his giving Wollstonecraft an Anglican funeral.

October
11 British ships defeat Dutch at Camperdown.
18 Treaty of Campo-Formio between France and Austria. War between them resumes on 12 March 1799.
26 Bonaparte forms an Army of England.
28 Publication by Cottle of Coleridge's *Poems, to Which Are Now Added, Poems by Charles Lamb and Charles Lloyd*. This month Coleridge finishes *Osorio* (eventually performed as *Remorse;* see 23 January 1813). Possibly this month he writes 'Kubla Khan' (see July).
Goethe's *Taschenbuch für 1798: Hermann und Dorothea* is published in Berlin by Vieweg. *Hermann and Dorothea*, Holcroft's verse translation, is published in 1801 by Longman, who also publish an anonymous prose translation in July 1804.
Thelwall moves to Llyswen Farm, near Brecon.

November

Early this month Austen's 'First Impressions' is rejected (unread) by Cadell and Davies. Between November and late December she makes, with her parents and sister, her first known visit to Bath. They stay with Austen's maternal uncle at 1 Paragon Buildings.

In early November Coleridge and the Wordsworths walk to Porlock and Lynmouth. William Wordsworth and Coleridge plan or start work on 'The Wanderings of Cain' (published, without permission, in *The Bijou for 1828*).

12–20 Wordsworth and Coleridge walk to places including Watchet. They plan *The Ancient Mariner*, intended at first as a collaborative work. By 20 Coleridge has composed 300 lines.

20 The *Anti-Jacobin, or Weekly Examiner* begins publication (until 9 July 1798). It is founded by George Canning (1770–1827) and edited by Gifford. They, with John Hookham Frere (1769–1846), are among the principal contributors. The targets of its satire include Erasmus Darwin, Paine, Southey, Wordsworth, Coleridge, Wollstonecraft and Godwin. It is succeeded by the monthly *Anti-Jacobin Review*.

23–5 Godwin reads Hays's *The Victim of Prejudice* in manuscript. It is published in two volumes by Joseph Johnson early in 1799.

29 Birth in Bergamo of Gaetano Donizetti (1797–1848).

From late this month until mid-December the Wordsworths are in London. William is further altering *The Borderers* for the stage, but it is rejected (by 13 December) by Covent Garden. They return to Alfoxden, via Bristol, on 3 January 1798.

December

13 Wordsworth is at Godwin's.

14 Lewis's *The Castle Spectre* is presented at Drury Lane with J.P. Kemble and Jordan. It runs for 48 nights. On 29, also at Drury Lane, Kemble and Siddons open in *Aurelio and Miranda*, a version of Lewis's *Monk*.

24 Scott and Charlotte Carpenter (originally Charpentier; 1770–1826) are married in Carlisle. They rent 50 George Street, Edinburgh, and then 19 Castle Street from later in 1798. In December 1801 they move into the newly built 39 Castle Street, finally sold during Scott's financial troubles in 1826. They also rent a cottage at Lasswade, near Edinburgh.

26   Death of John Wilkes (1725–97).
Barbauld's 'Washing-Day' is in *The Monthly Magazine*.
Coleridge visits Thomas Wedgwood (1771–1805) and Josiah Wedgwood the younger (1769–1843) at Westbury-on-Trym and meets Mackintosh. In January 1798, after much indecision, Coleridge rejects the Wedgwoods' gift of £100 a year, but soon accepts their renewed offer of £150.
Erasmus Darwin's *A Plan for the Conduct of Female Education, in Boarding Schools* is published by Joseph Johnson.
Kearsley publishes *The Laws of the Moral and Physical World, Translated from the French of M. Mirabaud*. The original *Système de la Nature* (1770) is by Paul-Henri, baron d'Holbach (1723–89), using the pseudonym Jean-Baptiste Mirabaud.
Harriet Lee's *The Canterbury Tales*, with some contributions from Sophia Lee, is published in five volumes between 1797 and 1805.
This year the first volume of *Hyperion, oder der Eremit in Griechenland*, by Friedrich Hölderlin (1770–1843), is published in Tübingen. The second appears in 1799.
Probably in 1797–8 Austen rewrites 'Elinor and Marianne' as *Sense and Sensibility*.
Shakespeare's *Dramatische Werke*, translated by August Wilhelm Schlegel (1767–1845) is published by Unger in Berlin, in nine volumes, between 1797 and 1810. Further plays, translated by Dorothea Tieck (1799–1841) and her husband Wolf Heinrich, Graf von Baudissin (1789–1878), are added between 1825 and 1833.
Between 1797 and 1805 Francisco de Goya y Lucientes (1746–1828) works on *The Clothed Maja* and *The Naked Maja*.

1798

January
8   Coleridge's 'Fire, Famine, & Slaughter. A War Eclogue' is in *The Morning Post*, signed 'Laberius'.
14   Coleridge preaches at the Unitarian Chapel in Shrewsbury and on 14–15 meets Hazlitt.
20   Dorothy Wordsworth begins her Alfoxden Journal (until May).
29   Publication by Joseph Johnson and by G.G. and J. Robinson of Wollstonecraft's *Posthumous Works*. It includes *The Wrongs of Woman; or, Maria. A Fragment*, 'Extract of the Cave of Fancy.

A Tale', a selection of letters, and 'Letter on the Present Character of the French Nation' (dated 15 February 1793). Johnson and the Robinsons also publish Godwin's *Memoirs of the Author of a Vindication of the Rights of Woman*. Its frank accounts of her sexual relationships and suicide attempts generate much abuse of both author and subject.

30   Coleridge begins a week-long visit to the Wedgwoods, returning to Stowey on 9 February.

Between January and March William Wordsworth writes 'The Old Cumberland Beggar'.

February

Between the second week of this month and 2 July the Wordsworths and Coleridge are often together.

17   Some time after this date Coleridge writes 'Frost at Midnight'.

March

At some point between 1 and 9 Wordsworth writes 'Lines Written at a Small Distance from my House' (later called 'To My Sister').

Early this month Coleridge and Lloyd quarrel over the parody of poems by the latter in Coleridge's sonnets published as the work of 'Nehemiah Higginbottom' in *The Monthly Magazine*. Lloyd in turn annoys Coleridge by basing on him aspects of the hero of his novel *Edmund Oliver*, published by Cottle in Bristol in early May. (They are reconciled in 1800.)

7–13   Wordsworth writes 'Goody Blake and Harry Gill'. In early March he also begins 'The Idiot Boy' (finished in May).

13   Holcroft's *He's Much To Blame* (partly after Goethe's *Clavigo*) is performed at Covent Garden.

19   Wordsworth writes at least part of 'The Thorn'. It is probably complete by 20 April.

23   By now Coleridge has completed *The Ancient Mariner*. This spring he also writes Part I of *Christabel* (but gives 1797 as the date in his 1816 Preface).

Scott's translation of Goethe's 'Erl–King' appears in *The Kelso Mail* (founded by James Ballantyne in 1796).

29   Robert Stewart, Viscount Castlereagh (1769–1822) is appointed Chief Secretary to the Lord Lieutenant of Ireland (until May 1802).

29   Helvetic Republic declared following the French invasion of Switzerland.

April

In April–May Wordsworth writes poems including 'Simon Lee, the Old Huntsman' and 'Anecdote for Fathers'.
In the second week of the month Coleridge is in Ottery St Mary.

12   Approximate date of Wordsworth's 'Lines Written in Early Spring'.
13   Coleridge, as 'Nycias Erythraeus', publishes 'Lewti' in *The Morning Post*. His 'The Recantation, An Ode' ('France. An Ode') follows there on 16.
16   *The Anti-Jacobin* carries the first part of 'The Loves of the Triangles', a parody of Erasmus Darwin's *The Loves of the Plants*. The second and third parts follow on 23 and on 7 May. The authors are Frere, George Canning and George Ellis (1753–1815).
20   Dorothy Wordsworth notes 'Peter Bell begun'. William Wordsworth continues sporadic work on the poem for many years (see April 1819).
20   Coleridge gives this date to 'Fears in Solitude'. This month he also writes 'The Nightingale; a Conversational Poem'.
21   Suspension of Habeas Corpus until 1 February 1799. Renewals prolong the suspension until 1 March 1800.
29–30 First performance, in Vienna, of Haydn's *Die Schöpfung* (*The Creation*), with text derived from the Bible and Milton.

May

8   Alderson marries John Opie (1761–1807), who was elected to the Royal Academy in 1787 and becomes Professor of Painting there in 1805.
11   Publication by Cadell and Davies of Sotheby's *Oberon: a Poem from the German*. Wieland's *Oberon: Ein Gedicht in vierzehn Gesängen* was published anonymously in Weimar in 1780.
16–17 The Wordsworths and Coleridge visit Cheddar. (Dorothy Wordsworth appears to misdate the trip 22 May: see Wordsworth [2002] p.299.)
18–22 William Wordsworth is in Bristol. He sees Lewis's *The Castle Spectre* at the Theatre Royal on 21.

19   Fitzgerald's hiding-place at 151 Thomas Street, Dublin is betrayed. He is seriously wounded while resisting arrest and dies in Newgate prison in Dublin on 4 June. His absence contributes to the failure of the imminent Irish rebellion.
c.20 Hazlitt stays at Alfoxden and then, from 22 for about three weeks, at Nether Stowey. Debate between Hazlitt and William Wordsworth inspires or influences Wordsworth's 'Expostulation and Reply' and 'The Tables Turned', written on about 23.
21   Byron succeeds his great-uncle, becoming 6th Baron Byron of Rochdale. He first sees the ancestral home, Newstead Abbey, with his mother in August.
23   Beginning of the Irish rebellion. Government forces defeat rebels at Vinegar Hill on 21 June.

John and Arthur Arch publish *Blank Verse* by Charles Lamb and Charles Lloyd. Poems include Lamb's 'The Old Familiar Faces'.

In Berlin the first issue of *Athenaeum: Eine Zeitschrift* comes out. It is edited by the brothers August Wilhelm Schlegel and (Karl Wilhelm) Friedrich Schlegel (1772–1829). Contributors, between now and the last issue in August 1800, include the editors and Novalis (Georg Philipp Friedrich von Hardenberg, 1772–1801).

June

Early this month Joseph Johnson publishes *Practical Education*, in two volumes, by Maria Edgeworth (1768–1849) and Richard Lovell Edgeworth. Their *Professional Education*, under R.L. Edgeworth's name only, follows in 1808.

11   Bonaparte captures Malta. It comes under British rule after a two-year siege in September 1800.
11   Hazlitt and Coleridge go to Bristol.
23   Joseph Johnson publishes *Essay on the Principles of Population, as it Affects the Future Improvement of Society*, by Thomas Robert Malthus (1766–1834). There is a second edition in 1803.
25   The Wordsworths, having moved out of Alfoxden, stay with Coleridge at Stowey. On 2 July they travel to Bristol.

Charlotte Smith's *Minor Morals, Interspersed with Sketches of Natural History, Historical Anecdotes, and Original Stories* is published in two volumes by Sampson Low.

The Rovers, a parody of Schiller's *Robbers*, appears in *The Anti-Jacobin*.

July

William and Dorothy Wordsworth visit Bath (8) and then Tintern Abbey, arriving back in Bristol on 13. 'Lines Written a Few Miles above Tintern Abbey' is composed on 11–13.

21   In Egypt, Bonaparte defeats the Mamelukes in the Battle of the Pyramids.

Southey begins work on his 'English Eclogues'.

August

1   Nelson's victory at the Battle of the Nile or Abu Qir (Aboukir) Bay. It inspires Thomas Dibdin's *The Mouth of the Nile*, given at Covent Garden on 25 October, the first of 27 performances this season. William Taylor's 'Nelson's Victory. An Ode' is in *The Monthly Magazine* for November; in 1799 Cadell and Davies publish, 'for the benefit of the widows and children of the brave men who fell', Bowles's *Song of the Battle of the Nile*. In 1799–1800 a 'naumachia' replays the events of the battle in Silver Street, off Fleet Street.

Early in the month Coleridge and the Wordsworths set off on a walking tour, visiting Thelwall at Llyswen.

22   French troops invade Ireland, landing at Killala, County Mayo. They surrender at Ballinanmuck, County Longford, on 8 September.

27   The Wordsworths and Coleridge reach London from Bristol, travelling via Blenheim and Oxford.

The anonymous *Gebir, a Poem in Seven Books* by Walter Savage Landor (1775–1864) is sold in London by Rivington. A second edition is brought out in Oxford in 1803 by Slatter & Munday.

September

Early this month Coleridge and Barbauld see each other in London.

14   Dorothy Wordsworth begins her 'Hamburgh' Journal (kept until 1 October).

14   Publication in New York, by Hocquet Caritat, of *Wieland; or, the Transformation. An American Tale* by Charles Brockden Brown (1771–1810).

16–19   Coleridge and the Wordsworths sail from Yarmouth to Hamburg. Before setting off William Wordsworth attempts, with some success, to interest Joseph Johnson in publishing

Lyrical Ballads. Johnson publishes Coleridge's *Fears in Solitude* volume this year.

21 Coleridge and William Wordsworth meet Friedrich Klopstock (1724–1803). Wordsworth talks to him again several days later.

24–27 Coleridge is in Ratzeburg, where he returns and moves into lodgings on 30.

By this month Joanna Baillie's *A Series of Plays: In Which it is Attempted to Delineate the Stronger Passions of the Mind*, volume one, is published by Cadell and Davies. A second volume appears in 1802 and a third in 1812.

October

2 Humphry Davy (1778–1829) arrives in Bristol, from Penzance, to begin work as assistant to Dr Thomas Beddoes (1760–1808) at the Pneumatic Institute at Hotwells. Davy is employed here until March 1801. He researches the properties of nitrous oxide or laughing gas, first breathing it unmixed on 11 April 1799 and writing *Researches, Chemical and Philsosophical: Chiefly Concerning Nitrous Oxide ... and its Respiration* (published in Bristol by Joseph Johnson). Through Beddoes (who has practised medicine in Bristol since 1793) he meets Cottle, Coleridge, Southey, Maria Edgeworth and William Wordsworth.

3 The Wordsworths leave Hamburg, reaching Brunswick on 5 and Goslar on 6, where they lodge at 107 Breitstrasse until February 1799. Here in late 1798 William Wordsworth writes poems including 'Nutting', 'The Fountain' and the 'Lucy poems', 'Strange fits of passion I have known', 'Song' ('She dwelt among th'untrodden ways') and 'A slumber did my spirit seal'. He also works on the poem now known as the 'Two-Part' *Prelude* (completed in November 1799).

4 Anonymous publication of *Lyrical Ballads, with a Few Other Poems*, by Cottle. It contains four poems by Coleridge and nineteen by Wordsworth.

11 Coleridge sets off on a visit to Lübeck and Kiel.

11 First performance of Inchbald's *Lovers' Vows*, adapted from a translation of Kotzebue's *Das Kind der Liebe*, at Covent Garden. It runs for 42 nights this season and is much performed in the provinces over the next few years. The text is

first published in late December. The play figures in Austen's *Mansfield Park* (1814).
29 Britain, Russia, Austria, Naples and the Ottoman Empire enter an alliance against France.
31 Tone is arrested after the defeat of French ships off Donegal. (He has served with the French army since 1796.) He is tried and condemned to death in Dublin on 10 November but dies from a self-inflicted wound on 19.

This year Austen starts 'Susan' (finished probably in summer 1799), forerunner of *Northanger Abbey*.

Joseph Johnson and Joseph Bell publish the anonymous *Appeal to the Men of Great Britain in Behalf of Women*, by Hays.

Kant's *Essays and Treatises on Moral, Political, and Various Philosophical Subjects*, translated by John Richardson, is published in London.

1799

January
20 About now Brockden Brown's *Ormond; or The Secret Witness* is published by Caritat in New York. A London edition by the Minerva Press follows in 1800.
23 French occupation of Naples, followed by the setting up of a pro-French republic. Nelson evacuated King Ferdinand IV and his family, with the Hamiltons, to Palermo on 23–26 December 1798. Here by February the sexual relationship between Nelson and Emma Hamilton is well established.

February
6 Coleridge leaves Ratzeburg to enrol as a student at Göttingen, which he reaches on 12.
11 Joseph Johnson, convicted of sedition for publishing *A Reply to Some Parts of the Bishop of Llandaff's Address ...* by Gilbert Wakefield (1756–1801), is sentenced to six months in prison. Wakefield himself receives a two-year sentence. In *An Address to the People of Great Britain* (1798) Richard Watson (1737–1816), Bishop of Llandaff, supports government policies including the imposition of income tax to finance the war with France.
23 The Wordsworths leave Goslar. They arrive in Nordhausen on 27.

This month Longman publishes Mary Robinson's *The False Friend: a Domestic Story* in four volumes. In March Longman also publishes her *A Letter to the Women of England, on the Injustice of Mental Subordination*, under the name Anne Frances Randall.
Publication of Goya's *Caprichos*.

March
4 John Constable (1776–1837) is admitted as a probationer to the Royal Academy Schools. He came to London in late February and lives there for much of his career, but until 1817 continues to spend long periods in and near his birthplace and frequent subject, East Bergholt in Suffolk.
7 Foundation in London of the Royal Institution of Great Britain. By June (when it first becomes 'Royal') it is using 21 Albemarle Street.
14 Scott's translation from Goethe, *Goetz of Berlichingen, With the Iron Hand*, is published by Joseph Bell. The title-page, in error, credits 'William Scott'. Scott is in London in March–April.
17 Between now and 21 May British forces successfully defend Acre against the French.
Moore enrols at the Middle Temple. He lodges at 44 George Street. He soon becomes known in fashionable society for his singing.
More's *Strictures on the Modern System of Female Education* is published in two volumes by Cadell and Davies.

April
4 Coleridge receives news of the death on 11 February of his second son Berkeley (born 14 May 1798).
10 Pope Pius VI is brought to France. He dies in Valence on 29 August.
12 Foundation, at the Castle and Falcon inn, Aldersgate, of the Society for Missions to Africa and the East, later the Church Missionary Society.
c.20 The Wordsworths reach Göttingen, where they see Coleridge. They reach Hamburg on 25 and Yarmouth at about the end of the month.
22 Lewis's *The East Indian* is performed at Drury Lane.
27 Charlotte Smith's *What is She?* opens at Covent Garden.

27 Publication by Mundell in Edinburgh of *The Pleasures of Hope* by Thomas Campbell (1777–1844). The London publishers are Longman and J. Wright.
29 The Royal Academy show includes seven watercolours and four oils by Turner.
Cowper writes 'The Cast-Away'.

May
6–18 Coleridge tours the Hartz Mountains.
10 Tipu Sultan is killed at Srirangapatna at the end of the fourth Anglo-Mysore war. Much of his territory, already diminished after the third war in 1792, comes under the control of the East India Company.
13 The Wordsworths come to stay with the Hutchinson family at Sockburn-on-Tees.
17 Austen, with her mother, brother Edward Austen and sister-in-law, is in Bath at 13 Queen Square until late June.
20 Honoré Balzac (later de Balzac, 1799–1850) is born at Tours.
20 Fuseli's 'Milton Gallery' opens at Christies, Pall Mall. It attracts relatively little interest and closes in late July. It opens again on 21 March 1800 but lasts only until 18 July.
24 Sheridan's *Pizarro*, adapted from Kotzebue's *Die Spanier in Peru* (1796), opens at Drury Lane. Siddons, John Philip Kemble and Jordan head the cast. It runs for 31 nights.
Holcroft lives in Hamburg and Paris between this month and October 1802. His *Travels from Hamburg, through Westphalia, Holland, and the Netherlands, to Paris* are published in two volumes in 1804.

June
6 Alexander Sergeyevich Pushkin (1799–1837) is born in Moscow.
24 Coleridge leaves Göttingen. After various visits he eventually reaches Cuxhaven on 18 July and sails for England. He is in Stowey by 29 July.
Nelson, acting for King Ferdinand, declares invalid the armistice arranged by Cardinal Ruffo with the Neapolitan republicans. Many of them are executed, imprisoned or exiled on and after 28. Nelson incurs particular ill-feeling in liberal circles for his role in the trial and hanging of Francesco Caracciolo (1752–99). Nelson is

honoured by Ferdinand as Duke of Brontë in August and censured in Parliament by Fox in February 1800.

July

12 Radical organizations including the London Corresponding Society and United Irishmen are banned under the law 'for the more effectual Suppression of Societies established for Seditious and Treasonable Purposes'. The 'Combination Act' or 'Act to prevent Unlawful Combinations of Workmen' is also passed on 12.

13 Southey begins writing *Thalaba*, working on it until July 1800.

25 French hunters find the boy, living wild, who becomes known as the 'Savage of Aveyron'. Mary Robinson's 'The Savage of Aveyron' is included in her *Memoirs* (1801).

August

Publication by Longman, in two volumes, of Mary Robinson's *The Natural Daughter. With Portraits of the Leadenhead Family. A Novel*.

Southey visits Coleridge at Nether Stowey (until September), completing a reconciliation begun in recent letters (see 14 November 1795).

Britain and Russia invade the Netherlands with some success but are driven back in September–October.

In August or September Byron's nurse, May Gray, is dismissed for sexually abusing and beating him.

In August–September Turner stays with Beckford at, and produces drawings of, Fonthill. He returns in summer 1800.

September

6 'The Devil's Thoughts', by Southey and Coleridge, appears anonymously in *The Morning Post*. (Southey expands it as 'The Devil's Walk' in 1827.) The two poets and their families are together in Exeter until the Coleridges leave for Stowey on 24.

October

9 Bonaparte, having left Egypt on 22 August, arrives back in France. He reaches Paris on 16.

c.16–22 Coleridge is in Bristol, where he sees Davy. Between 22 and 26 Coleridge and Cottle travel to Sockburn Farm, where the Wordsworths are meeting the Hutchinsons and Coleridge first meets Sara Hutchinson (1775–1835). On 27 William Wordsworth and Coleridge set off from Sockburn to walk in the Lake District. They are together until 18 November.

29 Mary Robinson's 'Sylphid' essays appear in *The Morning Post* between now and 31 January 1800.

Henry Crabb Robinson (1775–1867) visits Thelwall at Llyswen.

Goya, in Saragossa, witnesses some of the scenes in *Los Desastres de la Guerra*, which he works on between 1810 and 1820.

November

4 Turner is elected Associate Member of the Royal Academy.

9–10 Bonaparte overthrows the Directory and establishes the Consulate. He becomes one of three consuls and then on 12 December First Consul.

18–26 Coleridge is back in Sockburn, where he falls in love with Sara Hutchinson. He arrives in London, where he is to work as a staff writer on *The Morning Post*, on 27. He lives at 21 Buckingham Street.

December

2 Publication of Godwin's *St. Leon, A Tale of the Sixteenth Century* (4 volumes, Robinson).

16 Scott becomes Sheriff-Depute of Selkirkshire, holding the post for the rest of his life.

20 The Wordsworths move into a cottage at Town End, Grasmere, later called Dove Cottage.

21 Coleridge's 'Introduction to the Tale of the Dark Ladie' is published in *The Courier* and *The Morning Post*. It is a longer version of 'Love' as included in *Lyrical Ballads*, 1800. December 1799 to March 1800 is the period of many of his prose contributions to *The Morning Post*.

25 The Coleridges dine with Godwin. The intimacy between S.T. Coleridge and Godwin develops late this year and in 1800.

Completion of the Grand Pump Room at Bath (begun 1789).

Thomas Hope (1769–1831) buys the Duchess Street house in London where he will display paintings, sculpture and furniture; his *Household Furniture and Interior Decoration* is published in 1807.

1800

January

1 Robert Owen (1771–1858) arrives as manager of New Lanark cotton mills, where he is part-owner from 1799 until 1828. He works to improve workers' conditions of employment and accommodation and their children's education.

15 Mary Robinson entertains Godwin and Coleridge. 'Mrs. Robinson to the Poet Coleridge' appears in her *Memoirs* (1801). Coleridge also meets Sheridan this month.

Longman publishes Maria Edgeworth's *Castle Rackrent, An Hibernian Tale. Taken from Facts, and from the Manners of the Irish Squires, Before the Year 1782* in one volume. The novel goes into a fifth edition in 1810.

Early this year Wordsworth writes 'Hart-Leap Well' and 'The Brothers, a Pastoral Poem'.

February

By 11 Peacock is working as a clerk for Ludlow, Fraser and Company in the City of London.

23 Joseph Warton dies at Wickham in Hampshire. He is buried in Winchester Cathedral; he was headmaster of Winchester College 1766–93.

Work begins on the Isle of Dogs in London on the West India Docks, designed by William Jessop (1746–1814).

March

1 *The Farmer's Boy*, by Robert Bloomfield (1766–1823), is published by Vernor & Hood. Bloomfield, who works as a shoemaker, wrote the poem between May 1796 and April 1798. It reaches a third edition in September, a ninth in 1806.

19 Coleridge's 'Pitt and Bonaparte. Pitt' is in *The Morning Post* and, as 'A Pair of Portraits. Pitt and Bonaparte', in *The Courier*. (Coleridge in fact deals only with Pitt. The Bonaparte piece fails to materialize.) This month he socializes with Charles Lamb, Hays, Barbauld and Charlotte Smith.

By this month Wordsworth is working on *Home at Grasmere*, which is intended to become the first book of the first part of *The Recluse*.

In March or April Joseph Johnson publishes Erasmus Darwin's *Phytologia; or, the Philosophy of Agriculture and Gardening.*

April
6   Coleridge stays with the Wordsworths at Grasmere until 4 May.
14 The Southeys leave for Portugal (until June 1801). They live in Sintra between June and October 1800.
20 Coleridge completes the first part of his translation of Schiller's *Wallenstein*, working from a prompt-copy. The original trilogy is published this year; Coleridge translates only the second and third plays, *Die Piccolomini* and *Wallensteins Tod*.
25 Cowper dies at East Dereham in Norfolk.
25 Publication by Maradan, in Paris, of Staël's *De la Littérature considérée dans ses rapports avec les institutions sociales*. An English translation, *A Treatise on Ancient and Modern Literature*, is published by Cawthorn in 1803.
28 The Royal Academy exhibition includes Stubbs's *Hambletonian, Rubbing Down*, Blake's *The Loaves and Fishes* and Turner's *The Fifth Plague of Egypt* (actually showing the seventh plague). Beckford buys the Turner for 150 guineas.
29 First performance, at Drury Lane, of Baillie's *De Monfort*. Siddons and J.P. Kemble take the principal roles. There are eight performances this season; the play is most popular as a reading text but there are later productions including Edmund Kean's, opening at Drury Lane on 27 November 1821.

This spring Goya begins work on *The Family of Charles IV*.

May
14 Dorothy Wordsworth begins her *Grasmere Journal* (until 17 January 1803; the entries for 22 December 1800–9 October 1801 are lost).

Coleridge goes to Bristol and Stowey.

June
8   Godwin and Moore meet.
13 The Coleridges leave London for the Lakes, via Chester and Liverpool. They reach Grasmere on 29, where they stay with the Wordsworths until 23 July.

14 Bonaparte's victory over the Austrians at Marengo consolidates his power.
14 First performance, in Weimar, of Schiller's *Maria Stuart: Ein Trauerspiel*. It is published in 1801.
Late this month J. Stockdale publishes Moore's *Odes of Anacreon translated into English Verse*.

July
24 The Coleridges move into Greta Hall in Keswick. Contact with the Wordsworths remains frequent.

August
1 Mary Robinson's *Present State of the Manners, Society, &c. &c. of the Metropolis of England* is in *The Monthly Magazine* between now and November.
1 The Act of Union between Great Britain and Ireland receives Royal Assent. It was passed in May and confirmed by the Irish Parliament in June. Poems opposed to the union include Tighe's manuscript 'There was a young lordling whose wits were all toss'd up ...' (1799).
3 Moore is presented to the Prince of Wales, who this spring gave him permission to dedicate *Odes of Anacreon* to him.
Coleridge works on Part II of *Christabel*.
Artists paid by Thomas Bruce, Earl of Elgin (1766–1841), Ambassador in Constantinople from 1799 to 1803, start work copying and investigating ancient monuments in Athens. Firmans – letters of authorization – are issued by the Turkish authorities in May and July 1801. Elgin's agents then begin removing antiquities including much of the Parthenon frieze or 'Elgin marbles', eventually shipped to England in several consignments between 1803 and 1811.
Charles IV of Spain commissions David's painting of Bonaparte crossing the Alps on 20 May (finished 1803). David's several versions of the piece are much reproduced in Napoleonic France.

September
18 The Blakes go to live in a cottage at Felpham in Sussex in order to work on designs and engravings for Blake's patron Hayley.
Davy's first paper on galvanism ('Experiments on Galvanic Electricity', *Journal of Natural Philosophy, Chemistry and the Arts*).

In 1799 Alessandro Volta sent a paper to the Royal Society describing his pile, as published in *Philosophical Transactions of the Royal Society of London* in 1800.

October

By 6 Wordsworth and Coleridge (who is in Grasmere between 4 and 7) decide that *Christabel* will not be included in the second edition of *Lyrical Ballads*. To replace it, Wordsworth works on 'Michael. A Pastoral Poem' between now and December. *Christabel*, until its eventual publication in May 1816, circulates in manuscript.

25 Birth at Measham of Maria Jane Jewsbury (1800–33).
30 William Cobbett (1763–1835) launches *The Porcupine*, a daily newspaper.

November

9 Nelson and the Hamiltons arrive in London.
18 Sara Hutchinson comes to Grasmere. Coleridge and William Wordsworth meet her on the way, at Penrith. Coleridge is in Grasmere between 28 and 2 December.
27 Publication in two volumes by Joseph Bell, dated 1801, of *Tales of Wonder*, edited by Lewis and with contributions from him, Southey, Scott and others. Bell also publishes the anonymous *Tales of Terror*, often wrongly attributed to Lewis.

December

2 Coleridge returns to Grasmere until 6. The Wordsworths visit him in Keswick between10 and 14 and he is back with them on 20.
13 Single performance at Drury Lane of Godwin's *Antonio; or, The Soldier's Return*. The play is published by G.G. and J. Robinson on 22.
20 Nelson and the Hamiltons arrive to stay with Beckford at Fonthill amid grand festivities.
26 Death of Mary Robinson at Englefield Green, Old Windsor. Her *Lyrical Tales* was published in November and *The Memoirs of the Late Mrs. Robinson. Written by Herself. With Some Posthumous Pieces* (4 volumes, R. Phillips) appear in 1801. Memorials include Dacre's 'To the Shade of Mary Robinson' (*Hours of Solitude*, 1805).

This year *Letters from Italy* by Mariana Starke (1762–1838) is published in two volumes by R. Phillips. Starke lived in Italy between 1792 and 1798 and returns in 1817–19. The book is frequently revised and expanded.

In 1800–3 Matthew Flinders (1774–1814) leads the voyage of *The Investigator*, organized by Sir Joseph Banks, to Australia. Flinders is a prisoner of the French in Mauritius from 1803 to 1810.

1801

January

1   Stockdale publishes, in two volumes, Piozzi's *Retrospection: or a Review of the most striking and important Events … which the last eighteen hundred years have presented ….*

22   First meeting of the Parliament of Great Britain and Ireland.

c.25   Publication by Longman, dated 1800, of *Lyrical Ballads, with Other Poems*, in two volumes: a second edition of the 1798 *Lyrical Ballads* followed by a volume of new poems by Wordsworth. His name is on the title-page and his new preface (written in mid–late September 1800) much extends the 'Advertisement' of 1798. New material includes the definition of poetry as 'the spontaneous overflow of powerful feelings; it takes its origin from emotion recollected in tranquillity'. Wordsworth receives £80 from Longman. Davy proofreads the volumes and supervizes the printing.

Toussaint-L'Ouverture, in defiance of instructions from Bonaparte, invades Spanish Santo Domingo, the eastern part of the island of Hispaniola. He drafts a constitution, giving himself absolute power and granting only nominal authority to France. A French army is sent to remove him in 1802; he is captured on 6 November 1802, taken to France as a prisoner, and dies at the Fort de Joux on 7 April 1803. Saint-Domingue nevertheless achieves independence from France, as Haiti, in 1804.

February

3   Pitt offers his resignation. His support for the admission of Irish Catholics to the Westminster Parliament has caused conflict with the King. Henry Addington (1757–1844; Viscount Sidmouth from 1805) takes over as Prime Minister on 14 March.

9 Peace treaty between France and Austria.
c.15 Sara Hutchinson comes to stay with the Coleridges until late March.
24 *Deaf and Dumb*, by Holcroft, is at Drury Lane.

March
3 Establishment of the first regulated Stock Exchange in London.
4 Jefferson becomes President until 4 March 1809.
10 The first British national census begins. It records the population of England and Wales as 9,168,000 and of Scotland as 1,608,000. The 1831 figures are 13,896,000 and 2,364,000.
24 Alexander I (1777–1825) becomes Tsar of Russia after the assassination of Tsar Paul on 23 or 24.
28 Ludwig van Beethoven's (1770–1827) *Die Geschöpfer der Prometheus*, choreographed by Salvatore Viganò (1769–1821), is performed at the Theater an der Burg in Vienna.

Fuseli delivers his first three lectures – on 'Ancient Art', 'Art of the Moderns' and 'Invention' – as Professor of Painting at the Royal Academy (1799–1805 and 1810–25; he is also Keeper, 1804–25).

Davy is appointed assistant lecturer on chemistry and director of the laboratory at the Royal Institution. He gives his first lecture, on galvanism, on 25 April.

April
2 Victory of Nelson at Copenhagen, where the Danish fleet is destroyed.
2 Publication in Paris of Chateaubriand's *Atala, ou les amours de deux sauvages dans le désert*. An English translation is published in Boston in 1802. The original work is republished with *Le Génie du Christianisme* in 1802 and with *René ou les effets de la passion* in 1805. A translation of *René* follows in London in 1813.

In the first week of the month Longman publishes Amelia Opie's *The Father and Daughter: a tale, in prose; with an epistle from the Maid of Corinth to her Lover; and other poetical pieces*.

19 The Wordsworths visit Coleridge, who has been in poor health for some months.

24 First performance, in Vienna, of Haydn's *Die Jahreszeiten* (*The Seasons*), with text after James Thomson.
27 Turner's *Dutch Boats in a Gale*, commissioned for 250 guineas by the Duke of Bridgewater, is in the Royal Academy exhibition.

Late in April James Carpenter publishes *Poetical Works of the Late Thomas Little, Esq.* by Moore.

Byron starts at Harrow School.

Bonaparte is preparing, as on later occasions, to invade England.

May

1   Southey begins *The Curse of Kehama*.
4   Lewis's *Adelmorn* is performed at Drury Lane.
6   Coleridge drafts the Conclusion to *Christabel*, Part II. Between 7 and 15 he is in Grasmere.
22 Nelson is created Viscount. (He was made Baron Nelson of the Nile on 6 November 1798.)

Austen's father retires from active duties as Rector of Steventon and moves, with his wife and daughters, to Bath, where they lease 4 Sydney Place at the end of the month. From Bath they make a number of excursions to Hampshire, Kent and Devon. They holiday in Lyme Regis in November 1803 and the summer and autumn of 1804.

June

20 Turner sets off on his first tour of Scotland. He is in Edinburgh between 11 and 18 July and continues to Glasgow and Loch Lomond.

Rogers meets Wordsworth and Coleridge.

Joseph Johnson publishes Maria Edgeworth's *Belinda* in three volumes.

This summer Friedrich makes his first recorded visit to the island of Rügen. He returns in May 1802 and often thereafter; his best-known painting of the island is *The Cliffs on Rügen* (early 1818).

July

Southey's *Thalaba the Destroyer* is published by Longman. There is a revised edition in 1809.

16 Coleridge goes to Durham. He sees Sara Hutchinson at Bishop's Middleham and between 25 and 31 travels with her to her

brother's farm at Gallow Hill in Yorkshire, where he stays until 9 August.
21 Foundation of the Greenock Burns Club, first of many similar societies.
24 *The Gypsy Prince* opens at the Little Theatre in the Haymarket. The words are by Moore and he co-writes the music with Michael Kelly (1762–1826).

August
Coleridge returns to Keswick. Southey and his family stay.

September
11 Schiller's *Die Jungfrau von Orleans* opens in Leipzig. Schiller is present on 17 and is rapturously received.
15 Coleridge's 'On Revisiting the Seashore' is in *The Morning Post*.

October
31 George Frederick Cooke (1756–1811) makes his London debut as Richard III at Covent Garden.

November
2 Girtin goes to Paris until late April 1802.
3 Vincenzo Bellini (1801–35) is born in Catania.
6 Coleridge visits Grasmere and on 9 brings the Wordsworths back to Keswick (until 10).
10 Coleridge leaves for London, where he continues to write for *The Morning Post*. From late November he lives at 10 King Street.
Joseph Johnson publishes Maria Edgeworth's *Moral Tales for Young People* in five volumes.
In Sheffield Thelwall gives the first of many lectures on elocution. He tours extensively and in 1806 founds an Institute of Elocution in London at Bedford Place, moving to Lincoln's Inn Fields from 1813 to 1821. He continues to lecture on many other subjects: literature, drama, music, history, politics.

December
21 Godwin marries Mary Jane Clairmont or Vial (1768–1841).
24 Richard Trevithick (1771–1833) demonstrates his steam-driven locomotive *Puffing Devil* at Camborne in Cornwall. It

is lost in a fire following its third excursion on 28. Trevithick demonstrates another engine at Pen-y-Darren ironworks on 13 February 1804.
25 Davy is with Coleridge, who sets off for Stowey the following day, returning to London in mid-January.
28 Wordsworth is composing Book III of *The Prelude*.

1802

January
1 First number of Cobbett's *Annual Register*, later retitled *Weekly Political Register*. Initially Cobbett's stance is pro-government but by mid-decade he is becoming increasingly radical in his views on parliamentary reform, finance, and conditions for the rural poor.
15 Lewis's *Alfonso, King of Castile* opens at Covent Garden.
21 Davy gives his introductory discourse for a series of chemistry lectures at the Royal Institution. Coleridge is in the audience. *A Syllabus of a Course of Lectures on Chemistry* is published this year and Davy is promoted to Professor of Chemistry at the Institution on 21 May.
This month Vernor & Hood, and Longman, publish Bloomfield's *Rural Tales, Ballads and Songs*.

February
10 Turner is elected as a member of the Royal Academy.
24 Publication of the first, two-volume edition of Scott's *Minstrelsy of the Scottish Border* by Cadell and Davies. The second edition (three volumes, 25 May 1803) is published by Longman, who buys the copyright for £500 this summer. Work on the expanded version leads Scott to meet James Hogg (1770–1835) in April 1802.
26 Birth of Victor-Marie Hugo (1802–85) in Besançon.

March
2 Coleridge reaches Gallow Hill, where Sara Hutchinson is ill. He stays until 13 and on 15 is back in Keswick for the first time since November.

12–13   Wordsworth writes 'Alice Fell'. Beween March and July he writes 'To a Sky-Lark'. On 27 he begins the ode called from 1815 'Ode. Intimations of Immortality from Recollections of Early Childhood', continuing on 17 June and in the early months of 1804.
19–21   Coleridge visits the Wordsworths. They return the visit from 28 until 5 April.
25   Peace of Amiens (maintained until May 1803) allows travel between Britain and France. Many painters come to see the Louvre, including the art transferred there by Bonaparte from Italy. Among them are Fuseli and Joseph Farington (1747–1821) (in Paris between 27 August and early October) and Hoppner. John Flaxman comes and meets Ingres. Turner sets off for Paris on 15 July and travels extensively in Switzerland and back to Paris before returning to England in October, filling his Louvre and Swiss sketchbooks with about 400 drawings. Hazlitt, at this stage mainly a painter, arrives in Paris on 15 October for a four-month stay. The Opies come in August – Amelia Opie's 'Lines Written at Norwich on the First News of Peace' is in *The European Magazine* for July – and meet Helen Maria Williams and Fox (who is presented to Bonaparte on 3 September). Fanny Burney d'Arblay joins her husband in France on 20 April. (She remains there until August 1812.) Landor arrives in the summer. The Edgeworths come in November, stay until March 1803, and meet Stéphanie-Félicité, comtesse de Genlis (1746–1830). For the Wordsworths' visit see August. Joseph Forsyth (1763–1815) takes advantage of the peace to travel to Italy; he is arrested in France on 25 May 1803 and remains there as a prisoner until March 1814, writing *Remarks on Antiquities, Arts, and Letters, During an Excursion in Italy* (1813).

April
4–c.20   Coleridge writes 'A Letter to –' (revised as 'Dejection: an Ode'). He goes to Grasmere on 20 and reads the poem to the Wordsworths on 21.
14   Publication in Paris of Chateaubriand's *Le Génie du Christianisme; ou, Beautés de la religion chrétienne*. An English translation appears in Boston this year.

18   Concordat re-establishing Roman Catholicism in France.
18   Erasmus Darwin dies at Breadsall Priory, near Derby. His *The Temple of Nature; or, The Origin of Society: a Poem, with Philosophical Notes* is published in 1803 by Joseph Johnson.

May

3–9   Wordsworth writes 'The Leech Gatherer', published as 'Resolution and Independence' after rewriting in June and July. This month Coleridge and the Wordsworths continue much in one another's company and Coleridge's marriage reaches, and survives, one of its frequent crises.

June

7   Wordsworth, with some participation from Dorothy Wordsworth, further defines the ethos and subject-matter of *Lyrical Ballads*, particularly 'The Idiot Boy', in a letter to John Wilson (1785–1854).

12–13 and 23–30 Coleridge visits Grasmere.

The Rosetta Stone arrives at the British Museum. It was discovered in Egypt by French soldiers in July 1799 and passed to Britain by the Treaty of Alexandria of 2 September 1801.

Between this month and September 1806 Trimmer edits *The Guardian of Education*. Her *The Teacher's Assistant: consisting of lectures in the catethetical form* was first published by Rivington in 1800.

July

In mid-July Coleridge meets William Sotheby (1757–1833).

31   Wordsworth probably first writes now 'Composed Upon Westminster Bridge, Sept. 3, 1802'.

This month Muzio Clementi (1752–1832) and Field set off on a European tour. The aim is both to give concerts and to sell music and instruments. Clementi returns from St Petersburg; Field remains in Russia and makes his career there.

August

1–29   William and Dorothy Wordsworth are in Calais to see Vallon and Caroline. William Wordsworth writes 'It is a beauteous Evening, calm and free' and several other sonnets.

2   Bonaparte becomes Consul for Life.

2   Girtin's *Eidometropolis*, a panorama of London, opens at Wigley's Great Room, Spring Gardens, London. (Admission costs one shilling.)
2–9 Coleridge is on a walking tour of the Lakes.
14 Birth of Letitia Elizabeth Landon (1802–38) at 25 Hans Place, Chelsea.

The Lambs stay with the Coleridges from mid-August to early September.

September
6   Coleridge's 'The Picture, or The Lover's Resolution' (written in August) appears in *The Morning Post* under the name 'ΕΣΤΗΣΕ' – STC. It is followed on 11, under the same pseudonym, by 'Chamouni: The Hour Before Sunrise. A Hymn' (later 'Hymn Before Sun–rise, in the Vale of Chamouny'), which draws closely on Friederika Brun's' Chamounix beym Sonnenaufgange' (1791).

October
2   First issue of *The Edinburgh Review*, published by Archibald Constable. The founders are Sydney Smith (1771–1845), Francis Jeffrey (1773–1850), Henry Brougham (1778–1868) and Francis Horner (1778–1817). Smith is effectively the editor of the first three issues, succeeded by Jeffrey 1803–29. The first issue includes Jeffrey's hostile review of Southey's *Thalaba*, which identifies Southey as belonging to 'a sect of poets' whose other members are evidently Wordsworth and Coleridge.
4   Coleridge's 'Dejection: an Ode' is published in *The Morning Post*.
4   Wordsworth and Mary Hutchinson (1770–1859) are married at Brompton, near Scarborough. They reach Dove Cottage on 6. Coleridge visits them and Dorothy Wordsworth on 11–13 and brings them back with him to Keswick.
17 Coleridge's 'The Keepsake' is published in *The Morning Post*.
20 H.C. Robinson matriculates at the University of Jena. In Weimar he meets Goethe, Schiller and Staël. He returns to England in autumn 1805.
25 Birth of Richard Parkes Bonington (1802–28) at Arnold, near Nottingham. He moves with his parents to Calais in September 1817 and to Paris in late 1818.

30   Paine arrives in Baltimore having left France in August.
This month Amelia Opie's *Poems* is published.

November
4 and 9 Coleridge's open letters 'To Mr. Fox' appear in *The Morning Post*, again signed, transparently, 'ΕΣΤΗΣΕ'. He attacks Fox as a French sympathizer.
4–8   Coleridge travels to London, meeting Sara Hutchinson on 5 in Penrith. From London he goes on to stay with the seriously ill Tom Wedgwood and tours in Wales with him from 13.
9   Girtin dies in London.
13   Holcroft's *A Tale of Mystery*, based on Pixérécourt's *Coelina, ou l'enfant de mystère* (1800), opens at Covent Garden. It is published by Richard Phillips as *A Tale of Mystery, a Melo-Drama*: the first time an English play is so designated.
15   Romney dies in Kendal.
De Quincey lives, according to his *Confessions* (1821), in poverty in London until March 1803.
In November or December, dated 1803, Richard Phillips publishes Hays's anonymous six-volume *Female Biography; or, Memoirs of Illustrious and Celebrated Women, of all Ages and Countries*.

December
2   Austen accepts Harris Bigg-Wither's proposal of marriage but withdraws the next day.
8   The Glasgow Philosophical Society is established.
8   Staël's *Delphine* is published by J.J. Paschoud in Geneva and on 14 in Paris. The first English translation follows in 1803.
23   Birth of Sara Coleridge (1802–52) in Keswick. Coleridge arrives, with Tom Wedgwood, on 24. (Wedgwood stays until 30.)
Hanwell and Parker of Oxford publish *The Poetical Works of the Late Thomas Warton* in two volumes, edited by Richard Mant.
Publication in Paris of Vivant Denon's (1747–1825) *Voyage dans la Basse et la Haute Égypte pendant les campagnes du Général Bonaparte*.
Paley's *Natural Theology; or, Evidences of the Existence and Attributes of the Deity* is published by R. Faulder.
Traités de legislation civile et pénale, edited and translated from Bentham's manuscripts by Étienne Dumont, is published in Paris.

In 1802–3 Thomas Beddoes issues, in eleven parts, *Hygeia: or Essays Moral and Medical on the Causes Affecting the Personal State of Our Middling and Affluent Classes*.

1803

January
20   Coleridge sets off for Bristol. He spends time with Tom Wedgwood, and then with Poole in Somerset and Dorset until late February.

Rogers is preparing his new house at 22 St James's Place, London It is the setting for his art collection and for the breakfasts at which he entertains many of the best-known writers, artists and politicians of the first half of the nineteenth century.

February
7   Trial for high treason of Colonel Edward Despard (1751–1803). He is executed with six associates on 21. He was arrested on 16 November 1802 for allegedly conspiring to stage a coup a week later when Parliament opened. Despard had been involved with both the United Irishmen and the United Britons.

Cooper, aged thirteen, starts at Yale College. He is expelled in 1805.

March
22   Lewis's *The Captive* is performed at Covent Garden.

Coleridge is in London. He sees friends including the Lambs and meets Sir George Beaumont (1753–1827).

April
6   Death of Sir William Hamilton.
8   Coleridge arrives back in Keswick.
30 The United States buys Louisiana from France.

In April–May Scott visits London, Oxford and Blenheim. He meets Rogers and sees Lewis, at dinner with whom he meets the courtesan Harriette Wilson (1786–1845).

May
16   Nelson embarks on *Victory*.

25 Birth of Ralph Waldo Emerson (1803–82); and of Edward Bulwer (1803–73), later Lytton.
31 De Quincey initiates a correspondence with Wordsworth.

June
4 Between now and 4 January 1804 Charles Dibdin publishes a series of *British War Songs* commissioned by the government.
30 Thomas Lovell Beddoes (1803–49) is born in Clifton.
Longman publishes the third edition of Coleridge's *Poems*.

July
23 Emmet leads a failed rising in Dublin.
27 Act setting up the Caledonian Canal Commission. The engineers are Thomas Telford (1757–1834) and Jessop. Work starts in April 1804 and the canal, linking the North and Irish Seas via the Great Glen, opens in October 1822.
Longman publishes Southey's translation from Vasco Lobeira, *Amadis of Gaul*.
Hazlitt is in the Lake District in July and again in the autumn. He paints portraits of Coleridge and Wordsworth in July. Beaumont also comes to the Lakes.
This summer, as again in 1804 and 1805, Cotman travels and sketches in Yorkshire.

August
9 Rogers comes to see Wordsworth and Coleridge.
12 Blake forcibly removes a soldier, John Scolfield, from his garden in Felpham. On 15 Scolfield formally accuses him of making seditious statements – pro-French and anti-monarchical – and he is indicted at Petworth on 4 October. Blake is acquitted at Chichester Guildhall on 11 January 1804.
15 William and Dorothy Wordsworth and Coleridge set off for a tour of Scotland. They go to Burns's grave on 18, are in Glasgow on 22–3, and go on to the Trossachs. On 29 Coleridge intends to go to Edinburgh but instead goes to Glencoe, Fort William and Fort Augustus, where on 5 September he is briefly detained as a suspected spy. The Wordsworths continue through the Highlands. Dorothy Wordsworth's 'Recollections

of a Tour Made in Scotland, A.D. 1803', begun during the tour, are completed in May 1805 and added to in January–February 1806.

This month Keats starts at Rev. John Clarke's school in Enfield, near London, where he is a pupil until summer 1810. Clarke's son Charles Cowden Clarke (1787–1877) is a strong influence on Keats and his reading. (Keats writes 'To Charles Cowden Clarke' in September 1816.)

September
Early in the month the Southeys move to Greta Hall, Keswick, joining the Coleridges

3   William and Dorothy Wordsworth are at Glencoe. On 17 and between 19 and 23 they are with Scott, visiting places including Melrose and Dryburgh Abbeys. (On 18 they decide not to go to the Yarrow, prompting in October or November Wordsworth's 'Yarrow Unvisited'.) They reach Dove Cottage on 25. Coleridge returned to Keswick (via Edinburgh) on 15.

20 Execution of Emmet. He is the subect of Moore's 'Oh Breathe not his name' and later of P.B. Shelley's 'The Tombs' and 'On Robert Emmet's Tomb' (spring 1812).

25 Moore sets off for Bermuda, where he has been appointed Registrar of the Vice-Admiralty Court. He is in Norfolk, Virginia between 3 November and mid-December and arrives in Bermuda on 7 January 1804. Here he writes his 'Odes to Nea'.

The Blakes come back to London from Sussex, living at 17 South Molton Street until 1821.

Byron falls in love with Mary Chaworth (1785–1832) and does not return to Harrow until January 1804.

October

3   Amid fears of French invasion, Wordsworth enlists with the Grasmere Volunteers at Ambleside. Between now and March 1804 he writes 'She was a Phantom of delight.'

15 Bonaparte banishes Staël: she must stay at least forty miles from Paris. Later in the month she goes to Germany.

21 John Dalton (1766–1844) reads a paper to the Manchester Literary and Philosophical Society (published in 1805) on the

absorption of gases by water. An important supplement provides the first table of atomic weights. His ideas are developed in *A New System of Chemical Philosophy* (1808–27).
24 Hazlitt visits Keswick again. In November he has to leave the area after an incident involving a local woman.

November
29 Hazlitt is with Thelwall, who has installed his family in Kendal (until autumn 1805, when they move to Liverpool) but spends much time away on lecture tours.
29 Byron goes to stay at Newstead with Lord Grey de Ruthyn, who leases the estate between 1803 and 1808. In January 1804 Byron leaves and breaks off contact following, it is assumed, sexual advances by, or involvement with, Grey.

December
11 Birth of (Louis-)Hector Berlioz (1803–69) at La Côte-Saint-André.
14 Staël and Benjamin Constant (1767–1830) visit Weimar between now and 1 March 1804; Constant returns for 10–18 March. They meet, in January 1804, Goethe, Schiller, Wieland and H.C. Robinson.
20 Between now and mid-January Coleridge stays with the Wordsworths at Grasmere. He is ill for much of the time, suffering partly from the effects of laudanum.

By late 1803 Tighe has probably written much of her novel *Selena* but continues to revise it. It remains in manuscript until 2012.

1804

January
16 Coleridge goes to Liverpool. He reaches London on 23. He is preparing to go abroad.
31 Coleridge sees Richard 'Conversation' Sharp (1759–1835).

February
2 Coleridge is with the Lambs and Godwins. Between 7 and 17 he stays with Beaumont at Dunmow.
6 Priestley dies in Northumberland, Pennsylvania.

12 Death of Kant in Königsberg, where he has spent much of his life. He is buried in the cathedral after a grand public funeral. Temporary return of George III's illness.

March
Probable date of first composition of Wordsworth's 'I Wandered Lonely as a Cloud'. By 6 he has written a first version of 'Ode to Duty'. Since January he has been working on *The Five-Book Prelude*; he completes it on about 10 March. He then decides to produce a longer version and by 18 March revises the work into what becomes Books I–V of the *Thirteen-Book Prelude*, which is completed on about 20 May 1805.

7 A meeting at the London Tavern, Bishopsgate, establishes the British and Foreign Bible Society.
17 Schiller's *Wilhelm Tell. Ein Schauspiel* opens in Weimar. Constant is in the audience. An anonymous English translation comes out in 1829.
21 The Code Napoléon, officially the *Code civil des français*, is introduced in France.
21 Bonaparte's controversial execution of the duc d'Enghien, last of the Condé family and prince of the blood royal, after his seizure in Baden.
27 Coleridge goes to Portsmouth to board the *Speedwell*. In London he saw Beaumont, Sheridan, the Lambs and Campbell.

April
9 Coleridge sets off for Malta, reaching Gibraltar on 20.
25 Moore, leaving a deputy to fill his post as Registrar, sails from Bermuda. In early May he reaches New York and from there travels back to Virginia. He is in Washington in early June, where he is introduced to, and is unimpressed by, President Jefferson. He returns to New York (late June) via Baltimore and Philadelphia and leaves again on 4 July. He meets members of the Oneida Nation, visits Syracuse and Buffalo, and enters Canada on 21 July, seeing the Niagara Falls on 22 before going on to Montréal and, on about 20 August, Québec. He reaches Halifax, Nova Scotia in September, sails from there on 16 October and reaches Plymouth on 12 November.

Byron, staying with his mother at Burgage Manor, Southwell, meets his early friends Elizabeth Pigot (1783–1866) and her brother John (1785–1871). He lives at Southwell, often quarrelling with his mother, off and on between 1803 and 1807.
Turner opens his own gallery, having extended the house at 64 Harley Street which he moved into early in 1800. He retains the gallery here after moving house with his father to Isleworth and then, between 1806 and 1811, to Hammersmith. The gallery is later entered from Queen Anne Street, where Turner's new gallery is built from 1819, opening in 1822. Turner's main residence after 1826 is also in Queen Anne Street.

May
10   Pitt returns as Prime Minister.
18   Bonaparte becomes Emperor Napoleon I.
18   Coleridge, much delayed by difficult weather, arrives in Malta. On 20 he meets Sir Alexander Ball, the High Commissioner, and is soon employed by him as a secretary.

July
1   Birth of (Amantine) Aurore Dupin (George Sand) (1804–76).
4   Birth of Nathaniel Hawthorne (1804–64) at Salem, Massachusetts, as Nathaniel Hathorne.
This summer Scott and his family leave their country house at Lasswade, renting a larger house at Ashestiel, near Selkirk, until 1811.

August
10   Coleridge goes to Syracuse. He remains in Sicily until early November, visiting Catania and Etna before returning to Syracuse late in August.

October
13   Hazlitt is painting Lamb's portrait.
25   The Austen family rent 3 Green Park Buildings East in Bath.
Blake, writing to Hayley, says that he has been 'again enlightened with the light' after twenty years.
This autumn De Quincey, an undergraduate at Worcester College, Oxford, since December 1803, first takes opium in London

(according to his *Confessions*). His full addiction will develop in 1812–13.

November
8   Coleridge returns to Malta. He works again as a member of Ball's staff.

December
1   William Betty (1791–1874), known as 'the Young Roscius', makes his first appearance at Covent Garden in John Brown's *Barbarossa*. His debut was in Belfast in August 1803. He is at the height of his popularity in 1804–6.
2   Napoleon crowns himself Emperor in Notre-Dame cathedral. David's vast painting of the coronation is finished for display at the Salon of 1808.
21   Benjamin Disraeli (D'Israeli until 1822) (1804–81) is born in London.

Joseph Johnson publishes Maria Edgeworth's *The Modern Griselda* in one volume, dated 1805.

P.B. Shelley is at Eton College from 1804 to 1810.
Baillie's *Miscellaneous Plays* are published by Longman.
This year Blake begins *Milton* (printed 1810–11) and *Jerusalem* (1820). Canova begins work on his bust of Pope Pius VII. Between 1804 and 1808 he works on his statue of Pauline Borghese (1780–1825), Napoleon's sister, as Venus.

1805

January
12   Scott's *The Lay of the Last Minstrel; A Poem* is published by Archibald Constable in Edinburgh and Longman in London. It was composed between about autumn 1802 and August 1804. A sixth edition of 3,000 copies is published in 1807 and 27,000 copies of the poem are sold by 1815.
18   Coleridge is appointed Acting Public Secretary in Malta (until September).
21   Death of Rev George Austen (1731–1805), Jane Austen's father. His widow and daughters move to 25 Gay Street, Bath, on

25 March. While living here she writes, on about 20 April, 'Lines *supposed* ... to have been sent to an uncivil Dress maker'.
Southey's *Metrical Tales and Other Poems* is published by Longman.
Amelia Opie's *Adeline Mowbray; or the Mother and the Daughter; A Tale* is published in three volumes by Longman in London and by Archibald Constable in Edinburgh. There is a new edition in 1810.
Gifford's four-volume edition of *The Plays of Philip Massinger* appears. There is a revised edition in 1813. Gifford's *Works* of Ben Jonson follows in 1816 (nine volumes, published by Nicoll, Rivington and others) and his *Dramatic Works* of Ford in 1827 (two volumes, Murray).
Holcroft's *Theatrical Recorder* starts this month and continues until January 1806.
This month Park sets out on his second expedition to Niger. He dies in early 1806. *The Journal of a Mission to the Interior of Africa in the Year 1805 by Mungo Park* is published in 1815.
From early 1805 until 26 December 1808 Leigh Hunt is employed as a clerk at the War Office.

February
5 Death at sea of John Wordsworth (1772–1805), brother of William and Dorothy.
7 Between now and 11 April Davy gives his first course of lectures on geology at the Royal Institution. He repeats the course in 1806, 1808, 1809 and, in shortened form, 1811.
12 Coleridge decisively rejects Unitarianism.
15 Godwin's *Fleetwood: or The New Man of Feeling* is published (3 volumes, Phillips).
16 Inchbald's *To Marry, or not to Marry* opens at Covent Garden.

March
14 Scott enters partnership with James Ballantyne in his printing business.
Late in the month J.F. Hughes publishes in three volumes *Confessions of the Nun of St Omer, A Tale*, by Dacre as Rosa Matilda.
More's *Hints Towards Forming the Character of a Young Princess* (Princess Charlotte) is published in two volumes by Cadell and Davies.

April

2 Birth of Hans Christian Andersen (1805–75) in Odense.
7 First public performance of Beethoven's Third Symphony, the 'Eroica', at the Theater an der Wien. He wrote it in 1803 as 'Bonaparte' but tore through the title-page in disgust when the First Consul became Emperor in May 1804.

Southey's *Madoc* is published by Longman. He has worked on the poem off and on since 1794 or 1795. There is a second edition in 1807.

May

9 Death of Schiller.
12 Muhammad 'Alī (1769–1849) takes power as Pasha of Egypt. His position is confirmed by the Ottoman Empire, from which he achieves virtual independence, in 1806.

June

3 Lady Caroline Ponsonby marries William Lamb (1779–1848).

Between mid-June 1805 and mid-March 1806 Austen is away from Bath on visits in Kent, Sussex and Hampshire.

July

10 Tom Wedgwood dies.
19 Hazlitt's *An Essay on the Principles of Human Action...* is published anonymously by Joseph Johnson.

Tighe's *Psyche; or, the Legend of Love* (written 1801–3) is privately printed.

This summer William and Mary Jane Godwin set up their bookselling and publishing business; in August 1807 it, with the family, moves to 41 Skinner Street, London, where it is conducted in Mary Jane Godwin's name. The business publishes work, much of it in the Juvenile Library, by the Godwins, Charles and Mary Lamb, Eliza Fenwick and others, and often runs into financial difficulties, contributing to William Godwin's quest for loans or other sources of income.

August

2 Byron plays cricket for Harrow against Eton, shortly before leaving the school.

9   Britain, Austria and Russia enter an anti-French coalition.
11   Scott, Wordsworth and Davy are together in Keswick. They climb Helvellyn on 14. Scott also meets Southey, who comes to see him at Ashestiel in October.

About now Blake receives a commission to engrave his own illustrations for Blair's *The Grave* (edition of 1808) but in the event the publisher, Robert Cromek, uses Luigi Schiavonetti's engravings from Blake. The frontispiece of the edition is engraved from Thomas Phillips' portrait of Blake, displayed at the Royal Academy exhibition beginning in May 1807.

September
1   Publication in Heidelberg of the first part of *Das Knaben Wunderhorn. Alte Deutsche Lieder*, edited by Clemens von Brentano (1778–1842) and Achim von Arnim (1781–1831). Part Two follows on 3 September 1808.
23–4   Coleridge leaves Malta and goes to Syracuse. He reaches Catania on 30 and Messina on 4 October.

In late September Holcroft's *Bryan Perdue: a Novel* is published in three volumes by Longman.

Phillips publishes *The Novice of Saint Dominick*, in four volumes, by Sydney Owenson (later Lady Morgan, c.1778–1859).

October
18   Lewis's *Rugantino* begins a 30-night run at Covent Garden. It derives from *The Bravo of Venice, A Romance*, his version (published this year) of J.H.D. Zschökke's *Abällino, der grosse Bandit*.
20   Coleridge arrives in Naples, staying until 25 December.
21   Battle of Trafalgar: victory of British ships over the combined French and Spanish fleets. Nelson is fatally wounded on HMS *Victory*. His funeral is at St Paul's Cathedral on 8 January 1806. Wordsworth's 'Character of the Happy Warrior' (December 1805–January 1806) is inspired to a certain extent by Nelson. Turner paints a scene from the battle in 1805–8 and a much larger *Battle of Trafalgar* in about 1823; West paints *The Death of Lord Nelson* in 1806 and a more intimate version in 1808. In November Thelwall performs his 'The Trident of Albion' at the Lyceum in

Liverpool; in December he publishes *The Trident of Albion, an Epic Effusion; and an Oration on the Influence of Elocution on Martial Enthusiasm; with an Address to the Shade of Nelson* ... John Flaxman designs the monument to Nelson in St Paul's (1808–11).

21 M.J. Godwin publishes, in two volumes, *Fables, Ancient and Modern, adapted to the Use of Children*, by William Godwin writing as 'Edward Baldwin'.

24 Byron comes into residence at Trinity College, Cambridge. His attendances after the first term are in April–July 1806 and October–December 1807. He becomes romantically attached to a boy in Trinity choir, John Edleston (1789/90–1811) and meets friends including John Cam Hobhouse (1786–1869).

Southey goes to see Scott and Jeffrey in Edinburgh.

Crabbe takes up residence at Muston, where he has held the living since 1789.

November

5 Wordsworth writes 'The Solitary Reaper'.

6–12 Dorothy and William Wordsworth visit Ullswater. Her journal 'Excursion on the Banks of Ullswater' is later used by him in *Guide to the Lakes*.

14 Napoleon enters Vienna.

20 Beethoven's *Fidelio, oder Die eheliche Liebe*, is given its first performance at the Theater an der Wien.

26 Completion of Telford's Pontcysyllte aqueduct, carrying the Ellesmere (Llangollen) Canal (1794–1805) over the river Dee. Work began in 1795. Telford's Chirk aqueduct (1796–1801) took the canal over the river Ceiriog. Jessop was also involved in the engineering of the canal and aqueducts.

December

2 Napoleon's victory over Russian and Austrian forces at Austerlitz. France and Austria sign the Treaty of Pressburg on 26.

18 Byron takes lodgings in London, at 16 Piccadilly, between now and mid-April 1806 when he returns to Cambridge. Angelo teaches him fencing and he may well also go to Jackson for boxing, as he certainly does by 1808.

31 Coleridge arrives in Rome. He stays until May 1806 and meets Wilhelm von Humboldt (1767–1835) and Ludwig Tieck (1773–1853).

This month Peacock's *Palmyra, and Other Poems* is published by W.J. and J. Richardson, dated 1806.

This year the British Museum acquires the Townley collection of classical sculpture.

Poems by Tighe this year include 'Address to the West Wind, Written at Pargate, 1805' and probably 'Address to My Harp'.

1806

January

Early this month Maria Edgeworth's *Leonora* is published in two volumes by Joseph Johnson.

18 Foundation of the London Institution for the Promotion of Literature and Useful Knowledge. It is concerned especially with scientific education.

23 Death of Pitt. He is succeeded as Prime Minister on 11 February by William Wyndham Grenville, Lord Grenville (1759–1834), with Fox as Foreign Secretary. Soon afterwards Scott goes to London, anxious to secure his clerkship (see May this year) before it can be given to someone more congenial to the new ministry. Before leaving on 4 March he sees Frere, George Canning, Baillie, Lord and Lady Holland (Henry Vassall Fox [1773–1840] and Elizabeth Vassall Fox [1771?–1845]) and the Princess of Wales.

In January or February Vernor, Hood & Sharpe publish Bloomfield's *Wild Flowers; or, Pastoral and Local Poetry*.

March

6 Birth of Elizabeth Barrett (1806–61) at Coxhoe, County Durham.

27 At the King's Theatre the first British performance of a Mozart opera opens: *La clemenza di Tito*, with a cast including John Braham (1777–1856) as Sesto.

30 Death of Georgiana Cavendish, Duchess of Devonshire (1757–1806).

Austen returns to Bath and moves into lodgings taken by her mother in Trim Street.

April

25 The Lambs, William Wordsworth (who is in London between 4 April and about 20 May) and James Northcote (1746–1831) dine at Godwin's; Wordsworth and Godwin are with Charles Lamb on 26 and at Godwin's with Horne Tooke on 1 May. Wordsworth sees Godwin again on 16 and 19 May.

James Carpenter publishes Moore's *Epistles, Odes and Other Poems*.

Amelia Opie's four-volume *Simple Tales* is published late this month by Longman.

May

19 Fox and William Wordsworth are introduced by Rogers.

20 Wordsworth's 'Elegiac Stanzas, Suggested by a Picture of Peele Castle ... Painted by Sir George Beaumont' are written between about now and 27 June. Beaumont is a patron and friend of Wordsworth, Coleridge and Constable.

Publication by Longman, in three volumes, of *Zofloya; or, The Moor: A Romance of the Fifteenth Century*, 'by Charlotte Dacre, Better Known as Rosa Matilda'. Under the latter name her sequence of poems 'The Dream; or, Living Portraits' appears in *The Morning Post* in July.

Scott takes up the position of Principal Clerk to the Court of Session in Edinburgh (unpaid until 1812), resigning on 12 November 1830.

June

23 Coleridge, after about a month in Florence, Pisa and Livorno, sails for home on the *Gosport*. He lands in England on 17 August.

This summer J.F. Hughes publishes Maria Edgeworth's *Adelaide; or, the Chateau de St Pierre ... A Tale of the Sixteenth Century* in four volumes.

July

2 Austen leaves Bath for the last time. She stays in Clifton until late July, Adlestrop until 14 August, and Staffordshire until late September. She writes poems including 'Lines to Martha Lloyd'.

10 Death in London of Stubbs.

Britain, Russia and Prussia enter a new alliance against France.

Chateaubriand begins his tour of Greece, the Middle East and Spain, returning to Paris on 5 June 1807. His *Itinéraire de Paris à Jérusalem et de Jérusalem à Paris* comes out in 1811. A translation, Frederic Shoberl's *Travels in Greece, Palestine, Egypt and Barbary*, is published by Colburn in 1812.

August

6   Dissolution of the Holy Roman Empire. Franz II becomes Franz I of Austria.
11 A duel between Moore and Jeffrey at Chalk Farm is prevented. Moore's challenge is a response to Jeffrey's review of his *Epistles, Odes, and other Poems* in *The Edinburgh Review* for April. The two are soon reconciled. Farcical elements of the attempted fight attract much satire including Byron's in *English Bards and Scotch Reviewers* (1809).

Late this month Owenson's three-volume *The Wild Irish Girl: A National Tale* is published by Richard Phillips. It is much reprinted over the next few years.

Coleridge sees the Lambs in London.

September

1   John Constable's first dated work from his tour of the Lake District (until 19 October or soon afterwards). He meets William Wordsworth, probably on or after 8 September.
13 Death of Fox. Thelwall's 'A Monody on the Rt Hon Charles James Fox' is published in October.

This autumn Peacock goes on a walking tour in Scotland.

Ingres travels to Rome. He is in Italy until 1824 and paints there works including *Jupiter and Thetis* (1811), *The Dream of Ossian* (1813) and *La Grande Odalisque* (1814).

October

Early this month Moore goes to Dublin, staying until February 1807.

10–23   Coleridge stays with Clarkson at Bury St Edmunds.
14   Napoleon's victory at Jena. He enters Berlin on 27.
26   The Wordsworths and Hutchinson see Coleridge, in Kendal, for the first time since January 1804.
28   Charlotte Smith dies at Tilford in Surrey. She is buried at Stoke Park. Her *Beachy Head: With Other Poems* is published

by Joseph Johnson early in 1807. Hays's 'Mrs Charlotte Smith', begun by Smith herself, is in *Public Characters of 1800–1801* (Phillips, 1807).

30 The Wordsworths and Hutchinson come to live in Beaumont's property at Coleorton in Leicestershire, Hall Farm, until 10 June 1807, with a period in London between mid-April and early May. Coleridge is at Greta Hall from 30 October before coming to Coleorton, with his son Hartley, on 21 December.

Austen lives mainly in Southampton between this month and January 1808.

November

20 Davy gives first Bakerian lecture to the Royal Society, on the electrical nature of chemical affinity.

21 The Berlin Decrees establish the Continental Blockade or System. Napoleon binds much of Europe to end trade with Britain in an attempt to isolate and bankrupt it.

Distribution of Byron's (anonymous) *Fugitive Pieces*, privately printed by Samuel and John Ridge of Newark. Erotic material with sometimes transparent references to women in Southwell causes sufficient local offence for the author to recall and destroy most copies of the volume. Some of the offensive poems are omitted and new material added in the revised version printed by Ridge in December 1806 to January 1807 as *Poems on Various Occasions*.

December

10 Charles Lamb's farce *Mr. H* fails at Drury Lane.

23 First performance of Beethoven's Violin Concerto in D at the Theater an der Wien.

26 Beginning tonight, Joe Grimaldi (1778–1837) has one of his greatest successes as a clown in Thomas Dibdin's *Harlequin and Mother Goose; or, The Golden Egg*, at Covent Garden. It runs for 92 nights. Between 1800 and 1823 he plays in many such pantomimes, mainly at Covent Garden and Sadler's Wells.

Bowles's edition of *The Works of Alexander Pope* is published in ten volumes by Joseph Johnson and others.

Publication, between 1806 and 1809, of the 25 volumes of *The British Theatre; or, A Collection of Plays ... with Biographical and Critical Remarks by Mrs Inchbald*.

1807

January
22 Davy becomes joint secretary of the Royal Society, of which he was elected a Fellow on 17 November 1803.
28 Street gas lighting is used for the first time in Pall Mall.
28 Sophia Lee's *The Assignation* opens at Drury Lane.
31 Publication of Wilberforce's *A Letter on the Abolition of the Slave Trade* by Cadell and Davies and by Hatchard.

Coleridge dates this month his manuscript poem 'To William Wordsworth', written in response to Wordsworth's reading to him of *The Prelude*. Coleridge's revised piece becomes 'To a Gentleman' in *Sibylline Leaves* (1817).

Tales from Shakespear, Designed for the Use of Young Persons is published in two volumes under Charles Lamb's name by M.J. Godwin. Mary Lamb is the author of the work except for her brother's re-tellings of tragedies.

February
27 Henry Wadsworth Longfellow (1807–82) is born at Portland, Maine.

March
4 *The First Attempt; or Whim of a Moment*, a musical afterpiece with words by Owenson, is performed at the Theatre Royal, Dublin.
14 The first of three letters by Hazlitt, replying to Malthus's *Essay on Population*, is in Cobbett's *Weekly Register*. With the second and third letters (16 and 23 May) and some new material it is incorporated in *A Reply to the Essay on Population, by the Rev. T.R. Malthus. In a Series of Letters*, published by Longman late this summer.
20 Scott arrives in London, staying until 5 May with an excursion to places including the New Forest and the Isle of Wight in late March and early April. In or near London he meets John Philip Kemble and sees Wordsworth and the Princess of Wales. He also meets Coleridge for the first time.
25 Abolition of the Slave Trade Act passed. Abolition of slavery in the colonies will follow only after much further campaigning in 1833.
31 Portland succeeds Grenville as Prime Minister until 4 October 1809.

April
1   Lewis's *The Wood Daemon* opens at Drury Lane. A revised version, *One O'Clock! Or, The Knight and the Wood Daemon, A Grand Musical Romance* is at the Lyceum from 1 August 1811.
2   By now Byron is engaged on a successful campaign to lose weight.
9   John Opie dies in London. The funeral is at St Paul's Cathedral on 20. Amelia Opie goes back to live in Norwich but often comes to London.
28   Publication by Longman of Wordsworth's *Poems, in Two Volumes*. He is paid £105.

For much of April and May Coleridge is in London with the Wordsworths and (until 4 May) Hutchinson. Late in May he joins his wife in Bristol.

c.28   Cadell and Davies publish Dacre's *The Libertine* in four volumes.
30   Lewis's *Adelgitha; or, the Fruit of a Single Error* opens at Drury Lane.
30 (or 1 May)   Publication in Paris by Nicolle of Staël's *Corinne, ou l'Italie*. D. Lawler's English translation comes out this year. *The Corinna of England* (1809) is an anonymous parodic response.

May
4   David Wilkie's (1785–1841) *The Blind Fiddler* and Turner's *A Country Blacksmith Disputing Upon the Price of Iron* are among this year's exhibits at the Royal Academy.
6–8   Scott is at Coleorton with the Wordsworths. On 8 he goes on to Lichfield to meet Seward for the first time. He arrives in Edinburgh on 13.

June
6   Between now and late September Coleridge stays with Poole at Stowey. In July he meets De Quincey at Bridgwater; De Quincey goes to Bristol with Coleridge's family on 30 July.
14   Napoleon defeats the Russians at the Battle of Friedland.

Byron's *Hours of Idleness* is published, with the author's name, by Ridge of Newark. It is a revised version of *Poems on Various Occasions*. Hostile reviews, especially Brougham's in *The Edinburgh Review* for January 1808 (thought by Byron to be Jeffrey's), provoke Byron to write *English Bards and Scotch Reviewers*.
The first consignment of the 'Elgin marbles' goes on display in London in a purpose-built shed behind a house rented by Elgin in Park Lane. They are seen and enthusiastically admired by West, John Flaxman, Turner, Thomas Lawrence, Fuseli, Benjamin Robert Haydon (1786–1846) and other artists. Richard Payne Knight (1751–1824), whose *An Analytic Inquiry into the Principles of Taste* appeared in 1805, is prominent among dissenters. In late summer 1811 the marbles are moved to Burlington House, where the rest of the collection joins them in 1812. Byron sees Elgin as a plunderer in *Childe Harold's Pilgrimage*, Canto II.

July
7–9   Treaties are signed at Tilsit between France, Russia and Prussia.
10   The Wordsworth family returns to Grasmere.
Publication by Longman of Southey's *Letters from England by Don Manuel Espriella*.

August
2   Byron is working on a (lost) long poem about Bosworth Field.
17   Robert Fulton's steamboat *Clermont* begins its first voyage on the Hudson River.

September
2–5   Bombardment of Copenhagen by British ships. The aim is to prevent France pressurizing Denmark into using its ships and territory against Britain. The Danish fleet is surrendered into British hands on 7.

October
19   Davy isolates elemental potassium, soon followed by sodium. He gives his second Bakerian lecture on the subject on 19 November.
Crabbe's *Poems*, published by Hatchard, includes 'The Parish Register'. There is a favourable review by Jeffrey in *The Edinburgh Review* for April 1808.

November

De Quincey travels with Coleridge's family to Grasmere, where on 4 he meets the Wordsworths. He meets Southey in Keswick on 9 and is with Wordsworth until 12.

5   Death of Angelica Kauffman (1741–1807) in Rome. She left England in July 1781 but continued to exhibit regularly at the Royal Academy.

16   Wordsworth starts *The White Doe of Rylstone*. A first version is finished on 16 January 1808, revised in 1809 and 1814–15.

23   Coleridge arrives in London. He has been in Bristol since late September.

30   Jean-Andoche Junot (1771–1813) captures Lisbon. The Portuguese fleet and royal family have escaped to Brazil, aided by the British Royal Navy.

Jeffrey attacks Wordsworth's *Poems, in Two Volumes* in *The Edinburgh Review* for October, which is published this month.

December

16   Godwin's *Faulkener: a Tragedy* is at Drury Lane. It is published by Richard Phillips in 1808.

Possibly this year Blake writes or copies out the Pickering manuscript poems, including 'Auguries of Innocence'.

Between 1807 and 1819 Turner's *Liber Studiorum* is issued in fourteen parts. In 1807 he begins designing his own house at Twickenham, called first Solus Lodge and then Sandycombe Lodge. He and his father move there in 1812 or 1813 and he sells it in 1826.

1808

January

1   Cooper joins the United States navy as a midshipman, having served as a merchant seaman from October 1806. He leaves the navy soon after his marriage in January 1811.

3   Appearance of the first number of *The Examiner*, edited by Leigh Hunt and published by his brother John Hunt (1775–1848).

In the first week of January Byron moves into Dorant's Hotel, Albemarle Street.

15 At the Royal Institution Coleridge gives the first of his Lectures on the Principles of Poetry. Illness and other problems delay the second lecture until 5 February and the third until 30 March. He lectures more regularly during April and early May, including an extra two-hour talk on education on 3 May. It is uncertain how many times he speaks between then and his decision of 13 June to end the lectures; in all he seems to have given between eighteen and twenty (see Coleridge [1969–2002], 5.i.15, 16). One of the most regular attenders is H.C. Robinson. William Wordsworth comes on 30 March and 1 April and other listeners include the Lambs, Godwin, Rogers and De Quincey.

February

22 Scott's *Marmion; A Tale of Flodden Field* is published by Constable in Edinburgh and Murray and William Miller in London, reaching a third edition in May and selling 8,000 copies in a year. It was written between late 1806 and 22 January 1808.

27 Wordsworth arrives in London, staying until 3 April. He sees Coleridge, Hazlitt, Charles Lamb, Godwin and Southey.

Kleist's *Die Marquise von O ...* appears in *Phöbus – Ein Journal für die Kunst*, edited by Kleist and Adam Heinrich Müller and published monthly between January and December this year.

March

1 Charles Dibdin's entertainment *The Professional Volunteers* is at the Lyceum.

2 Kleist's *Der zerbrochne Krug* is staged at the Hoftheater in Weimar by Goethe.

24 Joachim Murat (1767–1815) and French forces enter Madrid.

Late in the month Byron's *Poems Original and Translated* is published by Ridge.

Baillie visits Scott.

April

Southey and Landor meet in Bristol. Southey visits him at Llanthony in August 1811.

Publication by James Power in London and William Power in Dublin of the first part of *A Selection of Irish Melodies* (1808–34) with words by Moore and music by Sir John Stevenson (1761–1833). The second instalment comes out soon afterwards and the third in spring 1810.

May
1 Hazlitt marries Sarah Stoddart (1774–1840) at St Andrew's, Holborn. On about 17 November they go to live at Winterslow in Wiltshire, from where he returns to London in 1811 and she in 1812.
2 Murat's forces suppress an insurrection in Madrid. Goya depicts the execution of Spanish prisoners the next day in *The Third of May 1808* (1814).
14 Peacock becomes Captain's Clerk (until 2 April 1809) on HMS *Venerable*, anchored off Deal.
16 Austen stays in London, at 16 Michael's Place, Brompton, with her brother Henry and his wife Eliza (until 14 June). Between then and 8 July she stays, as several times before, at Godmersham in Kent, the seat of her brother Edward Austen (who will take the name Knight in 1812).
22 Birth in Paris, as Gérard Labrunie, of Gérard de Nerval (1808–55).
24 About now the Wordsworths move into Allan Bank, Grasmere.
28 Mahmud II (1785–1839) becomes Sultan of the Ottoman Empire.
Late this month Baillie meets William and Dorothy Wordsworth in Ambleside and Grasmere.

June
16 Byron goes to Brighton. He visits Cambridge to receive his MA on 4 July and then returns to Brighton, with Hobhouse and others, until September, when he moves into Newstead.
Tighe composes 'Written at West-Aston. June, 1808'.
Davy isolates calcium, magnesium, barium and strontium, as reported in his 'Electro-Chemical Researches' in *Philosophical Transactions of the Royal Society of London*.
Publication by the Juvenile Library (M.J. Godwin) of Charles Lamb's *Adventures of Ulysses*.
Early this summer Carpenter publishes Moore's (anonymous) *Corruption and Intolerance: Two Poems ... Addressed to an Englishman by an Irishman*.

July
Austen returns to Southampton (until April 1809).

August
21   Sir Arthur Wellesley (1769–1852, Duke of Wellington from 1814), defeats the French at Vimeiro. For the ensuing Convention of Cintra see 27 December.

September
1   Coleridge comes to live with the Wordsworths.
20   Covent Garden Theatre burns down with the loss of 22 lives.
Charles Lamb's *Specimens of English Poets who Lived About the Time of Shakspeare* is published by Longman.
Maria Edgeworth's *The Match Girl. A Novel* is published by Hughes.

October
2–5   John Murray (1778–1843) visits Scott at Ashestiel. They are planning the launch of *The Quarterly Review*: see February 1809.
16   Moore plays David in Sheridan's *The Rivals* at the annual charity drama festival in Kilkenny. He plays other parts including, on 28, Spado in O'Keeffe's *The Castle of Andalusia*, and sings from *Irish Melodies*. In October 1809 he also takes several parts, repeating his Spado and playing Risk in Colman's *Love Laughs at Locksmiths*. And in 1810 he gives his Spado again; other parts include Sim in O'Keeffe's *Wild Oats*.

November
Early this month De Quincey comes to Allan Bank, remaining until February 1809. On 21 Oct 1809 he moves into Dove Cottage.
10   Death of Byron's Newfoundland dog, Boatswain. Byron writes the verse for the inscription on his tomb at Newstead on 20.
30   Scott starts work as secretary to the Commission on the Administration of Justice in Scotland, which meets between now and February 1809 and reports in 1810.

December
13   Madrid, which French forces abandoned on 30 July, surrenders to Napoleon.
16   Austen writes 'To the Memory of Mrs. Lefroy'.

22 A major Beethoven concert at the Theater an der Wien includes the first performances of his Fifth and Sixth Symphonies.
23 Dr Thomas Beddoes dies in Clifton.
27 The first part of Wordsworth's *Concerning ... the Convention of Cintra* is in *The Courier*, where the second appears on 13 January 1809; the whole work is published on 27 May 1809. At Cintra (Sintra) on 30 August it was agreed that the defeated French army would be evacuated from Portugal in British ships.

Late in the month, dated 1809, Longman publishes Owenson's *Woman; Or, Ida of Athens* in four volumes.

Cadell and Davies publish More's (anonymous) *Coelebs in Search of a Wife. Comprehending Observations on Domestic Habits and Manners, Religion and Morals*, in two volumes. It is often reprinted and first appears in German translation in 1816 and French in 1817.

Coleridge sends out prospectuses for *The Friend*.

Friedrich shows *The Cross in the Mountains* at his studio in Dresden.

Publication by M.J. Godwin of *Mrs. Leicester's School* (anonymous; dated 1809). Seven of its stories are by Mary Lamb and three by Charles Lamb.

Robert Cromek's *Reliques of Robert Burns* is published by Cadell and Davies. This year the same publishers bring out *Poems* by Browne (Hemans) (Liverpool, by subscription) and her *England and Spain; or, Valour and Patriotism*.

The revised *Faust: Eine Tragödie* (*Faust* Part One) appears in the eighth volume of *Goethe's Werke* (Tübingen: Cotta, 1806–10).

1809

January

16 General Sir John Moore (1761–1809) dies of wounds received in battle against Marshal Soult's army at Corunna (A Coruña). H.C. Robinson reports on the battle for *The Times*. Lewis's 'Monody on the Death of Sir John Moore' is first recited at Drury Lane on 14 February. 'The Burial of Sir John Moore', by Charles Wolfe (1791–1823) is published in the *Newry Telegraph* in April 1817 and *Blackwood's Magazine* that June.

By 19 Byron is at Reddish's Hotel, St James's Street.

19 Edgar Allan Poe (1809–49) is born in Boston.

February
3   Birth of Felix Mendelssohn (Bartholdy) (1809–47) in Hamburg.
12 Birth of Charles Darwin (1809–82) at The Mount, Shrewsbury.
12 Coleridge leaves Grasmere for Penrith. Over the next few months he also has periods in Keswick and Appleby.
24 The Theatre Royal, Drury Lane, burns down.
The Quarterly Review is founded, its first issue appearing on 1 March. It is published by Murray, Gifford is the first editor (to September 1825), and George Canning, Walter Scott and Southey are leading supporters and contributors. It is predominantly Tory and is conceived as a counter to the increasingly Whig *Edinburgh Review*.

March
Early this month James Cawthorn publishes the first, anonymous edition of Byron's *English Bards and Scotch Reviewers. A Satire*. The second edition is published under the author's name in mid-May. There are third and fourth editions in 1810 and some copies of a fifth are printed before Byron suppresses the work early in 1812.
4   James Madison (1751–1836) becomes President of the United States until 4 March 1817.
13 Byron enters the House of Lords.
23 Holcroft dies. He is buried in Marylebone. Hazlitt edits and completes *Memoirs of the Late Thomas Holcroft*, published in 1816.
25 Seward dies. She is buried in Lichfield Cathedral. Scott edits her *Poems* in three volumes (1810).
26 Piozzi, following the death of her husband, makes the last entry in *Thraliana*, the diary she has kept since 1776.

April
By early April Byron is back at Newstead. Some time after 12 Hobhouse, Charles Skinner Matthews (1785–1811) and James Wedderburn Webster (1788–1840) masquerade with him in monks' costumes and drink from a skull-cup. From 25 he stays at Batt's Hotel, Jermyn Street.
5   Scott visits London (until 15 June, with an excursion to Tunbridge Wells and Knole).
26 Wellesley lands at Lisbon. On 12 May he defeats the French at Oporto (Porto).
Publication by Longman of Campbell's *Gertrude of Wyoming; a Pennsylvanian Tale; and other Poems*. This month Longman also

publishes Waller Rodwell Wright's (1774/5–1826) *Horae Ionicae: a Poem, descriptive of the Ionian Islands* ....

May
Blake opens an exhibition of his watercolour and tempera paintings at his brother's home, 28 Broad Street, London. Apparently there are no sales. H.C. Robinson is at the exhibition on 23 April 1810 and probably takes the Lambs to it that June (Bentley [1969], 226).
13   French forces enter Vienna.
21–2   Napoleon loses the battle of Aspern-Essling to the Austrians, ending the myth that he cannot be defeated.
31   Haydn dies in Vienna.

June
1   First issue of Coleridge's *The Friend; A Literary, Moral and Political Weekly Paper*, which runs until 15 March 1810. Hutchinson assists.
Between June and early November William Wordsworth writes an introduction to Joseph Wilkinson's *Select Views in Cumberland, Westmorland, and Lancashire*, published in 1810.
8   Paine dies in New York.
13   Coleridge comes back to Allan Bank.
20–22   Byron and Hobhouse travel from London to Falmouth to begin their European tour. They sail for Lisbon on 2 July.
Joseph Johnson publishes Maria Edgeworth's *Tales of Fashionable Life* in three volumes. Volumes 4–6 follow in 1812.
Vernor, Hood & Sharpe, and Longman, publish Bloomfield's *Poems* in two volumes.

July
3   Marriage of Leigh Hunt and Marianne Kent (1787–1857).
5–6   Battle of Wagram, a significant French victory over Austria.
6   Pope Pius VII, who excommunicated Napoleon on 11 June, is detained in Savona.
7   Austen, with her mother and sister, moves into Chawton Cottage in Hampshire, near her brother Edward's Chawton Great House. During 1809–10 she revises *Sense and Sensibility*.
7   Byron and Hobhouse arrive in Lisbon. They visit Sintra between 12 and 16. Between 20 and 25 they travel, mainly riding, to Seville; on 28–9 they move on to Cadiz and on

3–4 August sail to Gibraltar, where on 15 they meet John Galt (1779–1839).
19   Scott, James Ballantyne and his brother John (1774–1821) set up the John Ballantyne publishing company. Scott's involvement in this and similar publishing ventures remains secret because it is deemed inappropriate to his position in the Court of Session.
27–8   Wellesley, who entered Spain in late June, wins the battle of Talavera. He is created Viscount Wellington on 4 September.

August
6   Birth of Alfred Tennyson (1809–92) at Somersby in Lincolnshire.
17   Boulton dies in Handsworth.
27–31   Byron and Hobhouse sail from Gibraltar to Malta with brief stops in Sardinia and Sicily. Galt is a fellow passenger. Byron and Hobhouse dine with Sir Alexander Ball on 1 September.

September
4   Byron and Hobhouse meet Constance Spencer Smith (1785–1829), with whom Byron falls briefly in love. His poems related to her include 'Written at Athens. January 16th, 1810' ('The spell is broke, the charm is flown'.) Byron and Hobhouse leave Malta for Greece and Albania on 19, reaching Prevesa on 29 and visiting the ruins of Nicopolis on 30.
18   The rebuilt Covent Garden opens with Siddons and Kemble in *Macbeth*. The performance founders amid 'Old Price' rioting – boxes have gone up from 6s. to 7 and the pit from 3s. 6d. to 4s. – which will continue until 14 December.
In late September and October the Lambs visit the Hazlitts at Winterslow. They come again in 1810.

October
5–11   Byron and Hobhouse are in Janina (Ioannina) in Epirus. On 12 they are at Zitsa and on 19 they arrive at Tepelene, where their host is Ali Pasha (1744?–1822), quasi-independent ruler of Albania, northern Greece and the Peloponnese. (He features in *Childe Harold's Pilgrimage* II.554–67.) They are back in Janina between 26 and 3 November. Here Byron begins *Childe Harold's Pilgrimage*, Canto I, on 31.

8 Klemens von Metternich (1773–1859, Prince from 1813) becomes Austrian foreign minister. He is also Chancellor from 25 May 1821.

November
Carlyle walks from Dumfriesshire to Edinburgh, where he studies at the University until 1813.

December
Tighe writes her last poem, 'On Receiving a Branch of Mezereon Which Flowered at Woodstock, December 1809'.

5 Byron and Hobhouse reach Vostitza, on 14 Salona (Amphissa), 22 Thebes and 24 or 25 Athens, where Byron finishes *Childe Harold's Pilgrimage*, Canto I, on 30. He and Hobhouse lodge until March 1810 with the family of Teresa Macri (1797–1875), the subject of 'Maid of Athens, ere we part' (published in 1812 as 'Song'.)

6 Publication of Irving's *A History of New-York from the Beginning of the World to the End of the Dutch Dynasty*, by Diedrich Knickerbocker.

20 Joseph Johnson dies.

25 John Wilson entertains the Wordsworths, Coleridge and De Quincey at Elleray.

Browne (Hemans) and her family move to Bronwlfa, near St Asaph.
Goethe's *Die Wahlverwandtschaften* (*Elective Affinities*) is published by Cotta in Tübingen.
In 1809–11 A.W. von Schlegel's *Über dramatische Kunst und Litteratur: Vorlesungen* is published in Heidelberg. Baldwin, Cradock and Joy bring out John Black's translation, *A Course of Lectures on Dramatic Art and Literature*, in 1815. The lectures discuss, influentially, the opposition of Classical and Romantic.
L'Histoire des républiques italiennes du Moyen-Age by Jean-Charles Simonde de Sismondi (1773–1842) comes out between 1809 and 1818.
La Description de l'Egypte is published between 1809 and 1829.

1810

January
14 Napoleon's marriage to the Empress Joséphine is annulled. He marries Archduchess Marie-Louise of Austria on 1 April.

17 Kleist's *Das Kätchen von Heilbronn oder die Feuerprobe* is performed in Vienna at the Theater an der Wien.
23 Byron and Hobhouse visit Sounion (then often called Cape Colonna) and Marathon.
29 Baillie's *The Family Legend*, with a prologue by Scott and an epilogue by Mackenzie, is performed at the Edinburgh Theatre, where Scott is a trustee and shareholder. Jeffrey is among those who see it. After three weeks of successful performances it is followed on stage by a production of Baillie's *De Monfort*. *The Family Legend* is shown again at Drury Lane in 1815.
Peacock goes to live, until 7 April 1811, at Maentwrog in Merionethshire.

February
21 Byron and Hobhouse see Galt in Athens. They are on the Acropolis with him on 28.
22 Death of Brockden Brown in Philadelphia.
23 Godwin and Leigh Hunt meet.
Hughes publishes Maria Edgeworth's *The Wife; or, a Model for Women. A Tale* in three volumes.

March
1 Frédéric (Fryderyk Franciszek) Chopin (1810–49) is born near Warsaw.
5–8 Byron and Hobhouse sail to Smyrna (Izmir). They visit Ephesus on 13. In Smyrna Byron finishes *Childe Harold's Pilgrimage*, Canto II, by 28. (He revises the two cantos mainly in 1811.)
24 Death of Tighe, of tuberculosis, at Woodstock, County Kilkenny. She is buried at Inistiogue. Her *Psyche, with Other Poems* is published by Longman in 1811. It reaches a third edition in 1816.

April
11 Byron and Hobhouse leave Smyrna. From 15 they are anchored near the presumed site of Troy, on 3 May Byron swims the Hellespont, and on 14 they land in Constantinople (Istanbul), where they remain until 14 July.
Longman publishes the first volume of Southey's *History of Brazil* (1810–19).

Crabbe's *The Borough: a Poem, in Twenty-Four Letters* is published by Hatchard. A revised second edition appears soon afterwards.

P.B. Shelley's *Zastrozzi, a Romance* is published by Wilkie & Robinson as the work of 'P.B.S'.

Late this month 'Memoir of Mr James Henry Leigh Hunt. Written by Himself' is in the *Monthly Mirror*.

Lucy Aikin's (1781–1864) *Epistles on Women, Exemplifying their Character and Condition in Various Ages and Nations* is brought out by Richard Taylor. Aikin is Barbauld's niece.

May

Early this month Coleridge leaves Grasmere for Keswick (until mid-October).

8   Publication by Ballantyne in Edinburgh and Longman and William Miller in London, of Scott's *The Lady of the Lake; A Poem*, begun in August 1809. 25,000 copies are sold by January 1811.

At about the end of the month Hookham publishes Peacock's *The Genius of the Thames: A Lyrical Poem, in Two Parts* (written in 1809).

In Malta Lady Hester Stanhope (1776–1839), Pitt's niece, and Michael Bruce (1787–1861) become lovers. They travel in the Middle East, including Egypt and Syria, and reach Palmyra on 17 March 1813. Bruce leaves for England that October while Stanhope remains in the Levant for the rest of her life.

June

8   Robert Schumann (1810–56) is born at Zwickau.

July

4   William Wordsworth sets off on a tour to Coleorton, the Midlands and Wales, returning to Grasmere at the beginning of September. He is with Dorothy Wordsworth until 6 August; she then visits Cambridge (11–12 August) and Bury St Edmunds (12 August–9 October), where she stays with the Clarksons. In London in mid-October she stays with the Lambs.

9   Cobbett, having protested at the flogging of militiamen who asked for a pay rise, begins a two-year prison sentence at Newgate. He is also fined £1,000.

10 Simón Bolívar (1783–1830) is in England between now and 21 September, as part of a delegation from the junta temporarily established in Caracas. Andrés Bello (1781–1865), another of the delegates, remains in London until 1829.
10 Byron attends an audience with Sultan Mahmud II.
16 Scott lands on Mull, visiting Staffa and Iona on 18.
17 Byron and Hobhouse reach Zea (Keos). Hobhouse sets off for home. Byron reaches Athens on 18, stays briefly again with the Macri family, and sets off on 21 for several weeks in the Peloponnese.
J.H. Reynolds becomes a clerk (until April 1816) at the Amicable Society for a Perpetual Assurance, Fleet Street, London.

August
c.19 Byron comes back to Athens. He stays at the Capuchin monastery built around the ancient 'Lantern of Demosthenes' (Monument of Lysikrates).
Keats begins his apothecary's apprenticeship.

September
2 Leigh Hunt's 'One Thousand Lashes!!' opposing military flogging, is in *The Examiner*. He and John Hunt are acquitted of seditious libel on 13 February 1811. Brougham leads their defence.
12 Byron meets Stanhope and Bruce in Athens.
18 Goethe visits Friedrich in Dresden.
29 Elizabeth Gaskell (1810–65) is born, as Elizabeth Stevenson, in Chelsea.
In September and early October Byron is in the Peloponnese with Nicolo Giraud (c.1795–1815), who boards at the monastery and is probably his lover.

October
11 From now until 5 March 1811 Wellington and British and Portuguese troops are besieged at Torres Vedras. Lack of supplies eventually forces a French withdrawal.
13 Byron is back at the Capuchin monastery in Athens.

26 Coleridge arrives in London. He becomes increasingly ill-disposed to William Wordsworth. (For details see Moorman [1965], pp. 191–209.)

November
3 Coleridge goes to live with John Morgan and his family at 7 Portland Place, Hammersmith, for much of the time between now and early October 1811. He meets H.C. Robinson.

December
11 Birth of Alfred de Musset (Louis-Alexandre-Alfred de Musset-Pathay, 1810–57) in Paris.
12–15 Kleist's *Über das Marionettentheater* appears in the *Berliner Abendblättern*.
c.20 (dated 1811) Stockdale publishes P.B. Shelley's *St. Irvyne; or, The Rosicrucian: a Romance*, as the work of 'a Gentleman of the University of Oxford'.
31 Tsar Alexander withdraws from Napoleon's Continental Blockade.

Byron visits Sounion again.

Between about December 1810 and March 1812 Wordsworth writes Books II–V of *The Excursion*.

Longman publishes Southey's *The Curse of Kehama*. A second edition follows in 1811.

This year Nicolò Paganini (1782–1840) begins his extensive concert tours of Italy. He also composes works including five violin concertos between 1816 and 1830.

Cotta in Tübingen publishes Goethe's *Zur Farbenlehre* (*On the Theory of Colours*).

Blake prints 'Chaucer's Canterbury Pilgrims', on which he began work in 1806.

Original Poetry by Victor and Cazire, by P.B. Shelley and his sister Elizabeth (1794–1831), is published by J.J. Stockdale. About a hundred copies are distributed; the rest are destroyed when it comes to light that one of the poems is plagiarized from 'The Black Canon of Elmham; or, Saint Edmond's Eve' in *Tales of Terror* (1800).

Friedrich paints *Mountain Landscape with a Rainbow*.

Barbauld provides an introduction and prefaces for the 50-volume *British Novelists* published by Rivington.

John Flaxman becomes Professor of Sculpture at the Royal Academy, where he was elected associate on 6 November 1797 and member on 10 February 1800.

1811

January

8   H.C. Robinson begins his diary: the first of 33 volumes.

Early this year, probably, Thomas Egerton agrees to publish Austen's *Sense and Sensibility* (at the author's expense).

February

5   George, Prince of Wales, becomes Regent under the terms of the Regency Act. His father's illness has returned permanently.

7   Peter Finnerty (c.1766–1822) goes on trial for libel at the court of King's Bench. He accused Castlereagh both of misconduct in Ireland and of attempting to prevent his exposure of the unsuccessful military expedition to Walcheren in 1809. Finnerty is sentenced to eighteen months in Lincoln gaol.

11   Wilkie is elected to the Royal Academy.

Late this month Owenson's *The Missionary: An Indian Tale* is published by J.J. Stockdale in three volumes.

Austen writes 'Lines on Maria Beckford'. She may also start *Mansfield Park* this month.

Publication in two volumes by Manners and Miller, Edinburgh, and Longman, London, of *Self-Control: A Novel* by Mary Brunton (1778–1818). It reaches a fourth edition in February 1812.

March

2–18   Byron works on *Hints from Horace*, revised in May–June and eventually published in 1832. He dates *The Curse of Minerva* 17; it is revised in London by mid-November. Byron decides against publishing it in May 1812 and it too is published by Murray in 1832, but the work is first pirated in 1815.

10   H.C. Robinson records showing Hazlitt Blake's engravings for Edward Young's *Night Thoughts*, and some of Blake's poems. Hazlitt judges the poems 'beautiful ... & only too deep for the vulgar' (Bentley [1969], p.229). On 24 July Robinson

says that Southey 'had been with Blake & admired both his designs & his poetic talents; At the same time that he held him for a decided madman'.

25 Moore marries Elizabeth (Bessy) Dyke (1796–1865).

25 P.B. Shelley and his friend Thomas Jefferson Hogg (1792–1862) are sent down from University College, Oxford, having refused to deny authorship of Shelley's *The Necessity of Atheism*, written in January. Shelley and Hogg both entered the college in October 1810.

29–30 Hazlitt, Coleridge, H.C. Robinson and Charles Lamb are together.

Austen is in London between about the end of this month and early May.

April

19 Between now and 27 September Coleridge writes most of his articles for *The Courier*.

22 Byron leaves Athens. Giraud travels with him as far as Malta, where Byron remains from 30 April to 2 June. He reaches Gibraltar on 17 June and lands in England on 14 July.

29 Lewis's *Timour the Tartar* is at Covent Garden.

29 Constable exhibits *Dedham Vale: Morning*, his most ambitious painting so far, at the Royal Academy.

May

5 Leigh Hunt and P.B. Shelley meet, for the first time, in London. Shelley has been living at 15 Poland Street since March.

9 Mozart's *Così fan tutte* receives its first British performance at the King's Theatre.

In late May or early June the Wordsworths move into the Rectory in Grasmere.

June

6 British premiere of Mozart's *Die Zauberflöte* at the King's Theatre.

19 The Prince of Wales celebrates his Regency in an extravagant evening fête ostensibly designed to honour the future Louis XVIII and his family.

July

2   Publication by Ballantyne in Edinburgh and Longman in London of Scott's *The Vision of Don Roderick*, written in spring and early summer this year.

17–19   Hobhouse joins Byron in Kent. They visit Canterbury.

18   Birth of William Makepeace Thackeray (1811–63) in Calcutta. He leaves for England in December 1816.

August

1   Death of Byron's mother. He reaches Newstead, where she has been living in his absence, on 3. On 7 he hears of the death (on 3) of his Cambridge friend Charles Skinner Matthews.

c.1   Bloomfield's *The Banks of the Wye: a Poem* is published by Vernor, Hood & Sharpe and by Longman.

28   P.B. Shelley and Harriet Westbrook (1795–1816) are married after eloping to Edinburgh, where they live at 60 George Street until the end of September; they are in York between early October and early November.

30   Birth at Tarbes of (Pierre-Jules-)Théophile Gautier (1811–72), who moves with his family to Paris in 1814.

This month Charles Robert Cockerell (1788–1863), who began his Grand Tour in April 1810, excavates the Temple of Apollo Epicurius at Bassae. In 1813 he persuades the British government to buy the frieze of the temple for the British Museum.

September

9   *M.P., or, The Blue-Stocking*, with words by Moore and music by Moore and Charles Horn, opens at the Lyceum.

In the second half of the month John Constable makes his first visit to Salisbury.

October

c.5   Byron goes to Rochdale. He owns land here but the leasehold and the right to mine coal were sold illegally by the 5th Lord Byron. (The leasehold is eventually recovered and Byron sells the estate for £11,255 in November 1823.) On 9 he is back at Newstead, where he learns that Edleston died in May; poems at least partly responding to his death include the 'Thyrza' poems which first appear in the first and second edition of *Childe Harold's Pilgrimage*, Cantos I–II. On 16 Byron is in Cambridge and from 28 in London at 8 St James's Street. He visits Cambridge again towards the end of November.

22 Birth of Franz Liszt (1811–86). He performs in public for the first time in November 1820 and studies in Vienna, in 1822–3, under Karl Czerny (1791–1857) and Salieri.

Publication by Egerton, on about 30, of *Sense and Sensibility*, 'By a Lady', in three volumes. During 1811–12 Austen revises 'First Impressions' as *Pride and Prejudice*.

November

The Shelleys live at Chestnut Cottage, east of Keswick, until late January 1812. P.B. Shelley has long conversations with Southey at Greta Hall in December and January.

4 Rogers introduces Byron to Campbell and Moore; Moore is conciliated after derogatory references to him in *English Bards and Scotch Reviewers* 287–8 and 464f (see 11 August 1806).

18 Coleridge gives the first of his Lectures on Shakespeare and Milton in Illustration of the Principles of Poetry at the London Philosophical Society, Scot's Corporation Hall, off Fleet Street. He continues on 21, 25 and 28; 2, 5, 9, 12, 16, 19 and 30 December; and 9, 13, 16, 20 and 27 January 1812. H.C. Robinson and John Payne Collier are regular attenders and note-takers. Mitford, Rogers and Aaron Burr (1756–1836) are present on 2 December, Charles Lamb on 5 December. Rogers goes again with Byron, probably on 16 December and certainly on 20 January. Mary Godwin is there on 13, 16, 20 and 27 January.

21 Suicide of Kleist and Henriette Vogel.

28 First performance of Beethoven's Piano Concerto no.5, the 'Emperor', in Leipzig. It was first published in London in 1810.

The fourth instalment of Moore's *Irish Melodies* is published.

December

19 Byron goes to Newstead, returning to St James's Street on 11 January 1812.

Late in the year *The Reflector* includes Charles Lamb's 'On Garrick, and Acting; and the Plays of Shakspeare, considered with reference to their fitness for Stage Representation' and 'Edax on Appetite'.

Turner gives his first lectures as Professor of Perspective at the Royal Academy (elected 1807). His final lectures are in 1828.
Friedrich paints *Winter Landscape with a Church*.

1812

January

3   P.B. Shelley initiates a correspondence with Godwin.
14 Hazlitt begins his lectures on philosophy at the Russell Institution, Great Coram Street. He speaks again on 21 and 28 January, 4, 11, 18 and 25 February and 3 March. He continues – fortnightly rather than weekly – on 17 and 31 March and 14 and 28 April. H.C. Robinson is present on most of these occasions. Other attenders include Charles Lamb, Thelwall and Ann Flaxman.
15 Hazlitt and H.C. Robinson are at tea with the Lambs.
19 British forces capture Ciudad Rodrigo; Viscount Wellington becomes an Earl on 18 February. He goes on to take Badajoz on 6 April.
20 Owenson marries Sir Thomas Morgan and writes from now on as Lady Morgan.

For Coleridge's lectures this month see November 1811.

February

7   Birth of Charles Dickens in Portsmouth.
10–13 Coleridge travels from London to Liverpool, where there is an (unfulfilled) possibility of lecturing. He reaches Keswick on 18 and stays there with his family and the Southeys until 26 March, without visiting the Wordsworths.
12   Barbauld's *Eighteen Hundred and Eleven, a Poem*, completed by December 1811, is published by Joseph Johnson's company.
21   The Literary and Philosophical Society of Liverpool is founded. William Roscoe becomes its President in 1817.
22   At Carlton House the Regent speaks against his former Whig allies; his daughter Princess Charlotte, it is reported, bursts into tears.
27   Byron's maiden speech in the House of Lords, opposing the 'Frame Work' Bill which seeks to impose the death penalty on 'frame breakers' after disturbances involving Nottinghamshire stocking-knitters. The bill passes into law.

27 H.C. Robinson, Hazlitt and Northcote dine with Thelwall. This month Hazlitt meets Haydon through Northcote.
28 Castlereagh takes office as Foreign Secretary.
P.B. Shelley arrives in Dublin, staying until April. He attempts, through speeches and pamphlets, to intervene in Irish politics.
Late in February Peacock's *The Philosophy of Melancholy: A Poem in Four Parts, with a Mythological Ode* is published by Hookham.

March

2 Byron's 'An Ode to the Framers of the Frame Bill' appears anonymously in *The Morning Chronicle*. There also, on 7, appears his anonymous 'Sympathetic Address to a Young Lady' (see 22 February). He is attacked by the Tory press when it appears under his name, as 'Lines to a Lady Weeping', with *The Corsair* in February 1814.

8 Moore's anonymous 'Parody of a Celebrated Letter', based on the Regent's letter justifying his abandonment of the Whigs, is printed (having circulated for some days) in *The Examiner*. Charles Lamb's satire 'The Triumph of the Whale', also aimed at the Prince, follows there on 15.

10 Publication by John Murray of Byron's *Childe Harold's Pilgrimage* Cantos I and II.

19 An article in *The Morning Post*, full of adulation for the Regent, prompts Leigh Hunt's attack on him in *The Examiner* on 22. In 'The Prince on St Patrick's Day' he calls him 'a violator of his word, a libertine over head and ears in debt' with no claim on 'the gratitude of his country or the respect of posterity'. Leigh and John Hunt are prosecuted for seditious libel. The trial is on 9 December, with Brougham again defending. Lord Ellenborough fines them each £500 and sentences them to two years' imprisonment, beginning on 3 February 1813, Leigh at Horsemonger Lane, John at Coldbath Fields. Leigh Hunt's visitors include Bentham (who met him in August 1812), Haydon, Byron, Moore, Hazlitt, the Lambs, the Edgeworths and John Scott (1784–1821).

25 Lady Caroline Lamb and Byron become lovers. He breaks with her in August but she is reluctant to accept the situation.

At the end of the month Opie's *Temper, or Domestic Scenes; A Tale* is published in three volumes by Longman.

April

Early in the month Hookham publishes a revised edition of Peacock's *The Genius of the Thames, Palmyra, and Other Poems*.

8   Davy is knighted. (He becomes a baronet on 20 October 1818). He gives his last lecture at the Royal Institution on 9 and marries Jane Apreece (1780–1855) on 11. Her money enables him to travel and to resign as Professor at the Royal Institution in 1813.

14   The Shelleys live at Nantgwyllt, Rhayader, Radnorshire (until 6 June).

14   Coleridge arrives back in London. He lives with John Morgan and his family at 71 Berners Street.

21   Byron speaks in the Lords on the Roman Catholic Claims Bill. He supports the successful motion to set up a committee to consider a petition by Irish Roman Catholics for equal civil rights. Actual reform is delayed until the 1820s.

27   Wordsworth arrives in London (until mid-June). The main aim of his visit is to achieve reconciliation with Coleridge. After further complications and mediation by Charles Lamb and H.C. Robinson, peace is made by 13 May. In London Wordsworth also sees De Quincey, Bowles, Baillie, Rogers and Davy.

Foundation by William Blackwood (1776–1834) of the Tory *Blackwood's Edinburgh Magazine*. From October its output is dominated by John Wilson as 'Christopher North', James Hogg and John Gibson Lockhart (1794–1854).

May

4   The Royal Academy show includes Turner's *Snowstorm: Hannibal and his Army Crossing the Alps* and Fuseli's 'Garrick and Mrs Pritchard in *Macbeth*' (inspired by his less visionary drawing of about 1766).

7   Birth of Robert Browning in Camberwell.

11   Assassination of Spencer Perceval (1762–1812), Prime Minister since October 1809. His killer, John Bellingham, is acting on a grudge against the government for not intervening to prevent his imprisonment for debt in Russia. He is hanged at Newgate on 18. Byron watches the execution.

11   Wordsworth probably meets Byron and Moore for the first time (Reed [1975], p. 498). He is with Byron at Rogers's on 26.

15   Scott takes possession of the farm he has bought for £4,200, Newarthaugh or Cartley Hole, near Melrose and Galashiels. He renames it Abbotsford, buys several adjoining farms in 1815–16, and builds the house here between 1817 and 1825 (in which year he entails it on his son Walter, thus preventing its forced sale amid his major financial problems of 1825–6).
19   Coleridge begins his Lectures on European Drama at Willis's Rooms, King Street, London. The First Series continues on 23, 26 and 29 May and 2 and 5 June. The Second Series begins on 9 June and may continue on 12 and 16 (Coleridge [1969–2002], 5.1.475).
25   Scott, as Sheriff-Depute of Selkirkshire, arrests weavers in Galashiels who are about to engage in frame-breaking.
25   Ninety-two workers are killed in an explosion at Felling Colliery, near Gateshead.
30   Coleridge and Wordsworth walk to Hampstead.
The Moores move to Kegworth in Leicestershire. In 1814 they move again to Mayfield Cottage, near Ashbourne.

June
4   Death of Wordsworth's younger daughter, Catherine (1808–12).
8   Robert Banks Jenkinson, Earl of Liverpool (1770–1828) becomes Prime Minister. He is in office until 9 April 1827.
5–12   Byron and Hobhouse are at Newstead.
6   The Shelleys spend three weeks at the Cwm Elan estate, near Rhayader, which P.B. Shelley first visited in July–August 1811. He works on 'Written at Cwm Elan' probably in July 1811 and 'The Retrospect: Cwm Elan, 1812' in May or June 1812. (Bowles's *Coombe Ellen* appeared in 1798.) From late June to late August the Shelleys live at Lynmouth in north Devon.
7–c.14   Mary Godwin sails from London to Dundee. She suffers from persistent skin eruption and her father has arranged, following a medical recommendation of sea-bathing, for her to stay at Broughty Ferry, near Dundee, with the Baxter family. She remains there until November and returns for a second visit between June 1813 and March 1814.
18   The United States declares war on Britain.

18   First British performance, at the King's Theatre, of Mozart's *Le nozze di Figaro*.
24   Napoleon launches his invasion of Russia.
c. 25   Byron is introduced to the Prince Regent.
29   Siddons retires with a performance as Lady Macbeth at Covent Garden. She will continue to act, mainly in benefit performances, until 1819.

Joseph Johnson's company publishes Davy's *Elements of Chemical Philosophy*. In 1813 Longman publishes his *Elements of Agricultural Chemistry*; he lectures annually to the Board of Agriculture between 1803 and 1812.

July
15   Wellington's major victory at Salamanca; on 3 October he is promoted Marquess. In August he enters Madrid (where Goya paints the first of several portraits of him) but the French recapture it in November.
30   Marriage of Browne and Captain Alfred Hemans (1781–1827). They live in Daventry and then, from 1813, at Bronwlfa. Earlier in 1812 her *The Domestic Affections and Other Poems* was published by Cadell and Davies.

William Moorcroft (1767–1825) travels in Tibet. In October to November he is imprisoned for a time in Nepal.

August
23   Byron is in Cheltenham until 24 October.

September
7   Napoleon wins the Battle of Borodino. He enters Moscow on 14.

Hatchard publishes Crabbe's *Tales*.

October
4   P.B. Shelley (living in London with his wife at Lewis's Hotel until November) meets William Godwin for the first time and comes back to see him at Skinner Street frequently over the next few weeks. He almost certainly first meets Mary Godwin there on 11 November. Shelley is much influenced by William Godwin's work and will provide him with considerable sums of

134 A Romantics Chronology, 1780–1832

money, especially in 1814–15. Probably this month or in early November Shelley also meets Peacock – they are introduced by the publisher Thomas Hookham (1787–1867).

10 Drury Lane, rebuilt by Benjamin Wyatt, re-opens with a production of *Hamlet*. Each night from now until 20 Robert Elliston delivers Byron's 'Address, Spoken at the Opening of Drury-lane Theatre' and it is published in *The Morning Chronicle* on 12. Also on 12 John Miller publishes *Rejected Addresses: or The New Theatrum Poetarum*, by James Smith (1775–1839) and his brother Horatio (Horace) Smith (1779–1849). This parodies Byron and other authors who are imagined submitting entries in the competition to provide the Drury Lane address.

12 Annabella Milbanke (1792–1860) refuses Byron's first marriage proposal, made through Elizabeth Lamb, Viscountess Melbourne (1751–1818), who is both her aunt and his close friend (and Lady Caroline Lamb's mother-in-law).

19 The French retreat from Moscow begins.

At some point before 24 Grimaldi and Byron are among guests at Berkeley Castle. On 24 Byron leaves Cheltenham to stay at Eywood in Herefordshire with Jane Harley, Countess of Oxford (1772–1824) and her husband the Earl. She and Byron become lovers.

November

3 Coleridge gives the first of his Lectures on the Belles Lettres at the Surrey Institution. The remaining lectures are on 10, 17 and 24 of this month, 1, 8, 15 and either 22 or 29 December (Coleridge [1969–2002], 5.1.493), and 5, 12, 19 and 26 January 1813. H.C. Robinson takes notes at many of the lectures. This month *Omniana, or Horae otiosiores*, by Coleridge and Southey, is published by Longman.

21 Byron goes to Cheltenham and then on 24 to Middleton Park, home of the Earl and Countess of Jersey. From 30 he is in London at Batt's Hotel, Dover Street.

Some time before 29 Egerton buys the copyright of *Pride and Prejudice* for £110.

30 Hazlitt starts work as parliamentary reporter for *The Morning Chronicle*. From September 1813 he also reviews plays there, becoming the regular theatre critic in January 1814.

In St Petersburg Field publishes his Nocturnes 1–3.

December

1 Wordsworth's second son, Thomas (1806–12), dies of complications following measles.
14 From about now until 17 January 1813 Byron is back at Eywood, engaged in his affair with Lady Oxford.
18 Maturin writes to Scott, beginning their correspondence.
19 Napoleon reaches Paris. Most of the survivors of his invasion army are still caught up in the retreat from Russia.

Much of Regent's Park in London, designed by John Nash (1752–1836), is laid out this year. He adds the Terraces during the 1820s. In 1813 work begins on Regent Street.

This year fairy-tales by Jacob Grimm (1785–1863) and Wilhelm Grimm (1786–1859) begin publication in Berlin: *Kinder- und Hausmärchen* (two volumes, 1812–15, with an expanded second edition in 1819–22). Edgar Taylor's (1793–1839) translation, *German Popular Stories*, appears in 1823–6.

1813

January

Between early January this year and late May 1814 Wordsworth completes *The Excursion*, Books VI–IX.

11 Scott's *Rokeby; A Poem* is published by Ballantyne in Edinburgh and Longman in London. It was completed on 31 December 1812. Scott visited Rokeby, in Northumberland, that September.
19 Byron returns to London. He lives at 4 Bennet Street. In London he is introduced to Princess Caroline.
23 Premiere of Coleridge's *Remorse* at Drury Lane. Coleridge himself, H.C. Robinson and William and Mary Godwin are in the audience. The production runs for twenty nights and there are three editions of the text this year. For Coleridge's lectures this month see 3 November 1812.
24 Godwin meets Robert Owen.
28 Egerton publishes *Pride and Prejudice*, 'by the Author of "Sense and Sensibility"', in three volumes.

February

6 First night at Teatro La Fenice in Venice of Rossini's *Tancredi*. His *L'italiana in Algeri* is given in Venice at Teatro San Benedetto

on 22 May. Rossini has been active as a composer of opera since 1810 and continues prolific until the early 1820s.

26 At Tanyrallt, near Tremadoc, where the Shelleys have lived since November 1812, there is or may be an incident in which P.B. Shelley fights off an intruder who, in different accounts, he claims to be either human or diabolical (see Bieri [2008], pp. 238–52).

John Howard Payne (1791–1852) arrives in England from America. His debut at Drury Lane is on 4 June as Young Norval in Home's *Douglas*.

March

1 Davy takes on Michael Faraday (1791–1867) as a laboratory assistant at the Royal Institution.

9 Anonymous appearance of Scott's *The Bridal of Triermain, or the Vale of St John: in Three Cantos* (Ballantyne, Edinburgh and Longman, London).

13 Coleridge and John Morgan visit Bexhill in Sussex.

16 Prussia declares war on France.

28 Byron is back at Eywood with Lady Oxford, returning to London by 24 April.

Moore's *Intercepted Letters, or, The Twopenny Post-Bag* is published by J. Carr as the work of 'Thomas Brown the Younger'.

P.B. Shelley's second Irish expedition (until April).

April

22 Between now and 1 May, and again between 19 May and June, Austen is in London, helping her brother Henry whose wife, Eliza (formerly de Feuillide), dies on 24 April (Le Faye [2013], 442). She stays with him again in September and November and in March to April, August to September and late November to early December 1814.

26 Wordsworth, through the patronage of the Earl of Lonsdale, becomes Distributor of Stamps (excise duties) in Westmorland and part of Cumberland.

Between April and July the Shelleys are in London, initially at Cooke's Hotel.

May
3   Turner's *Frosty Morning* and eight works by Thomas Lawrence are at the Royal Academy.
12 William, Mary and Dorothy Wordsworth and family move to Rydal Mount.
22 Richard Wagner (1813–83) is born in Leipzig.
Murray publishes Southey's *The Life of Nelson* in two volumes.
Byron meets Maria Edgeworth.
Hobhouse's *Journey Through Albania; and Other Provinces of Turkey ... during the Years 1809–1810* is published by Cawthorn.

June
1   Byron speaks in the House of Lords in support of John Cartwright's petition to be allowed to petition Parliament. The speech is published on 2 in *The Morning Chronicle* and *The London Gazette*.
5   Publication by Murray of the first edition of Byron's *The Giaour, a Fragment of a Turkish Tale*. Expansion continues until the seventh edition in December.
10 Publication by Longman of Opie's *Tales of Real Life* in three volumes.
20 Staël comes to England (until 10 May 1814). She meets Byron on 20 and they see each other again on 27 (at the Davys') and on 12 July. She meets many other people, including Southey, Mackintosh, Murray and Sheridan.
21 Wellington's victory at Vitoria.
In June–August Peacock visits Wales for the second time.

July
5   Lady Caroline Lamb attempts, or may attempt, to stab herself in front of Byron at a ball in London.
28 Byron dines with Rogers and Sheridan.
Austen probably finishes *Mansfield Park*.

August
1   Byron is with his half-sister, Augusta Leigh (1783–1851), at her home in Six Mile Bottom, near Newmarket. Their affair is in progress. They travel back to London together.

4   Godwin and Byron meet.
12   Austria declares war on France. On 26–7 Napoleon defeats Austrian, Prussian and Russian forces at Dresden but fails to consolidate his victory.
Scott visits Southey in Keswick.

September
2   Staël meets Coleridge in London.
Early this month Scott refuses the Prince Regent's offer of the post of Poet Laureate, following the death of Henry James Pye (1745–1813) on 11 August. Pye became Laureate in 1790. Southey takes up the appointment on 4 November.
c.17–25   Byron stays at Aston Hall, Rotherham, with James Wedderburn Webster and his wife Lady Frances Wedderburn Webster (1793–1837). He returns on about 5 October and the Websters stay with him at Newstead on 16–19 October. Byron pursues Lady Frances and sends Lady Melbourne a series of letters describing the pursuit, but in the end desists.
26   Southey meets Byron at Holland House. There on 30 Byron also meets John Philpot Curran (1750–1817).
Peacock visits Shelley in Bracknell.

October
Egerton produces second editions of *Pride and Prejudice* early in the month and of *Sense and Sensibility* at the end. A third edition of the former follows in 1817.
10   Birth of Giuseppe Verdi (1813–1901) at Le Roncole.
16–19   Napoleon is defeated at Leipzig with heavy losses.
c.20   Coleridge arrives in Bristol, where he raises money to help John Morgan and his family after the collapse of their finances this summer.
28   Coleridge begins his Lectures on Shakespeare and Education at the White Lion, Broad Street, Bristol, continuing on 2, 4, 9, 11, 16, 18 and 23 November. He also speaks on Milton and Poetry at Mangeon's Hotel, Clifton, on 10 and 17 November.
The Shelleys and Peacock live at 36 Frederick Street, Edinburgh, until December.

The Davys travel in Europe, with Faraday as assistant and valet. In Paris, Davy identifies iodine. Another area of research is volcanoes, extinct and active, including Vesuvius (May 1814). The group returns to England on 23 April 1815.

November

4 Murray publishes Staël's *De l' Allemagne*, which was prohibited from being printed in Paris in 1810. The translation, *Germany*, is also brought out by Murray.

14 Byron begins the journal which he keeps between now and 19 April 1814. It is published with some omissions in Moore's *Life* of 1830.

24–29 Coleridge is back in London before escorting John Morgan's wife Mary Morgan and sister-in-law Charlotte Brent to Bath.

December

2 Publication by Murray of Byron's *The Bride of Abydos. A Turkish Tale*. Eleven more editions follow in 1813–15.

3 Byron sees Galt. On 8 he is with Staël at Holland House and on 10 with Rogers and Sharp.

31 The Gas Light and Coke Company lights Westminster Bridge with gas.

Private distribution of P.B. Shelley's *Queen Mab; A Philosophical Poem: with Notes*, written mainly between spring 1812 and February 1813.

Publication by Sharpe & Hailes of Peacock's *Sir Hornbook; or, Childe Launcelot's Expedition: A Grammatico-Allegorical Ballad*, dated 1814. There are five editions by 1818.

This month Sherwood, Neely & Jones publish Maria Edgeworth's *The Ballad Singer; or, Memoirs of the Bristol Family: a Most Interesting Novel* in four volumes, dated 1814. At the end of December or in January 1814 her *Patronage*, also in four volumes, is published by Joseph Johnson's company.

The fifth instalment of Moore's *Irish Melodies* is published.

Coleridge spends much of the month ill in Bath before moving on to Bristol.

This year Sismondi's *De la Littérature du Midi de l'Europe* is published. A translation by Thomas Roscoe (1791–1871; son of William Roscoe) is published by Colburn in 1823: *Historical View of the Literature of the South of Europe*.

Robert Kerr's translation from Georges Cuvier (1769–1832), *Essay on the Theory of the Earth*, is published by Blackwood in Edinburgh.

1814

January
1   *Seren Gomer*, the first Welsh-language newspaper, is launched in Swansea. English-language newspapers published in Wales include *The Cambrian* (begun in Swansea in 1804) and *The North Wales Gazette* (Bangor, 1808).
11 Murat, as King of Naples (since 1 August 1808) abandons Napoleon, making peace with Austria.
17 Byron and Augusta Leigh set off for Newstead, where they remain until 6 February.
21 Austen starts work on *Emma*.
26 Kean's debut as Shylock at Drury Lane. (Hazlitt's enthusiastic review is in *The Morning Chronicle* on 27.) He repeats Shylock on 1 February and makes further Drury Lane debuts in roles including Richard III (12 February), Hamlet (12 March) Othello (5 May) and Iago (7 May). Cawthorn publishes Leigh Hunt's *The Feast of the Poets*, revised from the 1812 version in *The Reflector*.

February
1   Byron's *The Corsair* (begun on 18 December 1813 and completed on 1 January) is published by Murray. 'I sold on the Day of Publication, a thing perfectly unprecedented, 10,000 copies' (Murray [2007], p.72). Sales are helped by the inclusion in the same volume of 'Lines to a Lady Weeping'. There are six more editions this year.
9   Byron is back in London. On 19 he sees Kean's Richard III.

March
1   Byron, Rogers and Sheridan are together. Byron sees Rogers again on 14.
16 Crabbe is incumbent at Croxton-Kerrial, and at Trowbridge from 18.
28 Fanny Burney D'Arblay's (anonymous) *The Wanderer; or, Female Difficulties* is published in five volumes by Longman.

28 Byron moves into 2 Albany, London.
24 Friedrich shows *The Chasseur in the Woods* at the Exhibition of Patriotic Art, celebrating the defeat of Napoleon, in Dresden.
31 Paris surrenders and is entered by allied Russian, Prussian and Austrian forces.
Peacock's *Sir Proteus. A Satirical Ballad* is published, as the work of 'P.M. O'Donovan', by Hookham. This spring Peacock starts work on his unpublished poem 'Ahrimanes'.

April
Early this month Byron is at Six Mile Bottom with Leigh, returning to London on 7.
5 First of Coleridge's Lectures on Milton and Cervantes at the White Lion, Bristol. The others are on 7, 12, 14, 19 and 21.
6 Napoleon attempts to abdicate in favour of his son, Napoleon 'II' (1811–32), King of Rome. He abdicates without conditions on 11. Responses include Byron's *Ode to Napoleon Buonaparte*, published anonymously on 16. Another Murray publication, *Buonaparte. A Poem*, by Stratford Canning (1786–1880), comes out in May. The peace makes travel in Europe easier; P.B. Shelley and Mary Godwin, Thelwall and H.C. Robinson are in France in the late summer.
12 Death of Dr Charles Burney in Chelsea.
21 Wellington is appointed ambassador in Paris. He is created Duke on 3 May and arrives in Paris on 4.
26 Coleridge, at the White Lion in Bristol, gives the first of his intended three lectures on the French Revolution. Illness prevents him delivering the others.

May
2 Paintings at the Royal Academy exhibition include Thomas Phillips's Byron: *Portrait of a Nobleman in the Dress of an Albanian*.
3 Louis XVIII arrives in Paris.
4 Napoleon reaches Elba, to which he was exiled under the terms of the Treaty of Fontainebleau on 11 April.
5 Mary Godwin meets P.B. Shelley for either the first or more probably the second time. By June they are often together, usually accompanied by Mary Godwin's stepsister Jane (later Claire) Clairmont (1798–1879).

7	Byron sees Kean as Iago at Drury Lane. He goes again with Moore and Hobhouse on 19 and they meet Kean.
9	*Mansfield Park* is published by Egerton in three volumes. It sells out by November but Egerton cannot be persuaded to print a second edition.
12	Staël returns to Paris.
30	First Treaty of Paris restores France to its boundaries of 1 January 1792.

Hazlitt is dismissed from *The Morning Chronicle*. He writes for *The Champion* until March 1815, is theatre critic for *The Examiner* from May 1815, and later also writes for *The Edinburgh Review*.

Landor, having failed in his attempt to manage his estate at Llanthony, sets off for France via Jersey. He lives in Tours until 1815 before moving to Como (until 1818), Pisa (until 1821) and Florence.

June

23	Southey's 'The March to Moscow' is in *The Courier*.

July

1	Masked ball held by Watier's Club at Burlington House to honour Wellington. Participants include Byron, Hobhouse, Lady Caroline Lamb and Harriette Wilson. A similar celebration is held at Drury Lane in 1815.
3–7	Byron visits Six Mile Bottom and Cambridge.
7	Publication by Archibald Constable in Edinburgh and Longman in London of Scott's first novel, the anonymous *Waverley; or 'Tis Sixty Years Since* (three volumes). Scott first worked on it c.1808–10. Sales are high – a thousand copies in two days. The novel reaches a fourth edition in November.
18	William and Mary Wordsworth, with Hutchinson, set off for a tour of Scotland. They reach Lanark on 24, Glasgow on 25 and Callander on 1 August. They travel in the Highlands, reaching Glencoe on 11 August, and go on to Inverness on 14, Blair Atholl on 17 and Perth on about 21.
20	Byron goes to Hastings until 11 August.
28	After much unsuccessful expostulation from her father, Mary Godwin and P.B. Shelley, with Clairmont, elope for the Continent. They reach Paris on 2 August, Troyes on 12, and Switzerland on 19. Running out of money, they turn back at

the end of the month and in early September sail up the Rhine through Germany and go on by road to Rotterdam. They land at Gravesend on 13 September. Estranged from the Godwins, they live at a number of different London addresses between September 1814 and May 1815.

29 Beginning of the voyage in which Scott and the engineer Robert Stevenson (1772–1850) accompany the Commissioners for the Northern Lighthouse Service. They go to Shetland (3 August), Orkney (11), Harris (21), Skye (23), Iona (27), Staffa and Mull (29), cross to the Giants' Causeway, and arrive at Greenock on 8 September. The Bell Rock lighthouse, designed and built principally by Stevenson, was completed in 1811. Subsequently he is responsible for many others including those on the Isle of May (1816) and Sumburgh Head (1821).

Between summer 1814 and November 1818 Carlyle teaches, first at Annan Academy (1814–16) and then in Kirkcaldy (1816–18).

August

1 Bristol production of Coleridge's *Remorse*. This month he agrees to translate Goethe's *Faust* for Murray; he has abandoned the project by mid-October, but see September 1821.

Early this month Wordsworth's *The Excursion: Being a Portion of The Recluse* is published by Longman.

6 Publication by Murray of Byron's *Lara* (written between 15 May and 23 June) and Rogers's *Jacqueline: a Tale*.

10 Stendhal goes to Milan, where he spends several periods between now and 1821, when he becomes persona non grata to the Austrian authorities and leaves on 13 July. He knows Vincenzo Monti (1754–1828) and Silvio Pellico (1789–1854).

13 The first of Coleridge's *Essays on the Principles of Genial Criticism* is in *Felix Farley's Bristol Journal*. The series continues on 13, 20 and 27 and on 10 and 24 September.

20 Byron sets off from London for Newstead with Leigh, returning to London on 21 September.

20 Rogers sets off for Italy, at first with Mackintosh. He travels by way of Paris, Switzerland (where he parts from Mackintosh) and the Simplon Pass, in October reaching Milan (8), Venice (16) and Florence (31). He goes on to Rome on 24 November and Naples on 11 February 1815. The journey back is through

Rome, Florence, Innsbruck (13 April 1815), the Rhine and the Low Countries. He sails from Ostend for England on 6 May. During the journey Rogers keeps the journal which will inform his *Italy* (see January 1822). He goes to Italy again in 1821–2.

21 The first instalment of Hazlitt's review of Wordsworth's *The Excursion* is in *The Examiner*. It continues on 28 and on 2 October. Jeffrey's review of the poem, beginning 'This will never do,' is in *The Edinburgh Review* for November.

24 British troops capture and burn Washington, DC.

24 William and Mary Wordsworth and Hutchinson reach Linlithgow. They are in Edinburgh between 25 and 30. On 1 September they are with James Hogg by the Yarrow and Wordsworth writes 'Yarrow Visited' soon afterwards. They are back at Rydal Mount on 9 September. (Hogg arrived there, visiting Dorothy Wordsworth, on 7 September.)

September

9 Byron's second proposal of marriage to Milbanke. On 18 he learns that she has accepted him.

12 Coleridge recovers from his opium-related illness sufficiently to leave Bristol and move in with the Morgans at Ashley, near Bath.

18 The Congress of Vienna convenes. Its Final Act is issued on 9 June 1815.

John Wilson and De Quincey are among guests at Rydal Mount.

October

14 Byron and Kean dine.

15 Birth in Moscow of Mikhail Yuryevich Lermontov (1814–41).

November

2 Byron reaches Seaham in County Durham, the Milbanke family home, where he stays until 16. He is at Newstead on 17, Cambridge on 18–19 and 22–3 and Six Mile Bottom on 19, and arrives in London on 24.

Publication by Longman of Southey's *Roderick, the Last of the Goths*.

Between this autumn and April 1815 Byron writes many of the poems in *Hebrew Melodies* for melodies by Isaac Nathan.

December
2   Sade dies at Charenton asylum, where he has been detained since April 1803.
13 Brunton's *Discipline* is published by Longman.
24 Byron and Hobhouse set out for Seaham, visiting Six Mile Bottom on Christmas Day. They arrive in Seaham on 30.
24 The Treaty of Ghent officially ends hostilities in the Anglo-American War.
27 Death in London of Joanna Southcott (1750–1814), a prophet and religious writer who believes, from spring 1814, that she is about to give birth to Shiloh, the new Messiah.

This month Coleridge and the Morgans move to Calne in Wiltshire.

Picturesque Views on the Southern Coast of England, with engravings from Turner's drawings, is published by Murray between 1814 and 1826, remaining incomplete.

Clare writes manuscript poems in 'A Rustic's Pastime in Leisure Hours: Helpston 1814'.

Cawthorn and Martin publish J. H. Reynolds's *Safie: an Eastern Tale*.

1815

January
2   Scott's *The Lord of the Isles* (finished 16 December 1814) is published by Archibald Constable in Edinburgh and Longman in London.
2   Byron and Milbanke are married. They go to Halnaby, near Darlington, until 21, when they return to Seaham until 9 March.
15 Death of Emma Hamilton in Calais.

Stendhal's *Vies de Haydn, Mozart et Métastase* is published under the name Louis Alexandre Bombet. Murray publishes a translation, *The Life of Haydn ... followed by the Life of Mozart, with observations on Metastasio*, in 1817.

February
2   Leigh Hunt is released from prison (see 19 March 1812). Keats works on his sonnet 'Written on the Day that Mr. Leigh Hunt Left Prison'. Hunt's *The Defence of Liberty, a Mask* is published later this month by Gale, Curtis and Fenner.

24   Publication by Longman in London and Archibald Constable in Edinburgh of *Guy Mannering; or The Astrologer* (3 volumes) 'by the author of Waverley' – Scott's signature for many of his novels until 1827.
26   Napoleon leaves Elba.
Crabbe and Bowles meet for the first time.

March
1   Napoleon lands in France. Louis XVIII flees to Ghent on 13; Napoleon enters Paris on 20 and reassumes power for the 'Hundred Days' until 22 June.
12   The Byrons arrive at Six Mile Bottom. On 28 they go on to London, living from 29 at 13 Piccadilly Terrace. Leigh is with them from early April to late June.
16   Four regiments of British infantry are ordered to Ostend, the advance guard of a much larger force.
20   Liverpool's government, taking advantage of the distraction of the prospect of war, succeeds in passing its Corn Bill, keeping prices high at home by making foreign import of corn prohibitively expensive. Riots against the bill happen mainly earlier in the month.
26   Coleridge visits Bowles at Bremhill in Wiltshire.
29   Austen finishes *Emma*.
31   Byron suggests to Coleridge that he should write a Drury Lane tragedy for Kean. He produces instead a 'dramatic entertainment', called by December *Zapolya*.
This month Nash begins work on transforming the Prince Regent's Marine Pavilion and grounds into Brighton Pavilion. It is completed in 1823.

April
1   Mary Lamb's 'Essay on Needle-work' appears in *The British Lady's Magazine and Monthly Miscellany* under the name 'Sempronia'.
3   Advance copies of *Poems by William Wordsworth* (Longman, two volumes, published by 27) begin to be sent out.
4   Wellington arrives in Brussels to discuss military options with other allied commanders.

4   Hobhouse and the Byrons dine with Sir Francis Burdett (1770–1848).
5   Nathan publishes *A Selection of Hebrew Melodies*, with words by Byron. Murray's text of *Hebrew Melodies* follows in late May.
5   Scott arrives in London, staying until 11 June. He sees friends including Baillie, Opie and Wordsworth. He meets Byron for the first time on 7. The Prince Regent gives a dinner for him, probably on 22 or 29 (see Johnson [1970], vol.1, Notes p.li, n.14). He dines with him again in May.
10   Eruption of Mount Tambora on the Indonesian island of Sumbawa. Over 70,000 people die, many in the ensuing famine. The eruption is a main cause of the 'Year Without a Summer', 1816, when temperatures are unusually low and there are food shortages throughout the Northern Hemisphere.
20   Thomas Lawrence is knighted.

Publication of the sixth volume of Moore's *Irish Melodies*.

May

1   At the Royal Academy this season Sir Thomas Lawrence exhibits portraits of Wellington, Blücher and Metternich, commissioned in 1814 by the Prince Regent. Turner shows *Crossing the Brook* and *Dido Building Carthage; or the Rise of the Carthaginian Empire*. Beaumont, the most influential hostile critic of Turner's painting, attacks these works in particular (Farington [1978–82], 5 June).
c.5 William and Mary Wordsworth have brought Hartley Coleridge to Oxford, where he matriculates at Merton College on 6. (He graduates in 1818.) The Wordsworths go on to London, where they stay until 19 June and see the Lambs, H.C. Robinson, Haydon, Scott and Wilberforce.
13   P.B. Shelley and his father reach a financial settlement. One result of the agreement is that Shelley is able to provide Peacock with an annuity of £120.
25   Irving sails for England, where he lands at Liverpool and goes to Birmingham before his first visit to London in July.

Late this month Byron is appointed to the Drury Lane Sub-Committee of Management.

Between about the end of May and 19 September Coleridge composes the autobiographical and critical work which will become, after much expansion, *Biographia Literaria*.

June

2   Wordsworth's *The White Doe of Rylstone; or The Fate of the Nortons* is published by Longman: a revision of the version written in 1807.
15 Charlotte, Duchess of Richmond holds a ball in Brussels. Guests include many British officers, Wellington and Lord Uxbridge among them. The ball is referred to in Byron's *Childe Harold's Pilgrimage*, Canto III.
16 Battles of Ligny, where Napoleon defeats Prussian forces under Prince Gebhard Leberecht von Blücher (1742–1819), and Quatre-Bras, where Michel Ney (1769–1815) fights mainly Dutch, German and British contingents and prevents Wellington from reinforcing Blücher.
18 Battle of Waterloo: the final defeat of Napoleon by British forces commanded by Wellington and Prussian forces by Blücher. Responses include Scott's *The Field of Waterloo*, published on 23 October. (Scott visits the battlefield in August and meets Wellington and Tsar Alexander in Paris. Subsequently he draws on this expedition in *Paul's Letters to His Kinsfolk*, published on 25 January 1816.) Southey's *The Poet's Pilgrimage to Waterloo* comes out in 1816, following a visit in autumn 1815. Byron comes on 4 May 1816 and the battle features in *Childe Harold's Pilgrimage*, Canto III. Turner comes in August 1817 and shows his *The Field of Waterloo* at the Royal Academy exhibition in 1818.
22 Napoleon's second abdication.
Longman publishes Southey's *Minor Poems*.

July

1   Dacre marries Nicholas Byrne (d.1833), father of her three children and editor of *The Morning Post*.
8   Louis XVIII returns to Paris.
15 Napoleon surrenders himself to the captain of HMS *Bellerophon* at Rochefort. From 23 July to 4 August the ship remains off Plymouth, where curious and enthusiastic crowds gather. After much debate – the former Emperor's status is highly uncertain – the British authorities send him to St Helena. He sets off on HMS *Northumberland* on 7 August and arrives on 16 October.

28 Poe arrives in Liverpool with his adoptive parents, the Allans. After a period at Greenock they move to London in early October. Poe is a pupil at Manor House School, Stoke Newington between 1817 and 1820, when, on 14 June, the family sails for New York.

August
4   P.B. Shelley and Mary Godwin move to Bishopsgate, Windsor, their home until early March 1816. Between late August and about 10 September they go on a rowing expedition up the Thames to Reading, Oxford and Lechlade. With them are Peacock and Clairmont's brother Charles (1795–1850).
8   Austen begins work on the novel published in December 1817 as *Persuasion*.
14 Davy goes to Newcastle to meet colliery managers in preparation for his work on the miners' safety lamp.
15 Leigh joins the Byrons in London.
18 Wellington's ball for Blücher in Paris. On 30 Lady Castlereagh gives a ball for the Tsar, the Austrian Emperor and the King of Prussia. Scott is present on both occasions.
30 Byron goes to Six Mile Bottom, returning to London by 14.

September
9   Scott starts his return journey from Paris. He arrives in London on 12, dines with Byron on 14, and leaves on 15, reaching Abbotsford, via Carlisle, on 24.
10 P.B. Shelley starts *Alastor; or, the Spirit of Solitude*.

October
1   Keats becomes a student at Guy's Hospital in London. He lives at 28 St Thomas's Street, Southwark.
4   Austen comes to London (23 Hans Place, Chelsea) to stay with her brother Henry. She nurses him through illness, remaining until 16 December.
4   Rossini's *Elisabetta, regina d'Inghilterra*, is at Teatro San Carlo in Naples.
13 Murat is executed at Pizzo in Calabria. He took up Napoleon's cause again during the Hundred Days, was defeated at Tolentino

by the Austrians on 3 May and led an unsuccessful invasion of his former kingdom of Naples at the beginning of this month.
15 John Murray offers £450 for the copyright of *Sense and Sensibility*, *Mansfield Park* and the forthcoming *Emma*. Austen, in consultation with her brother Henry, rejects the offer in November. Instead Murray will publish the new novel and a second edition of *Mansfield Park*.

Davy devises his safety lamp. On 9 November he gives a paper to the Royal Society describing three possible versions. In a second paper there, on 11 January 1816, he presents the final form.

November
4 Byron sends Murray a copy of Coleridge's *Christabel* and encourages him to publish it.
13 At the request of the Prince Regent, who likes Austen's novels, she visits Carlton House, where she is told that he wishes her to dedicate a novel to him. She obliges with *Emma* and sends him a presentation copy in December.
19 Hunt's sonnet 'To Kosciusko' is in *The Examiner*. Tadeusz Kosciuszko (1746–1817) led the Polish uprising of 1794.
20 Second Treaty of Paris, restoring the French borders of 1790 and imposing indemnities on France.

Canova, who has been in Paris representing the Pope in discussions of the return of works of art taken there by Napoleon's régime, comes to London. He admires the Elgin Marbles.

December
Early this month Peacock's (anonymous) *Headlong Hall* is published in one volume by Hookham, dated 1816.
7 Ney is executed in Paris.
10 Birth of the Byrons' daughter, (Augusta) Ada Byron (1815–52), later Countess of Lovelace.
12 Maria Theresa Kemble's (1777–1838) *Smiles and Tears; or, The Widow's Stratagem*, adapted partly from Opie's *The Father and Daughter*, opens at Covent Garden.
19 Publication by Murray of Austen's anonymous *Emma* (dated 1816). Murray gives copies to Maria Edgeworth and Augusta Leigh.

This month J.H. Reynolds starts work for *The Champion*.

1816

January

Early in the year Henry Austen, on his sister's behalf, buys back the copyright of 'Susan' (later *Northanger Abbey*) from Crosby. She retitles the manuscript 'Catherine'.

1   January–1 April Lewis's first visit to his plantations in Jamaica. He lands in England on 5 June.

12 Kean's first Sir Giles Overreach, in Massinger's *A New Way to Pay Old Debts*, at Drury Lane.

15 Lady Byron and Ada leave London. On 2 February Lady Byron's father writes to Byron asking for his agreement to a separation. After further correspondence, charges and counter-charges, he signs the deed of separation on 21 April.

Leigh Hunt's *The Story of Rimini* is published by Murray in London and Blackwood in Edinburgh.

Coleridge completes *Zapolya*.

The Napoleon exhibition opens at the Egyptian Hall, Piccadilly. Its centrepiece is Napoleon's travelling carriage, which is taken to Bristol on 30 August and displayed there in Wellington Street.

February

13 Publication by Murray of Byron's *The Siege of Corinth* and *Parisina* in an edition of 6,000 copies. In April Byron accepts £1,050 for the copyrights from Murray, having earlier refused the money and asked for it to be divided between Godwin, Coleridge and Maturin.

15 Byron sends Coleridge a gift of £100.

19 Publication by Murray of the second edition of *Mansfield Park*. Austen completed revisions for it by 11 December 1815.

In mid-February P.B. Shelley's *Alastor; or, the Spirit of Solitude, and Other Poems* is published, at the author's expense, by Baldwin, Cradock and Joy.

20 First performance of Rossini's opera *Il barbiere di Siviglia*, with a libretto based on Beaumarchais' play, at Teatro Argentina, Rome. (It was originally called *Almaviva, ossia L'inutile precauzione*.)

29 First hearing of the Select Committee which considers the legitimacy of Elgin's obtaining of the Marbles and whether the

government should purchase them. Those questioned include Elgin himself, John Flaxman, Knight, Sir Thomas Lawrence and William Wilkins (1778–1839). The committee report is published in April and a price of £35,000 is agreed in a parliamentary debate on 7 June.
This month Longman publishes Opie's *Valentine's Eve* in three volumes.

March
4   Treaty ending the Anglo-Nepalese war of 1814–16. Nepal cedes territory to the East India Company.
15 Byron's 'Ode (From the French)', satirically ascribed to Chateaubriand, is in *The Morning Chronicle*.
18 (and 30) Byron writes the first drafts of 'Fare Thee Well' and 'A Sketch from Private Life'. These poems are printed for private circulation in early April and pirated in *The Champion* on 14 April as 'Lord Byron's Poems on his Own Domestic Circumstances'. 'A Sketch' in particular fuels the controversy over the Byrons' separation. Byron is ostracized in some social circles.
21 Inaugural lecture on comparative anatomy by William Lawrence (1783–1867), Professor of Anatomy and Surgery at the Royal College of Surgeons from 1815. His *Introduction to Comparative Anatomy and Physiology* is published in 1816. His materialist conclusions provoke controversy, particularly with his fellow professor at the Royal College, John Abernethy (1764–1831), who takes a more traditional vitalist approach.
P.B. Shelley and Mary Godwin are in London between March and May.

April
3   Byron, Hobhouse, Scrope Berdmore Davies (1782–1852) and Leigh Hunt dine together. Byron says goodbye to Rogers on 22.
10 Coleridge, who has been in London since mid-March, meets Byron. He recites 'Kubla Khan'. Byron submits Coleridge's *Zapolya* (recently rejected by Covent Garden) to Drury Lane. During the course of the year the Drury Lane management loses interest in performing the piece, especially once Byron and his friend Kinnaird are no longer on the committee and Thomas Dibdin is no longer involved in stage management (see Coleridge [1969–2002], 16.III.ii.1329–30).

15	Coleridge moves to live with Dr James Gillman (1782–1839) at Moreton House, Highgate. Gillman aims to cure his opium addiction.
20	Clairmont becomes Byron's lover. She introduces Mary Shelley to him, without yet telling her that the relationship is sexual, on 22.
21	Charlotte Brontë (1816–55) is born at Thornton, near Bradford.
23	Byron leaves London and on 25 England. Hobhouse and Davies accompany him as far as Dover and John William Polidori (1795–1821) goes on as his personal physician. They land at Ostend and travel to Bruges (27), Ghent (28) and Antwerp (30). Byron begins work on *Childe Harold's Pilgrimage*, Canto III, on 25.

May

1–6	Byron is in Brussels. The journey continues via Louvain (6), Cologne (8) and the Rhine, Basle (20) and Hôtel Angleterre, near Sécheron, Geneva (25).
2	Wedding of Princess Charlotte and Prince Leopold of Saxe-Coburg-Saalfeld (1790–1865) at Carlton House.
2–6	P.B. Shelley, Mary Godwin, their baby William, and Clairmont travel from London to Paris. They arrive at Sécheron on about 13–17. They meet Byron – Shelley for the first time – on the shore of Lake Geneva on 27.
4	Publication by Longman in London and Archibald Constable in Edinburgh of Scott's *The Antiquary* (three volumes), written mainly in the first three months of the year. It sells 6,000 copies before the end of May.
5	Keats's first published poem, 'O Solitude, if I must with thee dwell', is in *The Examiner*.
9	Maturin's *Bertram; or, The Castle of St Aldobrand* opens at Drury Lane with Kean in the title role. It runs for 22 nights. Maturin's *Manuel* with Kean is contrastingly unsuccessful when it opens at Drury Lane on 8 March 1817.
9	Colburn publishes Lady Caroline Lamb's *Glenarvon* in three volumes. It reaches a fourth edition in 1817.
16	Brummell, unable to pay his gambling debts, goes to Calais. He remains in France for the rest of his life.
25	Publication by Murray of Coleridge's *Christabel, Kubla Khan, and The Pains of Sleep*.

The first, anonymous edition of Hemans's *The Restoration of the Works of Art to Italy* is published by Pearson of Oxford and Ebers of London. The second edition, published by Murray, gives her name.

June

1   By this date the Shelley/Godwin party has moved into Maison Chappuis, Montalègre, near Cologny. Byron and Polidori are installed at Villa Diodati, nearby, from 10. Here, within a few days, the group start writing ghost or horror stories and discussing 'the nature of the principle of life' (*Frankenstein*, 1831 preface). Probably on 16 or 17, Mary Shelley begins an early version (completed in August) of *Frankenstein*. The result of Byron's participation in the story-writing competition is the fragment ('Augustus Darvell') published with *Mazeppa* in 1819.

2   Hazlitt attacks Coleridge's *Christabel* in *The Examiner*. A more fierce dismissal, in *The Edinburgh Review* for September, seems to be wrongly ascribed to Moore (see Murray [2007], p.193).

4   Opening of James Walker's Vauxhall Bridge, the first iron bridge across the Thames.

c.7   Publication by Colburn in London of Constant's *Adolphe*. He is in London between 25 January and July. During his visit, as earlier in Paris, he gives emotional readings from the novel. It is also published in Paris. The first English translation, by Alexander Walker, follows in September.

9–11   Constant visits Hobhouse at Whitton Park.

18   According to Polidori (1911), p.128, Byron's recitation of 'some verses of Coleridge's Christabel, of the witch's breast' sends P.B. Shelley into a shrieking fit.

23–30   Byron and P.B. Shelley tour Lake Léman (Geneva). They visit Chillon on 26, Vevey (among several sites connected with Rousseau and *La Nouvelle Heloïse*) on 27, and Lausanne, where they see the summer-house in which Gibbon finished his *Decline and Fall*, on 28. According to Mary Shelley (Shelley [1839], iii.35) P.B. Shelley conceives 'Hymn to Intellectual Beauty' during this 'voyage'.

July

4   Byron finishes *Childe Harold's Pilgrimage*, Canto III.

7	Sheridan dies. He is buried in Westminster Abbey on 13. Byron writes a first draft of 'Monody on the Death of the Right Honourable R.B. Sheridan' by 20 and revises it by 22; it is performed at Drury Lane on 7 September by Maria Davison (c.1780–1858). Moore's 'Lines on the Death of Sheridan' are in *The Morning Chronicle* on 5 August.
c.12	Byron visits Staël at Coppet and returns there several times this summer and autumn, including 7 and 12 September and 1 and 3 October. In July he meets A.W. von Schlegel here.
21–27	Shelley, Mary Godwin and Clairmont travel in the Alps, staying at the Hôtel de Londres, Chamonix, on 22–26. Shelley writes much of 'Mont Blanc' between 22 and 29.
25	Keats qualifies as a licentiate of the Society of Apothecaries.
25	The Shelleys see the Mer de Glace on Mont Blanc (the setting of *Frankenstein*, volume 2, chapter 2).

Between 27 July and 12 August Giovanni Belzoni (1778–1823) moves the colossal bust of the 'Younger Memnon' (Rameses II) from the Ramesseum to the Nile. He supervises its loading in November and its unloading at Alexandria in January 1817. It arrives in England in spring 1818 and is displayed at the British Museum from January 1819.

In late July or August of this 'Year Without a Summer' Byron writes 'Darkness', published in *The Prisoner of Chillon and Other Poems* (1816). His 'Prometheus', also published there, is written at about the same time.

August

6	Austen finishes *Persuasion*.
14	Lewis comes to stay with Byron at Villa Diodati. On 16 they visit Ferney. On 18 at Maison Chappuis there is a discussion on ghosts involving Lewis, Byron and P.B. Shelley, who writes versions of four ghost stories told by Lewis in Mary Shelley's Journal. During his visit Lewis also orally translates passages from Goethe's *Faust* to Byron. After Switzerland Lewis goes on, between now and September 1817, to Florence, Rome, Naples, Venice and Paris.
26	Hobhouse and Davies arrive at Villa Diodati.
29	Shelley, Mary Godwin and Clairmont set off for England, arriving in Portsmouth on 8 September. They are at Fontainebleau and Versailles on 2–3 and Rouen on 4.

29 Between now and 1 September Byron, Hobhouse and Davies visit Mont Blanc and Chamonix.

This month Byron begins his main period of work on *Manfred* (until mid-February 1817).

Keats visits Margate in August to September.

September

5 Davies leaves Villa Diodati for England. He carries with him manuscripts of Byron's *Childe Harold's Pilgrimage*, Canto III and *The Prisoner of Chillon*, and Shelley's notebook including alternative versions of 'Hymn to Intellectual Beauty' and 'Mont Blanc'. Davies keeps this material, leaving it in England when he goes abroad to escape his debts in January 1820; it is rediscovered only in 1976.

11 Ugo Foscolo (1778–1827) arrives in England. His *Ultime lettere di Jacopo Ortis* was published in 1802 (London edition by Murray 1817) and *Dei sepolcri* in 1807. In London this autumn he comes to know the Hollands and their circle, Rogers, Campbell and Brougham. Partly because of the expense of participating in this fashionable society, he soon runs into financial difficulties.

11 P.B. Shelley and Mary Godwin take lodgings at 5 Abbey Churchyard, Bath.

13 Between about now and 25 Shelley visits Peacock in Marlow. Mary Godwin joins them on 19.

c. 15 Byron dismisses Polidori from his service.

16 Macready's first appearance in London, in *The Distressed Mother*, by Ambrose Phillips, at Covent Garden.

17 Byron and Hobhouse go to Mont Blanc and Lausanne. They are at Vevey and Chillon on 18, Brientz on 24, Berne on 26 and Fribourg on 26–7. Between 17 and 28 (misdated '29') Byron keeps his *Alpine Journal* for Augusta Leigh. Extracts appear in Moore's *Life* of 1830.

October

1 Byron dines with Staël.

9 Suicide in Swansea of Fanny Imlay Godwin, Wollstonecraft's daughter and Godwin's step-daughter.

9	Keats is introduced to Leigh Hunt by Charles Cowden Clarke. By now Keats is living with his brothers at 8 Dean Street, Southwark (until November, when they move to 76 Cheapside); he studies to become a member of the Royal College of Surgeons but soon gives up in favour of a literary career.
12	Byron and Hobhouse, having left Switzerland on 5, arrive in Milan. At La Scala on 13 they are introduced to Ludovico di Breme (1781–1820). On 17 they meet Stendhal, Pellico and Monti. On 25 they are at a performance by the *improvvisatore* Tommaso Sgricci (1789–1836).
20	Keats and J. H. Reynolds meet. Reynolds's *The Naiad: a Tale, with Other Poems* was published by Taylor & Hessey in the summer.
31	Keats's 21st birthday, when, unknown to him, he becomes eligible for an £800 inheritance.

November

3	Possible first meeting of Hazlitt and Keats at Haydon's studio.
3–10	Byron and Hobhouse travel from Milan to Venice via Lake Garda (5), Verona (6–7 or 8), Vicenza and Padua. On 14 they take lodgings with Marianna Segati and her husband in the Frezzeria, near Piazza San Marco. (Hobhouse remains until 5 December.) She and Byron soon embark on a sexual relationship (until March 1818). This month Byron begins learning Armenian at the monastery on the island of San Lazzaro degli Armeni, continuing until late February or early March 1817.

In the first week of the month Cobbett starts issuing the twopenny version of his *Political Register*, aiming to broaden his readership; the price for the regular version remains one shilling and a halfpenny.

15	Henry 'Orator' Hunt (1773–1835) addresses a large reformist meeting at Spa Fields, Islington.
18	Murray publishes Byron's *Childe Harold's Pilgrimage*, Canto III.

December

1	Leigh Hunt's 'Young Poets', in *The Examiner*, draws attention to Keats, P.B. Shelley and J.H. Reynolds. They add strength to the (Romantic) school whose 'evident aspiration after real

nature and original fancy' recalls the virtues of earlier poetry. Keats's 'On First Looking into Chapman's *Homer*', written in October, is included in the article. In December he finishes 'I stood tip-toe upon a little hill' and probably *Sleep and Poetry*.

2   Spa Fields riot. Henry Hunt again addresses the crowd in the cause of constitutional reform but an attempted insurrection is led by the radical Arthur Thistlewood (1774–1820) and others. Thistlewood is arrested in May 1817 but a charge of high treason is dropped in June, after the acquittal of one of his colleagues on grounds of the unreliability of the government witness, an informer called Castle.

2   Blackwood in Edinburgh and Murray in London publish Scott's *Tales of My Landlord* (First Series), allegedly edited by Jedediah Cleishbotham. The first volume contains *The Black Dwarf* (completed this August) and the other three *The Tale of Old Mortality* (November).

4   Rossini's *Otello, ossia Il moro di Venezia* opens at Teatro del Fondo, Naples.

5   Publication by Murray of Byron's *The Prisoner of Chillon and Other Poems*.

11 Probable date when Leigh Hunt introduces Keats to P.B. Shelley.

16–17   Austen, in a letter to her nephew James Austen (later Austen-Leigh), refers to 'the little bit (two Inches wide) of Ivory on which I work with so fine a Brush, as produces little effect after much labour' (Austen [2014], p. 323).

30 Wedding of P.B. Shelley and Mary Godwin at St Mildred's Church, Bread Street, London. The marriage, and reconciliation with the Godwins, has been made possible by the suicide of Shelley's first wife, Harriet, on 9 or 10. P.B. Shelley has been in London since 17, Mary Godwin (Shelley) since 27 or 28. They go back to Bath on 1 January 1817.

This month Gale and Fenner publish Coleridge's *The Statesman's Manual; or, the Bible the Best Guide to Political Skill and Foresight: a Lay Sermon*.

Die Nachstücke, by Ernst Theodor Amadeus Hoffmann (1776–1822), appears in 1816–17.

1817

January

6   P.B. Shelley goes to London. Mary Shelley joins him on 26.
12 Birth, in Bath, of (Clara) Allegra Byron (1817–22), daughter of Byron and Clairmont.
12 Hazlitt's (anonymous) 'The Times Newspaper. On the Connexion Between Toad-Eaters and Tyrants' is in *The Examiner*.
17 Austen begins work on her unfinished novel 'The Brothers' (*Sanditon*).
19 P.B. Shelley's 'Hymn to Intellectual Beauty' is published in *The Examiner* (see also 5 September 1816).
25 First number of *The Scotsman, or Edinburgh Political and Literary Journal*.
25 Rossini's *La Cenerentola, ossia La bontà in trionfo* is given its first performance at Teatro Valle, Rome.

Leigh Hunt introduces P.B. Shelley to Hazlitt.
In late January or February Murray publishes Hanchen Wu's *Laou-Seng-Urh, or, 'An Heir in his Old Age'. A Chinese Drama*, translated by John Francis Davis (1795–1890).

February

1   The *Reformists' Register* is published between now and 25 October by William Hone (1780–1842).
3   The Elgin Room at the British Museum opens as a temporary display area for the Elgin Marbles. It is demolished in 1831 and the new Elgin Room opens in July 1832.
5   Mary Shelley meets Keats and J.H. Reynolds, at dinner with the Hunts at the house they have lived in since late 1815 in the Vale of Health, Hampstead. Keats returns on 12 and 15.
9–10 At the Hunts', where the Shelleys have been staying since 7, a debate on republicanism and monarchy continues until 3 a.m., with Hazlitt and P.B. Shelley taking the republican side (Shelley [1987], i.163 and n.). Hazlitt, his wife and Godwin visit on 16. On about 14, forty essays by Hazlitt and twelve by Hunt appear in the former's *The Round Table: a Collection of Essays on Literature, Men, and Manners* (two volumes, published by Longman in London and Archibald Constable in Edinburgh).

13 Southey's radical *Wat Tyler* (1794) is published, to the embarrassment of the now conservative author, by Sherwood, Neely & Jones. It cannot be suppressed because, as a seditious work, it is not protected by copyright. Southey's current position is attacked by Hazlitt in *The Examiner* for 9 March and defended by Coleridge in *The Courier* for 18 March.

At about mid-month P.B. Shelley writes *A Proposal for Putting Reform to the Vote Throughout the Kingdom*, published by Charles and James Ollier at the end of the month.

18 At some point between now and 28 Byron writes 'So We'll Go No More A Roving', published in Moore's *Life* of 1830.

27 The Shelleys stay with Peacock in Marlow (until 18 March).

March

1 or 2 Keats sees the Elgin Marbles for the first time with Haydon and as a result writes 'To B.R. Haydon, with a Sonnet Written on Seeing the Elgin Marbles' and 'On Seeing the Elgin Marbles'. Both poems are in *The Examiner* and *The Champion* on 9 March and in *Annals of the Fine Arts* for April 1818.

3 Keats's *Poems* is published by Ollier.

4 Habeas Corpus is suspended. The suspension is renewed on 27 June, remaining in force until March 1818.

4 Monroe takes office as President of the United States until 4 March 1825.

10 The 'Blanketeers' March: in St Peter's Field, Manchester, 5000 people, mainly textile workers, prepare to march to London to deliver a petition to the Prince Regent protesting at their economic distress and at the suspension of Habeas Corpus. Soldiers break up the march and there are many arrests.

11–13 Mary Shelley is in London.

18 As a result of illness, Austen gives up writing *Sanditon*.

18 Peacock's *Melincourt*, 'By the Author of Headlong Hall', is published in three volumes by Hookham and by Baldwin, Cradock and Joy.

18 The Shelleys move into Albion House, West Street, Marlow (until February 1818). They often see Peacock. Mary Shelley works intensively on *Frankenstein*; she fair-copies it between 18 April and 13 May. P.B. Shelley works on *Laon and Cythna*.

27 The Lord Chancellor, Lord Eldon, refuses P.B. Shelley custody of the children of his first marriage.

Late this month Keats and his brothers move to 1 Well Walk, Hampstead.

Publication by Gale and Fenner of Coleridge's *A Lay Sermon, Addressed to the Higher and Middle Classes, on the Existing Distresses and Discontents*.

April

Frankenstein has by now expanded into a draft two-volume novel.

2 Between now and 26 September 1818 Byron writes *Mazeppa*.
2–6 Godwin visits the Shelleys.
6 Leigh and Marianne Hunt and their children stay with the Shelleys in Marlow until 25 June.
10 Murray publishes *The History of Java* by Thomas Stamford Raffles (1781–1826), who was lieutenant governor there in 1811–15 during the temporary East India Company occupation. He is knighted on 29 May.
12 First British performance of Mozart's *Don Giovanni* at the King's Theatre.
14 Revival of Coleridge's *Remorse* at Drury Lane.
14 Keats travels to Southampton. He then goes to the Isle of Wight (until 23), Margate, Canterbury and the Sussex coast, returning to Hampstead on 10 June. Between about 18 April and 28 November he writes *Endymion: a Poetic Romance*. In late May he meets and probably has a sexual relationship with Isabella Jones.
17 Wordsworth writes 'Ode. – 1817', called 'Vernal Ode' from 1820.
17 Byron leaves Venice and goes to Ferrara, Bologna and (22–3) Florence. Having been to Ferrara he writes *The Lament of Tasso* and sends it to Murray from Florence. He proceeds to Terni, Foligno (26) and Rome (29), where he rejoins Hobhouse, lives at 66 Piazza di Spagna, and by 5 May revises the third act of *Manfred*.

May

5 John Constable's paintings at the Royal Academy exhibition include *Scene on a Navigable River*, known as *Flatford Mill*. Turner shows *The Decline of the Carthaginian Empire*.

5   Cobbett arrives in New York, fearing prosecution in England. He stays until October 1819. His *A Year's Residence in the United States of America* appears in 1818.
20 Byron leaves Rome. He is in Florence on 27 and returns to Venice on 28. Hobhouse goes to Naples.
23 The Shelleys come to London. They see *Don Giovanni* at the King's Theatre (23, as again on 10 and 21 February and 7 March 1818), go to the Royal Academy show (24) and see Hazlitt (25). P.B. Shelley returns to Marlow on 26 and Mary Shelley, having seen the Lambs (30), on 31.
24 Austen, seriously ill, moves to Winchester where better medical aid is available than in Chawton.

At the end of the month Longman publishes Moore's *Lalla Rookh*. He is paid 3,000 guineas for the copyright.

June

1   The first instalment of Leigh Hunt's review of Keats's *Poems* is in *The Examiner*, continuing on 6 and 13 July.
13 Coleridge sees Ludwig Tieck, as again on 24–5 and in November.
14 Hazlitt entertains the Godwins and the Lambs.
14 Byron moves into Villa Foscarini at La Mira.
16 Murray publishes Byron's *Manfred, a Dramatic Poem*.
18 *Frankenstein* is refused, on Gifford's advice, by Murray. Charles Ollier refuses it in August; Lackington accepts it in September.
18 Ceremonial opening of Waterloo Bridge on the second anniversary of the battle. John Constable produces a series of sketches of the occasion and finally exhibits *Whitehall Stairs, June 18th, 1817* at the Royal Academy in 1832. Godwin and Mary Shelley came to see the bridge on 30 May.

In mid-June Colburn publishes Lady Morgan's *France*, with some contributions by her husband Sir Charles, in two volumes. A French translation is published simultaneously.

23 John Philip Kemble's farewell performance, as Coriolanus, at Covent Garden. A farewell banquet, at the Freemasons' Tavern, follows on 27.
23 Crabbe comes to London until 24 July. He is in company with Moore, Rogers, Campbell, Lady Caroline Lamb, Murray and Foscolo.

26   (Patrick) Branwell Brontë (1817–48) is born at Thornton.
26   Byron writes *Childe Harold's Pilgrimage*, Canto IV, between now and 19 July. He makes extensive additions to it between this August and January 1818.
29   In the aftermath of the suppression of attempted rebellions by Midlands workers (see also 7 November) Leigh Hunt writes on 'Informers' in *The Examiner* and on 30 Hazlitt's 'On the Spy-System' appears anonymously in *The Morning Chronicle*. The focus of their protest is the government use of *agents provocateurs*.

This month Murray publishes, anonymously, Hemans's *Modern Greece, A Poem*. This summer Murray also publishes the first two cantos of Frere's *Prospectus and Specimen of an intended National Work by William and Robert Whistlecraft*. The third and fourth follow in 1818.

Cotman begins his first tour of Normandy, followed by further visits in the summers of 1818 and 1820; his etchings of *Architectural Antiquities of Normandy* are published in 1822.

At the end of the month R. Hunter, 'Successor to Mr. [Joseph] Johnson' brings out Maria Edgeworth's *Harrington, a Tale; and Ormond, a Tale* in three volumes.

July

c.3–8   Lewis is with Byron in Venice. In late July Lewis comes to La Mira; he leaves for England by 14 August.
12–26   Scott visits Loch Lomond and Rob Roy's Cave, Glasgow and Drumlanrig.
14   Staël dies in Paris. She is buried at Coppet. Her *Considérations sur les principaux événements de la Révolution française* is published in Paris in 1818.
17   Murray publishes Byron's *The Lament of Tasso*. There are three further editions this year.
18   Austen dies at 8 College Street, Winchester. Her last work, the poem 'When Winchester races...' ('Venta') was written on 15. She is buried in the cathedral on 24.
31   Disraeli is baptised as a Christian.

At the end of the month Stendhal's *Histoire de la Peinture en Italie* is published in Paris under the initials 'M.B.A.A.' ('M. Beyle, ancien auditeur' – from August 1810 he was auditor to the Conseil d'État).

Publication by Rest Fenner of Coleridge's *Biographia Literaria; or Biographical Sketches of My Literary Life and Opinions* and *Sibylline Leaves: A Collection of Poems* (including substantial revisions of *The Ancient Mariner*).

August
1   Belzoni penetrates the Great Temple of Rameses II at Abu Simbel.
6   The Lyceum introduces on-stage gas lighting; Drury Lane and Covent Garden follow suit on 6 September. It was first used at the Chestnut Street Theatre, Philadelphia, in November 1816.
10   Turner sets off on his second European tour, to the Rhineland and the Low Countries.
14   Robert Owen addresses a crowded meeting at the City of London Tavern, presenting his plans for ending poverty and stating his hostility to religion. The meeting reconvenes on 21. Owen's *Essays on the Principle of the Formation of the Human Character* appeared in 1813–14.
14   Southey visits Coleridge at Highgate.
30–3   September Irving stays with Scott at Abbotsford before going on to the Highlands. Lady Byron is another of Scott's visitors in August.
31   Hazlitt's 'On the Effects of War and Taxes' is in *The Champion*.
Stendhal is in London.
Byron's first encounter with Margarita Cogni (fl.1817–19), his principal lover in Venice in 1817–18.

September
3   Keats goes to visit his friend Benjamin Bailey (1791–1853) at Magdalen Hall, Oxford. They visit Stratford-on-Avon together on 2 October.
19–25   Leigh and Marianne Hunt visit Marlow.
23   Between now and late November P.B. Shelley is mostly in London.
This month Byron meets Richard Belgrave Hoppner (1786–1872), British consul general in Venice 1814–25 and son of John Hoppner.
This month and in October Coleridge stays at Littlehampton in Sussex, where he meets Henry Francis Cary (1772–1844). Cary's

translation of Dante's *Inferno* came out in 1805-6 and of the whole *Divina commedia*, at his own expense, in 1814. Coleridge's recommendations of the work result in increased sales and prompt Taylor & Hessey to issue a second edition in 1819.

Rome, Naples et Florence en 1817, Beyle's first publication as Stendhal, comes out in Paris. (A revised version appears in 1826.) An English translation from 'the Count de Stendal' is published by Colburn in 1818.

October

8-10   Probable date for the first draft of Byron's *Beppo*. Revisions and additions are made mostly between now and January 1818.

12   *The Champion* carries the first part of Hazlitt's 'What is the People?' There are further instalments on 19 and 26. The piece appears also in *The Yellow Dwarf* on 7 and 14 March 1818.

12   In the Valley of the Kings Belzoni discovers the tomb of Rameses I, followed a few days later by that of Seti I. He found the tomb of Ay here in October 1816.

13   Mary Shelley and Godwin (who has just read the proofs of *Frankenstein*) visit John Hampden's monument at Great Hampden (see *Frankenstein* vol.3, ch.2).

15   Death in Cairo of Johann Ludwig Burckhardt (1784-1817), who travelled extensively in the Middle East in the guise of a Muslim trader or pilgrim, visiting Mecca between September and November 1814. His *Travels in Nubia* and *Travels in Syria and the Holy Land* are published by Murray in 1819 and 1822 and *Travels in Arabia* by Colburn in 1829.

28   P.B. Shelley sends alterations to *Frankenstein* to the publishers (Lackington), some his own but most of them Mary Shelley's.

'On the Cockney School of Poetry. No. 1', by Lockhart writing as 'Z.', is in *Blackwood's* for this month, attacking Hunt and a school including, implicitly, Keats. No. 2 follows in the November *Blackwood's*, 3 and 4 in July and August 1818, 5 and 6 in April and October 1819, 7 in December 1822 and 8 in July 1825. Hunt is usually the main target; No. 4 savages Keats's *Poems* and *Endymion*. There are attacks also on Haydon and Hazlitt.

The steamer *Caledonia*, fitted with Boulton-Watt engines by James Watt, junior, crosses the Channel to Rotterdam and goes up the Rhine to Koblenz.

Emerson, aged fourteen, starts at Harvard, graduating on 29 August 1821.

November

1   Byron goes to Este, where he is leasing Villa I Cappuccini from R.B. Hoppner. (He never lives there.) On 13 he goes from La Mira to Venice.

Early this month the third Anglo-Maratha war begins. The defeat of the Marathas and their allies, completed between February and June 1818, substantially increases East India Company territory.

6   Publication by T. Hookham and C. and J. Ollier of the anonymous *History of a Six Weeks' Tour Through a Part of France, Switzerland, Germany and Holland* ... Most of the material is by Mary Shelley with some, including 'Mont Blanc', by P.B. Shelley.

6   Death of Princess Charlotte, daughter of the Prince Regent. Her funeral is on 19. Hyman Hurwitz (1770–1844) composes a Hebrew dirge, sung on 19, which Coleridge translates and adapts a few days later for publication, opposite the original, on about 12 December (Coleridge [1969–2002], 16.I.2.945–52, 16.II.2.1155). Hemans writes 'Stanzas on the Death of the Princess Charlotte' on 23 December (published in *Blackwood's*, April 1818, signed 'F.D.H.'). Thelwall writes and performs a 'Monody'.

7   Execution in Derby of the leaders of the attempted rising of Midlands workers at Pentrich in June. P.B. Shelley in *An Address to the People on the Death of the Princess Charlotte* (written on 11–12, signed 'The Hermit of Marlow', and published by Ollier) suggests that the executions are a more suitable cause for public mourning than the death of the princess. Similar points are made by Leigh Hunt in 'Death of the Princess Charlotte – Lamentable Punishments at Derby' in *The Examiner* on 19.

8–19   Mary Shelley joins P.B. Shelley in London. They see Godwin and the Hunts several times and Keats on 18.

13   Coleridge is back at Highgate.

22   Keats writes to his friend Benjamin Bailey about 'the holiness of the Heart's affections and the truth of Imagination'. Between 22 and 28 he finishes *Endymion* at the Fox and Hounds, Burford Bridge, near Mickleham in Surrey, where he stays until early December.

J.H. Reynolds is articled to a London solicitor, qualifying in 1822.
Coleridge's *Zapolya* is published by Rest Fenner (formerly Gale and Fenner). Originally it was to be published by Murray; the change has resulted in the breaking off of relations between Coleridge and Murray.
The Moores move to Sloperton Cottage, near Calne.
William Wordsworth is in London between late November and 19 January 1819.

December

1	Godwin's *Mandeville, a Tale of the Seventeenth Century in England* (three volumes, Constable) is published.
c.8	Publication by Ollier of P.B. Shelley's *Laon and Cythna: Or, The Revolution of the Golden City: A Vision of the Nineteenth Century*, written between March and autumn. Readers' complaints force the publisher to insist on changes to remove references to incest and the tyranny of religion, resulting in the revision published on 8 January 1818 as *The Revolt of Islam*.
10	Byron hears that Newstead Abbey has been sold to Thomas Wildman for £94,500.
18–20	Hone is tried at the Guildhall in London for blasphemy and seditious libel on the grounds of his publication and authorship, in January and February, of three anti-government pamphlets which parody the litany, including *The Late John Wilkes's Catechism of a Ministerial Member*. He is acquitted, and publishes *The Three Trials of William Hone* in 1818.
21	Keats, in a letter to his brothers, writes about 'Negative Capability'. His review of Kean's acting is in *The Champion*.
26–8	Horace Smith stays with the Shelleys.
27	An uneasy encounter between William Wordsworth and Coleridge takes place in London.
28	Haydon hosts what he calls the 'Immortal Dinner' for guests including Wordsworth, Keats and Charles Lamb.
30	The Lambs host a dinner: the guests include Coleridge, Wordsworth, H.C. Robinson and Thomas Noon Talfourd (1795–1854).
30	Scott's *Rob Roy* is published in three volumes, dated 1818, by Archibald Constable in Edinburgh and Longman in London. It was written between August and December. 10,000 copies sell in a fortnight. (This becomes from now on the standard size of first editions of Scott's novels.)

At the end of the month Austen's *Northanger Abbey* and *Persuasion*, with her brother Henry's 'Biographical Notice of the Author', are published in four volumes by Murray.

Baldwin, Cradock and Joy publish *The History of British India* by James Mill (1773–1836).

Murray publishes *On the Principles of Political Economy and Taxation*, by David Ricardo (1772–1823).

1818

January

1   Anonymous publication by Lackington of Mary Shelley's *Frankenstein: Or, the Modern Prometheus* (three volumes).
2   Foundation in London of the Institution of Civil Engineers. Telford is elected its President in 1820.
3   Keats calls on Wordsworth.
8   Hobhouse leaves Venice for England, taking with him for Murray the manuscript of *Childe Harold's Pilgrimage*, Canto IV.
11 P.B. Shelley's 'Ozymandias' appears in *The Examiner* as the work of 'Glirastes'.
13 Hazlitt's lectures on English poets begin at the Surrey Institution, continuing on 20 and 27 January, 3, 10, 17 and 24 February and 3 March. H.C. Robinson and Keats are regular attenders; others include John Hunt and the Landseers. Mitford comes several times, including for the last lecture on 3 March. Hazlitt repeats his lectures, beginning on 23 March, at the Crown and Anchor tavern in the Strand; Charles Lamb is there on 3 April and Moore on 13.
18 Hazlitt, Keats and William Bewick (1795–1866) dine with Haydon.
22 Keats writes 'On Sitting Down to Read *King Lear* Once Again' (published 1838). By 31 he also writes 'When I have fears that I may cease to be' (published 1848).
22 Byron sees Countess Teresa Guiccioli (1798–1873) for the first time.
27 Coleridge begins his Lectures on the Principles of Judgement, Culture, and European Literature at the London Philosophical Society. They continue on 30 January, 3, 6, 10, 13, 17, 20, 24 and 27 February and 3, 6, 10 and 13 March. H.C. Robinson is

in regular attendance. Charles Lamb is there on 17 February, Mackintosh on 20 February and Rogers on 27. Peacock, who comes to London on 29 January, is possibly there on 6 March (Coleridge [1969–2002], 5.2.197).
Coleridge's 'Treatise on Method' appears in the *Encyclopaedia Metropolitana*.
Probably at some point between January and March P.B. Shelley writes the review of *Frankenstein* eventually published after the 1831 edition: see 10 November 1832.

February
Early this month Peacock's anonymous *Rhododaphne* (finished in November 1817) is published by Hookham.
4   Keats, Shelley and Leigh Hunt write sonnets to the Nile.
5   *Fazio* by Henry Hart Milman (1791–1868) is at Covent Garden for the first of ten performances.
6 and 12   Coleridge writes letters expressing enthusiasm for Blake's *Songs of Innocence and Experience* (Bentley [1969], pp. 251–3).
9   Coleridge's *Zapolya* opens at the Surrey Theatre.
11   The Hunts entertain Keats, T.J. Hogg, Peacock, Clairmont and the Shelleys.
16   Marriage of Margaret (henceforth 'Marguerite') Power and Charles Gardiner, Earl of Blessington (1782–1829). Her salon flourishes at 11 St James's Square, London between now and 1822.
24   Murray publishes Byron's *Beppo, a Venetian Story*. There are six further editions this year (anonymous until the fifth).
Between about the end of this month and 27 April Keats writes 'Isabella; or, The Pot of Basil'.

March
2   Belzoni enters the pyramid of Khefren (Khafre).
6   Keats arrives at Teignmouth, in Devon, to take care of his brother, Tom (Thomas Keats, 1799–1818), who has tuberculosis.
8   The Shelleys meet the music publisher Vincent Novello (1781–1861) at the Hunts'.

10   Rossini's *Il barbiere di Siviglia* receives its first London performance at the King's Theatre. The Shelleys, the Hunts and Peacock are in the audience.

11   The Shelleys, with their children William and Clara, and Clairmont and her daughter Allegra Byron, set off for Italy. They reach Lyon on 21 and stay in Milan most of the time between 4 April and 1 May. Allegra is taken to Venice on 2 May and looked after at first by R.B. Hoppner and his wife Isabelle Hoppner. Much of the time between now and 1820 Clairmont will remain with the Shelleys in spite of recurrent tension with Mary Shelley.

25   Keats writes 'To J.H. Reynolds, Esq.'.

This month Longman publishes *Correction. A Novel* by Anne Raikes Harding (1781–1858) in three volumes.

April

c.6–13   Publication of Wordsworth's *Two Addresses to the Freeholders of Westmorland*, a revision of pieces in *The Kendal Chronicle* (14 February) and *The Carlisle Patriot* (7 March, reprinting a broadsheet of late February). He is canvassing, in the Tory interest, for the Lowther family.

c.16   Susan Ferrier's (1782–1854) *Marriage* is published in three volumes by Blackwood in Edinburgh and, several weeks later, by Murray in London.

20   Longman publishes Moore's *The Fudge Family in Paris* ('edited by Thomas Brown, the Younger'). On 23 Power publishes the first volume of *A Selection of Popular National Airs* with words by Moore and music by Stevenson; the second volume comes out in 1820, the third and fourth in 1822, the fifth in 1826 and the sixth in 1827.

28   Murray publishes Byron's *Childe Harold's Pilgrimage*, Canto IV. Murray also publishes Hobhouse's *Historical Illustrations of the Fourth Canto of Childe Harold*, which includes an 'Essay on the Present Literature of Italy' mainly by Foscolo.

30   British premiere of Rossini's *Elisabetta, regina d'Inghilterra* at the King's Theatre.

Robert Stodart and others publish Hazlitt's *A View of the English Stage; or, A Series of Dramatic Criticisms*.

In late April or May Taylor & Hessey publish Keats's *Endymion: a Poetic Romance*.

May

2–3   Keats writes to J.H. Reynolds comparing 'human life to a large Mansion of Many Apartments'.

Between about 5 and 11 Keats and his brother Tom travel back to Hampstead from Devon.

5   Karl Marx (1818–83) is born in Trier.

6–9   The Shelleys are at Le Tre Donzelle in Pisa. From 9 May to 11 June they are in Livorno, first at the Aquila Nera and then at the Croce di Malta. They meet Maria Gisborne (1770–1836), once a friend of Godwin and Wollstonecraft.

16   Lewis dies and is buried at sea while travelling back from Jamaica, where he arrived for a second visit on 24 January.

26   The Davys set off for the Continent, returning on 6 June 1820.

Publication by Murray of Hemans's *Translations from Camoens, and Other Poets, With Original Poetry*.

In late May or early June Taylor & Hessey publish Hazlitt's *Lectures on the English Poets* (see 13 January). There is a second edition in 1819.

June

In Venice in early June Byron moves into Palazzo Mocenigo.

8   A dinner is given to honour Moore at Morrison's Great Rooms, Dawson Street, Dublin. Daniel O'Connell (1775–1847) is the main organizer and Maturin is present. On 9 Moore is at the Theatre Royal for *Lalla Rookh*, based on his poem with music by Horn and a libretto by Michael O'Sullivan, which opened on 4.

11   The Shelleys move from Livorno to Casa Berti, Bagni di Lucca, until August.

13–21   Coleridge stays in Maldon with the surgeon Joseph Green (1791–1863), whom he met in June 1817.

22–3   Keats goes to Liverpool, from which his brother George (1797–1841) and sister-in-law Georgiana (1798-1879) are about to sail for America. With his friend Charles Brown (1786–1842), Keats embarks (24) on a walking tour to the Lakes, Scotland and Belfast. They call at Rydal Mount in Wordsworth's absence (27) and go on to Dumfries (where on 1 July Keats writes 'On Visiting the Tomb of Burns') and, via Portpatrick (6 July), to Ireland. After a brief visit to Belfast they return to Scotland on 8 July, visiting places including Ayr (11), and crossing to Mull fom Oban on 22. They see Iona and Staffa on 24 July and, back on the mainland, ascend Ben Nevis on 2 August. Keats is ill with tonsillitis and exhaustion and sails for England from Cromarty on 8 August.

25 Byron swims acros the Lagoon from Lido and up the Grand Canal.

This month Longman publishes Opie's *New Tales* in four volumes.

Murray publishes *A View of the State of Europe during the Middle Ages* (two volumes) by Henry Hallam (1777–1859).

Blake meets John Linnell (1792–1882), painter, patron and one of the main friends of his last years.

July

De Quincey becomes editor of the Tory *Westmorland Gazette*; he resigns on 5 November 1819.

3 Byron begins writing *Don Juan*.
25 Scott's *The Heart of Midlothian* is published by Archibald Constable in four volumes as *Tales of My Landlord*, Second Series, the work of 'Jedediah Cleishbotham'.
30 Emily Jane Brontë (1818–48) is born at Thornton.

August

18 Moore begins his Journal.
21–25 Byron and P.B. Shelley spend many hours talking at Palazzo Mocenigo and riding on the Lido. The conversations and the landscape are a significant source for Shelley's *Julian and Maddalo: a Conversation*, which he begins in late August or early September and completes probably by May 1819. Between August and the autumn he also writes the first act of *Prometheus Unbound*.
25 Wilberforce comes to stay at Rydal, near the Wordsworths, until 15 October.
28 First visit to the Wordsworths at Rydal Mount by Thomas Arnold (1795–1842).

31–5 September Mary Shelley and her children travel from Bagni di Lucca to Este, where Byron is letting the Shelleys occupy Villa I Cappuccini. In Venice P.B. Shelley has told Byron that his family and Clairmont are already in Padua, much nearer Este than the Bagni, in order to conceal from him the unwelcome fact that Clairmont is in Venice.

This summer Turner goes to Edinburgh to gather material for Scott's *The Provincial Antiquities of Scotland*.

September

From 22 P.B. Shelley is in Venice. On 24 he and Mary Shelley meet in Padua and take their sick daughter Clara to a doctor in Venice but she dies soon after arriving there. The Shelleys remain in Venice, often seeing Byron, until 29, when they go back to Este.

27 *The Quarterly Review* for April, published today, includes John Wilson Croker's (1780–1857) savage review of Keats's *Endymion* and Scott's favourable response to *Childe Harold's Pilgrimage*, Canto IV. A myth later develops that the Keats review caused his death: see, for example, P.B. Shelley's *Adonais*, and Byron's *Don Juan* XI.473–80. (Shelley and for a time Byron believe that Southey is the author of the review.)

Hemans and her husband separate. He moves to Rome, leaving her to bring up and provide for their five children.

Frances Wright (1795–1852) makes her first visit to America and Canada (until May 1820). On her return Longman publishes her *Views of Society in America – in a Series of Letters from that Country to a Friend in England, During the Years 1818, 1819, 1820*. She returns to America in 1824–7.

October

1 Publication of the seventh part of Moore's *Irish Melodies*.

At the beginning of the month Lockhart and John Wilson stay with Scott at Abbotsford.

3 Probable date for composition of most of P.B. Shelley's 'Lines Written Among the Euganean Hills, October 1818'.

12–31 Mary Shelley is in Venice. Her husband is with her except during 24–9, when he goes to Este and back to collect Allegra Byron. (His attempts to persuade Byron to let the child stay with Clairmont have failed.)

27   Keats writes to Richard Woodhouse (1788–1834) about his allegiance to a 'poetical Character ... distinguished from the wordsworthian or egotistical sublime': the poet as the 'most unpoetical of any thing in existence'. About now he begins *Hyperion*, which he eventually gives up on 21 April 1819.

November
1   The Shelleys set off from Este. They travel via Ferrara (6–8) and Bologna (8–11) to Rome (20). P.B. Shelley goes ahead to Naples (27).
3   Hazlitt begins his series of lectures at the Surrey Institution on the English Comic Writers, concluding on 5 January 1819. Attenders include Talfourd and H.C. Robinson. The lectures are published by Taylor & Hessey on 26 March 1819.
9   Ivan Sergeyevich Turgenev (1818–83) is born at Oryol.
17 Death of Queen Charlotte. The funeral is on 2 December.

At mid-month Peacock's *Nightmare Abbey*, 'By the Author of Headlong Hall', is published in one volume by Hookham and by Baldwin, Cradock and Joy. It was written between March and June.

At the end of the month Lady Morgan's *Florence Macarthy: an Irish Tale* is published in four volumes by Colburn.

December
1   The Shelleys move into 250 Riviera di Chiaia, Naples, their home until 28 February 1819. They visit Pompeii (22 December 1818 and 25 February 1819), the Bay of Baiae (Baia) (8 December), Paestum (24 February 1819) and other sites in the region.
1   Death in Hampstead of Tom Keats, nursed by his brother John, who now goes to live in Charles Brown's half of Wentworth Place, Hampstead (the present Keats House).
3   Payne's *Brutus; or, the Fall of Tarquin* opens at Drury Lane with Kean in the title role.
8   Murray purchases Crabbe's copyrights for £3,000.
13 Byron begins work on *Don Juan*, Canto II.
14 Coleridge begins two series of lectures at the Crown and Anchor tavern in the Strand, alternating philosophical topics with Shakespeare and other literature. He continues on 17, 28

and 31 of this month; 4, 7, 11, 14, 18, 21, 25 and 28 January 1819; 8, 11, 15, 18, 22 and 25 February 1819; and 1, 4, 8, 11, 15, 18, 22, 25 and 29 March 1819.
19   Hazlitt entertains Godwin and Irving.
19   Death of Brunton in Edinburgh. Murray publishes her unfinished novel *Emmeline* in April 1819.
25   Keats dines with Fanny Brawne (1800–65) and her family. Now or more likely some months later (see Roe [2012], p.288) Keats and Brawne reach an 'understanding' or unofficial engagement.
27   Birth in Naples of Elena Adelaide Shelley, possibly P.B. Shelley's daughter. In February 1819 she is registered as the Shelleys' child. She dies on 9 June 1820.

This year Friedrich produces what will become one of the best-known images of Romanticism, *The Wanderer Above the Sea of Mist*.

The Galignani six-volume Byron is published in Paris, to be followed by the sixteen-volume edition of 1822–5 and the works in one volume of 1826.

James Hakewill's *Picturesque Tour in Italy*, with engravings from Turner, is published by Murray in 1818–20; Thomas Whitaker's *History of Richmondshire*, also with Turner engravings, comes out between 1818 and 1822.

1819

January
1   Birth of Arthur Hugh Clough (1819–61) in Liverpool. He starts at Rugby School under Thomas Arnold in 1829.
18   Keats pays visits in Chichester and then (23 January–2 February) in Bedhampton. During this excursion he writes 'The Eve of St. Agnes' (revised in September).
28   British premiere of Rossini's *L'italiana in Algeri* at the King's Theatre.
29   Raffles, who is now East India Company Lieutenant-Governor at Bencoolen in Sumatra, lands in Singapore. A treaty with local powers on 6 February enables him to establish a trading post. In Singapore between April 1822 and June 1823 he lays extensive plans for its administration and development, establishes free trade and abolishes slavery. The population increases from roughly 5,000 in 1819 to roughly 10,000 in 1825.

February

8   John Ruskin (1819–1900) is born in London.
12 Godwin entertains Hazlitt and Irving.
15 A dramatization of Scott's *Rob Roy* opens at the Theatre Royal, Edinburgh.
28 The Shelleys leave Naples by way of Gaeta (1–3) and reach Rome on 5 March.

This month Murray publishes Rogers's *Human Life: A Poem* and Campbell's seven-volume *Specimens of the British Poets*.

March

1   John Miller prints *A Letter to William Gifford, Esq. from William Hazlitt, Esq*. Hazlitt is responding to reviews of his work in *The Quarterly Review*. Hazlitt's earlier attack, 'The Editor of the Quarterly Review', was in *The Examiner* on 15 June 1818.
7   In Rome the Shelleys move into Palazzo Verospi on the Corso; they are at 65 Via Sistina from 7 May.

April

1   Publication in *The New Monthly Magazine* of Polidori's novel as *The Vampyre: a Tale by Lord Byron*. Polidori writes to Colburn on 2 and in *The Courier* on 5 May stating that he is the author. In this and other letters he indicates that part of the original idea for the story was Byron's (as preserved in the 'Augustus Darvell' fragment). A separate edition by Sherwood, Neely & Jones is published at about the same time as the magazine version. On 3 Godwin complains to William Sherwood about the inclusion in the introductory letter of a claim that Mary Shelley and Clairmont have both been sexually involved with Byron. Godwin is successful in having the objectionable material removed from the Sherwood volume but not from the *New Monthly*. On 27 Byron writes to *Galignani's Messenger* to deny authorship.

By early April P.B. Shelley completes versions of acts II and III of *Prometheus Unbound*. Revisions and additions continue until May 1820.

2 or 3   Byron meets Guiccioli again and an affair between them soon begins. She goes to Ravenna with her husband on 12 or 13.

3	The Brawnes move into the other half of Wentworth Place, next door to Keats and Charles Brown.
11	Keats and Coleridge are introduced by Green. On 15 Keats describes, in his letter of 14 February–3 May to George and Georgiana Keats, the extraordinary range of topics raised by Coleridge during their brief encounter.
21	Keats writes 'La Belle Dame Sans Merci' (revised for publication in *The Indicator* on 10 May 1820). Late this month he also writes 'Ode to Psyche'.
c. 22	Publication of Wordsworth's *Peter Bell. A Tale in Verse*. J.H. Reynolds's partly pre-emptive parody *Peter Bell; a Lyrical Ballad* appears in instalments in *The Examiner* for 15 and 25 and for 2 May. Keats's anonymous review is in *The Examiner* on 25; Leigh Hunt reviews Wordsworth's original there on 2 May; P.B. Shelley, having read these sources, writes *Peter Bell the Third* mainly in October.

This month Walter Fawkes (1769–1825) exhibits his collection of watercolours, including many by Turner, at 45 Grosvenor Place, London. Since 1808 Turner has been a regular guest at Fawkes's Farnley Hall in Yorkshire.

In April or May Ollier publishes Shelley's *Rosalind and Helen: A Modern Eclogue; with Other Poems*.

This spring in Paris Bonington probably meets Eugène Delacroix (1798–1863). Bonington is a member of the studio of Jean-Antoine, baron Gros (1771–1835), between 1819 and 1822.

May

3	Paintings exhibited at the Royal Academy include Turner's *England: Richmond Hill* and Constable's *A Scene on the River Stour* (known as *The White Horse*).
18	Peacock is provisionally appointed assistant in the Examiner's office of the East India Company in London; the appointment is officially confirmed on 10 April 1821. At East India House he works under James Mill and (from 1823) with John Stuart Mill (1806–73). Through James Mill he knows Bentham.
24	Princess, later Queen, Victoria (1819–1901) is born at Kensington Palace.

P.B. Shelley works on *The Cenci. A Tragedy in Five Acts* between May and August. It is printed anonymously at Livorno in late summer and, under the author's name, by Ollier in London in early 1820 (dated 1819), followed by a second edition in 1821.

Murray publishes Hemans's *Tales, and Historic Scenes, in Verse*.

This month Keats writes 'Ode to a Nightingale' and 'Ode on a Grecian Urn'. Both poems are first published in *Annals of the Fine Arts* in 1820 (July and January respectively). 'Ode on Melancholy' also probably dates from May.

Moorcroft begins his expedition to Ladakh, Kashmir, Afghanistan (December 1823) and Bukhara. He dies in Afghanistan on 27 August 1825.

In late May or June Wordsworth's *The Waggoner: a Poem. To which are added, Sonnets* is published by Longman.

June

1   Byron sets off for Ravenna to see Guiccioli. He reaches Ferrara on 3, Bologna on 6 and Ravenna on 10. On 18 he begins *The Prophecy of Dante* (published with *Marino Faliero* in April 1821).

7   Death of William Shelley in Rome. He is buried in the 'Protestant' Cemetery. His parents leave Rome on 10, reach Livorno on 17, and move nearby into Villa Valsovano at Montenero on 24.

9   Siddons's last stage appearance, as Lady Randolph in *Douglas*, in a benefit for her brother Charles Kemble (1775–1854).

21 Scott's *Tales of My Landlord*, Third Series, by 'Jedediah Cleishbotham' – *The Bride of Lammermoor* and *A Legend of Montrose* – is published by Archibald Constable in Edinburgh. Publication in London, by Longman and by Hurst, Robinson, follows on 26.

23 Publication in America of the first instalment of Irving's *The Sketch Book of Geoffrey Crayon, Gent*. The last of the seven parts appears on 13 September 1820. The first four parts are published in one volume in London on 16 February 1820; following the financial failure of John Miller, Scott persuades Murray to bring out the remaining parts in a second volume in September 1820, as well as a second edition of the original four. *The Sketch Book* includes 'Rip van Winkle' and 'The Legend of Sleepy Hollow'.

26 Longman publishes Harding's *Decision. A Tale. By the Author of Correction* &c., in three volumes.
28 Murray publishes Byron's *Mazeppa, A Poem* and 'Venice. An Ode'.
28 Keats arrives at Shanklin, on the Isle of Wight, where he stays until 12 August. Between early July and about 5 September he writes *Lamia* (revised in mid-March 1820); from July he also works on revision of *Hyperion* as *The Fall of Hyperion* (abandoned by 21 September but worked on again possibly in November–December). In collaboration with Charles Brown he starts work on *Otho the Great*, finishing it by 23 August. The play is accepted by Drury Lane in December but performance is deferred; Brown submits it instead to Covent Garden, which refuses it.

July

1 The Duke of York lays the foundation stone of the new, Greek Revival St Pancras Church in London (consecrated 7 May 1822). The architects are William and Henry Inwood.
3 Murray publishes Crabbe's *Tales of the Hall*.
5 T.L. Beddoes's 'The Comet' is in *The Morning Post*.
15 Publication of Byron's *Don Juan*, Cantos I and II, by Murray, anonymously and without the publisher's name. Byron has been urged not to publish the work by Murray, Hobhouse and others and has agreed to the omission of the dedication attacking Southey.
c.15 Publication of Polidori's *Ernestus Berchtold; or, the Modern Oedipus. A Tale*, by Longman.
17 J.H. Reynolds' comedy *One, Two, Three, Four, Five; by Advertisement* opens at the English Opera House. It runs for 50 nights.

August

1 Birth of Herman Melville (1819–91).
1 Turner sails to Calais. He travels to Italy, for the first time, via Lyon and Mâcon. He works intensively in Venice (c.8–12 September), Rome (early October to the end of November, with an excursion to Naples, Vesuvius and Pompeii in late October and early November), Florence (late December to

early January) and many other places. Having filled twenty sketchbooks he reaches London on 1 February 1820.

9–10   The Guicciolis and then Byron travel from Ravenna to Bologna. Here on 11 he sees and is much affected by a production of Alfieri's *Mirra*.

10   Bolívar enters Bogotá. On 17 December he becomes President of the Republic of Gran Colombia (until April 1830), which includes for a time, once he has defeated Spanish forces there in 1820–2, the modern Venezuela, Ecuador and Panama. In 1823–4 Peru is also freed from Spanish rule and Bolívar becomes its dictator until 1826.

12   Keats travels from Shanklin to Winchester, where he stays until October apart from a brief visit to London on 11–15 September.

14   Hone publishes Hazlitt's *Political Essays, with Sketches of Public Characters*.

16   'Peterloo' massacre. Eleven people are killed and several hundred wounded when mounted militia disperse a public meeting in support of parliamentary reform at St Peter's Field, Manchester. Henry Hunt, attempting to address the meeting, is arrested and in March 1820 is sentenced to two and a half years in prison. Leigh Hunt's leader articles and related material in *The Examiner* on 22 and 29 influence P.B. Shelley's *The Mask of Anarchy*, written in September. Hone's *The Political House That Jack Built*, illustrated by George Cruikshank (1792–1878) and published in December, also responds to Peterloo; it goes through 40 editions this year.

25   Géricault's *The Raft of the Medusa* goes on show at the Paris Salon. It is in London at the Egyptian Hall, Piccadilly, in June 1820.

25   Watt dies in Handsworth. He is buried next to Boulton at St Mary's Church on 2 September.

Coleridge and the Gillmans stay in Ramsgate.

Goethe's *West-östlicher Divan* is published by Cotta in Stuttgart.

Probably this month Mary Shelley starts writing 'The Fields of Fancy'. It is completed in early September and then revised as *Mathilda*, which she dates 9 November but probably works on until February 1820.

Probably in late August or early September P.B. Shelley decides to add a fourth act to *Prometheus Unbound*. He completes it by 23 December.

September

5   Moore and Lord John Russell (1792–1878) sail from Dover. Moore's deputy in Bermuda (see 25 April 1804) has stolen £6,000 and Moore is liable for the debt; he goes abroad to avoid arrest. They are in Paris until 18, reach Geneva on 22 and cross the Simplon on 27–8. Having spent 1–5 October in Milan they separate, Russell going on to Genoa and Moore to Venice.

11 Publication in Paris of the first and second volumes of *Oeuvres complètes de Lord Byron* (ten volumes, 1819–21), translated by Amédée Pichot (1795–1877). Pichot's *Essai sur le génie et le caractère de Lord Byron* (1827) is prefaced to later editions.

12 Byron and Guiccioli leave Bologna for La Mira. Byron writes *Don Juan* Cantos III–IV, originally conceived as a single unit, between September and 30 November.

c.19 Keats writes 'To Autumn'.

21 Prince Leopold goes to see Scott at Abbotsford.

30 The Shelleys and Clairmont go to Pisa, where they meet Margaret King, Lady Mountcashell (1772–1835), known as 'Mrs Mason'. Wollstonecraft was her governess.

October

2   The Shelleys and Clairmont take lodgings in Florence at Palazzo Marini, Via Valfonda. Here their only child to survive infancy, Percy Florence Shelley (1819–89) is born on 12 November. In mid- and late October P.B. Shelley writes 'Ode to the West Wind'.

7–11 Moore visits Byron in La Mira and Venice. Byron gives him the manuscript of his Memoirs up to 1816, later sending him further material.This month Byron begins work on his translation *Morgante Maggiore di Messer Luigi Pulci*, completed on 21 February 1820 and published in *The Liberal* in July 1823.

c.8 Keats returns to London. He moves briefly to 25 College Street, Westminster, but is back at Wentworth Place by c.21. He may write 'Bright Star' this autumn; other possible dates include July (Roe [2012], pp. 331–2).

13 First number of Leigh Hunt's *The Indicator*, which runs until 21 March 1821.

16   Moore arrives in Florence, where he sees Lady Morgan. He is in Rome from 27 until 17 November and socializes with the Davys, Sir Thomas Lawrence, Canova and Turner. He is at the Falls of Terni on 18 November and back in Florence between 20 and 26 November; he reaches Chambéry via Mont Cenis on 5 December and Lyon on 6.
25   Macready's Richard III at Covent Garden is much acclaimed and much compared with Kean's more familiar performance in the same role. *A Critical Examination of the Respective Performances of Mr. Kean and Mr. Macready* (1819) finds Macready more reflective but less energetic than his rival.

A New Canto, probably by Lady Caroline Lamb, parodying *Don Juan*, is published anonymously by William Wright.

Blake begins his series of 'Visionary Heads'.

Hartley Coleridge has become a Probationary Fellow of Oriel College, Oxford; at a meeting of the fellows on 30 May 1820 it is decided that he cannot proceed to a fellowship because of his drinking habits and inattention to college rules. His father fails, during a visit to Oxford in mid-October 1820, to persuade the college authorities to reinstate him.

Probably this autumn Schubert composes his 'Trout' Quintet.

November

5   Hazlitt begins his Lectures on the Dramatic Literature of the Age of Elizabeth at the Surrey Institution. He continues on 12, 19 and 26 November and 3, 10, 17 and 24 December. The lectures are published by Stodart on 3 February 1820.
c.11 Guiccioli goes back to Ravenna with her husband.
15   Turner, Moore, Sir Thomas Lawrence and Canova are among those present at the Accademia Veneziana in Rome. Turner also sees Davy in Rome.
22   Mary Ann Evans (1819–80), who will write as George Eliot, is born near Nuneaton.
30   The 'Six Acts', introduced by the government on 23, are passed. They establish restrictions on public assembly and the press and include the Blasphemous and Seditious Libels Act.

Keats works on *The Cap and Bells* in November and December.

In November to December P.B. Shelley knows Sophia Stacey (1791–1874) in Florence. Poems including his 'The Indian Serenade' may be written for her.

In late November or early December (dated 1820) the Olliers publish *A Sicilian Story, with Diego de Montilla, and Other Poems* by Bryan Waller Procter (1787–1874), who writes as Barry Cornwall.

December

11   Moore arrives in Paris, his home until September 1821. His wife and children join him later in the month.

13   Hobhouse is arrested in response to his question, 'What prevents the people' from attacking the House of Commons, expelling the members, 'and flinging the key into the Thames?' in *A Trifling Mistake in Thomas Lord Erskine's recent Preface*. He remains in Newgate prison until 28 February 1820.

18   Publication in three volumes by Archibald Constable in Edinburgh of Scott's *Ivanhoe; a Romance* 'by the Author of Waverley', written between summer and early November and dated 1820. Publication in London, by Hurst, Robinson, follows on 31. 10,000 copies sell in two weeks.

21–4   Byron journeys to Ravenna via Bologna.

23   P.B. Shelley sends Leigh Hunt his sonnet 'England in 1819'. Shelley is aware that its attack on king and country make it unsafe to publish.

25   Keats's engagement to Brawne (see 25 December 1818).

In late 1819 and early 1820 P.B. Shelley works on his extended draft essay *A Philosophical View of Reform*.

John Richardson's translation of Kant, *The Metaphysical Works*, is published in two volumes by Simpkin & Marshall.

Publication of *Don John, or Don Juan Unmasked* and *Don Juan. Canto the Third* by Hone.

1820

January

1   Revolution in Spain begins. On 7 March King Ferdinand VII agrees to reinstate the constitution of 1812. Goya produces his 'Black Paintings'.

8   First British performance of Rossini's *La Cenerentola* at the King's Theatre.

c.12   Publication by Murray of Hemans's *The Sceptic. A Poem*. This month Murray also publishes John Herman Merivale's

(1779–1844) anonymous *The Two First Cantos of Richardetto*, 'freely translated' from Niccolò Forteguerri.

16 Publication by Taylor & Hessey of Clare's *Poems Descriptive of Rural Life and Scenery*. The volume reaches a third edition in May and a fourth in January 1821.
17 Birth of Anne Brontë (1820–49) at Thornton.
17 Coleridge, Frere, George Canning and Lord Liverpool dine together.
19 In Paris Moore, the Davys, Lady Morgan and Constant are at a gathering together.
26 The Shelleys move to Pisa, where from 29 they live at Casa Frassi.
29 Death of King George III and accession of George IV. George III is commemorated in Hemans's 'Stanzas to the Memory of the Late King'. Among other responses are Southey's *A Vision of Judgement* and Byron's answer *The Vision of Judgement*. The new king is celebrated by Dacre in *George the Fourth, a Poem* (1822).

This month the first issue of *The London Magazine* comes out. The editor is John Scott and contributors include Hazlitt, Procter and Horace Smith. It is conceived as a liberal answer to *Blackwood's*.

February
3 Keats recognizes definite symptoms of his own tuberculosis.
17 *Ivanhoe; or, The Saxon Chief* opens at the Adelphi and *Ivanhoe; or, The Jew's Daughter* at the Surrey Theatre. On 2 March *Ivanhoe; or, The Knight-Templar* is at Covent Garden and another adaptation of the novel, *The Hebrew*, is at Drury Lane.
23–4 Thistlewood and other conspirators are arrested in Cato Street, London. They plan to assassinate the Cabinet on 23, having been deceived about its whereabouts. Thistlewood kills a policeman. He is tried for high treason on 17–19 April and hanged, with four others, at Newgate on 1 May.

March
In early March Clare visits London, where he meets Cary and J.H. Reynolds. About a week after his return he marries, on 16, Martha Turner (1800–71) in Great Casterton.

3–6   P.B. Shelley is in Livorno, as again on 20–23 April, 28 April with Mary Shelley, 22–5 May, and 10–11 and 12 June.
6   About now Mary Shelley begins work on her historical novel about Castruccio Castracani, published as *Valperga* (1823). She finishes it, apart from some corrections, by 11 November 1821.
6   Barrett's *The Battle of Marathon* is privately printed on her fourteenth birthday.
10   First meeting of the Astronomical Society of London. (It becomes the Royal Astronomical Society on 7 March 1831.) Charles Babbage (1791–1871) is one of the founders and is awarded its gold medal in 1824.
11   Landon's 'Rome' is in *The Literary Gazette*. She will become one of the principal contributors to the *Gazette*, both of poems and reviews.
11   Publication in Paris of Lamartine's *Méditations poétiques*. His *Nouvelles méditations poétiques* appears on 27 September 1823.
11   Death of West. He is succeeded as President of the Royal Academy by Sir Thomas Lawrence, who returns this month having been abroad since autumn 1818, including periods in Vienna and Rome (where he paints Pope Pius VII).
23   Scott's *The Monastery. A Romance* (written mainly in late 1819 and early 1820) is published in three volumes by Archibald Constable and John Ballantyne in Edinburgh. Publication in London by Longman is on 30 (the same day that the title of baronet is conferred on Scott). On 26 he dines with Wellington. He also sees, before leaving London on 24 April, Baillie, J.W. Croker, Haydon and Irving.
25   Haydon's *Christ's Entry into Jerusalem* goes on show at the Egyptian Hall. It is seen and admired by visitors including Siddons, Hazlitt and Keats. (It features portraits of the latter two, Wordsworth, and the artist.)
25   Hobhouse is elected MP for Westminster.
Murray publishes Crabbe's *Poetical Works* in five volumes.
This spring P.B. Shelley writes 'The Sensitive-Plant'.

April
3   Radicals call for a general strike of workers in the central Scottish counties and are involved, over the next few days, in clashes with soldiers. Following trials in Glasgow and Stirling

in July and August three leaders are executed and many more people are transported.
4   Between now and 16 July Byron works on *Marino Faliero*.
8   The 'Venus de Milo', an ancient statue of Aphrodite, is discovered on Melos. After a (disputed) history of purchase or attempted purchase and a skirmish between French seamen and islanders, it is removed from the island. It goes on display in the Louvre in 1821.
20 The Brontë family moves into the parsonage at Haworth.
27 Opening, at the Royal Coburg Theatre, of William Moncrieff's *The Lear of Private Life! Or, Father and Daughter, a Domestic Drama*, adapted from Opie's *The Father and Daughter*. There are 53 performances, with Junius Brutus Booth (1796–1852) in the title role.
29 Scott's daughter, Charlotte Sophia (1799–1837), marries Lockhart.
29 Publication of *Lalla Roukh, ou la Princesse mogole*, translated from Moore's poem by Pichot.
Hatchard publishes Bulwer's *Ismael; an Oriental Tale*.
Publication, late in the month, of Wordsworth's *The River Duddon, a series of sonnets: Vaudracour and Julia: and other poems. To which is annexed, a Topographical Description of the Lakes in the North of England*.

May

3   Mary Shelley finishes her mythological drama *Proserpine* (published in revised form in November 1832). Soon afterwards she writes *Midas*, which remains unpublished until 1922.
4   First British performance of Rossini's *Tancredi* at the King's Theatre.
6   Keats moves to 2 Wesleyan Place, Kentish Town, London.
17 First performance, at Covent Garden, of James Sheridan Knowles's (1784–1863) *Virginius* with Macready in the title role. On 29 Kean fails in another *Virginius*, possibly by John Bidlake, put on at Drury Lane in competition with this production.
Pushkin, regarded as politically suspect following the circulation of such work as 'Ode. Liberty' (1817), is exiled: he is transferred from government service in St Petersburg to work in the Caucasus, Bessarabia and (1823–4) Odessa. Later in the summer of 1820 his *Ruslan and Lyudmila* is published.

P.B. Shelley writes 'Ode to Liberty'.

Baldwin, Cradock and Joy publish the two-volume *Memoirs of Richard Lovell Edgeworth, Esq. Begun by Himself and Concluded by his Daughter, Maria Edgeworth.*

June

6   Queen Caroline, who has been abroad for six years, arrives in London. Divorce proceedings are opened against her on the grounds of adultery.

15 The Shelleys and Clairmont move into the Gisbornes' house in Livorno, Casa Ricci, during their absence in England. Here P.B. Shelley writes *Letter to Maria Gisborne* (published in *Posthumous Poems*, 1824). Late in the month he writes 'To a Sky-Lark' (published with *Prometheus Unbound* in 1820).

19 Banks dies. Davy is elected to succeed him, on 30 November, as President of the Royal Society.

23 Keats, increasingly ill, moves in with Leigh Hunt and his family at 13 Mortimer Terrace, remaining there until, after a quarrel with Hunt on 12 August, he goes to the Brawnes' part of Wentworth Place. Late in June his *Lamia, Isabella, The Eve of St Agnes, and other Poems* is published by Taylor & Hessey. Favourable reviews include Jeffrey's (of this volume and *Endymion*) in *The Edinburgh Review* for August.

At about the end of the month Peacock's 'The Four Ages of Poetry' is published in *Ollier's Literary Miscellany*.

J.H. Reynolds' *The Fancy; A Selection from the Poetical Remains of the Late Peter Corcoran* is published by Taylor & Hessey.

July

1   Revolution in Naples. It collapses by the end of March 1821. See 26 September.

5   Opie's *Tales of the Heart* is published in four volumes by Longman.

John Constable and his family are in Salisbury between early July and about 23 August.

11 A party including William, Mary and Dorothy Wordsworth arrives in Calais at the beginning of an extensive tour, returning to England on 7 November. They visit the battlefield of Waterloo on 17. They travel in Switzerland, where H.C. Robinson joins

them on 16 August, and in northern Italy, from where they cross the Simplon Pass on 11 September. They reach Paris on 1 October and visit Annette Vallon, Caroline and her husband and children. In Paris Wordsworth also sees Moore and H.M. Williams. Dorothy Wordsworth's 'Journal of a Tour on the Continent, 1820' is written up by late August 1821.

12 The Pope has granted a separation between the Guicciolis.

Late in July Wordsworth's four-volume *Miscellaneous Poems* is published by Longman.

August

5 The Shelleys and Clairmont move into Casa Prinni, Bagni di San Giuliano, near Pisa.

11–12 Mary Shelley is in Lucca.

14–16 Having walked (11–13) from Bagni di San Giuliano to Monte Pellegrino and back, P.B. Shelley writes *The Witch of Atlas*. In London, on about 17, Ollier publishes Shelley's *Prometheus Unbound: a Lyrical Drama in Four Acts, with Other Poems*. The other poems include 'Ode to the West Wind', 'Ode to Liberty' and 'The Sensitive-Plant'.

16 At his new lodgings in London, 9 Southampton Buildings, Hazlitt meets and rapidly falls in love with Sarah Walker (1800–78).

17 The parliamentary bill designed to divorce Queen Caroline and deprive her of royal privileges is introduced in the House of Lords. Crowds show approval for her when she arrives and there is much support for her in opposition and radical circles. (Cobbett, for example, backs her in his *Political Register*.) The bill is withdrawn in November. P.B. Shelley's main response to the Queen Caroline affair is *Oedipus Tyrannus; or, Swellfoot the Tyrant*, written in late summer and autumn this year. (It is published anonymously in December but rapidly withdrawn.) Hone produces the Caroline-related pieces *The Queen's Matrimonial Ladder* (August) and *Non Mi Ricordo!* (September), both illustrated by Cruikshank. Hays includes a favourable account of the Queen in *Memoirs of Queens, Illustrious and Celebrated* (T. and J. Allman, 1821).

Charles Lamb's first essay as 'Elia', 'Recollections of the South-Sea House', is in *The London Magazine*. (He worked briefly at the South Sea House before joining the East India Company in 1792.) Byron is initiated into the Ravenna branch of the Carbonari, secret societies dedicated to the overthrow of foreign and papal rule in Italy. He is recruited by Guiccioli's father and brother, Count Ruggero Gamba Ghiselli (1770–1846) and Count Pietro (1800–26/7). In February 1821 Byron stores weapons and documents for the Carbonari.

Scott's guests at Abbotsford this month include Davy and Mackenzie.

September

1   In Paris Denon shows Moore his Egyptian drawings. They see each other again on 25 and on 14 October.

2   Scott's *The Abbot*, written mostly this summer, is published in three volumes by Archibald Constable and John Ballantyne in Edinburgh. Publication in London by Longman follows on 4. This month Scott starts work on *Kenilworth*.

Early in September Frere leaves for Malta, where he remains for much of the rest of his life.

17   Keats and Joseph Severn (1793–1879) sail for Italy. They are delayed by storms, land at Portsmouth on 28, and reach Naples on 21 October.

26   P.B. Shelley's 'Ode to Naples' is in *The Morning Chronicle*. *The Military Register* carries it on 1 and 8 October.

October

16   Byron's main work on *Don Juan* Canto V is between now and 27 November.

21   Clairmont takes up residence in Florence.

22   P.B. Shelley's cousin, Thomas Medwin (1788–1869) comes to stay with the Shelleys until 27 February 1821. On 29 October they move to Palazzo Galetti in Pisa.

31   Keats and Severn, after ten days in quarantine, stay at Albergo della Villa di Londra in Naples until 8 November.

John Constable begins painting a long series of sky studies on Hampstead Heath.

Pellico is arrested by the Austrian authorities as a member of the Carbonari. He is imprisoned in Venice and then at the fortress of

Spielberg in Moravia. He is released in 1830 and his *Le mie prigioni* is published in 1832.

November

1   Longman publishes Godwin's *Of Population: an Enquiry Concerning the Power of Increase in the Numbers of Mankind, being an answer to Mr. Malthus's essay on that subject.*

c.1 Maturin's *Melmoth the Wanderer* is published by Archibald Constable.

15 Keats and Severn arrive in Rome, where they lodge at 26 Piazza di Spagna.

17 Longfellow, aged thirteen, publishes 'The Battle of Lovell's Pond' in *The Portland Gazette* as 'Henry'.

29 Queen Caroline's supporters hold a service of thanksgiving at St Paul's Cathedral for her effective acquittal (see 17 August).

This month Cooper's first novel, *Precaution*, is published in two volumes, anonymously and at the author's expense, by A.T. Goodrich in New York. Colburn publishes it in London in February 1821.

Kean goes to America, acting in New York, Philadelphia, Boston and Baltimore between now and June 1821. He tours again in the United States and in Canada between autumn 1825 and December 1826.

Baillie visits Scott at Abbotsford.

December

9   Luigi dal Pinto, commandant of papal troops in Ravenna, is assassinated near Palazzo Guiccioli in Ravenna. Byron has the dead or dying man carried in and writes about the incident in *Don Juan V.*

19 Gifford's favourable review of Hemans's poems is in *The Quarterly Review* for October, published now.

21 The Shelleys see a performance by Sgricci in Pisa. This month they begin to enter Pisan social life more fully, meeting among others Sgricci and the future Greek independence leader Prince Alexandros Mavrokordatos (1791–1865), with whom Mary Shelley studies Greek.

23 Moore, in Paris, is with Irving and Russell.

Scott is elected President of the Edinburgh Royal Society.

Murray publishes Belzoni's *Narrative of the Observations and Recent Discoveries ... in Egypt and Nubia.* It includes an account of the women of Egypt, Nubia and Syria by Belzoni's wife, Sarah (1783–1870).

In late 1820 and early 1821 P.B. Shelley writes much of *Epipsychidion. Verses Addressed to the Noble and Unfortunate Lady Emilia V* (published anonymously, by Ollier, in 1821). The author first met 'Emilia' or Teresa Viviani (1801/2–36) in November.

James Mill's 'Government' is in the supplement to the *Encyclopaedia Britannica*. The essay is pilloried by Thomas Babington Macaulay (1800–59) in *The Edinburgh Review* for March 1829.

Campbell edits *The New Monthly Magazine* from 1820 to 1830.

1821

January
4   Byron keeps his Ravenna Journal from now until 27 February. Moore includes an edited version in his *Life* of 1830. On 13 Byron begins writing *Sardanapalus*, completing Acts I and II in May; Acts III–V are written more quickly on 13–27 May.
5   Mary Shelley sees Sgricci perform in Lucca, as again on 12. She and her husband watch him in Pisa on 22.
9   *Mirandola*, by Procter ('Barry Cornwall'), opens at Covent Garden with Macready and Charles Kemble.
15 Archibald Constable brings out Scott's *Kenilworth; A Romance* (three volumes) in Edinburgh. Hurst, Robinson follows in London on 18. The novel was completed on 27 December 1820.
19 In Pisa the Shelleys meet Edward Williams (1793–1822) and Jane Williams (1798–1884).

February
This month and in March P.B. Shelley writes *A Defence of Poetry*.
11 Scott arrives in London and stays until early April. He sees Wellington, Castlereagh, Beaumont and many others and sits to Sir Thomas Lawrence.
23 Death of Keats in Rome. On 26 he is buried in the Non-Catholic or 'Protestant' Cemetery.
24 The Carbonari uprising collapses.
27 John Scott, editor of *The London Magazine*, dies after wounds sustained in a duel with Jonathan Christie at Chalk Farm on

16. Christie is Lockhart's agent in London; the duel is the climax of Scott's dispute with Lockhart and *Blackwood's*. One element in the quarrel is the *Blackwood's* attacks on the 'Cockney' school. *The London* is taken over by Taylor & Hessey, who employ Thomas Hood (1799–1845) this summer as a sub-editor and frequent contributor.

March
5   The Shelleys move, within Pisa, to Casa Aulla.
25 Beginning of the Greek Revolution or War of Independence from the Ottoman Empire.
27 Blake and Linnell are at Drury Lane to see Sheridan's *Pizarro*.
31 Murray publishes Byron's *Letter to [John Murray], on the Rev. W.L. Bowles' Strictures*, written on 7–10 February. It defends Pope against Bowles's *The Invariable Principles of Poetry* (1819) as reviewed by D'Israeli in *The Quarterly Review* for July 1820, published on 4 November 1820. On 21 April Byron sends Murray *Observations upon Observations*, responding to Bowles's *Observations on the Poetical Character of Pope* (1821), but he decides against publication in view of his opponent's polite response to the *Letter*.

Late in the month J. Vincent in Oxford and G. & W.B. Whittaker in London publish T.L. Beddoes's *The Improvisatore, in Three Fyttes, with Other Poems*.

Longman publishes Baillie's *Metrical Legends of Exalted Characters* and pays her £1,000 for the copyright.

Clare finishes 'Sketches in the Life of John Clare Written by himself'.

April
6   The first volume of Hazlitt's *Table-Talk* is published by John Warren. Colburn publishes the second volume on 15 June 1822 and a second edition of the two together on 30 May 1824.
10 The Sultan responds to the Greek revolt by hanging Patriarch Grigorios V in Constantinople.
21 Byron's *Marino Faliero, Doge of Venice. An Historical Tragedy* is published by Murray with *The Prophecy of Dante*. Byron is insistent that the play should not be performed. An abbreviated version opens, in spite of Murray's attempt to have it stopped, at Drury Lane on 25.

23 George Soane's (1790–1860) version of Baron Friedrich de la Motte-Fouqué's *Ondine* (1811) is presented at Covent Garden.

Between this month and June P.B. Shelley writes *Adonais. An Elegy on the Death of John Keats, Author of 'Endymion', 'Hyperion'* etc. It is published in Pisa in July and in London in *The Literary Chronicle* in December.

Scott writes *The Pirate* between mid-April and October.

Southey's *A Vision of Judgement* is published by Longman.

May

1   An exhibition of Belzoni's discoveries, with models and a reconstruction of chambers in the tomb of Seti I, opens at the Egyptian Hall, Piccadilly.
2   Death of Piozzi at Clifton. She is buried at Tremeirchion on 16.
5   Death of Napoleon on St Helena.
5   First issue of *The Manchester Guardian*.
7   John Constable's *Landscape: Noon* (known as *The Hay-Wain*) is in the Royal Academy exhibition, where it interests French visitors including Charles Nodier (1780–1844) and Géricault. With two other Constables it is bought by the French dealers Arrowsmith and Schroth in 1824 (see 25 August 1824). Other paintings at the Academy include Sir Thomas Lawrence's portrait of Lady Blessington.
c.7   Publication by Blackwood in Edinburgh and Cadell in London, in one volume, of Galt's *Annals of the Parish; or the Chronicle of Dalmaling; During the Ministry of the Rev. Micah Balwhidder. Written by Himself. Arranged and Edited by the Author of 'The Ayrshire Legatees,'* &C.
7   Byron starts writing *The Vision of Judgement* but lays it aside (see 20 September).
8   The Shelleys move back from Pisa to Bagni di San Giuliano. Mavrokordatos visits them there on 21.
c.10   Publication of the eighth volume of Moore's *Irish Melodies*.
29   John Cartwright is convicted of sedition at Warwick. He is fined £100.

Publication, as the work of 'John Hamilton', of J.H. Reynolds's *The Garden of Florence and Other Poems*.

This month Faraday becomes acting Superintendent at the Royal Institution; from 1825 he is Director of the laboratory there. He lectures extensively at the Institution.

Coleridge's visitors include the Lambs and the comic actor Charles Matthews (1776–1835).

June

9   Hemans's *Dartmoor* wins a 50-guinea prize from the Royal Society of Literature.
11 Ignaz Moscheles (1794–1870) gives his first piano recital in London, where he settles in spring 1825 having been based in Vienna since 1808.
12 Byron writes *The Two Foscari* between now and c.14 July.
16 Death of John Ballantyne.

In mid-June Colburn publishes Lady Morgan's *Italy*. A French translation is published at the same time.

18 First performance of Weber's *Der Freischütz* (composed 1817–21) at the Schauspielhaus, Berlin.
26 Mavrokordatos sails for Greece. He is elected President by the National Assembly in 1822 but has little power against rival faction leaders. He defends Missolonghi when the Turks besiege it in October to December 1822 and returns there on 11 December 1823.

This month Blackwood in Edinburgh and Cadell in London publish, in one volume, Galt's *The Ayrshire Legatees; Or, The Pringle Family. By the Author of 'Annals of the Parish,'* &C. It was serialized in *Blackwood's Magazine* between June 1820 and February 1821.

July

10 Pietro Gamba is banished from the Romagna by the papal authorities, as is his father soon afterwards. Guiccioli joins them in Florence on 25.
16 Byron starts work on *Cain*, finishing it in September.
19 Coronation of George IV. Scott (who is in London until 26) is among those present. Sir Thomas Lawrence, as President of the Royal Academy, is part of the coronation procession. (He first painted the King as Regent in 1814–15 and produces several of the best-known portraits of him in the 1820s.) Queen Caroline is refused entry.

21	Jules Saladin's translation *Frankenstein, ou le Prométhée moderne*, is published in Paris.
29–2 August	P.B. Shelley is in Florence before setting off for Ravenna via Livorno.

August

1	Death of Inchbald in Kensington.
7	Death of Queen Caroline.
6–16	P.B. Shelley visits Byron in Ravenna. He arrives back in San Giuliano on 22.
8	Publication by Murray of Byron's *Don Juan*, Cantos III–V. This month he writes *The Blues*.
17	George IV makes a public entry into Dublin. O'Connell is prominent among his hosts. On 21 the King attends a production of Sheridan's *The Duenna* and *St Patrick's Day*. He leaves for England on 3 September.

September

1	Mary Shelley and Guiccioli meet. She arrived in Pisa with her father and brother late in August.
3–4	Faraday discovers electromagnetic rotation.
8–11	The Shelleys and Clairmont visit La Spezia, Massa and Carrara. On 17 the Shelleys are in Pisa, as often while they live at San Giuliano.
20	Byron's main period of work on *The Vision of Judgement* is between now and 4 October.
24–5	Moore and Russell travel from Paris to London.

Turner sketches in Normandy and the Île de France. This autumn Bonington is also in Normandy; he comes again in spring 1823.

Peacock spends most of the month in Wales.

Coleridge's anonymous translation, *Faustus: From the German of Goethe* is published by Boosey. (For evidence of the translator's identity see Coleridge [2007], xv–liv.) Among other recent *Faust* translations are extracts by George Soane (J.H. Bohte, January 1820) and by Daniel Boileau (Boosey, June 1820), both accompanying illustrations by Moritz Retzsch.

Clare's *The Village Minstrel* is published by Taylor & Hessey.

In September and October De Quincey's *Confessions of an English Opium-Eater* appears in *The London Magazine*. It is published in volume form in 1822.

October
1. Coleridge goes to Ramsgate until November; he is there again every autumn between 1822 and 1828.
3. First performance of a version of Kleist's *Friedrich Prinz von Homburg, oder die Schlacht bei Fehrbellin* (written 1809–10) at the Theater an der Berg in Vienna. The first Berlin performance is in 1828.
9. Byron starts work on *Heaven and Earth*. On 15 he begins his journal *Detached Thoughts*, kept in Ravenna and Pisa between now and mid-December with one further entry added on 18 May 1822.
10. Moore arrives in Dublin, where he visits his parents and sees Maturin and Morgan. He stays until 18 and is back in London on 22. In early November the Bermuda debt problem is resolved, meaning that he can safely stay in Britain.
25. The Shelleys move into rooms at Tre Palazzi di Chiesa in Pisa. P.B. Shelley writes much of *Hellas. A Lyrical Drama* this month. It is published by Ollier early in 1822.

Charles Lamb's 'Elia' essay 'Witches and other Night-Fears' is in *The London Magazine*.

Lady Blessington meets Count Alfred d'Orsay (1801–52) this autumn.

November
1. Byron, having left Ravenna on 29 October and travelled with Rogers from Bologna to Florence, moves into Palazzo Lanfranchi in Pisa.
11. Fyodor Mihailovich Dostoyevsky (1821–81) is born in Moscow.
14. Medwin comes to stay with the Shelleys in Pisa until 9 March 1822. He meets Byron for the first time on 20.

Late in the month Wordsworth visits Coleridge in Highgate.

December
12. Gustave Flaubert (1821–80) is born in Rouen.
19. Publication by Murray of Byron's *Sardanapalus, a Tragedy; The Two Foscari, a Tragedy; Cain, a Mystery*.

20	Publication of *Gedichte* by Heinrich Heine (1797–1856).
21 or 22	Archibald Constable in Edinburgh publishes Scott's *The Pirate* in three volumes, dated 1822. Longman publishes it in London on 24.
22	Publication in New York, by Wiley & Halsted, of Cooper's (anonymous) two-volume *The Spy: a Tale of the Neutral Ground*. The Whittakers publish it in London, in three volumes, in March 1822.

Charles Lamb's 'Elia' essay 'My First Play' appears in *The London Magazine*.

This year the Blakes move to 3 Fountain Court, near the Strand.
Also this year Blake's woodcuts for Robert Thornton's *The Pastorals of Virgil* are published.
Pushkin's *A Prisoner in the Caucasus* is published.

1822

January

9	Chateaubriand is appointed French ambassador in London. He leads the French delegation to the Congress of Verona and becomes foreign minister from January 1823 to June 1824.
14	Edward John Trelawny (1792–1881), who has recently arrived in Pisa, meets the Shelleys. On 15 he meets Byron.
17	Peel becomes Home Secretary in Lord Liverpool's government. He is in office until April 1827 and returns under Wellington from January 1828 to November 1830. He takes a particular interest in law and order, including crime, punishment and policing.
27	Hazlitt leaves for Scotland, seeking to divorce his wife in order to marry Walker. Under Scottish law remarriage after divorce is possible. He reaches Edinburgh on 4 February and moves to Renton Inn on 10.
27	At the court in Berlin members of the Prussian and Russian royal families and the Duke of Cumberland participate in a 'divertissement' with tableaux vivants, song and dance, derived from Moore's *Lalla Rookh*. The music is by Gaspare Spontini (1774–1851), who extends it into *Nurhamal, oder der Rosenfest von Caschmir*, performed at the Berlin Court Opera on 27 May.

P.B. Shelley works on his unfinished play about Charles I, probably begun late in 1821.

Longman publishes Rogers's (anonymous) *Italy, a Poem. Part the First*. The author's name is given in the enlarged edition published by Murray in 1823. Murray publishes the second part of *Italy* in 1828 and a lavish new edition of both parts in 1830 with engravings from Turner, Stothard and others. All the editions are published at Rogers's expense; the 1830 version costs him over £7,000 but sells very well.

Sara Coleridge's translation from Martin Dobrizhoffer, *An Account of the Abiphones, an Equestrian People of Paraguay*, is published by Murray.

Lady Blessington's *The Magic Lantern, or, Sketches of Scenes in the Metropolis* is published, anonymously, by Longman.

Bulwer starts at Trinity College, Cambridge, but transfers to Trinity Hall (until 1825) after the first term.

Between January and April Byron writes *Don Juan*, Canto VI; VII is finished by late June and VIII by late July.

February

2 The Shelleys and Jane Williams go for a forest walk. Soon afterwards, P.B. Shelley writes 'To Jane. The Invitation' and 'To Jane. The Recollection', published together as 'The Pine Forest of the Cascine, near Pisa', in *Posthumous Poems* (1824). 'With a Guitar. To Jane' follows in March.

5 Ali Pasha is killed by Ottoman soldiers in Janina. His war with the Sultan is, from the Greek rebels' point of view, a useful distraction.

7–11 P.B. Shelley and Edward Williams house–hunt in La Spezia.

18 Edward Williams mentions in his journal that Byron is thinking about putting on a production of *Othello*. Trelawny in 1825 says that Byron intended to play Iago to Trelawny's Othello and Mary Shelley's Desdemona (see Shelley [1980–8], i.470, n.7). The idea is given up by 28.

'On Some of the Old Actors', by Charles Lamb ('Elia'), is in *The London Magazine*.

March

11 Longman publishes Opie's *Madeline, a Tale* in two volumes.

15 Date given with the 'Preliminary Notice' to Peacock's *Maid Marian*, 'by the Author of Headlong Hall', published in one volume by Hookham and by Longman. It was written mostly in 1818. An operatic version by Henry Rowley Bishop and J.R. Planché, *Maid Marian; or, the Huntress of Arlingford*, is given at Covent Garden on 3 December 1822.

24 The 'Masi affair'. Following a scuffle between Major Stefano Masi and a group including Byron, P.B. Shelley and Pietro Gamba, Masi is badly wounded in an attack by Byron's coachman, Vincenzo Papi. The wounded man recovers but much scandal and ill-feeling has been generated and the English group is less welcome in Pisa than before the incident.

Publication by Longman of Wordsworth's *Memorials of a Tour on the Continent, 1820* and *Ecclesiastical Sonnets*.

The first part of *Noctes Ambrosianae* is in *Blackwood's* for March. The series includes contributions by William Maginn (1794–1842), Wilson, James Hogg and Lockhart. Maginn ('Odoherty'), Wilson ('Christopher North'), Hogg ('The Ettrick Shepherd') and De Quincey ('The English Opium Eater') feature in imaginary conversations. Wilson writes most of the material from 1825.

April

12 John Henry Newman (1801–90) is elected to a fellowship at Oriel College, Oxford. He becomes a tutor there between 1826 and 1832. He is joined by Richard Hurrell Froude (1803–36) as a fellow on 31 March 1826 and as a tutor from 1827.

12 Turkish troops begin massacres on Chios.

19 or 20 Death of Allegra Byron, of typhus, in the convent at Bagnacavallo.

20 Rogers visits Byron in Pisa.

20 Cherubini becomes Director of the Paris Conservatoire (called, between 1816 and 1831, the École Royale de Musique et de Déclamation).

30 The Shelleys and Clairmont move into Casa Magni, San Terenzo, near Lerici. Edward and Jane Williams join them soon afterwards. Mary Shelley is profoundly depressed during her time here.

Late in the month the first separate edition of Wordsworth's *A Description of the Scenery of the Lakes* is published by Longman.

Also late this month Baldwin, Cradock and Joy publish *May-Day with the Muses*, by Bloomfield.

May
Wilkie's *Chelsea Pensioners Reading the Gazette of the Battle of Waterloo* is at the Royal Academy, where it attracts unusually large crowds of viewers. Wellington, who commissioned the work, pays £1,260 for it.

6   Hazlitt repeats his 1818 lecture on Shakespeare and Milton at the Andersonian Institute in Glasgow. He speaks on Thomson, Cowper and Burns on 13. Between the two lectures he goes on a brief walking tour to Loch Lomond and the Trossachs. On 15–17 he sails to London, where he is discouraged by Walker. He then returns to Scotland, arriving in Edinburgh on 31.

13–16   Trelawny visits the Shelleys at Casa Magni.

16   First British performance of Rossini's *Otello* at the King's Theatre.

22   Hemans's 'The Meeting of the Bards' is read aloud at an 'Eisteddfod or meeting of Welsh Bards' in London. Her *A Selection of Welsh Melodies* – words to accompany airs by John Parry (1776–1851) – was published earlier this year.

c.22   From now until the beginning of July Byron and Guiccioli are at Villa Dupuy, Montenero, near Livorno. They then return to Pisa.

29   Archibald Constable in Edinburgh and Hurst, Robinson in London bring out Scott's *The Fortunes of Nigel* (completed in March) in three volumes. Sales are rapid.

Towards the end of the month Murray in England and Moses Thomas in America publish, in two volumes, Irving's *Bracebridge Hall; or the Humourists, A Medley*, under the name 'Geoffrey Crayon'. Murray bought the copyright for £1,050 in March.

Babbage has completed the first small version of his 'difference engine' or calculating machine.

This month and in June P.B. Shelley writes the unfinished *The Triumph of Life*.

Clare comes to London for the second time. He is in company with Cary, J.H. Reynolds, Charles Lamb and Hood.

June
8   Publication in Paris of Hugo's first collection, *Odes et Poésies diverses*.
16 Mary Shelley miscarries and almost dies from loss of blood.
26 The Godwins move to 195 The Strand.
28 The Royal Academy grants Blake – always poor – £25.
This month Shelley writes 'Lines Written in the Bay of Lerici'.
Blackwood in Edinbugh and Cadell in London publish, in one volume, Galt's *The Provost. By the Author of Annals of the Parish....*

July
1   Leigh and Marianne Hunt and their children arrive in Livorno. They set sail originally on 15 November 1821 but were driven back to Dartmouth by bad weather and set off again on 13 May, reaching Genoa on 15 June. On 1 P.B. Shelley and Edward Williams sail their boat, the *Don Juan*, to Livorno, where they see the Hunts on 2. Shelley then goes to Pisa to see Byron and Margaret King. The Hunts move into part of Casa Lanfranchi in Pisa – beneath Byron – on 3.
8   Shelley and Williams drown while sailing from Livorno for Lerici. Shelley's cremation, organized by Trelawny and with Byron and Leigh Hunt in attendance, is on 16 August. His ashes are buried in the 'Protestant' Cemetery in Rome in January 1823.
17 Hazlitt, in Edinburgh, is granted his divorce. Walker, however, has already effectively refused him. He is back in London by 21.
18 The Lambs go abroad for the first time. Mary Lamb is confined at Amiens after one of her mental crises. Charles Lamb continues to Versailles and, with John Howard Payne, to Paris, before returning to London in August. His sister, on her recovery, also goes to Versailles and Paris and reaches home in early September.
20 Mary Shelley moves back to Pisa until September. She sees much of Byron, Guiccioli and Trelawny.
Charles Lamb's ('Elia''s) 'Detached Thoughts on Books and Reading' is in *The London Magazine*.

August
12 Suicide of Castlereagh. He is succeeded as Foreign Secretary on 18 September by George Canning.

14-29   George IV's visit to Edinburgh, organized by Scott. George is the first Hanoverian monarch to visit the city. On Scott's initiative the royal party wears traditional highland dress, suggesting reconciliation after the suppression of the rising of 1745-6. Turner is present and afterwards paints, but never displays, *George IV at a Banquet in Edinburgh*. Cockerell and Wilkie are also there and the King knights Sir Henry Raeburn (1756-1823). Crabbe stays with Scott in Edinburgh and meets Lockhart, Mackenzie, Hogg and Wilson.

17   Stendhal's *De l'Amour* is published in Paris in two volumes by Mongie.

Byron begins *Don Juan*, Canto IX, this month. X and XI follow by mid-October.

Beckford opens Fonthill to visitors, announcing a sale by public auction for 8 October. In the event he sells privately, to John Farquhar, for £300,000, on 5 October. In October 1823 there is a sale of items from Beckford's collection at Fonthill, the subject of accounts by Hazlitt in *The Morning Chronicle* in August and September 1823. Beckford moves, that summer, to Lansdown Terrace, Bath (built by John Palmer in 1789-93). In 1826 he begins the tower on Lansdown hill, designed by himself and Henry Goodridge (1797-1864).

September

7   Brazil declares independence from Portugal.

11   Mary Shelley goes to Genoa, staying at first at the Croce di Malta. On about 25 she moves into Casa Negroto, Albaro (above Genoa), where the Hunt family joins her on 4 October.

15-21   Hobhouse comes to visit Byron in Pisa.

At mid-month Dorothy Wordsworth and Joanna Hutchinson (sister of Mary Wordsworth and Sara Hutchinson) start on a tour of Scotland, returning in late October. Dorothy Wordsworth revises her 'Recollections of a Tour Made in Scotland, A.D. 1803'.

Charles Lamb's ('Elia''s) 'A Dissertation upon Roast Pig' is in *The London Magazine*.

Jean-François Champollion (1790-1832) makes considerable progress, this month, in deciphering Egyptian hieroglyphs. He presents his findings in *Lettre à M Dacier* and develops them further in *Précis du système hiéroglyphique* (1824).

This autumn Lady Caroline Lamb's *Graham Hamilton* is published in two volumes by Colburn.

October

2 Mary Shelley's first entry in her new 'Journal of Sorrow'.
3 Byron, Guiccioli and Trelawny, having left Pisa on 27 September, arrive at Casa Saluzzo in Albaro.
13 Canova dies in Venice.
15 *The Liberal: Verse and Prose from the South* (published by John Hunt) includes in its first volume P.B. Shelley's translation of the Walpurgisnacht scene from Goethe's *Faust*, Part One, and Byron's *The Vision of Judgement,*.
19 Hemans's 'England's Dead' is in the *Literary Gazette*, signed 'H.'

Material included in Cobbett's *Political Register* between this month and November 1826 goes into the first edition of his *Rural Rides* (1830).

This month Schubert works on his 'Unfinished' Symphony.

Stendhal contributes a version of what becomes chapter 1 of his *Racine et Shakespeare* to the *Paris Monthly Review*. A version of chapter 2 follows there in January 1823 and the whole work is published in late February or early March 1823. Further material is added for a second part which appears in March 1825.

November

23 Murray publishes Byron's *Werner, a Tragedy*. Most of it was written in December 1821 and January 1822.

At the end of the month T.L. Beddoes's *The Brides' Tragedy* is published by Rivington.

December

12 First meeting, at Cutlers' Hall in Sheffield, of the Sheffield Literary and Philosophical Society. Montgomery is President in 1823 and 1827.

In mid-December (dated '1823') Blackwood in Edinburgh and Cadell in London publish, in three volumes, Galt's *The Entail: Or the Lairds of Grippy. By the Author of Annals of the Parish* ....

22 Birth at Laleham-on-Thames of Matthew Arnold (1822–88), son of Thomas Arnold.

23 Publication by Longman of Moore's *The Loves of the Angels*, dated 1823.
Blake works on *The Ghost of Abel*, a response to Byron's *Cain*.

1823

January
1 *The Liberal*, volume 2, includes Mary Shelley's 'A Tale of the Passions, or, the Death of Despina', P.B. Shelley's 'Song, Written for an Indian Air' (earlier called 'The Indian Serenade') and Byron's *Heaven and Earth, a Mystery*.
7 Publication of Scott's *Peveril of the Peak* (four volumes, Archibald Constable and Hurst, Robinson). This month he starts work on *Quentin Durward* (completed in May).
18–25 William Buckland (1784–1856) discovers, in a cave on the Gower peninsula, the bones of the 'Red Lady of Paviland', whom he identifies as a Roman-period woman. Much later investigation will reveal that the remains are male and about 33,000 years old. One of Buckland's other most significant discoveries is of hyena bones at Kirkdale Cavern in Yorkshire in 1821, published in his *Reliquiae Diluvianae* (1823).
25 The first part of Landon's series of poems *Medallion Wafers* is in *The Literary Gazette*. The rest of the series follows on 8 February and 1 March.
31 Foundation, at the King's Head tavern, of the London Society for Mitigating and Gradual Abolishing the State of Slavery Throughout the British Dominions (Anti-Slavery Society). Wilberforce is present at this and some other meetings. Prominent members include Zachary Macaulay (1768–1838) and Clarkson.

February
1 Cooper's *The Pioneers; or, The Sources of the Susquehanna* is published, anonymously, by Wiley in New York. Murray publishes it in London later in the month.
7 Radcliffe dies at 5 Stafford Row, Pimlico. She is buried at St George's, Hanover Square. She has published nothing since 1797; *Gaston de Blondeville, or the Court of Henry III Keeping*

Festival in Ardenne, A Romance (completed in 1803) and *St Alban's Abbey. A Metrical Tale* (c.1808) are published in four volumes by Colburn in 1826 with Talfourd's 'Memoir of the Life and Writings of Mrs Radcliffe'. Her 'On the Supernatural in Poetry' (originally intended as part of the introduction to *Gaston*) is in *The New Monthly Magazine* for January 1826.

10   Mary Shelley dates the first part of her unfinished life of her husband. She abandons it in March.

19   Publication by G. & W.B. Whittaker of Mary Shelley's *Valperga: or, the Life and Adventures of Castruccio, Prince of Lucca*, by 'the Author of *Frankenstein*'.

26   Death of John Philip Kemble in Lausanne.

Hood's 'Ode: Autumn', an evident homage to Keats, is in *The London Magazine*.

This month Hugo's *Han d'Islande* is published; an English abridgment follows in 1825, with etchings by Cruikshank.

March

3   London Greek Committee formed. The founders are John Bowring (1792–1872), who becomes secretary, and Edward Blaquiere (1779–1832). By 29 members include Hobhouse, Mackintosh, Burdett, Moore and Russell.

15   Mitford's *Julian, A Tragedy in Five Acts*, starring Macready, receives the first of eight performances at Covent Garden.

31   The Blessingtons arrive in Genoa. They have been travelling abroad since August 1822.

Murray publishes Lady Caroline Lamb's *Ada Reis, A Tale* in three volumes.

April

1   Rogers entertains Moore, Wordsworth (who came to London in late March), Henry Hallam, and Cary. On 4 there is a dinner for William and Mary Wordsworth, Coleridge, Rogers, Moore, the Lambs, Hutchinson and H.C. Robinson. Wordsworth is in London again in March and April 1824.

1   John Hunt publishes Byron's (anonymous) *The Age of Bronze; Or, Carmen Seculare et Annus Haud Mirabilis*, written mostly in December 1822.

1 The Blessingtons and Byron meet. Lady Blessington often sees him between now and 2 June.
5 Blaquiere and Andreas Louriotis (1789–1850), a representative of the provisional Greek government, visit Byron. He expresses willingness to go to Greece and is elected in May to the London Greek Committee.
26 *The Liberal*, volume 3, includes Byron's *The Blues, A Literary Eclogue*, Mary Shelley's 'Madame d'Houtetot', P.B. Shelley's 'Lines to a Critic' and Hazlitt's 'My First Acquaintance with Poets'.

May

5 Turner exhibits *The Bay of Baiae, with Apollo and the Sibyl*, at the Royal Academy show.
6 Byron finishes *Don Juan*, Canto XVI. XII–XVI have been composed in rapid succession.
7 Publication by Longman of *Fables for the Holy Alliance, Rhymes on the Road, &c. &c* by Moore, writing as 'Thomas Brown the Younger'.
7 First performance of Beethoven's Ninth Symphony, with parts of his Mass in D *(Missa Solemnis)*, at the Kärntnertortheater in Vienna.
8 *Clari; or, The Maid of Milan*, with words by Payne and music by Henry Bishop (1786–1855), is at Covent Garden. It includes the song 'Home, sweet home'.
8 Byron dates the fragment of *Don Juan*, Canto XVII.
9 John Hunt publishes Hazlitt's (anonymous) *Liber Amoris: Or, the New Pygmalion*.
12 O'Connell is one of the chief founders of the Catholic Association, designed to campaign for Roman Catholic emancipation.
17 William and Mary Wordsworth tour the Low Countries (until 11 June).
17 Publication in London by Hurst, Robinson of Scott's *Quentin Durward* in three volumes. Publication in Edinburgh by Archibald Constable is on 19. The work becomes immediately popular in France; illustrations include Delacroix's *The Murder of the Bishop of Liège* (1829) and Bonington's *Quentin Durward at Liège* (1828).This month Scott begins work on *St Ronan's Well* (until December).

21   Pushkin begins writing *Eugene Onegin*.
21   John Stuart Mill starts work as junior clerk in the Examiner's office of the East India Company.
Charles Lamb's 'Elia' essay 'Poor Relations' is in *The London Magazine*.
Between about May and July Mary Shelley writes the first version of her poem 'The Choice'. The revised version dates from July and later. See Shelley (2002), volume 4, pp. xxx–xxxi.

June
Murray publishes Hemans's *The Siege of Valencia: A Dramatic Poem ... With Other Poems*.
2   Byron sees Lady Blessington for the last time.
6   Maria Edgeworth arrives in Edinburgh. She sees Scott frequently, meets Raeburn, and travels on to Perth on 24. She returns to Edinburgh before staying with Scott at Abbotsford from 27 July to 11 August.
26   John Hunt publishes Byron's *The Island, or Christian and his Comrades*. (For Fletcher Christian see 28 April 1789.)

July
8   Death of Raeburn in Edinburgh.
14   *Melmoth the Wanderer: A Melo-Dramatic Romance, in Three Acts*, by B. West after Maturin, is performed at the Royal Coburg Theatre.
15   John Hunt publishes Byron's *Don Juan*, Cantos VI–VIII. Cantos IX–XI follow on 29 August.
16–21   Byron, Trelawny and Pietro Gamba sail from Genoa to Livorno on the *Hercules*. On 24 they sail for Greece.
25   Mary Shelley and her son Percy set off for England from Genoa, arriving in Turin on 27, Chambéry on 31 and Lyon on 2 August. In Paris, which they reach on 12 August, Horace Smith visits and Mary Shelley goes to see him and his family at Versailles from 15 to 18. They reach London on 25 August.
28   First night of Richard Brinsley Peake's *Presumption; or, the Fate of Frankenstein* at the English Opera House (the Lyceum), with Thomas Potter Cooke (1786–1864) as the creature. It runs for 37 performances. Mary Shelley and her father see it on 29 August.

28 First performance, at the Hoftheater in Kassel, of Louis Spohr's (1784–1859) *Jessonda*.
30 *The Liberal*, volume 4, includes Byron's *Morgante Maggiore di Messer Luigi Pulci* and Mary Shelley's 'Giovanni Villani'.

August
3 Byron and his party land at Argostoli in Cephalonia. (The island has been under British control since 1815.) He visits Ithaca on 11–17 and moves from Argostoli to Metaxata on 4 September. Trelawny leaves for the mainland on 6 September and becomes involved with the warlord Odysseus Androutsos (c.1788–1825).
11 G. & W.B. Whittaker publish a second edition of *Frankenstein*. Revisions are minor.
19 Bloomfield dies at Shefford in Bedfordshire. He is buried at Campton.
30 Charles Lamb sees Mary Shelley. This month the Lambs move out of London to Islington. They move to Enfield in September 1827.

September
8 Mary Shelley and her son move into 14 Speldhurst Street, Brunswick Square. At about mid-month she meets Procter and probably soon afterwards T.L. Beddoes. (Both are guarantors of P.B. Shelley's *Posthumous Poems* in 1824.) She also sees much of the Novello family and the Lambs over the next few years.
28 and 30 Byron writes entries in his 'Journal in Cephalonia'. A third follows on 17 December and a fourth (written in Missolonghi) on 15 February 1824. 'The Dead have been awakened – shall I sleep?' precedes the entries.

Manzoni completes *Fermo e Lucia*, the first version of *I promessi sposi*. Between now and September 1825 the Hunt family lives in Florence.

October
c.1 *The London Magazine* includes De Quincey's 'On the Knocking at the Gate in Macbeth' and Lamb's 'Letter of Elia to Robert Southey, Esquire'. Lamb is responding

to Southey's accusation of lack of sound 'religious feeling' in *Elia* in the *Quarterly Review* for January, which appeared on 8 July. (Extracts from the 'Letter of Elia' are included in the first issue of the medical journal *The Lancet* on 5 October.) Lamb and Southey are soon reconciled.
1 First meeting of the Institution for the Encouragement of the Fine Arts, later the Royal Manchester Institution.
20 Peake's burlesque *Another Piece of Presumption* is at the Adelphi Theatre.

Byron meets George Finlay (1799–1875).

This autumn Schubert works on *Die Schöne Müllerin* (published 1824).

November
13 Byron agrees to lend £4,000 to the Greek provisional government. He is also acting as a commissioner for a much larger loan from the London Greek Committee. (£800,000 is promised and about £300,000 delivered, the first instalment arriving after his death.)
23 Foundation of the Edinburgh Oil Gas Light Company, with Scott as chairman. It merges with the Edinburgh Coal Gas Company in March 1828 to form the Edinburgh Gas Light Company.

The Gillmans and Coleridge move to 3 The Grove, Highgate.

December
3 Belzoni dies at Gwato in Benin. He intended to go on to the Niger and Timbuctoo.
10 Mary Anning (1799–1847) of Lyme Regis discovers the first complete Plesiosaurus fossil. Her later finds include a Pterodactyl in 1828.
13 Rossini comes to London, leaving in late July 1824. Several of his operas are put on at the King's Theatre. He conducts his *Zelmira* there on 24 January 1824.
17 Byron's *Don Juan*, Cantos XII–XIV, published by John Hunt.
23 Unsuccessful performance of Hemans's *The Vespers of Palermo* at Covent Garden. The play is better received in Edinburgh (5 April 1824). Her 'The Lost Pleiad' is in *The New Monthly Magazine* for December. (She uses the same title for the longer poem published in 1829.)

27 Publication by Archibald Constable and Hurst, Robinson of Scott's *St Ronan's Well* (three volumes), dated 1824.
29 Byron sets off from Cephalonia, via Zante (Zakynthos) on 30, for Missolonghi on the Greek mainland.

The Lambs adopt Emma Isola (1809–91; later Moxon).

Lord Francis Leveson-Gower's (1800–57) translations *Faust; and Schiller's Song of the Bell* are published by Murray.

The first edition of the Second Series of D'Israeli's *Curiosities of Literature* comes out this year.

Turner's *Rivers of England* is published between 1823 and 1827.

1824

January
5 Byron lands at Missolonghi. In the middle of the month he recruits a force of 500 Suliotes and writes a 'War Song of the Suliotes', but finds them faction-ridden and unreliable and disbands most of them on 15 February.
18 Coleridge sees the Lambs. Mary Shelley may also be there. Her 'Recollections of Italy' is in *The London Magazine* for this month.
20 A Turkish fleet blockades Missolonghi.
22 Byron writes 'January 22nd 1824. Messalonghi', often known as 'On this day I complete my thirty sixth year'. It is published in *The Morning Chronicle* on 29 October.
26 Géricault dies in Paris.

First issue of *The Westminster Review*, founded by Bentham and edited by Bowring as a vehicle of radical thought.

February
c.9 Dickens, aged twelve, starts work at Warren's blacking warehouse (probably until June). Subsequently he is sent to school at Wellington House Academy until spring 1827.
10 Finlay is in Missolongi between now and 21 March.
15 Byron suffers a convulsive fit in Missolonghi. On 24 his *The Deformed Transformed; a Drama* is published by John Hunt. It was begun in January 1822 and worked on further in 1823 but remained incomplete.

In mid-April Longman publishes Moore's *Memoirs of Captain Rock, The Celebrated Chieftain ... Written by Himself.*
26 Publication by Colburn of the first volume of Godwin's *History of the Commonwealth of England*. The remaining three volumes appear on 24 April 1826, 13 June 1827 and 25 October 1828.
27 Rossini signs a contract with the French monarchy. In September he becomes joint director of the Théâtre-Italien in Paris.

March
16 Coleridge is elected to the Royal Society of Literature (founded in 1820).
26 John Hunt publishes Byron's *Don Juan*, Cantos XV–XVI.
Schubert composes his 'Death and the Maiden' String Quartet (published 1831).
Mary Shelley's 'On Ghosts' is in *The London Magazine*. Her 'The Bride of Modern Italy' follows in the April number.
Taylor & Hessey publish the first volume of Landor's *Imaginary Conversations of Literary Men and Statesmen*. Colburn publishes the second in 1828 and James Duncan the third and fourth in 1829.

April
Coleridge and Wordsworth see each other early this month.
7 Meeting at the Bridgwater Arms, Manchester, to establish the Manchester Mechanics' Institute. Dalton is one of the founders.
c.8 Hazlitt marries his second wife, Isabella Bridgwater (1791–1869) in Scotland. They stay at Melrose, returning to London on about 5 May. The marriage founders in early autumn 1827.
9 Byron develops a fever after riding in heavy rain. He dies on 19. There are many tributes in verse and prose. Barrett's 'Stanzas on the Death of Lord Byron' is in *The Globe and Traveller* on 30 June. Bowring's 'Lord Byron in Greece' is in *The Westminster Review* for July. Rossini's *Il pianto delle muse in morte di Lord Byron*, with the composer as soloist, is performed at Almack's Assembly Rooms in London on 11 June. Dionysios Solomos (1798–1857) writes his 'Lyrical Poem on the Death of Lord Byron' in 1824–5 and Andreas Kalvos (1792–1869) 'The Britannic Muse' in 1826.

May

By this month, when they go to the Royal Academy together, Blake knows Samuel Palmer (1805–81). They are introduced by Linnell.

10 The National Gallery opens to the public at 100 Pall Mall, London. Beaumont, who gives sixteen important paintings, is influential in its founding. Work on the Trafalgar Square building, by Wilkins, begins in 1832.

17 Burning of Byron's unpublished Memoirs at John Murray's, 50 Albemarle Street. Their destruction is agreed by Murray, Hobhouse, Moore and representatives of Lady Byron.

At mid-month Mitford's *Our Village; Sketches of Rural Character and Scenery* is published by Whittaker. There are second and third editions later this year and in 1825. Volumes II, III, IV and V follow in 1826, 1828, 1830 and 1832.

20 Clare comes to London, returning to Helpston on 8 August. He visits, among others, the Lambs and Sir Thomas Lawrence. In early July he meets Coleridge and Hazlitt.

Wilhelm Meister's Apprenticeship. A Novel, Carlyle's three-volume translation from Goethe's *Wilhelm Meisters Lehrjahre* (1795–6), is published by Oliver and Boyd in Edinburgh and Whittaker in London. The sequel, *Wilhelm Meister's Travels; or, The Renunciants*, from *Wilhelm Meisters Wanderjahre oder die Entsagenden* (1821) first appears in *Specimens of German Romance* (1827), published in Edinburgh and London by Tait.

At the end of the month the first volume of Constant's *De la Religion* (five volumes to April 1831) appears.

In about May Stendhal's *Vie de Rossini* is published in Paris by Boulland. A translation, *Memoirs of Rossini* (1824) is brought out by Hookham.

June

2 Scott finishes work on *Redgauntlet. A Tale of the Eighteenth Century*. It is published in three volumes by Archibald Constable and Hurst, Robinson on 14.

Early this month Blackwood in Edinburgh and Cadell in London publish Ferrier's *The Inheritance* in three volumes.

Also early in the month John Hunt publishes *Posthumous Poems of Percy Bysshe Shelley*, edited by Mary Shelley. It is withdrawn in August, after 309 of the 500 copies have been sold, at the insistence of Sir Timothy Shelley, who thinks the work will bring his family into disrepute.

c.4 Publication by Longman of James Hogg's one-volume *The Private Memoirs and Confessions of a Justified Sinner: Written by Himself*.

5 Carlyle sets off for London, where he lives until March 1826. This month he and Gabriele Rossetti (1783–1854), an Italian political exile who settles in England this year, are among Coleridge's visitors.

5 Liszt plays for the first time in London at the Argyll Rooms. He has been established in Paris since December 1823. He is at the Argyll Rooms again on 21 and Drury Lane on 29. He performs at Windsor for the King on 27 July and in Manchester at the Theatre Royal on 4 August, as again during his next visit to England in June 1825.

21 Mary Shelley and her son move to 5 Bartholomew Place, Kentish Town.

Catherine Gore's (1798–1861) *Theresa Marchmont; or, the Maid of Honour. A Tale* is published in one volume by J. Andrews as the work of 'Mrs. Charles Gore'. (Catherine Moody married Lieutenant Charles Gore at St George's, Hanover Square, on 15 February 1823.)

John Buckstone's *The Revolt of the Greeks; or, The Maid of Athens* is at Drury Lane.

July

16 Byron is buried at Hucknell Torkard in Nottinghamshire. Hobhouse, Moore, Rogers, Campbell and Pietro Gamba are present.

17 Mary Shelley sees Moore, whom she helps considerably in the compilation of his *Letters and Journals of Lord Byron* (1830), and is introduced to Irving.

19 John Hunt is fined £100 for publishing Byron's *The Vision of Judgement*.

22 First English performance of Weber's *Der Freischütz, or the Seventh Bullet*, at the English Opera House (Lyceum). The cast includes Braham and Thomas Simpson Cooke (1782–1848). Mary Shelley goes to several performances in August.

The Improvisatrice and Other Poems by Landon (as L.E.L.) is published by Hurst, Robinson in London and Archibald Constable in

Edinburgh. There are five further editions by the end of the year. She receives £300 for the copyright.

August

10 Charlotte Brontë, aged eight, starts at the Clergy Daughters' School, Cowan Bridge, Lancashire, where her elder sisters Maria and Elizabeth are already pupils. The six-year-old Emily follows in November. Following outbreaks of disease, probably typhus or typhoid, Maria and Elizabeth are taken home to Haworth in 1825 and die of consumption on 6 May and 15 June respectively. The younger sisters are withdrawn from the school not long before Elizabeth's death. Lowood is Charlotte Brontë's version of the school in *Jane Eyre* (1847).

10 Turner leaves London to tour the Meuse, Moselle and Rhine, and to visit Dieppe. He returns on about 15 September.

21 Pushkin arrives in his new place of exile, his mother's estate at Mikhailovskoe. He has been dismissed from government service partly because of a letter in which he describes atheism as 'plausible'. His exile ends in 1826 but he is still kept under close surveillance.

25 John Constable's *Hay-Wain* and Delacroix's *The Massacres of Chios* are among works displayed at the Salon in Paris. (Delacroix admires Constable's landscapes, which he first saw in June.) Constable, Bonington and Copley Fielding (1787–1855) are awarded gold medals by King Charles X.

27 William and Mary Wordsworth and their daughter Dora (1804–47) begin a tour of North Wales (until mid-September).

Lafayette revisits the United States after nearly 40 years. He stays until September 1825.

September

1 Hazlitt and his new wife set out for Paris. While there he meets Stendhal.

23 Death in London of John Cartwright. His last important work was *The English Constitution Produced and Illustrated* (1823).

October

23 Publication by Colburn of Medwin's *Journal of the Conversations of Lord Byron*.

30 Maturin dies at 37 York Street, Dublin. He is buried at St Peter's Church, where he was curate from 1804.

November
The ninth volume of Moore's *Irish Melodies* is published.

December
Publication of Pushkin's *The Fountain of Bakhchisaray*.

Dorothy Wordsworth begins an occasional journal (until 1835).
The first American edition of Wordsworth's *Poetical Works* is published in four volumes by Cummings, Hilliard in Boston.
Canzoni by Giacomo Leopardi (1798–1837) is published this year in Bologna. His *Versi* comes out in 1826 and *Canti* in 1831.
In 1824–6 J.S. Mill assists Bentham in the preparation of his *Rationale of Judicial Evidence: Specially Applied to English Practice* (Hunt and Clarke, 1827). Bentham's *Rationale of Reward* (1825) and *Rationale of Punishment* (1830) originally appeared together, in French, in 1811.
Picturesque Views of England and Wales, with engravings from Turner, is published in parts by Charles Heath between 1824 and 1838.

1825

January
3 Robert Owen buys land to set up a model community at New Harmony, Indiana, where he arrived on 16 December 1824. He then goes to Philadelphia and Washington, DC, to explain his ideas for the reform of society to public figures including President Monroe and President-elect Adams. He also visits Jefferson at Monticello before returning to New Harmony on 13 April. He leaves to return to Scotland in June but comes back in 1826. By the time he leaves again in June 1827 the experiment at New Harmony has largely failed.
11 Publication by Colburn of Hazlitt's (anonymous) *The Spirit of the Age: or Contemporary Portraits*. Galignani publishes an edition in Paris, with some additions and omissions, on 19 May.
14 Hazlitt leaves Paris for Italy, arriving on 5 February in Florence, where he sees Leigh Hunt and meets Landor. The tour continues to Rome, back to Florence, and to Venice,

Milan, Lake Como and (7 June) Vevey. He and his wife reach London in October. His series of letters to *The Morning Chronicle* is published as *Notes of a Journey Through France and Italy* in May 1826.

The first instalment of *Memoirs of Harriette Wilson, Written by Herself* is published by J.J. Stockdale. Her wealthy and aristocratic customers can buy exemption from mention for £200. Wellington is one of the most famous not to pay.

February

9 Campbell, in *The Times*, proposes the establishment of a university in London (see 11 February 1826).

21 Coleridge produces the first draft of 'Work Without Hope' (published late in 1827, without his permission, in *The Bijou for 1828*).

Baldwin, Cradock and Joy publish *Odes and Addresses to Great People*, by Hood and J.H. Reynolds.

Pushkin's *Eugene Onegin*, chapter 1 is published at the end of the month.

March

2 Work begins on a tunnel beneath the Thames from Rotherhithe to Wapping, designed by Marc Isambard Brunel (1769–1849). His son Isambard Kingdom Brunel (1806–59) assists on the project, which runs into major difficulties in January 1828 and is completed only in 1842.

4 John Quincy Adams (1767–1848) becomes United States President until 4 March 1829.

6 First performance of Beethoven's String Quartet in E flat major (op.127), beginning the 'Late Quartets'.

7 Opening of the University of Virginia, founded in Charlottesville by Jefferson.

9 Death of Barbauld in Stoke Newington. Her *Works* in two volumes, edited with a memoir by Aikin, are published this year by Longman.

29 Lamb retires from the East India Company. His 'Elia' essay 'The Superannuated Man' is in *The London Magazine* for May.

Blake's *The Book of Job* is published.

April

16　Fuseli dies at Putney Hill. He is buried in St Paul's Cathedral on 25.

Publication by Knight & Lacey of William Parry's *The Last Days of Lord Byron*, ghost-written by Thomas Hodgskin (1787–1869). Parry (1773–1859) was with Byron at Missolonghi as 'fire master' – officer in charge of explosives – from 7 February 1824.

May

John Constable's *Landscape* (called *The Leaping Horse*) is exhibited at the Royal Academy.

7　Death of Salieri in Vienna.

10　Burdett's Catholic Relief Bill passes in the Commons but is defeated in the Lords on 17.

14　Lamartine's *Le Dernier Chant du pèlerinage d'Harold* is published in Paris. It is translated in 1827 as *The Last Canto of Childe Harold's Pilgrimage*.

16　*Faustus: a Romantic Drama* by George Soane, after Goethe, opens at Drury Lane and runs for 24 nights.

24　Delacroix arrives in London, staying until late August. He sees Bonington in July and August and meets Sir Thomas Lawrence, Cockerell, and probably John Constable.

18　Coleridge delivers his lecture 'Prometheus' at the Royal Society of Literature.

23　Jewsbury visits the Wordsworths at Rydal Mount and is with them again at Kent's Bank, Lancashire, in July. Her *Phantasmagoria, or, Sketches of Life and Literature* has just been published, as the work of 'M.J.J.', by Hurst, Robinson in London and Archibald Constable in Edinburgh and is dedicated to William Wordsworth. He and Mary Wordsworth, with Hutchinson, return the visit in Manchester in mid-November.

c.25　Coleridge's *Aids to Reflection in the Formation of a Manly Character on the Several Grounds of Prudence, Morality, and Religion* is published by Taylor & Hessey. A second edition is published by Hurst, Chance in 1831.

30　The Godwins move to 44 Gower Place, London. Their bookselling business has gone bankrupt.

This month Hemans's *The Forest Sanctuary; and Other Poems* is published by Murray; an expanded second edition follows in December

1828. She begins, as 'F.H.', a sequence (1825–7) of *Records of Woman* in the *New Monthly Magazine*.

June

11   Trelawny, caught up in fighting between Greek factions, is shot and seriously injured on Mount Parnassus. He recovers and goes to Cephalonia in 1826 and to England in 1828.

Archibald Constable and Hurst, Robinson bring out Scott's *Tales of the Crusaders* in four volumes. The tales are *The Betrothed* and *The Talisman*.

July

Publication of Landon's *The Troubadour; Catalogue of Pictures, and Historical Sketches* by Hurst, Robinson in London and Archibald Constable in Edinburgh; the first of four editions.

11   Mary Shelley entertains the Godwins, the Lambs and Payne (whose declaration of love she rejected on 25 June).

14   Scott reaches Dublin, having sailed from Glasgow to Belfast. On 18 he is at Trinity College to receive an LLD. He travels to Edgeworthstown to see Maria Edgeworth and on to Limerick and Killarney with her. He is back in Dublin on 13 August and sails for Holyhead on 17. He visits the 'Ladies of Llangollen'.

27   T.L. Beddoes enters the university of Göttingen. He studies subjects including physiology and chemistry until his expulsion for alcohol-related offences in April 1829. During his time here he works on an early version of *Death's Jest-Book, or, the Fool's Tragedy*. After his expulsion he continues his studies at Würzburg.

August

6   Upper Peru, following the end of Spanish rule, renames itself the Republic of Bolivia in honour of Bolívar, who serves as the first President until January 1826.

20–23   Scott and George Canning stay at Lake Windermere. Wordsworth, Lockhart and John Wilson are also present. On 23 Scott, Wilson and Lockhart visit Wordsworth and Southey.

25 Publication by Carey and Lea in Philadelphia and Murray in London of Irving's *Tales of a Traveller* (two volumes), under the name 'Geoffrey Crayon'. Murray gives £1,575 for the copyright.
11 Opie is admitted to the Society of Friends. She has been going to Quaker meetings since 1814. (Earlier she was a Unitarian.) This year she publishes *Illustrations of Lying in All its Branches*. *The Black Man's Lament; or, How to Make Sugar* follows in 1826 and *Detraction Displayed* in 1828.

Mary Shelley is in Windsor for ten days.

Late this month Turner begins a tour of the Low Countries and the Rhine.

T.B. Macaulay's 'Milton' is in *The Edinburgh Review* for August.

September

27 George Stephenson's (1781–1848) steam locomotive *Locomotion No. 1* makes its first journey on the newly completed line between Stockton and Darlington, work on which began on 13 May 1822.

About now (see Bentley [1969], p.302 n.2) Blake visits Shoreham in Kent, a place particularly important to Samuel Palmer and other young 'Ancients' or Blake disciples.

October

Early this month Disraeli visits Scott and Lockhart at Abbotsford.

c.6 Longman publishes Moore's *Memoirs of the Life of the Right Honourable Richard Brinsley Sheridan* in two volumes.
8 Jewsbury sends 'Farewell to the Muse' in a letter to Dora Wordsworth. It is included *in The Poetical Album* (1828–9), edited by Alaric Watts.
14 Leigh and Marianne Hunt and family arrive in London after three years in Italy.
20 Lockhart becomes Editor of *The Quarterly Review*.
29 Moore comes to Abbotsford, meeting Scott for the first time.

November

7 Dacre dies at Lancaster Place, London. She is buried at St Mary's, Paddington on 11.

Scott starts work on *Woodstock*. On 20 he begins his Journal.

December

1 Tsar Alexander I dies at Tagenrog. He is succeeded by his brother Nicholas I (1796–1855).

26 The 'Decembrists' – liberal army officers in St Petersburg – lead an attempted revolt. Five Decembrists are executed on 25 July1826; many more are exiled to Siberia and other parts of the Russian empire. Pushkin knows many of the rebels but is already in exile from the capital.

29 David dies in Brussels, where he settled in January 1816.

Hemans's 'Evening Prayer at a Girls' School' is in *Forget Me Not; A Christmas and New Year's Present for 1826*. Between 1825 and 1835 approximately 100 poems by Hemans are published in such annuals as *Forget Me Not* and *The Keepsake* (see Hemans [2000], pp. 435–6). Late this year the first authorized American edition of her work begins to appear in Boston (four volumes, published by Hilliard, Gray, dated 1826–8).

Wright begins her 'colony', Nashoba, in Tennessee. In theory, slaves will buy their freedom by working the land. Following the collapse of the experiment, Wright takes the slaves to Haiti in 1830.

Coleridge meets Blake probably this year (Bentley [1969], pp. 301, 325).

Fairy Legends and Traditions of the South of Ireland, by Thomas Crofton Croker (1798–1854) is published by Murray in three volumes between 1825 and 1828. The Grimms translate part of the work into German (Leipzig, 1826).

Nash rebuilds Buckingham Palace between 1825 and 1830.

1826

January

10 and 13 Coleridge sees Frere, who is visiting from Malta.

From mid-month Scott is plunged into financial crisis by the failure of the publishers Constable and Hurst, Robinson and his own James Ballantyne printing company. He owes £121,000. His creditors set up a trust into which he pays subsequent literary earnings; his debt is reduced to £53,000 by the time of his death.

23 *The Last Man*, by 'The Author of *Frankenstein*', is published in three volumes by Colburn. Mary Shelley started writing it probably early in 1824 and finished it by November 1825.
30 Telford's Menai suspension bridge opens. His Conwy suspension bridge is also completed this year.

February
2 A paper by Somerville is read at a meeting of the Royal Society. It is published as 'On the Magnetizing Power of the More Refrangible Solar Rays' in *Philosophical Transactions of the Royal Society of London* for 1826, the first such contribution by a woman. Murray publishes her *Mechanism of the Heavens* in 1831.
4 Cooper's *The Last of the Mohicans; a Narrative of 1757* is published in two volumes by Carey and Lea in Philadelphia. It is published by Miller in London, in three volumes, this spring.
11 Foundation of the University of London (later University College, London), which provides, unlike Oxford and Cambridge at this time, education for non-Anglican students. Campbell, Brougham and James Mill are involved. Building to designs by Wilkins begins in 1827 and the university opens in October 1828.
14 Poe enters the University of Virginia, where he studies until 21 December.
15 Irving arrives in Madrid. Research there and in Seville informs his *A History of the Life and Voyages of Christopher Columbus*, published by Murray in January 1828 (four volumes). In 1829, in Granada, Irving lives in part of the Alhambra (see May 1832) before leaving Spain to take up an appointment as secretary to the American Legation in London (until 1832). His *Chronicle of the Conquest of Granada* is published in 1829.
In late February Blackwood in Edinburgh and Cadell in London publish, in one volume, Galt's *The Omen*.

March
5 Weber arrives in London, where he completes *Oberon*, which is first performed at Covent Garden on 12 April with Braham as Huon. J.R. Planché's libretto derives from Wieland's *Oberon* (1780).

8   At Covent Garden Weber conducts a selection from *Der Freischütz*.
c.20 In Paris an unauthorized Galignani edition of Mary Shelley's *The Last Man* appears.
25 Barrett's *An Essay on Mind with Other Poems* is published by James Duncan.

April
'F.H.' (Hemans) publishes 'To the Author of the Excursion and the Lyrical Ballads' (later called 'To Wordsworth') in the *Literary Magnet*.
4   Bonington sets off for Italy, returning to Paris via Switzerland in early July. His stay in Venice (April–mid-May) provides material for a series of major oil paintings of 1826–8.
22 Colburn publishes Disraeli's (anonymous) *Vivian Grey* in two volumes; three further volumes follow in 1827. The novel generates much scandal and abuse and contributes to Disraeli's nervous illness over the next few years. There is a new edition in 1827.
25 Fall of Missolonghi to the Turks. Turkish forces recapture much of central Greece, taking Athens on 5 June 1827.
28 Publication of Scott's *Woodstock; or The Cavalier. A Tale of the Year Sixteen Hundred and Fifty-One*, in three volumes, by Archibald Constable and Longman.
28 Publication of Hazlitt's (anonymous) *The Plain Speaker. Opinions on Books, Men and Things*, in two volumes, by Colburn.
Alfred de Vigny's (1797–1863) *Cinq-Mars, ou Une Conjuration sous Louis XIII* is published in two volumes by Urbain Canel in Paris.

May
3   Work begins on Telford's St Katharine's Docks in London, completed in October 1828.
9   Joseph Paxton (1803–65) arrives at Chatsworth to take up his post as head gardener.
15 Death of Scott's wife, Charlotte. She is buried at Dryburgh Abbey.
15 An exhibition in aid of Greece opens at Galerie Le Brun in Paris. Paintings include Delacroix's *Greece on the Ruins of Missolonghi* and his Byron-inspired *The Combat of the Giaour and Hassan*.
Jewsbury is physically and mentally ill this month.

June

1 Cooper and his family set sail for Europe from New York. They live in Paris (until 1833) and travel in Switzerland, Italy, the Low Countries and Britain. While abroad Cooper publishes works including *The Prairie, A Tale* (three volumes, Colburn, London and two volumes, Carey and Lea, Philadelphia, 1827), *Notions of the Americans: Picked up by a Travelling Bachelor* (two volumes, Colburn and Carey and Lea, 1828) and *The Bravo* (three volumes, Colburn and Bentley and two volumes, Carey and Lea, 1831). He becomes a close friend of Lafayette.

3 Coleridge sends Eliza Aders 'The Two Founts: Stanzas Addressed to a Lady on her Recovery with Unblemished Looks, from a Severe Attack of Pain' (published late in 1827, without the author's permission, in *The Bijou for 1828*).

5 Rev. Patrick Brontë's gift of toy soldiers to his son Branwell begins the fantasy and role-play which will soon lead into the children's written sagas, dominated at first by Branwell and Charlotte but involving Emily and Anne also. Among other influences is the siblings' reading of Scott, Byron and *Blackwood's Edinburgh Magazine*.

5 Weber dies in London. He is buried on 21 at the Roman Catholic chapel of St Mary Moorfields, with Braham singing in Mozart's *Requiem*. (Weber's remains are later removed to Dresden.)

10 *Le Monstre et le magicien*, an adaptation of *Frankenstein* by Jean Toussaint Merle and Antoine Nicolas Béread, begins its run of 94 performances at the Théâtre Porte Saint-Martin, Paris. Thomas Potter Cooke, as in *Presumption*, plays the creature.

19 Longfellow arrives in Paris to begin travel and study prefatory to taking up his post teaching languages at Bowdoin College, Maine, from which he graduated in 1825. He visits Spain between March and November 1827, tours Italy for much of 1828, and is at Göttingen between February and June 1829 before starting work at Bowdoin in August 1829.

July

4 Death of Jefferson at Monticello.

13 The Hunts entertain Mary Shelley, the Lambs, H.C. Robinson and Peter George Patmore (1786–1855).

Hazlitt returns to Paris to work on his Life of Napoleon. During his stay he meets Lafayette, Cooper and Constant.

August
Early this month Disraeli leaves on a three-month trip to Switzerland and Italy. He is rowed on Lake Léman by Byron's former boatman.
Between c. 5 and 2 September Mary Shelley is in Brighton and then at Sompting. Her 'A Visit to Brighton' is in *The London Magazine* in December.
6 Mendelssohn completes his *A Midsummer Night's Dream* overture. It is first performed in Stettin on 20 February 1827.
Hemans's 'Casabianca' is published in *The Monthly Magazine* for August under the initials 'F.H.'
In August and September Turner sketches in Normandy, Brittany, and on the Loire between Nantes and Orléans.

September
10 Beaumont and Rogers visit Wordsworth. The three are with Southey on 19 and again at the end of the month.
Robert Dale Owen (1801–77), Robert Owen's son, becomes editor of *The New Harmony Gazette* (see 3 January 1825).

October
17 Scott arrives in London. He is received by George IV at Windsor on 20. He sees Rogers and Moore on 23 and leaves for France on 26, reaching Paris on 29. He sees Hazlitt on 30.
17 Marriage of Carlyle and Jane Baillie Welsh (1801–66). They live at Comely Bank in Edinburgh and then, from 1827, at Craigenputtoch.
Pushkin's *Eugene Onegin*, chapter 2 is published at the end of the month.
Mary Shelley's review of books about Italy is in *The Westminster Review*; she covers further accounts there in July 1829.
Colburn publishes Jameson's *A Lady's Diary*, retitled in the second edition *Diary of an Ennuyée*.
This autumn J.S. Mill suffers a mental breakdown or crisis.
In October and November unsigned articles in *The Wasp* attack Landon. From about 1825 rumours circulate that she is the lover of William Jerdan (1782–1869), editor of *The Literary Gazette*.

November
3 In Paris, Scott and Cooper meet (as again on 4 and 6). Scott also speaks to King Charles X, whom he had known in exile. Back

in London, from 10, he sees Wellington and Peel several times and is introduced to Burney (Mme D'Arblay) by Rogers on 18. He leaves London on 20.

15   Campbell is elected Rector of Glasgow University. He is twice re-elected, serving until 1829.

De Quincey's 'Gallery of the German Prose Classics' begins to appear in *Blackwood's Edinburgh Magazine*. His translation of Lessing's *Laokoon* is in the November 1826 and January 1827 numbers. He came to Edinburgh in October and lives in or near the city permanently from 1830.

Hemans, as 'F.H.', publishes 'The Illuminated City' in *The Monthly Magazine*.

December

7   John Flaxman dies. He is buried in St Pancras graveyard.

First publication of 'The Queen of Prussia's Tomb' by 'F.H.' (Hemans) in the *Monthly Magazine*.

Longman publishes Landon's *The Golden Violet with its Tales of Romance and Chivalry: and Other Poems* (dated 1827).

Browning probably writes his Byron-influenced *Incondita* this year. In 1826 or 1827 he first reads P.B. Shelley in *Miscellaneous Poems* (1826).

At the end of his life, in 1826–7, Blake produces watercolour illustrations to Dante and engraves seven of them for Linnell.

Katsushika Hokusai (1760–1849) begins work on *Thirty-Six Views of Mount Fuji*.

1827

January

7   Count Ioannis Kapodistrias (1776–1831) arrives in Nauplion on his way to take office as Governor – i.e. President – of Greece.

22   Davy travels in Europe between now and 6 October.

Between now and April Wordsworth writes 'Scorn not the Sonnet'.

February

De Quincey's 'On Murder Considered as One of the Fine Arts' appears in *Blackwood's*.

7   Death of Beaumont at Coleorton. He leaves £100 each to Wordsworth, Southey and Sara Coleridge; S.T. Coleridge is

offended at his exclusion. (Lady Beaumont leaves him £50 at her death in July 1829.)

23 Scott publicly admits his authorship of the *Waverley* novels at the Theatrical Fund dinner in Edinburgh.

Schubert begins *Winterreise* Book I; he works on Book II from October. The complete work is published in 1828.

March

12 Branwell Brontë's 'Battell Book' is the first dated manuscript of the Brontës' juvenilia. Charlotte Brontë probably writes 'There was once a little girl' at about the same time. Branwell and Charlotte work together on the Glasstown or Angria saga until the mid-1830s, initially with the younger sisters also (but see January 1831).

26 Beethoven dies in Vienna.

Hazlitt's 'On the Feeling of Immortality in Youth' appears anonymously in *The Monthly Magazine*.

'The Deserted House', by 'F.H.' (Hemans) is in the *New Monthly Magazine*.

This month Dickens starts work as a solicitor's clerk.

Late this month Bulwer's *Falkland* (one volume) is published by Colburn.

April

12 Heine sets off for England, where he stays until August. His *Englische Fragmenten* are in *Nachträge zu den Reisebildern*, published in January 1831.

20 Publication by Jackson of Louth of *Poems by Two Brothers*, mainly by Alfred and Charles Tennyson (1808–89) with a few contributions from their brother Frederick (1807–98).

Taylor & Hessey publish Clare's *The Shepherd's Calendar; with Village Stories, and Other Poems*.

Charles Darwin leaves Edinburgh University, which he entered in October 1825, without a degree.

First appearance of 'The Homes of England' by 'F.H.' (Hemans) in *Blackwood's*.

May

4 Bonington's *Scene on the French Coast* is at the Royal Academy. He comes to London this spring and again between January

and early summer in 1828. During this second trip he meets Sir Thomas Lawrence.

7 Publication in Boston, by Calvin Thomas, of Poe's *Tamerlane and Other Poems*. On 26 Poe, as Edgar Allan Perry, joins the United States Army. He obtains his discharge on 15 April 1829. In September 1830 he becomes a cadet at the United States Military Academy, West Point; on 28 January 1831 he is court-martialled and dismissed for neglect of duty and disobeying orders.

Wordsworth's *Poetical Works* in five volumes is published by Longman.

Liszt arrives in London for his third visit.

In late May or early June Andrews brings out Gore's one-volume *The Lettre de Cachet; a Tale. The Reign of Terror; a Tale*.

June

7 Scott completes *The Life of Napoleon Buonaparte, Emperor of the French. With a Preliminary View of the French Revolution*. Publication in nine volumes (1827–8) by Cadell (Edinburgh) and Longman (London) begins later this month.

15 Manzoni's *I promessi sposi, storia Milanese del secolo XVII* is published in three volumes by Ferrario in Milan. A translation by Charles Swan, *The Betrothed Lovers*, is brought out in Pisa in 1828 by Niccolò Capurro.

29 Longman publishes Moore's *The Epicurean, A Tale*.

Carlyle's 'Jean-Paul Friedrich Richter' is in *The Edinburgh Review* for June 1827; 'Jean Paul Friedrich Richter Again' follows there in January 1830. Work by Richter (1763–1825), who writes as 'Jean Paul', includes *Hesperus, oder 45 Hundposttage* (1795) and *Titan* (1800–3). Over the next few years Carlyle contributes many pieces on German literature, including Goethe, Schiller and Novalis, to the *Edinburgh* and *The Foreign Review*.

July

Early this month *The Christian Year; Thoughts in Verse for Sundays and Holy Days Throughout the Year* by John Keble (1792–1866) is published in Oxford (anonymously) by J.H. Parker. There is a second edition in November. Keble, who was elected as a fellow of Oriel College in 1812, has been acquainted with Newman for some time; they become friends this year.

24 Between now and 26 October Mary Shelley lives in Sussex, at Worthing, Sompting and Arundel. She is working on *Perkin Warbeck*.

This month Henry Hallam's *The Constitutional History of England from the Accession of Henry VII to the Death of George II* is published by Murray.

From late this month until early September Turner stays with Nash at East Cowes Castle (built by Nash himself in 1798–1802). He displays two paintings of the second Cowes Regatta at the Royal Academy in 1828. In October and again in December he is at Petworth House, the home of his patron George Wyndham, third Earl of Egremont (1751–1837). He first stayed there in 1809 and returns regularly from about 1825. In the late 1820s Turner produces a series of oil paintings which are set into the panelling of the Carved Room at Petworth.

August
8   Death of George Canning (Prime Minister since 12 April). On 31 Frederick Robinson, Viscount Goodrich (1782–1859) takes office as his successor.
12 Death of Blake at 3 Fountain Court. He is buried at Bunhill Fields on 17. Contrasting verdicts on him are passed in *The Literary Gazette* on 18 (an excellent artist and a good man) and *The Literary Chronicle* on 1 September (more eccentric than able): Bentley (1969), pp. 348–53.
15 Balzac becomes a partner in a printing business in Paris. It fails disastrously in 1828.
29 Bulwer marries Rosina Doyle Wheeler (1802–82).

Publication by Urbain Canel in Paris of the anonymous *Armance ou quelques scènes d'un Salon de Paris, en 1827* (three volumes). Stendhal is named as the author in an edition of 1828.

September
11 The Irish actor Harriet Smithson (1800–54) plays Ophelia to Charles Kemble's Hamlet at the Odéon in Paris and Juliet to his Romeo on 15. (She will spend most of her career in France.) Berlioz, who is in the audience for these performances, is overwhelmed both with enthusiasm for Shakespeare and with passion for Smithson. She rejects him in 1829 but marries him in 1833. Their relationship is a source for Berlioz's *Symphonie fantastique*.

The company also performs, later in the season, *Othello, Macbeth, King Lear, Richard III* and *The Merchant of Venice*. Delacroix is at some of these productions but it is not known which. Hemans's 'The Image in Lava' appears anonymously in the *New Monthly Magazine*.

October
2-8   Scott is in Northumberland and Durham, where receptions are being held for Wellington. He also sees Sir Thomas Lawrence.
c.9   Colburn publishes *The Mummy! A Tale of the Twenty-Second Century*, in three volumes, by Jane Webb (later Loudon, 1807–58).

Some time between 9 and 13 Wright visits Mary Shelley in Arundel. Wright came back to Europe in June with Robert Dale Owen, who joined her at Nashoba in May.

20   Battle of Navarino. British, Russian and French ships under Admiral Sir Edward Codrington (1770–1851) defeat the Turks and Egyptians off the Peloponnese. The official intention is only to stop the fighting in the Greek War of Independence; the effect is to make Greek independence possible.
24   Lady Morgan's *The O'Briens and the O'Flahertys; A National Tale* is published in four volumes by Colburn, who pays £1,300 for the copyright.
27   In Harrow Wright introduces Mary Shelley to Frances (Fanny) Trollope (1779–1863). On 31 Wright visits Godwin with Mary Shelley, Robert Owen and Robert Dale Owen. Wright, Trollope and three of her children are about to sail (14 November) for America. Shelley has declined, and Trollope accepted, Wright's invitation to join her at Nashoba.
27   Bellini's *Il pirata* is at La Scala, Milan.
30   Scott's *Chronicles of the Canongate* (First Series) is published in two volumes by Cadell (Edinburgh) and Simpkin & Marshall (London). Scott (see 23 February) signs the preface.

Late this month Pushkin's *Eugene Onegin*, chapter 3 is published.
Heine's *Das Buch der Lieder* is published in Hamburg.

November
4   Delacroix shows *The Execution of Marino Faliero* at the Salon in Paris. He adds *The Death of Sardanapalus* in February 1828.

6   Davy resigns, because of ill health, as President of the Royal Society.
Hemans (as 'F.H.') publishes 'Woman on the Field of Battle' and 'Supplement: to the Memory of Lord Charles Murray ...' in *Blackwood's Edinburgh Magazine*. Murray, a Philhellene volunteer, died of disease in Greece on 11 August 1824.
10 Tennyson enters Trinity College, Cambridge. He leaves without taking a degree at the end of February 1831.
24 An adaptation of Mozart's *Die Entführung aus dem Serail* is performed at Covent Garden.
Mary Shelley and her son Percy move to 51 George Street, Portman Square, London.
Publication of the first issue of *The Keepsake* (for 1828).

December
1   D'Orsay marries Harriet Gardiner, daughter of the Earl of Blessington, in Florence.
5   Hugo's *Préface de Cromwell* is published: a manifesto of French Romanticism.
15 Helen Maria Williams dies in Paris and is buried in Père Lachaise cemetery.
15 The Egyptian collections of the Louvre open in Paris.
15 Publication by Cadell (Edinburgh) and Simpkin & Marshall (London) of Scott's *Tales of a Grandfather: Being Stories Taken from Scottish History* (First Series), dated 1828. The Second Series follows on 1 September 1828 ('1829'), the Third on 21 December 1829 ('1830'), and the Fourth – *Being Stories Taken from the History of France* – On 20 December 1830 ('1831'). Scott starts work on an incomplete Fifth Series in 1831.
29 Faraday gives his first Christmas chemistry lectures, particularly aimed at young people, at the Royal Institution. He continues on 1, 3, 5, 8 and 10 January 1828. The first such lectures at the Institution were given by the Professor of Mechanics there, John Millington (1779–1868).
This month Nerval's translation of Goethe's *Faust* is published (dated 1828). Berlioz sets parts of it as *Huit scènes de Faust* (1829). In 1827–8 Berlioz writes his *Waverley* overture.

1828

January

Charles Darwin begins his studies at Christ's College. He passes his degree examinations in January 1831 and remains in Cambridge for several months.

9   Leigh Hunt's *The Companion* runs from today to 23 July.
11 The first two volumes of Hazlitt's *Life of Napoleon Buonaparte* are published by Hunt and Clarke. The third and fourth volumes come out in 1830.
13 Meetings all over Ireland take place as part of O'Connell's campaign for Catholic rights.
22 Wellington becomes Prime Minister until 15 November 1830.
25 Lady Caroline Lamb dies. She and her husband separated in 1825.

Bonington visits London and sees Sir Thomas Lawrence.

In late January Colburn brings out Leigh Hunt's *Lord Byron and some of his Contemporaries*. Amid hostile reviews a second edition soon follows.

February

4   Delacroix's *The Execution of Marino Faliero* goes on show at the British Institute.
13 First performance of *Amy Robsart*, Hugo's adaptation of Scott's *Kenilworth*, at the Odéon in Paris, with costumes by Delacroix.
23 Clare comes to London for the last time, leaving in late March.

Pushkin's *Eugene Onegin* (chapters 4 and 5) is published.

March

14 Newman is inducted as Vicar of the University Church of St Mary in Oxford.

April

9   Scott arrives in London. On the way south he visits (7–8) Kenilworth, Warwick Castle and Stratford-upon-Avon. In London in April–May he sees Murray, Rogers, Coleridge, Baillie, Russell, Wellington, J.W. Croker, Cooper, Sydney Smith,

William Wordsworth, Southey, Godwin, Peel, Lord Sidmouth and many others. He dines with George IV on 11 May and is presented to the young Princess Victoria on 19. He visits Brighton on 20–22 May and Hampton Court, with Rogers, Moore and William and Mary Wordsworth, on 25. He reaches Abbotsford on 2 June.

11   Mary Shelley is in Paris until 26 May. She contracts smallpox but recovers to meet, in May, Lafayette and writers including Constant and Prosper Mérimée (1803–70). (Her reviews of his recent work appear in *The Westminster Review* in January 1829 and October 1830.)

16   Goya dies in Bordeaux, where he settled in September 1824.

27   The Zoological Society of London (founded in 1826) opens its gardens in Regent's Park to members and those they vouch for. In 1831 the collection is joined by the animals of the royal menagerie, until then at the Tower of London.

Carlyle's 'Goethe's Helena' is in *The Foreign Review* for April and his 'Goethe' in the July number.

Publication of Pushkin's *Eugene Onegin*, chapter 6.

May

2   Three works by Bonington are included in the Royal Academy exhibition.

9   Repeal of the Test and Corporation Acts. Catholics can hold public office and attend universities.

12   Birth of Dante Gabriel Rossetti (1828–82). His father Gabriele Rossetti becomes Professor of Italian at King's College, London in 1831.

15   Scott's *Chronicles of the Canongate*, Second Series – *St Valentine's Day; or, the Fair Maid of Perth* – is published in three volumes by Cadell in Edinburgh and Simpkin & Marshall in London. It was written between December 1827 and the end of March 1828.

c. 15   Colburn publishes Bulwer's *Pelham; or the Adventures of a Gentleman* in three volumes. Colburn gives him £500. There is a second edition this year, a third in 1829, and a New York edition in 1829.

Blackwood in Edinburgh and Cadell in London publish Hemans's *Records of Woman: With Other Poems*, which reaches a fourth edition

in October 1830. (For earlier versions of the *Records* see May 1825.) Her 'The Dying Improvisatore' is published in the *New Monthly Magazine* for May. Correspondence begins between Hemans and Baillie, the dedicatee of *Records of Woman*.
Between late May and 23 June Mary Shelley is in Dover, and then until early August in Hastings. Godwin joins her during 25–30 June.

June
21 Wellington leads a meeting to establish King's College, London. Peel is also present. The college, which receives its royal charter on 14 August 1829 and opens on 8 October 1831, is conceived in reaction to the secular and Dissenting base of the University of London but does not restrict student membership to Anglicans.
21 Coleridge, Wordsworth and his daughter Dora tour the Low Countries and the Rhineland, returning to London on 6 August. They visit A.W. Schlegel in Bonn. Meanwhile, Dorothy Wordsworth and Joanna Hutchinson visit the Isle of Man (described in Dorothy Wordsworth's journal).
Wright becomes co-editor, with Robert Dale Owen, of *The Free Enquirer*.
In June–July William Pickering publishes *The Poetical Works of S.T. Coleridge* in three volumes. There is a second edition in May 1829.

August
Early this month Turner goes to France on the way to his second Italian tour. From Paris he travels to Provence and by way of Nice, Genoa, Livorno, Pisa and Florence to Rome, where he has a studio in Charles Eastlake's (1793–1865) house. In December he exhibits *View of Orvieto*, *Regulus* and *The Vision of Medea* at Palazzo Trulli. (Hobhouse sees and dislikes the works, as do many German and Italian artists.) Turner leaves Rome in January 1829, crossing the Alps in heavy snow and reaching London in early February.
7 Mary Shelley goes to live with the Robinson family at Park Cottage, Paddington, until December, as again in April–May 1829.
By 16 Thomas Arnold has become Headmaster of Rugby School.
18 The Franco-Tuscan expedition to study hieroglyphs and antiquities, led by Champollion, arrives in Alexandria. The group is in Egypt until autumn 1829.

20 Rossini's *Le Comte Ory* is at the Opéra in Paris.
This summer Jewsbury and her sister Geraldine (1812–80) visit Hemans at Rhyllon, her house near St Asaph since 1825. Later this year Hemans moves to Wavertree, Liverpool, where she lives until 1831.
Between now and October Schubert works on *Schwanengesang* (published this year).

September
9   Birth of Count Lev Nikolayevich Tolstoy (1828–1910) at Yasnaya Polyana.
c.22 Shaka Zulu (1787–1828), centralizing Zulu king since 1816, is assassinated by his bodyguard and half-brothers.
23 Death in London, from tuberculosis, of Bonington. He travelled from Paris to London early this month. The funeral, attended by Sir Thomas Lawrence, is at St James' Chapel, Pentonville.

October
Arthur Hallam (1811–33) enters Trinity College, Cambridge. By early summer 1829 he and Tennnyson are close friends. They are members of the Cambridge Conversazione Society (founded 1820), known as the Apostles.
20 Poe's 'Dreams' is in *The North American*, Baltimore.
This month Marsh and Capen of Boston publish, anonymously and at the author's expense, Hawthorne's *Fanshawe: A Tale*.
Late this month Browning begins going to lectures at the London University, where he was enrolled on 22 April. He withdraws from the university in May 1829.

November
7   Dorothy Wordsworth sets off for Whitwick in Leicestershire (near Coleorton), where she looks after the house of her nephew, John, until June 1829. She visits Jewsbury at Manchester on the way.
15 Mary Shelley and Trelawny meet for the first time since 1823.
19 Schubert dies in Vienna.
23 Edward Bouverie Pusey (1800–82) is ordained priest, as requisite to his taking up the post of Regius Professor of Hebrew

at the University of Oxford, for which Wellington nominated him earlier in the month.

Dickens becomes a shorthand reporter at Doctors' Commons.

The Keepsake for 1829 is published this month. It includes Coleridge's 'The Garden of Boccaccio' and 'Epigrams' and, as the work of the 'Author of Frankenstein', Mary Shelley's 'The Sisters of Albano' and 'Ferdinando Eboli: a Tale'. There are contributions also by Moore, Hemans, Landon, Scott and Southey.

This autumn Longman publishes Moore's *Odes upon Cash, Corn, Catholics and other Matters, Selected from the Columns of the Times Journal*.

In late November or early December Colburn publishes Bulwer's *The Disowned* in four volumes.

Hood edits *The Gem* for 1829. Contributors include J.H. Reynolds, Scott, Charles Lamb and Clare.

December

24   Mary Shelley moves to 4 Oxford Terrace, London, until April 1829.

Hemans's 'Woman and Fame' is in *The Amulet; or Christian and Literary Remembrancer* for 1829.

Arthur Hallam and Richard Monckton Milnes (1809–85) visit Coleridge this year.

Jewsbury's *Letters to the Young* is published by Hatchard.

The Galignani edition of Wordsworth – a piracy of his 1827 *Poems* – comes out in Paris.

William Taylor's *Historic Survey of German Poetry* is published in three volumes in 1828–30.

Publication of *Konrad Wallenrod*, by Adam Mickiewicz (1798–1855).

1829

January

19   Hugo's *Les Orientales* comes out in Paris.
28   Hanging in Edinburgh of William Burke (1792–1829), who with William Hare (b.1792?) murdered about fifteen people and sold the corpses for medical dissection. (Hare was released having given evidence against Burke and others involved.) Scott watches the execution.

February

3 Publication of Hugo's *Le Dernier jour d'un condamné*.
10 John Constable is elected to the Royal Academy after several unsuccessful earlier attempts. He has been an Associate since 1 November 1819.
11 *Henri III et sa cour*, by Alexandre Dumas (1802–70), opens at the Théâtre-Français. *Catherine of Cleves*, Gower's translation of the play, is published in 1832.

Late this month Jewsbury's *Lays of Leisure Hours* is published by Hatchard in two volumes.

J.S. Mill visits Coleridge at Highgate.

Thackeray matriculates at Trinity College, Cambridge. Here his friendship with Edward FitzGerald (1809–83) begins.

March

4 Andrew Jackson (1767–1845) takes office as President of the United States until 1837.
21 Wellington and George Finch-Hatton, Earl of Winchilsea (1791–1858) duel at Battersea Fields, both firing wide. Winchilsea objects to his opponent's support for Catholic emancipation and failure to restrict King's College to Anglicans.

Balzac's *Le Dernier Chouan; ou, La Bretagne en 1800* (later *Les Chouans*) is published in Paris.

April

Early this month Hookham publishes Peacock's *The Misfortunes of Elphin*, 'By the Author of Headlong Hall', in one volume.

13 The Roman Catholic Relief Act becomes law, bringing further emancipation to Catholics.
21 Mendelssohn begins his first visit to Britain (until late November). He conducts a revised version of his First Symphony in London on 25 May and begins his *Hebrides* overture during a summer tour of Scotland, including, on 8 August, Staffa and Fingal's Cave.

At the end of April or beginning of May Colburn publishes Gore's (anonymous) *Romances of Real Life* in three volumes.

May

4 Turner shows *Ulysses Deriding Polyphemus – Homer's Odyssey* at the Royal Academy.

13 Mary Shelley moves to 33 Somerset Street, Portman Square. She sees Moore on 20 and 22, as quite frequently at this time.
20 Publication in three volumes by Cadell in Edinburgh of Scott's *Anne of Geierstein; or The Maiden of the Mist* (begun in summer 1828, completed late this April.) Simpkin & Marshall bring it out in London on 25.
29 Death of Davy in Geneva. He left England on 29 March 1828. His recently completed *Consolations in Travel, or, The Last Days of a Philosopher* is published by Murray in 1830.
29 Death of the Earl of Blessington in Paris, where the Blessingtons and D'Orsays have lived since late in 1828.

June
1   The first volume of Scott's edition of the 'Waverley' novels or 'Magnum Opus' (1829–33) is published.
6   Tennyson wins the Chancellor's Medal at Cambridge for his 'Timbuctoo'. Thackeray's 'Timbuctoo', a parodic version of an entry for the prize on the same prescribed topic, was in *The Snob* on 29 April.
19 Peel's Metropolitan Police Improvement Act becomes law. The new officers are on the streets from 29 September.
30 Publication by Colburn in three volumes of Bulwer's *Devereux. A Tale*.
Robert Dale Owen moves to New York, where he continues to edit *The Free Enquirer*.
Jewsbury visits the Wordsworths at Rydal Mount.
Carlyle's 'Signs of the Times' is in *The Edinburgh Review* for June.

July
14 Hemans, who visits Scotland this month, meets Scott. She stays at Chiefswood, a cottage in the grounds of Abbotsford. She comes to Abbotsford itself and spends the day with him on 20. She also meets Jeffrey in Edinburgh.
This summer Opie visits Paris. She sees Lafayette and sits to Pierre-Jean David d'Angers (1788–1856). She returns in summer 1830, soon after the July Revolution.

August
3   Opening of Rossini's last opera, *Guillaume Tell*, at the Paris Opéra. He has lived mainly in Paris since 1824.

Turner returns to Normandy and visits Guernsey.
At the end of the month Wordsworth sets off for several weeks' extensive tour of Ireland.

September
3   Marriage at Crosthwaite, near Keswick, of Sara Coleridge and her cousin Henry Nelson Coleridge (1798–1843), future editors of the works of her father, S.T. Coleridge.
21   Death of William Turner (1745–1829), Turner's father, helper and close companion.

Poe's 'Fairy-Land' is published in *The American Monthly Magazine*.
Stendhal's *Promenades dans Rome* is published in Paris by Delaunay.

October
4   Publication in Paris of Musset's version of De Quincey, *L'Anglais mangeur d'opium*.
5   London debut of Fanny Kemble (1809–93), niece of Siddons and John Philip Kemble, as Juliet.
6–14   Robert Stephenson's (1803–59) *Rocket* wins in steam locomotive trials at Rainhill for the Liverpool and Manchester Railway (see 15 September 1830).
7 or 8 Mary Shelley is with Moore while he sits to Sir Thomas Lawrence.
24   *Le More de Venise*, Vigny's adaptation of *Othello*, opens at the Théâtre-Français.

Publication by Longman of Landon's *The Venetian Bracelet, The Lost Pleiad, A History of the Lyre, and Other Poems*.
Jeffrey's favourable review of the second editions of Hemans's *Records of Woman* and *The Forest Sanctuary* appears in *The Edinburgh Review* for October.

November
11   Mary Shelley's 'The False Rhyme' is in *The Athenaeum*. The story is published also, this month, in *The Keepsake* for 1830, as are 'The Mourner' and 'The Evil Eye'. The 'Author of Frankenstein' is credited. 'The False Rhyme' is further reprinted in May 1830 in *The Casket, Flowers of Literature, Wit & Sentiment* and in *The Polar Star of Entertainment and General Science, and Universal Repertorium of General Literature* (1830).

December

c. 15   Publication by Galignani in Paris of *The Poetical Works of Coleridge, Shelley, and Keats*, edited by Cyrus Redding.

23   Poe's *Al Aaraaf, Tamerlane and Minor Poems* is published in Baltimore by Hatch and Dunning. An extract appeared in *The Baltimore Gazette and Daily Advertiser* on 18 May.

Hurst, Chance publish Coleridge's *On the Constitution of the Church and State* (dated 1830). There is a second edition probably in April 1830.

James Mill's *Analysis of the Phenomena of the Human Mind* is published in two volumes by Baldwin and Cradock.

1830

January

7   Death of Sir Thomas Lawrence. Turner's painting of Lawrence's funeral in St Paul's on 21 is in this year's Royal Academy exhibition.

9   Publication of Musset's first volume of poems *Contes d'Espagne et d'Italie*.

18   Publication by Murray of the first volume of Moore's *Letters and Journals of Lord Byron*; the second volume follows in late November or early December.

'The Diver', by Hemans, is in the *New Monthly Magazine*. This year it is reprinted among the 'Miscellaneous Poems' in her *Songs of the Affections, with Other Poems* (Edinburgh: Blackwood and London: Cadell).

Colburn and Bentley bring out Galt's *Lawrie Todd; or the Settlers in the Woods* (three volumes). They publish his second three-volume novel with a North American setting, *Bogle Corbet*, in 1831.

February

4   O'Connell takes his seat at Westminster as MP for County Clare.

25   Opening night of Hugo's *Hernani, ou l'Honneur castellan* at the Théâtre-Français. It runs for 39 performances, amid clashes between traditionalists and Hugo's supporters, who include Nerval and Gautier. Gower's English translation of *Hernani* appears this year.

March

4 Godwin's *Cloudesley: a Tale* is published in three volumes by Colburn and Bentley as the work of 'the author of Caleb Williams'.
11 Bellini's *I Capuleti e i Montecchi* is at La Fenice, Venice.
17 Chopin performs his Piano Concerto in F Minor at a large public concert in Warsaw. He gives his E Minor concerto on 11 October, before leaving for Vienna on 1 November.
25 Mary Shelley hosts a social gathering where the guests include Godwin, Moore, Bulwer, Irving and J.W. Croker. The first three are among the guests at another party on 7 June.

April

30 Publication by Colburn and Bentley of Bulwer's *Paul Clifford* (three volumes).

Westley & Davis publish Jewsbury's *The Three Histories*.

May

3 The Royal Academy Exhibition includes Sir Thomas Lawrence's portrait of Moore and Delacroix's *The Murder of the Bishop of Liège*, which is shown also at the Salon from 14 April 1831.
13 Mary Shelley's *The Fortunes of Perkin Warbeck, A Romance*, is published in three volumes by Colburn and Bentley, who bought the copyright for £150 in January.
28 Disraeli sets off from London on his Grand Tour. He arrives in Gibraltar in mid-June, tours Andalucia between 14 July and 8 August, and reaches Malta on 19 August. He is in Corfu in early October and travels in Albania and Greece before going to Constantinople on 10 December. In January 1831 he goes on to Smyrna and Cyprus and visits Jaffa and Jerusalem before landing in Alexandria in March 1831. He is in Egypt until that summer and returns to England, via Malta, in late October 1831.

June

14 France invades Algeria. 'Abd al-Qādir (1808–83), who takes the title Amir in 1832, becomes the most important resistance leader.
16 or 17 Jewsbury meets Mary Shelley.
26 Death of King George IV, succeeded by his brother William IV.

26 Scott meets Fanny Kemble in Edinburgh, where he watched her perform on 16 and 17.

Tennyson's *Poems, Chiefly Lyrical* is published by Effingham Wilson, London.

Murray publishes the first volume of Sir Charles Lyell's (1797–1875) *The Principles of Geology: Being an Attempt to Explain the Former Changes of the Earth's Surface, by reference to causes now in operation*. The second comes out in 1832.

'Swing riots' begin in Kent, becoming more serious between August and November and spreading to other southern and western counties. Protests against conditions of agricultural labour are exacerbated by bad harvests in 1829 and 1830. About 250 people are hanged and about 750 transported.

July

2 Tennyson and Arthur Hallam set off for the Pyrenees via Paris. They liaise with representatives of the dissident Spanish Constitutionalists. In the Pyrenees Tennyson has his first idea of 'Mariana in the South'. Beween 8 and 12 September they sail from Bordeaux to Dublin and then on to Liverpool, arriving in Manchester on 20.

27–29 The July Revolution in France removes Charles X. Attempts to restore the Republic fail and Louis-Philippe becomes King. Delacroix paints *Liberty Leading the People* later in the year and exhibits it at the Salon from 14 April 1831.

28 Publication in Paris of Gautier's *Poésies*.

Mary Shelley spends much of the month in Southend with her son Percy.

In July and August Hemans and three of her children stay at Dove Nest, a cottage near Ambleside. She goes to see the Wordsworths at Rydal Mount and is visited by Jewsbury. In August the Hemans family goes on to Scotland and then to Dublin.

August

5 Mary Shelley comes to stay with the Robinsons again at Park Cottage, Paddington, until 4 November, when she returns to 33 Somerset Street.

September
In early September Galt's *Life of Lord Byron* is published by Colburn. There are four more editions in the next few months.
7   Lady Morgan's *France in 1829–30* is published in two volumes by Saunders and Otley.
11 Poe's 'Sonnet' is in *The United States Saturday Post*. It reappears as 'Sonnet – To Science' in *The Casket* in October.
15 Opening of the Liverpool and Manchester Railway with Wellington as the guest of honour. William Huskisson (1770–1830), MP for Liverpool since 1823 and President of the Board of Trade in 1823–7, dies after being hit by *Rocket*. Wellington stays on his train when angry crowds impede his progress in Manchester.
18 Death of Hazlitt at 6 Frith Street, Soho.

This autumn Pushkin, trapped at Boldino by an outbreak of cholera, largely finishes *Eugene Onegin* and writes other works including *The Little House in Kolomna*, *The Stone Guest* and *Tales of Belkin*.

J.S. Mill and Harriet Taylor (1807–58) meet at the house of the Unitarian minister William Johnson Fox (1786–1864). Harriet Martineau (1802–76) is also present.

October
4   First number of Leigh Hunt's *The Tatler*. The last is on 13 February 1832. He writes almost all of it himself.
4   Belgian independence is proclaimed by the provisional government following the withdrawal of Dutch troops on 27 September. (Belgium and the Netherlands were united as the Low Countries in 1815.) The National Congress elected on 3 November ratifies a new constitution on 7 February 1831 and elects Prince Leopold of Saxe-Coburg-Gotha (until 1826 Saxe-Coburg-Saalfeld) as King Leopold I on 4 June. He is crowned on 21 July.

Carlyle begins work on what becomes *Sartor Resartus*.

November
2   Wellington, in the House of Lords, declares against any kind of parliamentary reform. On 16 he resigns as Prime Minister, to be succeeded on 22 by Charles, Earl Grey (1764–1845).

Publication in Paris, by Levasseur, of Stendhal's *Le Rouge et le noir, Chronique de 1830*, dated 1831. On 25 Stendhal arrives in Trieste having been appointed French consul there, but the Austrian authorities block the appointment. Eventually he becomes consul instead, on 17 April 1831, in Civitavecchia.

Mary Shelley's stories 'Transformation' and 'The Swiss Peasant' and her poems 'Absence', 'A Dirge', and 'A Night Scene' are in *The Keepsake* for 1831. 'Transformation' appears also in *The Spirit of the Annuals* for 1831.

Beginning of the unsuccessful Polish uprising of 1830–1 against Russian rule. Many refugees settle in Paris. In 1831 Campbell founds the Association of Friends of Poland.

Lady Blessington, with the D'Orsays, leaves Paris for London.

December

1–2   Performances, badly received, of Musset's *La Nuit vénitienne* at the Théâtre de l'Odéon in Paris.
5   First performance of Berlioz's *Symphonie fantastique* at the Paris Conservatoire. He meets Liszt.
5   Birth of Christina Rossetti (1830–94) in London.
10   Birth of Emily Dickinson (1830–86) in Amherst, Massachusetts.
c.10 Southey joins William Wordsworth on a visit to Cambridge.
17   Bolívar dies in Santa Marta.
24   Wordsworth (who is in London much of the time until April 1831) visits Coleridge. On 27 he visits Baillie.
26   Donizetti's *Anna Bolena* opens at Teatro Carcano, Milan. The first performance in England is at the King's Theatre on 8 July 1831.

Lucia Elizabeth Vestris (1797–1856) leases, and soon makes a success of, the Olympic Theatre in London. It is licensed mainly for musical entertainments.

Pushkin's *Boris Godunov*, originally completed in 1825, is published, dated 1831.

1831

January

9   J.S. Mill's 'The Spirit of the Age' is in *The Examiner*.
14   Death of Mackenzie in Edinburgh.

17 Charlotte Brontë becomes a pupil at Margaret Wooler's school, Roe Head, Mirfield (until summer 1832). Soon afterwards Emily and Anne Brontë start work on the Gondal saga, separate from their siblings' Glasstown cycle.
30 Lockhart, Murray and Mary Shelley are among guests of the geologist Roderick Impey Murchison (1792–1871) and his wife.
Hazlitt's 'On the Punishment of Death' is in *Fraser's Magazine* for January.

February
12 Jewsbury's 'Literary Sketches No.1. Felicia Hemans' is published anonymously in *The Athenaeum*. The companion piece, her 'Literary Women – No. 2 Jane Austen' follows on 27 August.
At mid-month Peacock's *Crotchet Castle* is published by Hookham. This month Peacock becomes opera critic for *The Examiner*. He held the same position with *The Globe and Traveller* in 1830.

March
1 Russell presents government proposals for electoral reform. In the ensuing debate T.B. Macaulay is among those who speak most notably in favour of reform, and Peel against. The bill passes its second reading on 22 by a single vote but is lost on a Tory 'wrecking amendment' on 19 April. Having convincingly won the general election in May the Grey administration reintroduces the bill on 24 June. It passes in the Commons (second reading 6 July and third 21 September) but is rejected in the Lords on 7 October.
6 First performance of Bellini's *La sonnambula* at Teatro Carcano, Milan. Its English premiere is at the King's Theatre on 28 July.
16 Publication in Paris of Hugo's *Notre-Dame de Paris. 1482*.
27 Poe's *Poems* is published by Elam Bliss in New York.

April
1 Publication of the Colburn and Bentley edition of *Caleb Williams* with Mary Shelley's 'Memoir of William Godwin'.
12 William Wordsworth calls on Haydon. The visit results in 'To B.R. Haydon, on Seeing his Picture of Napoleon Buonaparte on the Island of St. Helena' (completed by 11 June).
Ferrier's *Destiny* is published by Cadell in three volumes.
Late in April Hemans, in failing health, moves to Dublin.

May

2   Public opening of the Royal Academy exhibition. It includes seven oils by Turner.

31–7 June   'Merthyr Rising'. People in Merthyr Tydfil take back property removed by the Court of Requests and are involved in fighting with constables and troops. At least sixteen protesters are killed when soldiers open fire on 3 June.

Heine settles in Paris.

June

3   First British performance by Paganini at the King's Theatre in London. From August he tours in Ireland, Scotland and England, returning to London in March 1832 and then leaving for Paris. (Since 1828 he has toured Austria, Bohemia, Germany, Poland and France.)

8   Siddons dies. She is buried at St Mary's, Paddington, on 15.

25   Landon's 'The Hall of Statues' is in *The Literary Gazette*.

27   William Roscoe dies in Liverpool.

30   Mary Shelley agrees terms with Colburn and Bentley for the publication of her revised edition of *Frankenstein*. She sells them the copyright.

July

7   Cobbett is tried for seditious libel and acquitted. The government regards him as having incited and encouraged the 'Swing riots' (see June 1830).

14   Gore's *The School for Coquettes* opens at the Haymarket and runs for 37 performances.

At mid-month Longman publishes Moore's *The Life and Death of Lord Edward Fitzgerald* in two volumes.

August

13   Poe's 'A Dream' is in *The Saturday Evening Post*, Philadelphia.

29   Faraday discovers electromagnetic induction.

Turner visits Scott at Abbotsford. He is to illustrate Cadell's new edition of the *Poetical Works*. He moves on to Mull, Staffa and Iona.

Arthur Hallam's anonymous review of Tennyson's *Poems, Chiefly Lyrical* is in *The Englishman's Magazine*.
Balzac's *La Peau de chagrin* is published in Paris.
Fanny Trollope returns to England. In early 1828 she was briefly with Wright at Nashoba before living in Cincinnati and, in 1830–1, visiting Washington, DC, Philadelphia, New York and the Niagara Falls.
Charles Darwin is in North Wales with Adam Sedgwick (1785–1873), Woodwardian Professor of Geology at Cambridge since 1818.
Thomas Carlyle comes to London, where Jane Carlyle joins him in October. They return to Scotland in April 1832.

September

8   Coronation of William IV. Among those present in Westminster Abbey are John Constable and Mary Shelley.

10   T.L Beddoes qualifies in medicine at the university of Würzburg. He is expelled from the city in July 1832 because of involvement in radical politics.

19–22   William and Dora Wordsworth visit Scott at Abbotsford. Over the next three weeks they tour in Scotland as far as Mull. The ailing Scott travels to London.

21   The Second Reform Bill is passed by the House of Commons but rejected by the House of Lords on 22.

22   Coleridge is visited by J.S. Mill and James Stephen (1789–1859).

27   Foundation, in York, of the British Association for the Advancement of Science.

28   Scott arrives in London, where he sees friends including J.W. Croker, Moore and Irving.

Chopin settles in Paris.
Field comes to London for medical treatment. He remains until 1832, giving recitals and meeting Moscheles and Mendelssohn.

October

William Wordsworth composes 'Yarrow Revisited'.

1 and 12   Clara Wieck (later Schumann, 1819–96) plays for Goethe in Weimar.

9   Kapodistrias is assassinated in Nauplion by the son and brother of the imprisoned Petros Mavromikhalis (1765–1848), leader of the Maniots.
22 Mary Shelley's introduction to the revised *Frankenstein* first appears in *The Court Journal*, which is owned by Colburn and Bentley. Here she gives the most detailed version of the genesis of the novel in 1816.
23 Scott reaches Portsmouth. He sails on HMS *Barham* on 29, landing in Malta on 28 November (where he sees Frere and, on 1 December, is honoured by the British garrison with a 'Grand Ball') and Naples on 25 December. He visits Pompeii on 9 February 1832, and again on the way to Paestum in March. Sir William Gell (1777–1836) accompanies him to these and other sites. Scott sets off for Rome on 16 April 1832 and is there until 11 May; he then travels via Florence to Venice (19 May), Munich (30), Cologne (8 June), Nijmegen (9) and London (13).
29 Riots in Bristol (witnessed by Crabbe) in response to the arrival of Sir Charles Wetherell (1770–1846), Attorney-General and opponent of Reform (see 1 March). There are also riots in Nottingham and Derby.
31 The revised *Frankenstein* is published by Colburn and Bentley with Mary Shelley's name on the title-page. (The volume also includes the first part of a translation of Schiller's *Der Geisterseher, The Ghost-Seer*.) The edition is reprinted in 1832.

This month Peacock visits Wales.

Cholera reaches north-east England. The disease arrived in Russia in 1830, closing Moscow University and interrupting the studies of Lermontov and Alexander Herzen (1812–70); measures against it cause riots in St Petersburg in summer 1831. It reaches Hamburg in September 1831. Over 32,000 people die of cholera in Britain during 1831–3.

November
14 Georg Wilhelm Friedrich Hegel (1770–1831) dies in Berlin.
21 First performance of Giacomo (Jakob) Meyerbeer's (1791–1864) *Robert le Diable* at the Paris Opéra.

Schumann's *Papillons* is published.
Bulwer becomes editor of *The New Monthly Magazine*.

Mary Shelley's 'The Dream', by the 'Author of Frankenstein', is in *The Keepsake* for 1832, published this month. Her *Proserpine* is in *The Winter's Wreath* for 1832.

December
1nbsp; Cadell in Edinburgh and Whittaker in London publish in four volumes (dated 1832) Scott's *Tales of My Landlord* (Fourth Series) – *Count Robert of Paris* and *Castle Dangerous*.
3   Wordsworth begins revising *The Prelude*, working on it until spring 1832.
10   *La Tour de Nesle*, by Dumas, opens at the Théâtre de la Porte Saint-Martin in Paris.
12   The third Reform Bill is introduced.
20   Gore's *Lords and Commons* opens at Drury Lane.
26   Bellini's *Norma* has its premiere at La Scala, Milan.
27   Samuel Sharpe (d.1832) leads a slave rebellion in Jamaica, savagely suppressed in January 1832. Over five hundred slaves are killed. Sharpe is hanged on 23 May 1832.
27   Charles Darwin sails from Devonport on the *Beagle*, after the ship has twice been forced back into port. The voyage continues until 1836.

Carlyle's 'Characteristics' is in *The Edinburgh Review* for December 1831.
Colburn and Bentley publish Trelawny's *Adventures of a Younger Son*. Late in the month they publish Bulwer's *Eugene Aram* (three volumes), dated 1832.
Dorothy Wordsworth, as a result of illness, breaks off her Journal until October 1832.
Tennyson writes *The Palace of Art* probably between autumn 1831 and spring 1832.

Landon's *Romance and Reality* is published by Colburn and Bentley. Berlioz composes overtures to *King Lear* and Scott's *Rob Roy*.

1832

January
1   Delacroix sets off for Morocco. He is in North Africa until the summer.
13   Barrett's poem 'The Pestilence' is in *The Times* (see October 1831).

14   Poe's 'Metzengerstein' is published in *The Philadelphia Saturday Courier*.
16   Darwin, on *The Beagle*, reaches the Cape Verde Islands. He goes on to Brazil on 28 February, Montevideo on 26 July and Tierra del Fuego on 18 December.

Publication by Murray of the first part of *Finden's Landscape Illustrations* of Byron (1832–3). The engravings are from artists including Turner.

Galt's political satire *The Member: an Autobiography. By the Author of 'The Ayrshire Legatees, etc. etc.'* is published by James Fraser. Galt's *The Radical* follows in May.

Pushkin's *Eugene Onegin*, chapter 8 is published.

In the early part of the year Dickens starts work for *The Mirror of Parliament*. He reports parliamentary proceedings also for *The True Sun* (first number 5 March).

Early this year Leigh Hunt circulates his privately printed *Christianism; or, Belief and Unbelief Reconciled*.

February

3   Crabbe dies at Trowbridge. He is buried there at St James's Church.
13   The Sultan recognizes the independence of Greece.
22   Leigh Hunt's first visit to the Carlyles.
26   Chopin plays at the Salle Pleyel in Paris for the first time. Liszt is in the audience.

Disraeli's *Contarini Fleming; a Psychological Autobiography* (four volumes) is published by Murray.

Publication of the first part of Martineau's *Illustrations of Political Economy* (1832–4).

March

3   Poe's 'The Duke de L'Omelette' is in *The Philadelphia Saturday Courier*.
19   Publication by Whittaker & Treacher, in two volumes, of Fanny Trollope's *The Domestic Manners of the Americans*.
22   Death of Goethe in Weimar. Carlyle's 'Death of Goethe' is in *The New Monthly Magazine* for June, followed by 'Goethe's Works' in *The Foreign Quarterly Review* for August. *Faust: Der*

Tragödie. Zweiter Teil (*Faust* Part Two) is published posthumously this year as volume 41 of Goethe's *Werke* (Stuttgart and Tübingen: Cotta, 1827-42). Part of the work, *Helena. Klassisch-romantische Phantasmagorie*, first appeared separately in 1827.
30 Godwin, Mary Shelley and Gabriele Rossetti are together at a gathering.

April
13 The third Reform Bill is passed in the Lords but put in jeopardy by a 'wrecking amendment' on 7 May. Following the temporary (9-15 May) resignation of Grey, the King threatens to create enough Whig peers to carry the bill and most Tories withdraw their opposition to it.
27 Work begins on Birmingham Town Hall, a neoclassical concert hall.
Publication by Blackwell in Edinburgh of De Quincey's novel *Klosterheim, or, the Masque*.
Between April and June Mendelssohn pays his second visit to Britain. The first performance of his *Hebrides* overture is given by the Philharmonic Society in London on 14 May.

May
7 Turner's *Staffa. Fingal's Cave* and *Childe Harold's Pilgrimage - Italy* are among his six exhibits at the Royal Academy. On Varnishing Day he adds a red buoy to his seascape *Helvoetsluys*, apparently upstaging John Constable's more colourful *Opening of Waterloo Bridge*.
12 First performance of Donizetti's *L'elisir d'amore* at the Teatro Cannobiana, Milan.
18 Publication of George Sand's *Indiana*, her first novel as sole author.
18 First British performance of Beethoven's *Fidelio* at the King's Theatre in London. Browning sees it there some time between now and late June.
21 Irving arrives in New York after seventeen years' absence in Europe. His *Tales of the Alhambra: a series of Tales and Sketches of the Moors and Spaniards* is published this month, as the work of 'the Author of the Sketch Book', by Colburn in London and by Carey and Lea in Philadelphia.

24 A select committee of the House of Commons is set up to consider the possibility of effecting 'the extinction of slavery throughout the British Dominions'. Members of the committee include Peel and Russell. Proceedings close on 11 August. Its report influences the Abolition Act of 1833.
In about May Tennyson completes the first version of 'The Lady of Shalott'.

June
4   The third Reform Bill is passed, becoming law on 7.
6   Bentham dies at Queen Square Place. His body is preserved, in accordance with his will, as an 'auto-icon'.
9   Poe's 'A Tale of Jerusalem' appears in *The Philadelphia Saturday Courier*.
15 Mary Shelley goes to Sandgate in Kent until late September. Trelawny comes to Sandgate for most of August. Percy Florence Shelley starts at Harrow School on 29 September.
31 Arthur Hallam and Tennyson set off from London on a tour of the Rhineland, including Cologne and Bonn. They return to England early in August.
Landor, who visits England this summer, sees Wordsworth and then Southey.

July
Early this month Jameson's *Characteristics of Women, Moral, Poetical and Historical* is published by Saunders and Otley.
4   Act to establish Durham University receives the Royal Assent.
11 Great Reform Banquet at the Guildhall in London. Reformers present include Grey, Burdett and Thelwall.
11 Lamartine sails from Marseille for Greece and the Middle East.
Publication of Longfellow's collection *Saggi de' Novellieri Italiani d'ogni secolo*. His *Elements of French Grammar* (1830) is followed by several essays on European literature in 1831–2.
Lady Blessington's *Journal of Conversations with Lord Byron* is serialized in *The New Monthly Magazine* between now and December 1833.

August
1   Jewsbury marries Rev. William Kew Fletcher. (The ceremony is performed by Hemans's brother.) On 19 September they sail for

India, where she will die of cholera in 1833. Her 'Extracts from a Lady's Log-Book' are in *The Athenaeum* on 1 and 22 December and 'The Outward-Bound Ship', the first poem of *The Oceanides*, on 29.
3 Henry Hunt presents to the House of Commons, on behalf of Mary Smith, an unsuccesful petition for the franchise to be extended to women without husbands and who fulfil the same property qualifications as men. Under the 1832 legislation, as not explicitly before, all women are banned from voting.
Turner is in Paris, gathering material connected with Scott's Life of Napoleon. He meets Delacroix.

September
8 William Godwin, Jr. (1803–32), dies in the cholera outbreak.
21 Death of Scott at Abbotsford, where he returned on 11 July. He is buried at Dryburgh Abbey on 26.
29 Landor visits Coleridge with H.C. Robinson.

October
8 Mary Shelley returns to Somerset Street. She is working on *Lodore* (1835).
11 Death of Hardy. His *Memoir of Thomas Hardy* is published soon afterwards. Thelwall speaks at the funeral.
22 Browning sees Kean as Richard III at the King's Theatre, Richmond. He may begin *Pauline* soon afterwards.
Publication of Gautier's *Albertus*.

November
10 Poe's 'A Decided Loss' (a version of 'Loss of Breath') is in *The Philadelphia Saturday Courier*.
10 Medwin publishes P.B. Shelley's review of *Frankenstein* in *The Athenaeum*.
22 Hugo's *Le Roi s'amuse* is performed at the Comédie Française. Its banning after one night is among the signs that the new government is less liberal than was at first supposed by many supporters of the 1830 revolution.
26 Macready plays Iago to Kean's Othello at Drury Lane.
The Keepsake for 1833 includes Mary Shelley's 'Stanzas' beginning 'I must forget thy dark eyes' love-fraught gaze' and 'To love in solitude

and mystery', and her stories (as the 'Author of Frankenstein') 'The Brother and Sister: an Italian Story' and 'The Invisible Girl'.

Landon's 'On the Ancient and Modern Influence of Poetry' appears anonymously in *The New Monthly Magazine*. (For the authorship of this essay see Landon [1997], p. 277 n.48.)

December

1   Poe's 'The Bargain Lost' appears in *The Philadelphia Saturday Courier*.
5   Publication by Moxon of Tennyson's *Poems*, dated 1833.
22 Emerson resigns from the Second Church, Boston, where he has been pastor since 1829. He sails for England on 25.
24 Moscheles conducts the first English performance of Beethoven's *Missa Solemnis* at the house of Thomas Alsager at 26 Queen Square, London.
25 Turner spends Christmas at Petworth.

Late in the year, after financial difficulties and delays, part of Babbage's Difference Engine no.1 is assembled.

John Genest's (1764–1839) *Some Account of the English Stage: from the Restoration in 1660 to 1830* is published in ten volumes in Bath this year by H.E. Carrington.

Publication of *Fifty-Three Stations of the Tokaido*: landscape prints by Utagawa Hiroshige (1797–1858).

Briefe eines Verstorbenen by Hermann, Fürst von Pückler-Muskau (1785–1871), published in Munich and Stuttgart in 1830–2, is translated by Sarah Austin (1793–1867) and published by Effingham Wilson as *Tour in England, Ireland, and France, in the Years 1828 and 1829* and *Tour in Germany, Holland and England in the Years 1826, 1827, and 1828*.

Ingres paints *Portrait of M. Bertin*.

Sources

There is a wealth of important information in such reference works as *Oxford Dictionary of National Biography: from the Earliest Times to the Year 2000*, ed. H.G.C. Matthew and Brian Harrison (Oxford: Oxford University Press, 2004), *The New Grove Dictionary of Music and Musicians*, ed. Stanley Sadie (London: Macmillan, 1980) and *The London Stage, 1660–1800*, ed. William Van Lennep (Carbondale: Southern Illinois University Press, 1960). Among the other works I have consulted I have found the following especially useful:

Austen, Jane (2014), *Jane Austen's Letters*, ed. Deirdre Le Faye, fourth edition (Oxford: Oxford University Press).

Bate, Jonathan (2004), *John Clare: a Biography* (London: Picador).

Bentley, G.E., Jr (1969), *Blake Records* (Oxford: Clarendon Press).

Bentley, G.E., Jr (1988), *Blake Records Supplement* (Oxford: Clarendon Press).

Bieri, James (2008), *Percy Bysshe Shelley: a Biography* (Baltimore: Johns Hopkins University Press).

Brown, Susan, Patricia Clements and Isobel Grundy (2006), *Orlando: Women's Writing in the British Isles from the Beginnings to the Present*. Cambridge: Cambridge University Press Online, http://orlando.cambridge.org

Burns, Robert (1968), *The Poems and Songs of Robert Burns*, ed. James Kinsley, 3 vols (Oxford: Clarendon Press).

Burns, Robert (2014–), *The Oxford Edition of the Works of Robert Burns*, ed. Nigel Leask, 1 vol. so far (Oxford: Oxford University Press).

Burwick, Frederick, Nancy Moore Goslee and Diane Long Hoeveler (2012) eds, *The Encyclopedia of Romantic Literature* (Chichester: Wiley-Blackwell).

George Gordon Byron, Lord Byron (1973–82), *Byron's Letters and Journals*, ed. Leslie A. Marchand, 12 vols (London: John Murray).

Coleridge, Samuel Taylor (1969–2002) *The Collected Works*, ed. Kathleen Coburn and Bart Winer, 16 vols (Princeton: Princeton University Press).

Coleridge, Samuel Taylor (2007), *Faustus from the German of Goethe*, ed. Frederick Burwick and James McKusich (Oxford: Clarendon Press).

Farington, Joseph (1978–82), *The Diary of Joseph Farington*, ed. Kenneth Garlick and Angus Macintyre, 10 vols (New Haven: Yale University Press).

Garrett, Martin (2002), *A Mary Shelley Chronology* (Basingstoke and New York: Palgrave Macmillan).

Garside, P.D., J.E. Belanger and S.A. Ragaz, *British Fiction 1800–1829: A Database of Production, Circulation & Reception*, designer A.A. Mandal<http.//www.british-fiction.cf.ac.uk>[date accessed 20.8.15].

Godwin, William (2010), *The Diary of William Godwin*, ed. Victoria Myers, David O'Shaughnessy, and Mark Philp (Oxford: Digital Library), http://godwindiary.bodleian.ox.ac.uk.

Hemans, Felicia (2000), *Selected Poems, Letters, Reception Materials*, ed. Susan J. Wolfson (Princeton: Princeton University Press).
Johnson, Edgar (1970), *Sir Walter Scott: the Great Unknown* (London: Hamilton).
Jones, Stanley (1989), *Hazlitt: a Life. From Winterslow to Frith Street* (Oxford: Clarendon Press).
Knight, David M., *Humphry Davy: Science and Power* (Oxford: Blackwell, 1992).
Landon, Letitia Elizabeth (1997), *Selected Writings*, ed. Jerome J. McGann and Daniel Riess (Peterborough, Ontario: Broadview Press).
Le Faye, Deirdre (2006), *A Chronology of Jane Austen and her Family* (Cambridge: Cambridge University Press).
Moore, Thomas (1983–91), *The Journal of Thomas Moore*, ed. Wilfred S. Dowden, 6 vols (Newark: University of Delaware Press).
Moorman, Mary (1965) *William Wordsworth, a Biography: The Later Years, 1803–1850* (Oxford: Oxford University Press).
Murray, John (2007), *The Letters of John Murray to Lord Byron*, ed. Andrew Nicholson (Liverpool: Liverpool University Press).
Peacock, Thomas Love (2001), *The Letters of Thomas Love Peacock*, ed. Nicholas A. Joukovsky (Oxford: Clarendon Press).
Polidori, John William (1911), *The Diary of John William Polidori 1816 Relating to Byron, Shelley, etc.*, ed. William Michael Rossetti (London: Elkin Mathews).
Poplawski, Paul (1998), *A Jane Austen Encyclopedia* (London: Aldwych Press).
Purton, Valerie (1993), *A Coleridge Chronology* (Basingstoke: Macmillan).
Reed, Mark L. (1967), *Wordsworth: the Chronology of the Early Years, 1770–1799* (Cambridge, MA: Harvard University Press).
Reed, Mark L. (1975), *Wordsworth: the Chronology of the Middle Years, 1800–1815* (Cambridge, MA: Harvard University Press).
Robinson, Henry Crabb (1938), *Henry Crabb Robinson on Books and their Writers*, ed. Edith J. Morley, 3 vols (London: Dent).
Roe, Nicholas (2012), *John Keats: a New Life* (New Haven: Yale University Press).
Royal Academy of Arts Collections, http.//www.racollection.org.uk.
Scott, Walter (2013), *The Walter Scott Digital Archive*, http//www.walterscott.lib.ed.ac.uk.
Shelley, Mary Wollstonecraft (1987), *The Journals of Mary Shelley 1814–1844*, ed. Paula R. Feldman and Diana Scott-Kilvert, 2 vols (Oxford: Clarendon Press).
Shelley, Mary Wollstonecraft (1980–8), *The Letters of Mary Wollstonecraft Shelley*, ed. Betty T. Bennett, 3 vols (Baltimore: Johns Hopkins University Press).
Shelley, Percy Bysshe (1839), *The Poetical Works of Percy Bysshe Shelley*, ed. Mary Wollstonecraft Shelley, 4 vols (London: Edward Moxon).
Shelley, Percy Bysshe (1964), *The Letters of Percy Bysshe Shelley*, ed. Frederick L. Jones (Oxford: Clarendon Press).

Smith, Charlotte (2005–7), *The Works of Charlotte Smith*, ed. Stuart Curran and others (London: Pickering and Chatto).
Uglow, Jenny (2002), *The Lunar Men: the Friends Who Made the Future, 1730–1810* (London: Faber).
Wollstonecraft, Mary (1989), *The Works of Mary Wollstonecraft*, ed. Janet Todd, Marilyn Butler and Emma Rees-Mogg, 7 vols (London: Pickering).
Wordsworth, Dorothy (2002), *The Grasmere and Alfoxden Journals*, ed. Pamela Woof (Oxford: Oxford University Press).
Wordsworth, William (1975–2007), *The Cornell Wordsworth*, ed. Stephen Parrish and Mark L. Reed, 18 vols (Ithaca, NY: Cornell University Press).

Author/Name Index

Notes:
bold = extended discussion or rite of passage;
fp = first performed;
'London' = present-day (2015) Greater London.

A Lady (Austen) 128
'Abd al-Qādir (Algeria) 240
Abernethy, J. 152
Adams, J. 66
Adams, J.Q. 215, **216**
Aders, E. 223
Aeschylus 45
Agricola (pen-name) 30
Aikin, Lucy 122, 216
Alexander I 86, 124, 148, 149, **220**
Alfieri, V. 15, 180
Ali Pasha (Albania) 119, **198**
Allans, the 149
Allman, T. and J. (publisher) 188
Alsager, T. 253
Andersen, H.C. **102**
Andrews, J. (publisher) 213, 227
Androutsos, O. 208
Angelo, H. Sr 56, 104
Angelo, H. Jr 56
Anning, M. 209
Anonymous 9, 21–2, 25, 30–2, 35–6, 41–2, 56, 59, 63, 68, 72, 74–6, 79, 84, 93, 102, 108, 110, 114, 116–17, 130, 136, 140–1, 150, 154, 159, 163, 166, 168–9, 178, 184, 188, 190–1, 195, 197–8, 204–6, 215, 222, 224, 226–9, 234, 236, 246, 253
Aphrodite 186
Arch, J. and A. (publisher) 73
Armour, J. 15, 22, 25, 28
Arnim, A. von 103
Arnold, M. 203

Arnold, T. 172, 175, 203, 233
Arrowsmith and Schroth (art dealers) 193
Atholl, Duke and Duchess of 26
Austen, Cassandra (mother of Jane) 69, 78, 118, 100–1
Austen, Cassandra Elizabeth (sister) 13, 19, 69, 100–1, 118
Austen, Edward 78, 114, 118
Austen, Eliza (wife of Henry) 50, 114, **136**
Austen, Rev G. 69, 87, **100**, 118
Austen, Henry 50, 114, 136, 149–51, 168
Austen, James (later Austen-Leigh) 158
Austen, Jane vi, 13, 19, 27, 35, 40, 46, 49–50, 60–1, 64–5, **69**, 70, 76, 99, **100–1**, 102, 105–6, 108, 114–15, 118, 125–6, 136, 146, 149, **150–1**, 155, 159, 168, 244, 254–5
  illness and death (1817) 160, 162, **163**
  rejects marriage proposal (1802) 93
Austin, Sarah 253
Ay (tomb discovered, 1816) 165

Babbage, C. 185, 200, 253
Bach, J.C. **8**
Bage, R. 65
Bailey, B. 164, 166
Baillie, J. 17, 75, 82, 100, 106, 113–14, 121, 131, 147, 185, 190, 192, 231, 233, 243

Author/Name Index

Baldwin, E. (Godwin pen-name) 104
Baldwin and Cradock (publisher) 239
Baldwin, Cradock and Joy (publisher) 120, 151, 160, 168, 174, 187, 199, 216
Ball, Sir Alexander 99, 100, 119
Ballantyne, James (publisher) 14, 101, 119, 220
Ballantyne, John (publisher) 119, 122, 127, 135–6, 185, 189, **194**
Balzac, H. de 78, 228, 236, 246
Banks, Sir Joseph 8, 85, **187**
Barbauld, A.L. 7, 34, 37, 70, 74, 81, 122, 124, 129, **216**
Barras, J-N. 58
Barrett, E. vi, **105**, 185, 211, 222, 248
Bate, J. 254
Baudissin, W.H. Graf von 70
Baxter family 132
Beaumarchais, P.A.C. de 10, 17, 151
Beaumont, Lady **226**
Beaumont, Sir George 94–5, 97–8, 106, 108, 147, 191, 212, 224, **225**
Beaupuy, M. de 42
Beckford, W. 4, 8, 9, 12, 17, 22, 24, **63–4**, 79, 82, 84, 202
Beddoes, Dr Thomas (1760–1808) 75, 94, **116**
Beddoes, Thomas Lovell (1803–49) **95**, 179, 192, 203, 208, 218
  qualifies in medicine (1831) 246
Beethoven, L. van 86, 102, 104, 108, 116, 128, 206, 216, **226**, 250, 253
Bell, J. (publisher) 15, 41, 43, 49, 61, 76–7, 84
Bellingham, J. **131**
Bellini, V. **88**, 229, 240, 244, 248
Bello, A. 123
Belsches, W. 58
Belzoni, G. 155, 164, 165, 169, 190–1, 193, **209**
Belzoni, S. 191
Bentham, J. 33, 47, 130, 177, 210, 215, **251**

Bentley, G.E., Jr 219, 220, 228, 254
Berlioz, L.-H. **97**, 228, 230, 243, 248
Bernardin de St Pierre, J.-H. 27
Betty, W. ('Young Roscius') 100
Bew (publisher) 11
Bewick, W. 168
Beyle, H. (Stendhal) **12**
Bidlake, J. 186
Bieri, J. 136, 254
Bigg-Wither, H. 93
Bishop, E. (*née* Wollstonecraft) 15, 27
Bishop, (Sir) Henry Rowley 199, 206
Blachford, M. *see* Tighe, M.
Black, J. 120
Blackwood, W. (publisher) 131, 139, 151, 158, 170, 193–4, 201, 203, 212, 221, 232
Blair, H. 13, 14, 23
Blake, C. 31, 35, 83, 96, 197
Blake, R. **24**
Blake, W. vi, 4, 10, 14, 17, 19, 24, 27, 30–1, 33, 35, 39, 49, 55, 60, 63, 65, 82–3, 95–6, 99–100, 103, 112, 118, 124–6, 169, 172, 182, 192, 197, 204, 212, 216, 220, 225, 254
  death (1827) 228
  grant from Royal Academy (1822) 201
Blamire, R. (publisher) 11, 45
Blanchard, J.-P. 18
Blaquiere, E. 205, 206
Blessington: Charles Gardiner, Earl of 205–6, 230, **237**
  marries Margaret Power (1818) 169
Blessington: Marguerite (*née* Margaret Power), Countess of **32**, **169**, 193, 196, 198, 205–7, 237, 243, 251
Bligh, W. 31
Blood, F. 15, **20**
Bloomfield, R. 81, 89, 105, 118, 127, 200, **208**

Blücher, Prince G.L. von   147, 148, 149
Bohte, J.H.   195
Boileau, D.   60, 195
Bolívar, S.   123, 180, 218, **243**
Bombet, L.A. (Stendhal pen-name)   145
Bonaparte, J. (*née* de Beauharnais)   61, 120
Bonaparte/Buonaparte, N.   vi, 47, 58, 62, 65, 67–8, 73–4, 83, 85, 87, 93, 96, 104, 107–8, 110, 115, **193**, 227, 244, 252
  abdication (1814)   141
  arrives safely in Paris, 1812 (army in retreat from Moscow)   135
  becomes Emperor (1804)   99, 100, 102
  Consul for Life (1802)   91
  excommunication (1809)   118
  exiled to Elba (1814–15)   vi, 141
  final defeat and second abdication (1815)   148
  First Consul (1801–4)   80, 99, 102
  'Hundred Days' (1815)   146, 149
  marriage (1796)   61
  marriage (1810)   120
  overthrows Directory (1799)   80
  safe return to Paris, 1799 (army remains in Egypt)   79
  surrender to captain of HMS *Bellerophon* (1815)   148
  transfer of art from Italy to Louvre   90
  travelling carriage (exhibited, 1816)   151
  see also Napoleonic Wars
Bonington, R.P.   **92**, 177, 195, 206, 214, 217, 222, 226–7, 231–2, **234**
Bonneville, N. de   8
Boosey (publisher)   195
Booth, J.B.   186
Borghese, P.   100
Boscawen, F.   13
Boswell, J.   8, 16, 22, 28, 38, 57

Boucher, C.   10
Boulland (publisher)   212
Boulton, M. (1728–1809)   6, 33, 61, **119**, 180
Boulton, M.R. (1770–1842)   61
Bowles, Rev. W.L.   30, 68, 74, 108, 131, 132, 146, 192
Bowring, (Sir) John   205, 210, 211
Boydell, J.   23, 34
Braham, J.   105, 213, 221, 223
Brandenburg-Ansbach, E., *Markgräfin* of   8
Brawne, F.   175, 177, 183, 187
Breme, L. di   157
Brent, C.   139
Brentano, C. von   103
Bridgewater, Duke of   87
'Bristol Milkwoman' (A. Yearsley)   19
Brontë family   186
Brontë, A.   **184**, 223, 244
Brontë, C.   **153**, **214**, 223, 226, 243
Brontë, Elizabeth   **214**
Brontë, Emily Jane   **172**, 214, 223, 244
Brontë, M.   **214**
Brontë, Rev. Patrick   223
Brontë, Patrick *Branwell*   **163**, 223, 226
Brougham, H.   92, 111, 123, 130, 156, 221
Brown, Charles   171, 177, 179
Brown, Charles Brockden   74, 76, **121**
Brown, J.   100
Brown, L. 'Capability'   **12**
Brown, T., the Younger (Moore pen-name)   170, 206
Browning, R.   **131**, 225, 234, 250, 252
Bruce, M.   122, 123
Brummell, G. 'Beau'   52, 153
Brun, F.   92
Brunel, I.K.   216
Brunel, M.I.   216
Brunton, M.   125, 145, **175**

260 Author/Name Index

Brydone, P.   25
Buckland, W.   204
Buckstone, J.   213
Buisson (publisher)   34
Bulwer, E.G. (later 1st Baron
    Lytton)   95, 186, 198, 226, 232,
    235, 237, 240, 247–8
  marries Rosina Wheeler
    (1827)   228
Bulwer, R.D. (*née* Wheeler)   228
Burckhardt, J.L.   165
Burdett, Sir Francis   205, 217, 251
Bürger, G.A.   62, 64
Burke, E.   8, 24, 28–30, 36–7, 64, 67
  Crabbe's patron (1781–)   6, 13
Burke, W.   235
Burney, C.   15, **141**
Burney, F. *see* D'Arblay, F.
Burns, G.   5, 15
Burns, R.   vi, 5, 7, **12–55** (with
    gaps), 63, 88, 95, 116, 172,
    200, 254
Burr, A.   128
Butler, Lady Eleanor   56
Byrne, N.   **148**
Byron, Catherine Gordon   28,
    99, **127**
Byron, Clara *Allegra*   **159**, 170,
    173, **199**
Byron, fifth Lord   127
Byron, G.G.   vi, **28**, 79, 87, 96–7,
    99, 104, 107, 110, **111–211**,
    222–5, 249, 254–5
  burial (1824)   213
  cricketer (1805)   102
  death (1824)   209, **211**
  journal (1813–14; published
    1830)   139
  loan to Greek provisional
    government (1823)   209
  maiden speech in House of Lords
    (1812)   129
  marriage to A.I. Milbanke
    (1815)   145
  Paris editions (1818, 1822–5,
    1826)   175
  portrait by Phillips (1814)   141
  separation from wife (1816)
    151, 152
  sixth Baron Byron of Rochdale
    (from 1798)   73
  social ostracism (1816)   152
  swims up Grand Canal
    (1818)   172
  unpublished memoirs burnt
    (1824)   212
Byron, J.   **39**
Byron, Lady (*née* Milbanke)   134,
    144–7, 149–50, 164, 212
  marriage to Byron (1815)   145
  separation from husband
    (1816)   151, 152

Cadell (publisher)   6, 21, 22, 28–9,
    33, 46, 193–4, 201, 203, 212,
    221, 227, 229–30, 232, 237,
    245, 248
Cadell & Davies (publisher)   53, 55,
    59, 63, 65–6, 69, 72, 74–5, 77,
    89, 101, 109–10, 116, 133
Calvert, R.   55
Camoens, L. de   171
Campbell, T.   98, 117, 128, 156,
    162, 176, 191, 213, 216, 221,
    225, 243
Canel, U. (publisher)   222, 228
Canning, G.   69, 72, 106, 117, 184,
    201, 218, **228**
Canning, S.   141
Canova, A.   3, 8, 27, 100, 150,
    182, **203**
Caracciolo, F.   78
Capurro, N. (publisher)   227
Carey and Lea (publisher)   219,
    221, 223, 250
Caritat, H. (publisher)   74, 76
Carlyle, T.   60, 120, 143, **212**,
    213, **227**, 232, 237, 242, 246,
    248–9
  marries Jane Welsh (1826)   224
Carlyle, J.B. (*née* Welsh)   **224**,
    246, 249

Author/Name Index 261

Caroline of Brunswick
  Princess (of Wales)   56, 60, 106, 109, 135
  Queen   187–8, 190, 194, **195**
Carpenter, J. (publisher)   87, 106, 114
Carr, J. (publisher)   136
Carrington, H.E. (publisher)   253
Carter, E.   13, 15
Cartwright, Rev. E.   19
Cartwright, J.   3, 137, 193, **214**
Cary, H.F.   164–5, 184, 200, 205
Castle (informer)   158
Castlereagh, Lady   149
Castlereagh: R. Stewart, Viscount   71, 125, **130**, 191, **201**
Castracani, C.   185
Catherine II, the Great   64
Cawley, A.   13
Cawthorn, J. (publisher)   82, 117, 137, 140
Cawthorn and Martin (publisher)   145
Cervantes Saavedra, M. de   141
Chalmers, M.   27
Champollion, J.F.   202, 233
Charles IV (Spain)   83
Charles X (France)   214, 224, **241**
Charlotte, Queen (consort of George III)   11, 22, 28, **174**
Charlotte Augusta, Princess   60, 101, 129, **166**
  marries Prince Leopold of Saxe-Coburg-Saalfeld (1816)   153
Chastenay, V. de   51
Chateaubriand, F.-R. de   46, 66, **86**, 90, 107, 151
  Ambassador of France to UK (1822)   197
  foreign minister (1823–4)   197
Chatterton, T.   11
Chaworth, M.   96
Chénier, A.   52
Cherubini, L.   18, 66, 199
Chopin, F.F.   **121**, 240, 246, 249
Christian, F.   31, 207
Christie, J.   **191–2**
Christie, T. (publisher)   29
Churchill, T.   17
Clairmont, C.   149
Clairmont, J. (later Claire)   141–2, 153, 155, 159, 170, 173, 176, 181, 187–9, 195, 199
Clare, J.   **46**, 145, 184, 192, 195, 200, 212, 226, 231, 235, 254
Clare, M. (*née* Turner)   184
Clarke, C.C.   96, 157
Clarke, Rev. J.   96
Clarkson, T.   22, 25, 107, 122, 204
Cleishbotham, J. (Scott penname)   158, 172, 178
Clementi, M.   91
Clough, A.H.   **175**
Cobbett, W.   84, 122, 157, 162, 188, 203, 245
Cockerell, C.R.   127, 202, 217
Codrington,
  Admiral Sir Edward   229
Colburn, H. (publisher)   34, 66, 107, 139, 153–4, 162, 165, 174, 176, 190, 194, 203, 205, 211, 214–15, 221–4, 226, 229, 231–2, 235–7, 242, 250
Colburn and [R.] Bentley (publisher)   223, 239–40, 244–5, 247–8
Coleridge, B.   77
Coleridge, Hartley   63, 108, 147, 182
Coleridge, Henry Nelson
  marries Sara Coleridge (1829)   238
Coleridge, Rev. J.   **7**
Coleridge, S.T.   vi, 7, 10, 40, 46, **48–110**, 112, **113**, 115–18, 120, 122, 124, 126, 128–9, 131–2, 134–6, **138**, 139, 141, 143–7, **150–4**, 158, 160–1, **164–9**, 171, **174–5**, 177, 180, 184, 194–6, 205, 209–13, 216–17, 220, 223, 225, 231, 233, 235–6, 238–9, 243, 246, 252, 254–5
  breach with Murray (1817)   167
  legacy from Lady Beaumont (1829)   226

Coleridge, S.T. – *continued*
  marries Sara Fricker (1795) 58
  rejects Unitarianism (1805) 101
Coleridge, Sara (*née* Fricker,
  1770–1845) 58, 62–3, 67, 79–80,
  82–3, 86, 92, 96, 110, 225
Coleridge, Sara (1802–52) **93**, 198
  marries H.N. Coleridge (1829) 238
Collier, J.P. 128
Colman, G., the Younger 26, 61, 115
Comberbache, S.T. (Coleridge) 49
Condé family 98
Condorcet: N. de C., marquis de **50**
Constable, A. (publisher) vii, 92,
  100–1, 113, 145–6, 142, 153,
  159, 167, 172, 183, 185, 189–91,
  197, 200, 204, 206, 210, 212–13,
  217–18, 222
  financial failure (1826) 220
Constable, J. vii, 77, 106–7, 126–7,
  161–2, 177, 187, 189, **193**, 214,
  217, **236**, 246, 250
Constant, B. 97, 98, 154, 184, 212,
  223, 232
Cooke, G.F. 88
Cooke, T.P. 207, 223
Cooke, T.S. 213
Cooper, James Fenimore **32**, 94, 112,
  190, 197, 204, 221, **223**, 224, 231
Cooper, Joseph (publisher) 32
Corni, M. 164
Cornwall, B. 183, 191
Cort, H. 12
Cotman, J.S. **9**, 65, 163
Cotta (publisher) 116, 120, 124,
  180, 250
Cottle, J. (publisher) 58–60, 62, 65,
  68, 71, 75, 79
Courtenay, W. 17
Cowley, H. 3, 12, 28, 40
Cowper, W. 9, 11, 19, 29, 38, 43,
  49, 78, 82, 200
Crabbe, G. vi, 3, 4, 6, 9, 13, 14, 44,
  104, 111, 122, 140, 146, 162,
  179, 202, 247, **249**
  deacon (1781), priest (1782) 8

Crayon, G. (Irving pen-name)
  200, 219
Creech, W. (publisher) 22
Croker, J.W. 173, 185, 231,
  240, 246
Croker, T.C. 220
Cromek, R. (publisher) 103, 116
Crosby (publisher) 52, 151
Cruikshank, G. 180, 188, 205
Cruttwell, R. 30, 54
Cumberland, Duke of 197
Cumberland, R. 51, 56, 57
Cummings, Hilliard (publisher) 215
Curran, J.P. 138
Cuvier, G. 139
Czerny, K. 128

d'Arblay, A. **47**, 90
d'Arblay, F. (*née* Burney) 9–10, 15,
  22, **47**, 56, 63, 90, 140, 225
d'Enghien, duc **98**
d'Holbach, P.-H. baron 70
D'Israeli, I. 41, 192, 210
  see also B. Disraeli
d'Orsay, Count Alfred 196, **230**,
  237, 243
d'Orsay, H. (*née* Gardiner) 230,
  237, 243
Dacre, C. 81, 101, **106**, 110,
  184, **219**
  marries Nicholas Byrne (1815) 148
Dalton, J. 96–7, 211
Dante 45, 178, 225
Danton, G. 46, 50
Darby, A. III 5
Darwin, C.R. **117**, 226, 231, 246,
  248–9
Darwin, E. 6, 12, 31, 39, 51, 60,
  69–70, 72, 82, **91**
David, J.-L. 17, 31, 43, 46–8, 60,
  83, 100, **220**
David d'Angers, P.-J. 237
Davies, S.B. 152, 153, 155–6
Davies, T. (publisher) 7
Davis, J.F. 159
Davison, M. 155

Davy, Sir Humphry   75, 79, 83,
    85–6, 89, 101, 103, 108–9, 111,
    114, 136–7, 139, 149–50, 171,
    182, 184, **187**, 189, 225, 230,
    237, 255
  knighted (1812), baronet
    (1818)   131
  marries Jane Apreece (1812)   131
Davy: Jane, Lady (*née* Apreece)   131,
    137, 139, 171, 182, 184
Day, T.   6, 15
De Quincey, T.   19, 93, 95, 99–100,
    110, 112–13, 115, 120, 131,
    144, 172, **196**, 199, 208, **225**,
    238, 250
Delacroix, F.V.E.   177, 206,
    214, 217, 222, 229, 231, 240–1,
    248, 252
Delaunay (publisher)   238
Demosthenes   123
Denon, V.   93, 189
Dent, J.   32
Desdemona   198
Desmoulins, C.   50
Despard, Colonel E.   **94**
Devonshire: G. Cavendish,
    Duchess of   105
Dibdin, C.   5, 18, 33, 63, 95, 113
Dibdin, T.   55, 74, 108, 152
Dickens, C.J.H.   vi, **viii**, **129**, 210,
    226, 235, 249
Dickinson, E.   **243**
Diderot, D.   **16**
Dilly, C. (publisher)   20, 35, 38
Disraeli, B. (*né* D'Israeli)   **100**, 219,
    222, 224, 240, 249
  baptism (1817)   163
  see also I. D'Israeli
Dobrizhoffer, M.   198
Dodsley, J. (publisher)   6, 11, 13, 18
Donizetti, G.   69, 243, 250
Dostoyevsky, F.M.   **196**
Dumas, A.   236
Dumont, É.   93
Duncan, J. (publisher)   222
Dunlop, F.   30

Dupin, A.A. *see* G. Sand

Eastlake, C.   233
Ebers of London (publisher)   154
Eccles, J.   7
Edgeworth, M.   73, 75, 81,
    87–8, 90, 100, 105–6, 115,
    118, 121, 137, 139, 150, 163,
    187, 207, 218
Edgeworth, R.L.   6, 73, 130, 187
Edleston, J.   104, **127**
Effingham Wilson (publisher)   241
Egerton, T. (publisher)   60, 125,
    128, 134, 135, 142
Egremont: G. Wyndham,
    third Earl of   228
Elam Bliss (publisher)   244
Eldon, Lord   161
Elgin: T. Bruce, Earl of   83,
    111, 151–2
Elia (pen-name of Charles
    Lamb)   189, 196, 197–8, 201–2,
    207–9, 216
Eliot, G. (*née* Mary Ann Evans)   **182**
Ellenborough, Lord   130
Ellis, G.   72
Elliston, R.   134
Elmy, S.   14
Emerson, R.W.   **95**, 166, 253
Emmet, R.   55
Equiano, O.   28
Erskine, T.   54
'ESTEESI' (Coleridge pen-name)   67
Ettrick Shepherd (pen-name)   199
Eusebia (pen-name)   42
Evans and Becket (publisher)   41
Eyre, Lord Chief Justice   54
ΕΣΤΗΣΕ ('STC'; Coleridge pen-
    name)   92, 93

Faraday, M.   **39**, 136, 139, 194, 195,
    230, 245
Farington, J.   90, 147, 254
Farley, F.   143
Farquhar, J.   202
Faulder, R. (publisher)   20, 93

264 Author/Name Index

Fawkes, W. 177
Fox, C.J. 8, 12, 14, 28, 30, 79, 90, 93, 106, **107**
  Foreign Secretary (1806) 106
Fox, W.J. 242
Fenwick, E. 56, 102
Ferdinand IV (Naples) 76, 78–9
Ferdinand VII (Spain) 183
Ferrario (publisher) 227
Ferrier, S. 170, 212, 244
Feuillide, E. de (*née* Hancock; later Austen) 50
Feuillide, J.C. de **50**
Field, J. 50, 91, 134, 246
Fielding, C. 214
Finlay, G. 209, 210
Finnerty, P. 125
Fitzgerald, Lord Edward 57, **73**
FitzGerald, E. 236
Fitzherbert, M. 20, 56
Flaubert, G. **196**
Flaxman, A. 27, 129
Flaxman, J. 14, 27, 36, 45, 90, 104, 111, 125, 152, **225**
Fletcher Rev. W.K. **251–2**
Flinders, M. 85
Forsyth, J. 90
Forteguerri, N. 184
Foscolo, U. 156, 162, 170
Franklin, B. 13, 19, 20, 30, **34**
Franz I (Austria) 107, 149
Fraser, J. (publisher) 249
Frederick the Great **22**
Frederick William III (King of Prussia) 149
Frend, W. 42, 46, 56
Frere, J.H. 69, 72, 106, 163, 184, 189, 220, 247
Friedel, A.C. 8
Friedrich, C.D. 55, 87, 116, 123–4, 129, 141, 175
Froude, R.H. 199
Fulton, R. 111
Fuseli, H. (H. Füssli) 9, 23, 27, 29, 34, 44, 63, 78, 86, 90, 111, 131, **217**

Gainsborough, T. 3, 16, **29**
Gale, Curtis and Fenner (publisher) 145
Gale and Fenner (publisher) 158, 161, 167
Galignani (publisher) 175, 215, 222, 235, 239
Galt, J. 119, 121, 139, 193–4, 201, 203, 221, 239, 242, 249
Gamba Ghiselli, Count Pietro 189 194, 199, 207, 213
Gamba Ghiselli, Count Ruggero 189
Garrett, M. 254
Garrick, D. 20, 131
Gaskell, E. (*née* Stevenson) i, **123**
Gautier, P-J-T. **127**, 239, 241, 252
Gell, Sir William 247
Gemmingen, H. von 49
Genest, J. 253
Genlis, S.-F. comtesse de 90
'Gentleman of University of Oxford' (Shelley pen-name) 124
George III 11, 12, 22, 25, 30, 85, 98, **125**, **184**
  coach attacked (1795) 58
George IV **184**, 195, 213, 224, 232, **240**
  coronation (1821) 194
  death of daughter (1817) 166
  marriage to Princess Caroline (1795) 56
  Prince of Wales 3, 14, 20, 30, 52, 56, 60, 83, 125
  Prince Regent (1811–20) **125**, 126, 129, 130, 133, 138, 146–7, 150, 160, 194
  visit to Edinburgh (1822) 202
Géricault, T. **39**, 180, 193, **210**
Gerrald, J. 48, 49
Gibbon, E. 8, 26, 29, **49**, 65, 154
Gifford, W. 20, 69, **101**, 117, 162, 190
Gilchrist, A. 4
Gillman, Dr J. 153, 180, 209
Gilpin, W. **11**, 45
Giraud, N. 123, 126

Author/Name Index 265

Girtin, T. 66, 88, 92, **93**
Gisborne, M. 171, 187
Glencairn: J. Cunningham, Earl of 23
Glirastes (P.B. Shelley pen-name) 168
Godwin, F. 51, 57, **156**
Godwin, M.J. (*née* Vial) **88**, 97, 143, 158, 201, 218
Godwin, M.J. (publisher) 102, 104, 109, 114, 116, **217**
Godwin, M.W. *see* M.W. Shelley
Godwin, W. 40, 44–5, 52–4, 56, 59–61, 63, 68, **69**, 71, 80–2, 84, 102, 133–5, 156, 201, 207, 101, 106, 112–13, 121, 129, 138, 151, 159, 161–2, 165–7, 171, 175–6, 190, 195, 211, 217–18, 229, 232, 233, 240, 244, 254
  marriage to M.J. Clairmont or Vial (1801) 88
  marriage to Wollstonecraft (1797) 66
Godwin, W. Jr 195, **252**
Goethe, J.W. von vi, 21, 23, 29, 34, **36**, 43, 68, 71, 92, 97, 113, 120, 123–4, 143, 180, 212, 217, 227, 230, 246, **249–50**, 254
Goodrich, A.T. (publisher) 190
Goodrich: F. Robinson, Viscount 228
Goodridge, H. 202
Gordon, Duke and Duchess of 26
Gordon, Lord George 3–4
Gordon, Lady Margaret 17
Gore, Lieutenant Charles 213
Gore, C. **213**, 236, 245, 248
Göschen (publisher) 36
Goya y Lucientes, F. de 70, 77, 80, 82, 114, 133, 183, **232**
Gray, M. (nurse of Byron) 79
Green, J. (surgeon) 171, 177
Grenville, Lord 59, 106
Grey: Charles, Earl **242**, 244, 250, 251
Grey de Ruthyn, Lord 97
Grigorios V, Patriarch 192
Grimaldi, J. 108, 134

Grimm, J. 135, 220
Grimm, W. 135, 220
Gros, J-A., baron 177
Grose, F. 37
Guiccioli, Count Alessandro 176, 180, 182, **188**
Guiccioli, Countess Teresa 168, 176, 178, 181, 189, 194, 195, 200–1, 203
  separation from husband (1820) 188
Gustav III **42**

Hakewill, J. 175
Hallam, A. 234, 235, 241, 246, 251
Hallam, H. 172, 205, 228
Hamilton: Emma, Lady 21, 47, 76, 84, **145**
Hamilton, J. (pen-name of J.H. Reynolds) 193
Hamilton, Sir William 4, 21, 47, 76, 84, **94**
Hampden, J. 165
Handel, G.F. 50
Hannibal 131
Hanwell and Parker (publisher) 93
Harding, A.R. 179
Hardy, L. 52
Hardy, T. 41, 44, 51–4, **252**
Hare, W. 235
Harrison, B. 254
Hart, E. (*née* Lyon; later Lady Hamilton, *qv*) 9, 21
Hastings, W. 24, 25, 28
Hatch and Dunning (publisher) 239
Hatchard (publisher) 109, 111, 122, 133, 186, 235–6
Hawkins, Sir John 24
Hawthorne, N. (*né* Hathorne) **99**, 234
Haydn, F.J. 36, 38, 49, 72, 87, **118**, 145
Haydon, B.R. 111, 130, 147, 157, 160, 165, 167–8, 185, 244
Hayley, W. 17, 23, 43, 83, 99

266 Author/Name Index

Hays, M. 7, 21, 29, 42, 44, 54, 59–60, 64, 68–9, 76, 81, 93, 108, 188
Hazlitt, I. (née Bridgwater) **211**, 214
Hazlitt, S. (née Stoddart) **114**, 119, 159, 197, (201)
Hazlitt, W. vi, 53, 70, 73, 90, 95, 97, 99, 102, 109, 113, 117, 119, 125–6, **129**, 130, **134**, 140, 142, 144, 154, 157, **159–60**, 162–5, **168**, 170–1, 174–6, 180, 182, 184–5, 188, 192, 197, 200–2, 206, 212, 214, 222–4, 226, 231, **242**, 244, 255
  divorce (1822) 201
  marriage to Sarah Stoddart (1808–22) 114, 201
  marries Isabella Bridgwater (1824) 211
Heath, C. (publisher) 215
Hegel, G.W.F. **247**
Heine, H. 197, 226, 229, 245
Hemans, A. **133**, 173
Hemans, F.D. (née Browne) vi, **47**, 116, 120, **133**, 154, 163, 166, 171, 178, 183–4, 190, 194, 200, 203, 207, 209, 217–18, 220, 224–6, 229–30, 232–5, 237–8, 241, 244, 251, 255
  separates from husband (1818) 173
Henley, S. 22
Herder, J.G. 17
Hermit of Marlow (P.B. Shelley pen-name) 166
Herschel, C. 6
Herschel, W. 6
Herzen, A. 247
Higginbottom, N. (Coleridge pen-name) 71
Hilliard, Gray (publisher) 220
Hiroshige Utagawa 253
Historicus (Franklin pen-name) 34
Hobhouse, J.C. 104, 114, **117–21**, 123, 127, 137, 142, 145, 147, 152–6, **157**, 161–2, 168, **170**, 179, 183, 202, 205, 212–13, 233
  elected MP (1820) 185

Hodgskin, T. 217
Hoffmann, E.T.A. 158
Hogg, J. 89, 131, 144, 199, 202, 213
Hogg, T.J. 126, 169
Hokusai Katsushika 225
Holcroft, T. 4, 7, 17, 20, 20, 24, 41–2, 44, 49, 54, 56–7, 68, 71, 78, 86, 93, 101, 103, **117**
Hölderlin, F. 70
Holland, Lord and Lady (H. Fox and E.V. Fox) 106, 156
Holman, J. 8
Home, J. 135
Homer 38, 236
Hone, W. 159, 167, 180, 188
Hood, T. 192, 200, 205, 216, 235
Hookham (publisher) 35, 122, 130–1, 141, 150, 160, 169, 174, 199, 212, 236, 244
Hookham, T. (1787–1867) 134, 166
Hookham and Carpenter (publisher) 50, 60
Hookham and Miller (publisher) 38
Hope, T. 80
Hoppner, J. 16, 56, 90, 164, 170
Hoppner, R.B. 164, 166, 170
Horn, C. 127, 171
Horner, F. 92
Hucks, J. 52
Hughes, J.F. (publisher) 101, 106, 115, 121
Hugo, V.-M. **89**, 201, 205, 230–1, 235–6, 239, 244, 252
Humboldt, W. von 105
Hunt, H. 'Orator' 157, 158, 252
Hunt, James Henry Leigh 10, **17**, 101, 112, 121–3, 126, 130, 140, 145, 150–2, 157–9, 161–6, 169, 177, 180–1, 183, 187, 201–2, 208, 217, **215–16**, 223, 231, 242, 249
  marriage to Marianne Kent (1809) 118
Hunt, John (publisher) 112, 123, 130, 168, 203, 205–7, 209–12
  fined (1824) 213

Author/Name Index 267

Hunt, M. (*née* Kent) **118**, 159, 161, 164, 166, 169, 201–2, 208, 216, 219, 223
Hunt & Clarke (publisher) 231
Hunter, R. 163
Hurst, Chance (publisher) 217, 239
Hurst, Robinson (publisher) 178, 183, 191, 200, 204, 206, 210, 212–13, 217–18
    financial failure (1826) 220
Hurwitz, H. 166
Huskisson, W. **242**
Hutchinson family 78
Hutchinson, J. 202, 233
Hutchinson, S. 80, 84, 86, 87–9, 93, 107, 108, 110, 118, 142, 144, 202, 205, 217

Iago vi, 140, 142, 198, 252
Imlay, F. *see* Godwin, F.
Imlay, G. 44, 51, 56, 57
Inwood, W. and H. 179
Inchbald, E. 16, 19, 24, 37, 44, 61, 66, 75–6, 101, 108, **195**
Ingres, J-A. **4**, 60, 90, **107**, 253
Ireland, W.H. 60, 62
Irving, W. 12, 120, 147, 164, 175–6, 178, 185, 190, 200, 213, 219, **221**, 240, 246, 250

Jackson, A. 236
Jackson, J. 'Gentleman' 56, 104
Jackson of Louth (publisher) 226
Jayadéva 40
Jameson, A.B. (*née* Murphy) **52**, 224, 251
'Jean Paul' (Richter pen-name) 227
Jefferson, T. 19, 25, 50, 86, 98, 215, 216, **223**
Jeffrey, F. 92, 104, 107, 111–12, 121, 144, 187, 237–8
Jeffries, J. 18
Jenner, E. 62
Jerdan, W. 224
Jersey, Earl and Countess of 134
Jessop, W. 81, 95, 104
Jewsbury, G. 234

Jewsbury, M.J. **84**, 217, 219, 222, 234–7, 240–1, 244, 251, **252**
Johnson, E. 147, 255
Johnson, James 25, 51
Johnson, Joseph (publisher) 7, 9, 11–13, 17, 19, 23–4, 27, 29–31, 36–41, 44–5, 50–1, 53, 57, 59, 61, 69–71, 73–6, 82, 87–8, 91, 100, 102, 105, 108, 118, **120**, 163
    Joseph Johnson company 129, 133, 139
Johnson, S. vi, 7, 8, 16, **17**, 20
Jones, I. 161
Jones, R. 35, 37, 47
Jones, Sir William 11, 14, 18, 21, 32, 40, 50, **51**
Jonson, B. 101
Jordan, D. 20, 54, 69, 78
Jordan, J.S. 37, 41
Joseph II **5**
Junot, J.-A. 112

Kalvos, A. 211
Kant, I. 8, 14, 30, 76, **98**, 183
Kapodistrias, Count I. 225, **247**
Kauffman, A. **112**
Kean, E. vi, 27, 82, **140**, 142, 144, 146, 151, 153, 167, 174, 182, 186, 190, 252
Kearsley (publisher) 70
Kearsley & Forster (publisher) 9
Keats, George 161, 167, 171, 177
Keats, Georgiana 171, 177
Keats, J. vi, **59**, 96, 123, 145, 149, **153–91**, 193, 205, 239, 255
Keats, T. 161, 167, 169, 171, **174**
Keble, J. 227
Kelly, M. 88
Kemble, C. 178, 191, 228
Kemble, F. 238, 241
Kemble, J.P. 14, 50, 56, 61–2, 69, 78, 82, 109, 119, **162**, 205, 238
Kemble, M.T. 150
Kerr, R. 30, 139
Keymer, W. (publisher) 19
King, M. 201

Kingsborough, Lord and Lady   23
Kinnaird, D.   152
Kleist, H. von   43, 113, 121, 124, **128**, 196
Klopstock, F.   75
Knight & Lacey (publisher)   217
Knight, R.P.   111, 152
Knowles, S.   186
Kosciuszko, T.   150
Kotzebue, A.F.F. von   75, 78

L.E.L. (L.E. Landon)   213
Laberius (Coleridge pen-name)   70
Lackington (publisher)   162, 165
Laclos, P.C. de   9
'Ladies of Llangollen'   56, 218
Lady Macbeth   18, 50, 133
Lafayette: M.-J. du Motier, Marquis de   3, 17, 32, 35, 214, 223, 232, 237
Lamartine, A. de   **36**, 185, 217, 251
Lamb, Lady Caroline (née Ponsonby)   **20**, 130, 134, 137, 142, 153, 162, 182, 203, 205, **231**
  marries W. Lamb (1805)   102
  separation from husband (1825)   231
Lamb, Charles   vi, 10, 42, 60, 62–4, 67–8, 73, 81, 99, 1020, 108–9, 113–16, 126, 128–31, 168–9, 189, 196–7, 198, 200, 202, 207–9, 216, 235
Lamb, Charles and Mary   vi, 53, 92, 94, 97–8, 106–7, 113, 118–19, 122, 129–30, 147, 162, 167, 194, 201, 205, 208, 212, 218, 223
  adopt Emma Isola   210
Lamb, Mary   **63**, 102, 109, 116, 146
Lamb, W. (second Viscount Melbourne)
  marries Lady Caroline Ponsonby (1805)   102
Landon, L.E.   vi, **92**, 185, 204, 213–14, 218, 224–5, 235, 238, 245, 248, 253, 255

Landor, W.S.   74, 90, 113, 142, 211, 215, 251–2
Landseer, John, Thomas and Edwin   168
Lane, W. (publisher)   56, 65
'Laura' (Robinson pen-name)   30
'Laura Maria' (Robinson pen-name)   30
Lavoisier, A.   30
Lawrence, Sir Thomas   34, 40, 111, 137, 152, 182, 185, 191, 193–4, 212, 217, 227, 229, 231, 234, 238, **239**, 240
  knighted (1815)   147
Lawrence, W.   152
Lee, C.   5
Lee, H.   5, 70
Lee, S.   5, 15, 62, 70, 109
Lefroy, T.   61
Leigh, A.   137, 140–1, 143, 146, 149–50, 156
Lemprière, J.   30
Leopardi, G.   215
Leopold I
  King of Belgians (1831–65)   242
  marries Princess Charlotte (1816)   153
  Prince of Saxe-Coburg-Gotha/Saalfeld   181, 242
Leopold II (Holy Roman Emperor)   **42**
Lermontov, M.Y.   **144**, 247
Lessing, G.E.   **6**, 225
Levasseur (publisher)   242
Leveson-Gower: Francis, Lord   210, 236, 239
Lewis, M.G.   15, 34, 43, 51, 61, 69, 72, 77, 87, 89, 94, 103, 110, 116, 126, 151, **155**, 163, **171**
Linnell, J.   172, 192, 212, 225
Liszt, F.   **128**, 213, 227, 243, 249
Little, T. (Moore pen-name)   87
Liverpool: R.B. Jenkinson, Earl of   132, 146, 184, 197
Lloyd, C.   63, 64, 68, 71, 73
Lloyd, M.   106

Lobeira, V. 95
Lockhart, C.S. (*née* Scott) **186**
Lockhart, J.G. 131, 165, 173, 192, 202, 218, 244
 marries Charlotte, daughter of Sir Walter Scott (1820) 186
Longfellow, H.W. **109**, 190, 223, 251
Longman, T.N. (publisher) 68, 77–9, 81, 85–6, 89, 95, 100–3, 106, 109–11, 115–18, 121–2, 124–5, 127, 130, 133–7, 142–6, 148, 150, 152–3, 159, 162, 167, 170, 172–3, 178–9, 185, 187–90, 192–3, 197–9, 204, 206, 211, 213, 216, 219, 222, 225, 227, 235, 238, 245
Lonsdale, Earl of 136
Loudon, J. (*née* Webb) 229
Louis XVI 32, 34–5, 38–9, **45**, 57
Louis XVII 57
Louis XVIII vi, 126, 141, 146, 148
Louis-Philippe 241
Louriotis, A. 206
Loutherbourg, P.J. de 5, 8
Lovelace, Countess of (*née* A.A. Byron) **150**, 151
Lowther family 170
Ludlow, Fraser and Company 81
Lyell, Sir Charles 241

M.B.A.A. (M. Beyle, *ancien auditeur*) 163
Macartney: G., Viscount (later Earl) 47
Macaulay, C. 35
Macaulay, T.B. 191, 219, 244
Macaulay, Z. 204
Mackenzie, H. 18, 23, 121, 189, 202, **243**
Mackintosh, Sir James 37, 70, 137, 143, 169, 205
Macpherson, J. 61
Macready, W.C. **45**, 182, 186, 191, 205, 252
 first appearance in London (1816) 156

Macri family 123
Macri, T. 120
Madison, J. 117
Maginn, W. 199
Mahmud II, Sultan 114, 123, 192, 198, 249
Malone, E. 8, 17, 22, 36, 57, 62
Malthus, Rev. T.R. 73, 109, 190
Manners & Miller (publisher) 64, 125
Mant, R. 93
Manzoni, A. **18**, 208, 227
Maradan (publisher) 82
Marat, J.-P. 37, **46**
Margarot, M. 44, 48, 49
Maria Theresia **5**
Marie-Antoinette 7, 35, **48**
Marie-Louise, Empress 120
Marsh & Capen (publisher) 234
Marshall, J. 39
Martin, J. 49
Martin, S. ('Bath Butcher') 24
Martineau, H. 242, 249
Marx, K.H. **171**
Massinger, P. 101, 151
Mathew, Rev. A.S. 14
Mathew, H. 14
Matthew, H.G.C. 254
Matthews, Charles 194
Matthews, Charles Skinner 117, **127**
Maturin, C.R. **4**, 135, 151, 153, 171, 190, 196, 207, **215**
Mavrokordatos, Prince Alexandros 190, 193, 194
Mavromikhalis, P. 247
Maxwell, J. 26
McLehose, A. 27, 40
Medwin, T. 189, 196, 214, 252
Melbourne: E. Lamb, Viscountess 134, 138
Melville, H. **179**
Mendelssohn Bartholdy, F. **117**, 224, 236, 246, 250
Mendoza, D. 24, 56
Merchant, T. (T. Dibdin) 55
Mérimée, P. 232

Author/Name Index

Merivale, J.H.   183–4
Metastasio, P.   145
Metternich, (Prince) K. von   120, 147
Meyerbeer, G.   247
Mickiewicz, A.   235
Mill, James   168, 177, 191, 221, 239
Mill, John Stuart   177, 207, 215, 224, 236, 242–3, 246
Miller, J. (publisher)   134, 176, 178, 221
Miller, W. (publisher)   26, 113, 122
Millington, J.   230
Milman, H.H.   169
Milnes, R.M. (first Baron Houghton)   235
Milton, J.   18, 72, 100, 128, 138, 141, 200, 219
Mirabaud, J.-B. (pseudonym for P.-H., baron d'Holbach)   70
Mirabeau: H.G. Riqueti, comte de   37
Mitford, M.R.   27, 128, 168, 205, 212
Moncrieff, W.   186
Mongie (publisher)   202
Monroe, J.   49, 160, 215
Montagu, B. (Sr and Jr)   58
Montagu, E.   13, 17, 19, 32
Montgomery, J.   52, 55, 60–1, 203
Monti, V.   143
Moorcroft, W.   133, **178**
Moore, B. (*née* Dyke)   126, 132, 167
Moore, General Sir John   116
Moore, Dr John   26
Moore, T.   55, 77, 82–3, 87–8, 96, **98**, 106, **107**, 114–15, 127–8, 130–2, 136, 139, 142, 154–5, 160, 162, 167–8, 170–3, **181**, 182–4, 188–91, 193, 195, 204–5, 211–3, 215, 219, 224, 227, 232, 235, 237–40, 245–6
  journal   **172**, 255
  marries E. Dyke (1811)   126
  visits Dublin (1821)   196
Moorman, M.   124
More, H.   13, 15, 17, 19, 25, 32, 56, 77, 101, 116
Morgan, J.   124, 136, 138–9, 196
Morgan, Lady (*née* Owenson)   103, 107, 109, 116, 125, **129**, 144–5, 162, 174, 182, 184, 194, 229, 242
Morgan, M.   139
Morgan, Sir Thomas Charles   **129**, 144–5, 162
Moscheles, I.   194, 246, 253
Motte Fouqué, Baron Friedrich de la   193
Mountcashell: Margaret King, Lady ('Mrs Mason')   181
Moxon (publisher)   253
Moxon, Emma (*née* Isola)   210
Mozart, W.A.   5, 10, 21, 27, 29, 33, 39, **40**, 126, 133, 145, 223, 230
  opera (UK fp, 1806)   105
Mrs Mason (pseudonym)   181
Muhammad 'Alī   102
Muir, T.   47, 49
Müller, A.H.   113
Mundell (publisher)   78
Murat, J.   113, 114, 140, **149–50**
Murchison, R.I.   244
Murray, Lord Charles   230
Murray, J. (publisher)   41, 101, 113, 115, 117, 125, 130, 137, 139–41, 143, 145, 147, 150–1, 154, 156–9, 161–3, 165, 167–72, 174–6, 178–9, 183–4, 190, 192, 195–6, 198, 200, 203–5, 207, 210, 212, 217, 219–21, 231, 237, 239, 241, 244, 249, 255
Musset, A. de   **124**, 238, 239, 243

Napoleon I *see* Bonaparte, N.
Napoleon II ('King of Rome')   141
Nash, J.   135, 146, 220, 228
Nathan, Isaac   144, 147
Necker, J.   29
Nelson, Admiral Lord   47, 74, 76, **78–9**, 84, 86, 94, **103–4**
  Baron (1798) and Viscount (1801)   87
  Duke of Brontë (1799)   79
Nerval, G. de (*né* G. Labrunie)   **114**, 230, 239

Newman, J.H. 199, 227, 231
Ney, Marshal 148, **150**
Nicholas I 220
Nichols, J. 4
Nicoll (publisher) 101
Nicolle (publisher) 110
Nodier, C., 193
Noehden, G. 13, 26
North, Lord 8, 12, 14
North, C. *see* John Wilson
Northcote, J. 106, 130
Nourse (publisher) 5
Novalis (G.P.F. von Hardenberg) 73, 227
Novello family 208
Novello, V. 169
Nycias Erythraeus (Coleridge pen-name) 72

O'Connell, D. 171, 195, 206, 231, 239
O'Donovan, P.M. (Peacock pen-name) 141
O'Keeffe, J. 115
O'Sullivan, M. 171
Oliver and Boyd (publisher) 212
Ollier, C. and J. (publisher) 160, 162, 166, 167, 177, 178, 183, 191, 196
Ophelia 228
Opie, A. (*née* Alderson) 36, 52–4, **72**, 86, 90, 93, 101, 106, 110, 130, 137, 147, 150, 152, 172, 186–7, 198, **219**, 237
Opie, J. 72, 90, **110**
  marries A. Alderson (1798) 72
Orléans: Philippe 'Égalité', Duke of **48**
Otway, T. 16
Outram, B. 52
Overreach, Sir Giles (theatrical role) 151
Owen, Robert 81, 135, 164, 215, 224, 229
Owen, Robert Dale 224, 229, 233, 237

Owenson, S.
  marries Sir Thomas Morgan (1812) 129
  see also Lady Morgan
Oxford, Earl of 134
Oxford: Jane Harley, Countess of 134, 135, 136

P.B.S. 122
  see also P.B. Shelley
Paganini, N. 124, 245
Paine, T. 6, 21, 25, 29, 33, 37–8, 40–1, 69, 93, **118**
  arrested in Paris 49
  convicted of seditious libel 45
  elected deputy in French Convention 43
  made French citizen 43
Paisiello, G. 10, 31
Paley, W. 20, 54, 93
Palmer, J. 16, 202
Palmer, S. 212, 219
Palmer, T.F. 47, 49
Papi, V. 199
Park, M. 57, **101**
Parker, J. 10
Parker, J.H. (publisher) 227
Parry, J. 200
Parry, W. 217
Paschoud, J.J. (publisher) 93
Patmore, P.G. 223
Paul, Tsar 64, 86
Paul Positive (pen-name) 61
Paxton, J. 222
Payne, J.H. 136, 174, 201, 206, 218
Payne, T. (publisher) 33, 63
Peacock, T.L. 20, 81, 105, 107, 114, 121–2, 130–1, 134, 137–9, 141, 147, 149–50, 156, 160, 169, 174, 177, 187, 195, 199, 244, 247, 255
Peake, R.B. 207, 209
Pearson of Oxford (publisher) 154
Peel, Sir Robert 197, 225, 232–3, 237, 244, 251
Pellico, S. 143, **189–90**

272 Author/Name Index

Perceval, S. **131**
Percy, T. 8
Phillips, J. (publisher) 22
Phillips, R. (publisher) 85, 93, 101, 103, 107–8, 112
Phillips, T. 103, 141
Pichot, A. 181, 186
Pickering, W. (publisher) 233
Pigot, E. 99
Pigot, J. 99
Pinto, L. dal **190**
Piozzi, G.M. **16**, 58, **117**
Piozzi, H. (previously Thrale; née Salusbury) **16**, 21, 58, 85, **193**
Pitt, W., the Younger 9, 10, 14, 16, 19, 30, 47, 54, 59, 81, **106**, 122
 resignation (1801) 85
 return as PM (1804) 99
Pius VI 77
Pius VII 100, 118, 150, 185, 188–9
Pixérécourt, R.-C.G. de 93
Planché, J.R. 199, 221
Poe, E.A. **116**, 149, 221, 234, 238–9, 244–5, 249, 251–3, **227**, 242
Pole, E.C., marries Erasmus Darwin (1781) 6
Polidori, J.W. 153–4, 156, 176, 179, 255
Ponsonby, S. 56
Poole, T. 53, 62, 66, 94, 110
Pope, A. 11–12, 108, 192
Portland: W.C. Bentinck, Duke of 12, 109
Power, J. (publisher) 113, 170
Power, W. (publisher) 113
Prévost, Abbé A.-F. 21
Price, R. 36
Price, U. 29
Priestley, J. 5, 6, 11, 36, 39, 50, **97**
Pritchard, Hannah 131
Procter, B.W. 183, 184, 191, 208
Prometheus 86, 155, 168, 172, 176, 180, 187, **188**, 217
Pückler-Muskau: Hermann, Fürst von 253
Pusey, E.B. 234–5

Pushkin, A.S. 78, **186**, 197, 207, 214–16, 220, 229, 231–2, 242–3, 249
Pye, H.J. **138**

Qianlong, Emperor 47

Radcliffe, A. 35, 40–1, 51, 55, 65, **204–5**
Radcliffe, W. 51
Raeburn, Sir Henry 202, **207**
Raffles, Sir Thomas *Stamford* 161, **175**
Rameses I 165
Rameses II 164
Randall, A.F. (M. Robinson) 77
'Red Lady of Paviland' 204
Redding, C. 239
Reed, M.L. 131, 255
Reeve, C. 19, 38
Reeves, J. 44
Repton, H. **29**
Rest Fenner (publisher) 164, 167
Retzsch, M. 195
Revett, N. 33–4
Reynolds, J.H. **53**, 123, 145, 150, 157, 159, 167, 170–1, 177, 179, 184, 187, 193, 200, 216, 235
Reynolds, Sir Joshua vii, 3, 8, 13, 15, 16, **41**
Ricardo, D. 168
Richardson, J. 14, 76, 183
Richardson, S. 65
Richardson, W. (publisher) 25
Richardson, W.J. & J. (publisher) 105
Richmond: Charlotte, Duchess of 148
Richter, J.-P. F. 227
Riddell, M. 38
Riddell, R. 38
Ridge, S. and J. (publisher) 108, 111, 113
Rivington (publisher) 7, 74, 91, 101, 124, 203
Robert (Bruce) 51

Author/Name Index

Robespierre, M. 46, **52**, 53
Robinson family 233
Robinson, G.G. and J. (publisher)
    8, 11, 12, 30, 37, 43, 45, 51, 52,
    59, 61, 64, 66, 70–1, 80, 84
Robinson, H.C. 80, 92, 97, 113,
    116, 118, 124, **125**, 125–6,
    128–31, 134–5, 141, 147,
    167–9, 174, 187–8, 205, 223,
    241, 252, 255
Robinson, M. ('Perdita') 3, 7, 30, 41,
    48, 50, 54, 60–1, 64, 77, 79–81,
    83, **84**
Rockingham: C. Watson-Wentworth,
    Marquess of 8, **10**
Roe, N. 175, 181, 255
Rogers, S. 42, 87, 94–5, 106, 113,
    128, 131, 137, 139–40, **143–4**,
    152, 156, 162, 169, 176, 196,
    198, 199, 205, 213, 224–5,
    231–2
Roland, M-J. 48
Romney G. 3, 9, 23, 43, **93**
Rosa Matilda (C. Dacre) 101, **106**
Roscoe, T. 139
Roscoe, W. 65, 129, 139, **245**
Rossetti, C. 243
Rossetti, D.G. 232
Rossetti, G. 213, 232
Rossini, G. **41**, 135–6, 149, 151,
    158–9, 170, 175, 183, 209, 211,
    234, 237
Rousseau, J.-J. 53
Rowley, T. 11
Ruffo, Cardinal 78
Ruskin, J. i, **176**
Russell, Lord John **181**, 190, 195,
    205, **231**, 251
Rutland, Duke of 9

Sade: D.-A-F., marquis de 38, **145**
Saladin, J. 195
Salieri, A. 16, 28, 128, **217**
Sampson Low (publisher) 73
Sancho, C.I. 5
Sand, G. (*née* A.A. Dupin) **99**, 250

Saunders & Otley (publisher)
    242, 251
Schiavonetti, L. 103
Schiller, J.C.F. von 10, 13, 15, 19,
    26, 29, 60, 82–3, 88, 92, 97–8,
    102, 210, 227, 247
Schlegel, A.W. 70, 73, 120,
    155, 233
Schlegel, K.W.F. 73
Schubert, F. 65, 182, 203, 209, 211,
    226, **234**
Schumann, C. (*née* Wieck) 246
Schumann, R. **122**, 247
Scolfield, J. 95
Scott, C. (*née* Charpentier) 69, **222**
Scott, John vii, 130, 184, **191–2**
Scott, Sir John (later Earl of
    Eldon) 54
Scott, Sir Walter vi, vii, **14**, 23, 39,
    43–4, 58, 64–5, 71, 77, 80, 84,
    89, 94, 96, 99–101, 103–4, 106,
    109–10, 113, **117**, 119, 121–3,
    127, 132, 135, 138, 143, 145,
    146–7, **148**, 149, 153, 163–4, 167,
    172, **173**, 176, 178, 181, 183,
    189–91, 193–4, 200, 202, 204,
    206–7, 209, **218**, 223, **224–5**, 227,
    229, **230–2**, 235, 237, 241, 245,
    246–7, 248, 255
  admits authorship of *Waverley*
    novels (1827) 226
  begins Journal (1825) 219
  created baronet (1820) 185
  death (1832) 252
  first novel 142
  marriage to C. Carpenter
    (1797) 69
  personal financial crisis
    (1826) 220
Scott, Walter Jr 132
Sedgwick, A. 246
Segati, M. 157
Sempronia (M. Lamb
    pen-name) 146
Seti I 165, 193
Severn, J. 189, 190

Author/Name Index

Seward, A. 56, 110, **117**
Sgricci, T. 157, 190, 191
Shaka Zulu **234**
Shakespeare, W. 36, 60, 62, 70, 115, 128, 138, 174, 200, 228
Sharp, R. 'Conversation' 97, 139
Sharpe, S. **248**
Sharpe & Hailes (publisher) 139
Shelburne: W. Petty, Earl of 10, 12
Shelley, C. 170, **173**
Shelley, E.A. **175**
Shelley, H. (*née* Westbrook) **127**, 128, 131–3, 136, 138, **158**
Shelley, M.W. (*née* Godwin) vi, **68**, 128, 132–3, 135, 141, 149, 152–6, **159–60**, 161–2, 165–7, **169**, 170–1, 173–6, 180–1, 184–206, **207–8**, 210–11, 213, 218–19, 221, 223–4, 228–30, 233–5, 237–8, 240–1, **243**, 244–8, 251–5
  elopement with P.B. Shelley (1814), **142–3**
  journal 155
  marries P.B. Shelley (1816) **158**
  miscarriage (1822) 201
  smallpox (1828) 232
Shelley, P.B. vi, **43**, 96, 100, **122–208** (with gaps), 225, 239, 244, 252, 254–5
  drowned (1822) **201**
  marries Harriet Westbrook (1811) 127
  marries Mary Godwin (1816) **158**
  notebook 156
  refused (1817) custody of children of first marriage 161
Shelley, P.F. **181**, 207, 208, 213, 230, 241, 251
Shelley, T. (later Sir Timothy, Bt.) 43, 147, 213
Shelley, W. 153, 170, 173, **178**
Shepperson & Reynolds (publisher) 42
Sheridan, R.B. 4, 8, 12, 24, 28, 65, 78, 81, 98, 115, 137, 140, **155**, 192, 195, 219

Sherwood, W. 176
Sherwood, Neely & Jones (publisher) 139, 160, 176
Shiloh 145
Shoberl, F. 107
Siddons, S. 11, 14, 16, 18, 50, 56, 62, 69, 78, 82, 119, 185, 238, **245**
  last stage appearance 178
  retirement (1812) 133
Sidmouth, Lord 85, 232
Simpkin & Marshall (publisher) 14, 183, 229–30, 232, 237
Shylock 140
Sismondi, J.-C. S. de 120, 139
Skirving, W. 48, 49
Slatter & Munday (publisher) 74
Smith, A. 35
Smith, C. 16, 17, 21, 28, 33, 40, 43, 46, 49, 53, 55, 73, 77, 81, **107–8**, 255
Smith, C.S. 119
Smith, H. 134, 167, 184, 207
Smith, J. 134
Smith, M. 252
Smith, S. 92, 231
Smithson, H. 228
Soane, G. 193, 195, 217
Solomos, D. 211
Somerville, M. (*née* Fairfax) **5**, 221
Sotheby, W. 72, 91
Soult, Marshal N. 116
Southcott, J. 145
Southerne, T. 11
Southey, E. (*née* Fricker) 59, 82, 96, 129
Southey, R. 42, 47, **52–3**, 54–6, 58, 60, 64, 66–7, 69, 74–5, **79**, 82, 84, 87–8, 92, 95–6, 101–4, 111–13, 117, 121, 124, 126, 128–9, 134, 137–8, 142, 144, 148, 160, 164, 173, 179, 184, 193, 208–9, 218, 224, 232, 235, 243, 251
  legacy from Beaumont (1827) 225
  marriage (1795) 59
  Poet Laureate (1813) 138

Author/Name Index 275

Spencer, W.R. 62
Spohr, L. 208
Spontini, L. 197
Stacey, S. 182
Staël-Holstein: A.-G., baronne de (née Necker) 65, 82, 92–3, 97, 110, 137–9, 142, 155–6, **163**
 banishment (1803) 96
Stanhope, Lady Hester 122, 123
Stanley, J.T. 62
Stedman, J.G. 39
Stendhal **12**, 143, 145, 163–5, 202–3, 212, 214, 228, 238, 242–3
Stephen, J. 246
Stephenson, G. 219
Stephenson, R. **143**, 238
Stevenson, Sir John 114
Stockdale, J. (publisher) 15, 83, 85
Stockdale, J.J. (publisher) 124, 125
Stodart, R. (publisher) 170, 182
Stoddart, Sir John 13, 26
Storace, S. 34
Stothard, T. 4, 198
Strahan (publisher) 6, 29
Strahan, Cadell & Creech (publisher) 13, 22
Stuart, C.E. ('Young Pretender') 28
Stuart, J. ('Athenian') 33–4
Stubbs, G. 21, 82, **106**
Swan, C. 227
'Sylvander and Clarinda' 27

Tait (publisher) 212
Talfourd, T.N. 167, 174, 205
Talleyrand-Périgord, C.-M. de 35, 41
Taylor, E. 135
Taylor, H. 242
Taylor, J. (publisher) 192
Taylor, W. 36, 62, 74, 235
Taylor & Hessey (publisher) 165, 171, 174, 184, 187, 195, 211, 217, 226
Telford, T. 95, **104**, 168, 221, 222
Tennyson, A. **119**, 226, 230, 234, 237, 241, 246, 248, 251, 253

Tennyson, C. 226
Tennyson, F. 226
Thackeray, W.M. **127**, 236
Thelwall, J. 32, 45–6, 48, 51, 53–4, 58, 61–3, 67–8, 80, **88**, 97, **103**–4, 107, 129–30, 141, 166, 251–2
Thistlewood, A. 158, 184
Thomas, C. (publisher) 227
Thomas, M. (publisher) 200
Thomson, G. 46, 51
Thomson, J. 87, 200
Thornton, R. 197
Tieck, D. 70
Tieck, L. 105
Tighe, H. **48**
Tighe, M. (née Blachford) 42, **48**, 56, 83, 97, 102, 105, 114, 120, **121**
Tipu Sultan (Mysore) 15, 78
Tolstoy, Count L.N. **234**
Tone, T.W. 40, 76
Tooke, J. H. 24, 41, 49, 51, 53–4, 106
Toussaint-l'Ouverture, F.-D. 39, **85**
Trelawny, E.J. 197–8, 200–1, 203, 207–8, 218, 234, 248
Trevithick, R. **88–9**
Trimmer, S. 28, 91
Trollope, F. 229, 246, 249
Turgenev, I.S. **174**
Turner, J.M.W. vi, 33, 34, 62, 78–80, 82, 87, **89**, 90, 99, 103, 110–12, **129**, 137, 145, 147–8, 161, 164, 173, 175, **177**, **179–80**, 182, 195, 198, 202, 206, 210, 214, 219, 224, **228**, **233**, 236, 238–9, 245, 249–50, 252–3
Turner, W. **238**
Tytler, A. 8

Unger (publisher) 70
Urbani, P. 51
Uxbridge, Lord 148

Vallon, A. 40, 42, 44, 91, 188
Verdi, G. **138**
Vernor (publisher) 60

Vernor & Hood (publisher) 81, 89
Vernor, Hood & Sharpe (publisher) 105, 118, 127
Vesey, E. 13
Vestris, L.E. 243
Victoria, Princess (later Queen) **177**, 232
Vieweg (publisher) 68
Viganò, S. 86
Vigny, A. de 222
Vincent, J. (publisher) 192
Virgil 197
Viviani, Teresa 'Emilia' 191
Vogel, H. **128**
Volney: C.-F. de C., comte de 39
Volta, A. 84
Voltaire 38

Wagner, R. **137**
Wakefield, G. 76
Walker, A. 154
Walker, S. 188, 197, 200, 201
Walpole, H. 13, 15, **66**
Walsh, J. 67
Warton, J. 8, 11–12, **81**
Warton, T. 11, 18, 22, **35**, 93
Washington, G. 14, 31
Watson, R. (Bishop of Llandaff) 76
Watt, J. 6, 16, 61, **180**
Watt, J., the younger 61, 165
Watts, A. 219
Weber, C.M. von **23**, 194, 221, **223**
Webster, Lady Frances Wedderburn 138
Webster, J.W. 117, 138
Wedgwood, J. 6, 34–5, **55**
Wedgwood, J., the younger 70, 71
Wedgwood, T. 70, 71, 93, 94, **102**
Wellington, Duke of
  Ambassador of UK to France (1814) 141
  Duke (1814) **141**, 142, 146–7, **148**, 149, 185, 191, 200, 216, 225, 229
  Earl (1812) 129, 133
  Marquess (1812) 133, 137
  Prime Minister (1828–30) 197, **231**, 233, 235–6, **242**
Viscount (1809) 119, 123, 129
Wellesley, Sir Arthur 115, 117, 119
Wesley, J. 15, **37**
West, B. 23, 41, 103, 111, **185**, 207
Westley & Davis (publisher) 240
Wetherell, Sir Charles 247
Whitaker, T. 175
White, B. (publisher) 30
White, G. 30
Whitehead, W. 18
Whittaker, G. & W.B (publisher) 192, 205, 208, 212, 248
Whittaker & Treacher (publisher) 249
Wieland, C.M. 43, 97, 221
Wilberforce, W. 4, 16, 31–2, 37–8, 45, 66, 109, 147, 172, 204
Wildman, T. 167
Wiley (publisher) 204
Wiley & Halsted (publisher) 197
Wilkes, J. **70**
Wilkie, (Sir) David 110, 125, 200, 202
Wilkie & Robinson (publisher) 122
Wilkins, W. 152, 212, 221
Wilkinson, J. 118
William IV **240**, 250
  Coronation (1831) 246
  Duke of Clarence 20
Williams, E. 191, **198**, 199, **201**
Williams, H.M. 22, 27, 40, 48, 90, 188
Williams, J. 191, 198, 199
Wilson, E. (publisher) 253
Wilson, H. 94, 142, 216
Wilson, John ('Christopher North') 91, 120, 131, 144, 173, 199, 202, 218
Wilson, John (printer) 22
Wolcot, J. ('Peter Pindar') 9
Wolfe, C. 116
Wollstonecraft, E. 15, 27

Wollstonecraft, M. vi, 7, 15, 20–1, 23, 29, 36, 39–41, 44, 51, 53, 56–8, 60–1, 63, **68**, 69–70, 171, 181, 156, 256
  marriage to W. Godwin (1797) 66
Woodhouse, R. 174
Wordsworth, A.-C. **44**, 91, 188
Wordsworth, C. 132
Wordsworth, Dora 214, 219, 233, 246
Wordsworth, Dorothy vi, 50, 58, 67, 69, 70, **72–4**, 76–8, **80**, **82**, 83–4, 86–8, 92, **95–6**, 97, 104, 122, 137, 144, **187–8**, 202, 234, 241, 256
  moves into (later called) Dove Cottage (1799) 80
  occasional journal (1824–35) 215, 233, 248
  visit to France (1802) 90, 91
  journals 172, 255
Wordsworth, John (brother of Dorothy and William) **101**
Wordsworth, John (nephew) 234
Wordsworth, M. (*née* Hutchinson) 92, 97, 107–8, 110–12, 114–15, 120, 126, 129, 137, 142, 144, 147, 172, **187–8**, 202, 205–6, 214, 217, 232, 237, 241
Wordsworth, T. **135**
Wordsworth, W. vi, 27, 35, 37, 40, 42, 44–5, 47, 49–50, **55–148** (with gaps), 161, 167–8, 170, 172, 177–8, 185–6, **187–8**, 196, 199, 205–6, 211, 214–15, 217–18, 222, 224, 227, 232–3, 237–8, 241, 243–4, 246, 251, 255–6
  legacy from Beaumont (1827) 225
  marries Mary Hutchinson (1802) 92
  moves into (later called) Dove Cottage (1799) 80
  visit to France (1802) 90, 91
Wright, F. 173, 220, 229, 233, 246
Wright, J. (publisher) 78
Wright, J. (painter), of Derby 12, 18, 60, **68**
Wright, W.R. 118
Wu Hanchen 159
Württemberg, Duke of 10
Wyatt, B. 134
Wyatt, J. 63
Wyndham, W. 54
Wynn, C.W.W. 67

Yearsley, A. 19, 45
York, Duke of 179
Young, A. 25, 47
Young, E. 63
'Young Roscius' 100
'Younger Memnon' (Rameses II) 155

'Z' (pen-name of Lockhart) 165
Zschökke, J.H.D. 103

Title Index

Abällino, der grosse Bandit (Zschökke, 1793) 103
Abbot, 3v (Scott, 1820) 189
'Absence' (M. Shelley, 1830) 243
Account of Abiphones of Paraguay (Dobrizhoffer; Sara Coleridge translation, 1822) 198
Ada Reis, 3v (Lady Caroline Lamb, 1823) 205
'Address to Edinburgh' (Burns, 1786) 23
'Address to My Harp' (Tighe, 1805) 105
Address to Opposers of Repeal of Test and Corporation Acts (Barbauld, 1790) 34
Address to People of Britain (Tooke and Martin, 1794) 49
Address to People of Great Britain (Watson, 1798) 76
Address to People on Death of Princess Charlotte (P.B. Shelley, 1817) 166
'Address to Unco Guid, or the Rigidly Righteous' (Burns, c.1784–6) 17
'Address to West Wind' (Tighe, 1805) 105
'Address, Spoken at Opening of Drury-lane Theatre' (Byron, 1812) 134
Adelaide (Alderson, 1786, 1791) 36
Adelaide; or Chateau de St Pierre, 4v (Edgeworth, 1806) 106
Adelgitha; or, Fruit of Single Error (Lewis, 1807) 110
Adeline Mowbray, 3v (Opie, 1805) 101
Adelmorn (Lewis, 1801) 87
Adolphe (Constant, 1816) 154

Adonais: Elegy on Death of Keats (P.B. Shelley, 1821) 173, 193
'Adventures on Salisbury Plain' (Wordsworth, 1795–6) 59
Adventures of Ulysses (Charles Lamb, 1808) 114
Adventures of Younger Son (Trelawny, 1831) 248
'Ae fond kiss' (Burns, 1792) 40
Age of Bronze; or, Carmen Seculare et Annus Haud Mirabilis (Byron, 1823) 205
'Ahrimanes' (Peacock, unpublished poem) 141
Aids to Reflection in Formation of Manly Character (Coleridge, 1825) 217
Al Aaraaf, Tamerlane and Minor Poems (Poe, 1829) 239
Alastor; or, Spirit of Solitude (P.B. Shelley, 1816) 149, 151
Albertus (Gautier, 1832) 252
Albion (newspaper) 29
Alfonso, King of Castile (Lewis, 1802) 89
Alfoxden Journal (D. Wordsworth) 70, 256
'Alice Fell' (Wordsworth, 1802) 90
All Religions are One (Blake, 1788) 30
Almaviva, ossia L'inutile precauzione see *Barbiere di Siviglia*
Almeyda, Queen of Granada (Lee, 1796) 62
Alpine Journal (Byron, 1816/1830) 156
Amadis of Gaul (Lobeira; Southey translation, 1803) 95
Ambrosio; or, Monk (Lewis, 1798) 62
America a Prophecy (Blake 1793) 49
American Monthly Magazine 238

Title Index 279

Amulet; or Christian and Literary Remembrancer 235
Amy Robsart (Hugo; fp 1828) 231
'An die Freude' (Schiller, 1786) 19
Analysis of Phenomena of Human Mind, 2v (James Mill, 1829) 239
Analytic Inquiry into Principles of Taste (Knight, 1805) 111
'Ancient Art' (Fuseli, 1801) 86
Ancient Mariner (Coleridge, 1798) 71
 planned as collaborative work (Coleridge/Wordsworth) 69
 revision (1817) 164
'Ancients' (Blake disciples) 219
'Anecdote for Fathers' (Wordsworth, 1798) 72
Anecdotes of Late Samuel Johnson (Piozzi, 1786) 21
Angelina, 3v (Robinson, 1796) 60
Animadversions on Some Poets (Maxwell, 1788) 26
'Animal Tranquillity and Decay' (Wordsworth) 65
'Animal Vitality' (Thelwall, 1793) 45
Anna Bolena (Donizetti, 1830) 243
 England fp (1831) 243
Anna St Ives: a Novel, 7v (Holcroft, 1792) 42
Annals of Fine Arts 160, 178
Annals of Parish (Galt, 1821) 193, 201, 203
Anne of Geierstein, 3v (Scott, 1829) 237
Annual Anthology (1800) 67
Annual Necrology, 1797–1798 (1800) 68
Annual Register (Cobbett) 89
Anti-Jacobin Review 69
Anti-Jacobin, or Weekly Examiner 69, 72, 73
Antiquary (Scott, 1816) 153
Antiquities of Athens (Stuart and Revett, 1762–1830) 33–4
Antiquities of Scotland, v2 (Grose, 1791) 37

Antonio; or, Soldier's Return (Godwin, 1800) 84
Appeal to Men of Great Britain on Behalf of Women (Hays, 1798) 76
Appeal to popular opinion, against kidnapping and murder (Thelwall, 1796) 63
Architectural Antiquities of Normandy (Cotman, 1822) 163
Arkwright's Cotton Mills by Night (Wright, 1782–3) 12
Armance ou quelques scènes d'un Salon de Paris, en 1827, 3v (Stendhal, 1827) 228
'Art of Moderns' (Fuseli, 1801) 86
Asiatick Miscellany 18
Asiatick Researches 18, 21
Assignation (S. Lee, 1807) 109
Atala, ou les amours de deux sauvages dans le désert (Chateaubriand, 1801) 86
Athenaeum 238, 244, 252
Athenaeum: Eine Zeitschrift 73
'Auguries of Innocence' (Blake, c.1807) 112
'Augustus Darvell' (Byron, 1819) 154, 176
'Auld Lang Syne' (Burns, 1788) 30
Aurelio and Miranda (Lewis, 1797) 69
Authentic Account of Shakspearian Manuscripts (Ireland, 1796) 62
'Autobiographical Letter' (Burns, 1787) 26
Ayrshire Legatees (Galt, 1821) 194, 249

Ballad Singer; or, Memoirs of Bristol Family, 4v (Edgeworth, 1813) 139
Baltimore Gazette 239
Banished Man: Novel, 4v (C. Smith, 1794) 53
Banks of Wye (Bloomfield, 1811) 127
Barbarossa (J. Brown, 1804) 100
Barbiere di Siviglia (Rossini, fp 1816) 151; London fp (1818) 170

Title Index

'Bard from Gray' (Blake, 1785)   19
'Bargain Lost' (Poe, 1832)   253
Bas Bleu, or, Conversation (More, 1786)   13
'Battell Book' (B. Brontë, 1827)   226
'Battle of Lovell's Pond' (Longfellow, 1820)   190
Battle of Marathon (Barrett, 1820)   185
Battle of Trafalgar (Turner, 1823)   103
Baviad (Gifford, 1791)   20
Bay of Baiae, with Apollo and Sibyl (Turner, 1823)   206
Beachy Head: With Other Poems (C. Smith, 1807)   107–8
Belinda, 3v (Edgeworth, 1801)   87
Belle's Stratagem (Cowley, 1780)   3
Beppo, a Venetian Story (Byron, 1818)   165, 169
Berliner Abendblättern   124
Bertram; or, Castle of St Aldobrand (Maturin, 1816)   153
Betrothed (Scott, 1825)   218
Betrothed Lovers (Manzoni; Swan's translation, 1828)   227
Bible   32, 72, 98
Bibliotheca classica (Lemprière, 1788, 1797)   30
Bijou   69, 216, 223
Biographia Literaria (Coleridge, 1817)   147, 164
Biographical and Imperial Magazine   32
'Biographical Notice of Author [Jane Austen]' (Henry Austen, 1817)   168
'Birks of Aberfeldey' (Burns, 1787)   26
'Black Canon of Elmham' (1800)   124
Black Dwarf (Scott, 1816)   158
Black Man's Lament (Opie, 1826)   219
'Black Paintings' (Goya, 1820)   183
Blackwood's Edinburgh Magazine   116, 131, 165–6, 184, 192, 195, 199, 223, 225–6, 230

Blank Verse (Charles Lamb and Charles Lloyd, 1798)   73
Blind Fiddler (Wilkie, 1807)   110
Blues, A Literary Eclogue (Byron, 1823)   195, 206
Bogle Corbet, 3v (Galt, 1830)   239
Bold Stroke for Husband (Cowley, 1783)   12
Bonaparte Crossing Alps (David, 1800–3)   83
Book of Ahania (Blake)   60
Book of Job (Blake, 1825)   216
Book of Los (Blake)   60
Book of Thel (Blake, 1789)   33
Borderers (Wordsworth, 1842)   64, 69
Boris Godunov (Pushkin, 1830; dated '1831')   242, 243
Borough: Poem, in Twenty-Four Letters (Crabbe, 1810)   122
Botanic Garden (Darwin)
part one (1792, dated 1791)   31, 35, 39
part two (1789)   31
Bracebridge Hall, 2v (Irving, 1822)   200
Bravo (Cooper, 1831)   223
Bravo of Venice, A Romance (Lewis, 1805)   103
Bridal of Triermain (Scott, 1813)   136
Bride of Abydos (Byron, 1813)   139
Bride of Lammermoor (Scott, 1819)   178
'Bride of Modern Italy' (M. Shelley, 1824)   211
Brides' Tragedy (Beddoes, 1822)   203
Briefe eines Verstorbenen (Pückler-Muskau, 1830–2)   253
'Bright Star' (Keats, 1819)   181
'Brigs of Ayr, a Poem' (Burns, 1786)   23
Bristol Journal   143
'Britannic Muse' (Kalvos)   211
British Lady's Magazine   146
British Novelists, 50v (with introduction by Barbauld, 1810)   124

British Theatre; or, A Collection of Plays, 25v (Inchbald, 1806–9) 108
British War Songs (C. Dibdin, 1803–4) 95
'Brother and Sister: Italian Story' (M. Shelley, 1832) 253
'Brothers' (Austen, unfinished) 159
 see also *Sanditon*
'Brothers, Pastoral Poem' (Wordsworth, 1800) 81
Brutus; or, Fall of Tarquin (Payne, 1818) 174
Bryan Perdue: a Novel, 3v (Holcroft, 1805) 103
Buonaparte. A Poem (Stratford Canning, 1814) 141
'Burial of Sir John Moore' (Wolfe, 1817) 116

Cabinet (radical periodical) 53
Cain, a Mystery (Byron, 1821) 194, 196, 204
Caleb Williams (Godwin) 52, 240
 performed at Drury Lane (1796) 61
 1831 edition 244
 see also *Things as They Are*
Caledonian Mercury 55
Cambrian (newspaper) 140
Cambridge Intelligencer 64
Camilla: or, Picture of Youth, 5v (Burney d'Arblay, 1796) 63
Candidate: Poetical Epistle to Authors of Monthly Review (Crabbe, 1780) 4
Canterbury Tales, 5v (H. Lee, 1797–1805) 70
Canti (Leopardi, 1831) 215
Canzoni (Leopardi, 1824) 215
Cap and Bells (Keats, 1819) 182
Caprichos (Goya, 1799) 77
Captive (Lewis, 1803) 94
Carlisle Patriot 170
'Casabianca' (Hemans, 1826) 224
Casket, Flowers of Literature, Wit & Sentiment (1830) 238, 242
'Cast-Away' (Cowper 1799) 78

Castle of Andalusia (O'Keeffe, 1782) 115
Castle Dangerous (Scott, 1831; dated '1832') 248
Castle Rackrent (Edgeworth, 1800) 81
Castle Spectre (Lewis, 1797–8) 69, 72
'Catherine' (Austen) 151
 see also *Northanger Abbey*
Catherine of Cleves (Dumas; Gower's translation, 1832) 236
'Cave of Fancy' (Wollstonecraft, 1786) 23
Cecilia, or Memoirs of Heiress, 5v (Burney, 1782) 9–10, 63
Cenci (P.B. Shelley, 1819) 178
'Chamouni: Hour Before Sunrise' (Coleridge, 1802) 92
'Chamounix beym Sonnenaufgange' (Brun, 1791) 92
Champion 142, 150, 164, 165, 167
Chapter of Accidents (Lee, 1780) 4
'Character of Happy Warrior' (Wordsworth, 1805–6) 103
'Characteristics' (Carlyle, 1831) 248
Characteristics of Women (Jameson, 1832) 251
'Charles I' (unfinished play by P.B. Shelley) 198
Chase, The, and William and Helen (Scott, 1796) 64
Chasseur in Woods (Friedrich, 1814) 141
'Chaucer's Canterbury Pilgrims' (Blake, 1810) 124
Cheap Repository Tracts (1795–) 56
Chelsea Pensioners Reading Gazette (Wilkie, 1822) 200
Childe Harold's Pilgrimage (Byron)
 Cantos I and II (1812) 111, 119–21, 128, **130**
 Canto III (1816) 148, 153, 154, 156, **157**
 Canto IV (1818) 163, 168, **170**, 173

282 Title Index

Childe Harold's Pilgrimage – Italy (Turner, 1832) 250
'Choice' (M. Shelley) 207
Choleric Fathers (Holcroft, 1785) 20
Christ's Entry into Jerusalem (Haydon, 1820) 185
'Christ's Hospital' (Hunt, 1801) 10
'Christ's Hospital Five-and-Thirty Years Ago' (Charles Lamb, 1820) 10
Christabel (Coleridge, 1816) 83, 84, 87, 150, 153, 154
Christian Year (Keble, 1827) 227
Christianism; or, Belief and Unbelief Reconciled (Hunt, 1832) 249
Chronicle of Conquest of Granada (Irving, 1829) 221
Chronicles of Canongate
  First Series, 2v (Scott, 1827) 229
  Second Series, 3v (Scott, 1828) 232
Cinq-Mars, ou Une Conjuration sous Louis XIII, 2v (Vigny, 1826) 222
Clari; or, Maid of Milan (Payne/ Bishop, 1823) 206
Clavigo (Goethe, 1774) 71
Cliffs on Rügen (Friedrich, 1818) 87
Clothed Maja (Goya, 1797–1805) 70
Cloudesley, 3v (Godwin, 1830) 240
Coelebs in Search of Wife, 2v (More, 1808) 116
Coelina, ou l'enfant de mystère (Pixérécourt, 1800) 93
Combat of Giaour and Hassan (Delacroix, 1826) 222
'Comet' (Beddoes, 1819) 179
Comic Songs (T. Dibdin, 1794) 55
Companion (Hunt, 1828) 231
'Composed Upon Westminster Bridge, Sept. 3, 1802' (Wordsworth, 1802) 91
'Concerning Convention of Cintra' (Wordsworth, 1808–9) 116
Conciones ad Populum. Or Addresses to People (Coleridge, 1795) 59
'Conference of People called Methodists' (1784) 15

Confessions (Rousseau, 1782) 11
Confessions of English Opium-Eater (De Quincey, 1821, 1822) 93, 100, **196**
Confessions of Nun of St Omer (Dacre, 1805) 101
Confessions of W.H. Ireland (1805) 62
Considerations on Bills concerning Treasonable Practices (Godwin, 1795) 59
Considérations sur les principaux événements de la Révolution française (Staël, 1818) 163
Consolations in Travel (Davy, 1830) 237
Constitutional History of England (Hallam, 1827) 228
Contes d'Espagne et d'Italie (Musset, 1830) 239
Contarini Fleming, 4v (Disraeli, 1832) 249
Coombe Ellen (Bowles, 1798) 132
Corinna of England (anonymous, 1809) 110
Corinne, ou l'Italie (Staël, 1807) 110
Coriolanus 162
Correction, 3v (Harding, 1818) 170, 179
Corruption and Intolerance (Moore, 1808) 114
Corsair (Byron, 1814) 130, 140
Così fan tutte (Mozart, 1790) 33
  UK fp (1811) 126
'Cotter's Saturday Night' (Burns, 1785–6) 20
Count Robert of Paris (Scott, 1831; dated '1832') 248
Country Blacksmith Disputing Upon Price of Iron (Turner, 1807) 110
Courier 80, 81, 116, 126, 142, 160, 176
Course of Lectures on Dramatic Art and Literature (A.W. Schlegel; Black's translation, 1815) 120
Court Journal 247
Creation (Haydn, 1798) 72

Critical Examination of Respective
 Performance of Kean and Macready
 (anonymous, 1819) 182
Cross in Mountains (Friedrich,
 1808) 116
Crossing the Brook (Turner,
 1815) 147
Crotchet Castle (Peacock, 1831) 244
Cupid and Psyche (Canova,
 1787–93) 27
Curiosities of Literature (D'Israeli,
 1791–1823) 41, 210
Curse of Kehama (Southey,
 1810) 87, 124
Curse of Minerva (Byron) published
 by Murray (1832) 125; pirated
 edition (1815) 125
Cursory Remarks on Propriety of Social
 Worship (Hays, 1791) 42
Cursory Strictures on Charge Delivered
 by Lord Chief Justice Eyre
 (Godwin, 1794) 53–4

Daily Universal Register 18
Dangers of Coquetry (Opie, 1790) 36
'Darkness' (Byron, 1816) 155
Dartmoor (Hemans) 194
Das Buch der Lieder (Heine,
 1827) 229
Das Kätchen von Heilbronn oder die
 Feuerprobe (Kleist, 1810) 121
Das Kind der Liebe (Kotzebue) 75
Day in Turkey, or Russian Slave
 (Cowley, 1791) 40
De l'Allemagne (Staël, 1813) 139
De l'Amour, 2v (Stendhal, 1822) 202
De l'influence des passions (Staël,
 1796) 65
De la Littérature (Staël, 1800) 82
De la Littérature du Midi de l'Europe
 (Sismondi, 1813) 139
De la Religion, 5v (Constant,
 1824–31) 212
De Monfort (Baillie, 1800) 82, 121
'Dead have been awakened – shall
 I sleep?' (Byron, 1824) 208

Deaf and Dumb (Holcroft, 1801) 86
'Death and Dying Words of Poor
 Mailie' (Burns, 1782) 13
'Death of Goethe' (Carlyle,
 1832) 249
Death and Maiden String Quartet
 (Schubert 1824/1831) 211
Death of Nelson (West, 1806,
 1808) 103
'Death of Princess Charlotte –
 Lamentable Punishments at
 Derby' (Hunt, 1817) 166
Death of Sardanapalus (Delacroix,
 1828) 229
Death's Jest-Book, or, Fool's Tragedy
 (Beddoes) 218
'Decided Loss' (Poe, 1832) 252
Decision, 3v (Harding, 1819) 179
'Declaration of Rights of Man and of
 Citizen' (1789) 32
Decline of Carthaginian Empire
 (Turner, 1817) 161
Dedham Vale: Morning (Constable,
 1811) 126
Defence of Poetry (Shelley,
 1821) 191
Deformed Transformed (Byron,
 1824) 210
Dei sepolcri (Foscolo, 1807) 156
'Dejection: Ode' (Coleridge,
 1802) 90, 92
Delphine (Staël, 1802) 93
Der deutsche Hausvater (Gemmingen,
 1779) 49
Der Freischütz (Weber, fp 1821) 194
 CG (1826) 222
 England fp (1824) 213
Der Geisterseher (Schiller,
 1787–9) 60, 247
Der zerbrochne Krug (Kleist,
 1808) 113
Des Knaben Wunderhorn. Alte
 Deutsche Lieder, 2v (Brentano
 and Arnim, 1805, 1808) 103
Description of Scenery of Lakes
 (Wordsworth, 1822) 199

Title Index

Descriptive Sketches (Wordsworth, 1793) 35, 45
Deserted Daughter (Holcroft, 1795) 57
'Deserted House' (Hemans, 1827) 226
Desmond (C. Smith, 1792) 43
Destiny, 3v (Ferrier, 1831) 244
Detached Thoughts (Byron journal, 1821–2) 196
'Detached Thoughts on Books and Reading' (Charles Lamb, 1822) 201
Detraction Displayed (Opie, 1828) 219
Devereux, 3v (Bulwer, 1829) 237
'Devil's Thoughts' (Southey and Coleridge, 1799) 79
'Devil's Walk' (Southey, 1827) 79
'Diary', 33v (H.C. Robinson, 1811–67) **125**, 125–6
Diary of Ennuyée (Jameson, 1826) 224
Dido Building Carthage (Turner, 1815) 147
Die Entführung aus dem Serail (Mozart, 1782) 10, 230
Die Geschöpfer der Prometheus (Beethoven, 1801) 86
Die Italienische Reise (Goethe, 1816–29) 21, 23
Die Jahreszeiten (Haydn, 1801) 87
Die Jungfrau von Orleans (Schiller, 1801) 88
Die Marquise von O (Kleist, 1808) 113
Die Nachstücke (Hoffmann, 1816–17) 158
Die Piccolomini (Schiller; Coleridge's translation, 1800) 82
Die Räuber (Schiller, 1782) 8, 73
Die Schöpfung (Haydn, 1798) 72
Die Schöne Müllerin (Schubert, 1824) 209
Die Spanier in Peru (Kotzebue, 1798) 78
Die Verschwörung des Fiesko zu Genua (Schiller, 1783) 13
Die Wahlverwandtschaften (Goethe, 1809) 120
Die Zauberflöte (Mozart, 1791) 40
UK fp (1811) 126
'Dirge' (M. Shelley, 1830) 243
Discipline (Brunton, 1814) 145
Discourse of Love of Our Country (Price, 1790) 36
Discourse on Institution of Society (Jones, 1784) 14
Disowned, 4v (Bulwer, 1828) 235
Dissertation on Government (Paine, 1786) 21
'Dissertation upon Roast Pig' (Charles Lamb, 1822) 202
Distressed Mother (Ambrose Phillips) 156
'Diver' (Hemans, 1830) 239
'Diverting History of John Gilpin' (Cowper, 1782) 11
Divina commedia (Dante; Cary's translation, 1814) 165
Dom Karlos, Infant von Spanien (Schiller, 1787) 26
Domestic Affections and Other Poems (Browne/Hemans, 1812) 133
Domestic Manners of Americans, 2v (F. Trollope, 1832) 249
Don Carlos, Infant of Spain (Schiller; Noehden and Stoddart translation, 1798) 26
Don John, or Don Juan Unmasked (Hone, 1819) 183
Don Juan (Byron)
Cantos I and II (1819) 174, 179
Cantos III–V (1821) 181, 189, 190, 195
Cantos VI–VIII (1823) 198, 207
Cantos IX–XI (1823) 173, 202, 207
Cantos XII–XIV (1823) 206, 209
Cantos XV–XVI (1824) 206, 211
Canto XVII 206
parodied (1819) 182
Don Juan. Canto the Third (Hone, 1819) 183
Douglas (Home, 1756) 135, 178
Dramatic Works, 2v (Ford, 1827) 101

Title Index   285

Dramatische Werke, 9v (Shakespeare; A.W. Schlegel translations, 1797–1810)   70
'Dream' (Burns, 1786)   22
'Dream' (Poe, 1831)   245
'Dream' (M. Shelley, 1831)   248
'Dream; or, Living Portraits' (Dacre, 1806)   106
Dream of Ossian (Ingres, 1813)   107
'Dreams' (Poe, 1828)   234
Dreams, Waking Thoughts and Incidents (Beckford, 1783)   12
Duenna (Sheridan)   195
'Duke de L'Omelette' (Poe, 1832)   249
Dumfries Journal   55
'Dumfries Volunteers' (Burns, 1795)   55
Duplicity (Holcroft, 1781)   7
Dutch Boats in Gale (Turner, 1801)   87
'Dying Improvisatore' (Hemans, 1828)   233

East Indian (Lewis, 1799)   77
Ecclesiastical Sonnets (Wordsworth, 1822)   199
'Edax on Appetite' (Charles Lamb, 1811)   128
Edinburgh Courant   55
Edinburgh Evening Courant   26
Edinburgh Herald   37
Edinburgh Magazine   26, 37
Edinburgh Review   92, 111, 112, 117, 142, 144, 154, 187, 191, 219, 227, 237–8, 248
'Editor of Quarterly Review' (Hazlitt, 1818)   176
Edmund Oliver (Lloyd, 1798)   71
Edwy and Elgiva (Burney D'Arblay, 1795)   56
'Effusion XXXV' (Coleridge, 1795)   57
Egmont: Ein Trauerspiel (Goethe, 1788)   36
'Eidometropolis' (Girtin, 1802)   92

'Eidophusikon, or Representation of Nature' (Loutherbourg, 1781–2, 1786)   5
Eighteen Hundred and Eleven, a Poem (Barbauld, 1812)   129
'Electro-Chemical Researches' (Davy, 1808)   114
Elegiac Sonnets, and Other Essays (C. Smith, 1784)   16
'Elegiac Stanzas, Suggested by Picture of Peele Castle' (Wordsworth, 1806)   106
'Elegy on Captain Matthew Henderson' (Burns, 1787)   24
Elements of Agricultural Chemistry (Davy, 1813)   133
Elements of Chemical Philosophy (Davy, 1812)   133
Elements of Chemistry (Lavoisier; Kerr translation, 1790)   30
Elements of French Grammar (Longfellow, 1830)   251
'Elinor and Marianne' (Austen, 1795)   60, 70
see also *Sense and Sensibility*
Elisabetta, regina d'Inghilterra (Rossini, 1815)   149
UK fp (1818)   170
Emigrants: Poem (C. Smith, 1793)   46
'Eminent Contemporaries' (Coleridge, 1794–5)   54
Emma (Austen, 1815; dated '1816')   140, 146, **150**
Emmeline (Brunton, 1818)   175
Emmeline, Orphan of Castle (C. Smith, 1788)   28
'Enchanted Fruit, or, Hindu Wife' (Jones, 1785)   18
Encyclopaedia Britannica (1820)   191
Endymion (Keats, 1818)   161, 165–6, **171**, 173, 187, 193
England: Richmond Hill (Turner, 1819)   177
'England in 1819' (P.B. Shelley)   183

England and Spain; or, Valour and Patriotism (Browne/Hemans, 1808) 116
'England's Dead' (Hemans, 1822) 203
Englische Fragmenten (Heine, 1831) 226
English Bards and Scotch Reviewers (Byron, 1809) 107, 111, 117, 128
English Comic Writers (Hazlitt lectures, 1818) 174
English Constitution Produced and Illustrated (Cartwright, 1823) 214
'English Eclogues' (Southey) 74
Englishman's Magazine 246
Enquirer, Reflections on Education, Manners and Literature (Godwin, 1797) 66
Enquiry Concerning Nature of Political Justice, 2v (Godwin, 1793) 45
Entail: or Lairds of Grippy, 3v (Galt, 1822) 203
'Eolian Harp' (Coleridge 1795/1817) 57
Epea Pteroenta, or Diversions of Purley (Tooke, 1786, 1798, 1805) 24
Esquisse d'un tableau historique des progrès de l'esprit humain (Condorcet, 1794) 50
Epicurean, A Tale (Moore, 1827) 227
'Epigrams' (Coleridge, 1828) 235
Epipsychidion (P.B. Shelley, 1821) 191
Epistle to Wilberforce (Barbauld, 1791) 37
Epistle on Women (Aikin, 1810) 122
Epistles, Odes and Other Poems (Moore, 1806) 106, 107
'Erl-King' (Goethe; Scott's translation, 1798) 71
Ernestus Berchtold; or, Modern Oedipus (Polidori, 1819) 179
Essai sur le génie et le caractère de Lord Byron (Pichot, 1827) 181

Essai sur les révolutions anciennes et modernes (Chateaubriand, 1797) 66
Essay on Corruptions of Christianity, 2v (1782) 11
Essay towards Definition of Animal Vitality (Thelwall, 1793) 45
Essay on Mind with Other Poems (Barrett, 1826) 222
'Essay on Needle-work' (M. Lamb, 1815) 146
Essay on Picturesque (Price, 1794) 29
'Essay on Present Literature of Italy' (Foscolo, 1818) 170
Essay on Principles of Human Action (Hazlitt, 1805) 102
Essay on Principles of Population (Malthus, 1798, 1803) 73, 109
Essay on Slavery and Commerce of Human Species (Clarkson, 1786) 22
Essay on Theory of Earth (Cuvier; Kerr translation, 1813) 139
Essay on Writings and Genius of Pope, v2 (J. Warton, 1782) 11
Essays on Formation of Human Character (Owen, 1813–14) 164
Essays on Moral, Political and Various Philosophical Subjects (Kant; Richardson's translation, 1798) 76
Essays on Principles of General Criticism (Coleridge, 1814) 143
Ethelinde, or Recluse of Lake, 5v (C. Smith, 1789) 33
Études de la Nature (Bernardin de St Pierre, third edition, 1787) 27
Eugene Aram, 3v (Bulwer, 1831; dated '1832') 248
Eugene Onegin (Pushkin, 1823–32) 207, 216, 224, 229, 231, 232, 242, 249
Europe (Blake, 1794) 55
European Magazine 90
'Eve of St. Agnes' (Keats, 1819) 175
Evelina (Burney, 1778) 10, 63

'Evening Prayer at Girls' School' (Hemans, 1825) 220
Evening Walk (Wordsworth, 1793) 45
'Every Inch a Sailor' (C. Dibdin, 1789) 33
'Evil Eye' (M. Shelley, 1829) 238
Examiner 112, 123, 130, 142, 144, 150, 153, 154, 159–60, 162–3, 168, 176–7, 180, 243, 244
Excursion: Being Portion of The Recluse (Wordsworth, 1814) 66, 124, 135, **143**, 144
'Excursion on Banks of Ullswater' (D. Wordsworth, 1805) 104
Execution of Marino Faliero (Delacroix, 1827) 229, 231
'Experiments on Galvanic Electricity' (Davy, 1800) 83
Experiments and Observations on Different Kinds of Air (Priestley, 1790) 36
'Expostulation and Reply' (Wordsworth, 1798) 73
'Extract of Cave of Fancy' (Wollstonecraft, 1798) 70–1
'Extracts from Lady's Log-Book' (Jewsbury, 1832) 252

Fables, Ancient and Modern (Godwin, 1805) 104
Fables for Holy Alliance (Moore, 1823) 206
Fairy Legends of South of Ireland, 3v (Croker, 1825-8) 220
'Fairy-Land' (Poe, 1829) 238
Falkland (Bulwer, 1827) 226
Fall of Hyperion (Keats, 1819) 179
Fall of Robespierre: Historic Drama (Coleridge, 1794) 53
False Friend: Domestic Story (Robinson, 1799) 77
'False Rhyme' (M. Shelley, 1829) 238
Family of Charles IV (Goya, 1800) 82

Family Legend (Baillie, 1810) 121
Family Magazine 28
Fancy: Selection from Poetical Remains of Corcoran (J.H. Reynolds, 1820) 187
Fanshawe (Hawthorne, 1828) 234
'Fare Thee Well' (Byron, 1816) 152
Farewell Odes, for the Year 1786 (Wolcot) 9
'Farewell to Muse' (Jewsbury, 1828–9) 219
Farmer's Boy (Bloomfield, 1800) 81
Fashionable Lover (Cumberland, 1772) 57
Fate of Sparta (Cowley, 1788) 28
Father and Daughter (Opie, 1801) 86, 150, 186
Faulkener: a Tragedy (Godwin, 1807–8) 112
Faust (Goethe) 143, 203
  Ein Fragment (1790) 36
  Leveson-Gower's translation (1823) 210
  Nerval's translation (1827; dated '1828') 230
  Part One (revised edition, 1808) 116
  Part Two (1832) 249–50
Faustus: From German of Goethe (Coleridge's translation, 1821) 195, 254
Faustus: Romantic Drama (Soane, 1825) 217
Fazio (Milman, 1818) 169
Fears in Solitude (Coleridge, 1798) 72, 75
Feast of Poets (Hunt, 1814) 140
Federal Gazette 34
Female Biography, 6v (Hays, 1802) 93
'Ferdinando Eboli' (M. Shelley, 1828) 235
'Fermo e Lucia' (Manzoni) 208
Fidelio, oder Die eheliche Liebe (Beethoven, 1805) 104
  UK fp (1832) 250

Title Index

Field of Waterloo (Scott, 1815)   148
Field of Waterloo (Turner, 1818)   148
'Fields of Fancy' (M. Shelley, 1819–20)   180
Fiesco; or Genoese Conspiracy (Schiller; Noehden and Stoddart translation, 1796)   13
Fifth Plague of Egypt (Turner, 1800)   82
Fifty-Three Stations of Tokaido (Hiroshige, 1832)   253
Finden's Landscape Illustrations (1832–3)   249
'Fire, Famine, & Slaughter' (Coleridge, 1798)   70
First Attempt; or Whim of Moment (Owenson, 1807)   109
First Book of Urizen (Blake, 1794)   55
'First Impressions' (Austen, 1796–7)   64, 69, 128
   see also *Pride and Prejudice*
Fishermen at Sea (Turner, 1796)   62
Flatford Mill (Constable, 1817)   161
Fleetwood; or New Man of Feeling, 3v (Godwin, 1805)   101
Florence Macarthy, 4v (Morgan, 1818)   174
Florence Miscellany (Piozzi, Merry et al., 1785)   19
Follies of Day (Holcroft, 1784)   17
Foreign Quarterly Review   249
Foreign Review   227, 232
Forest Sanctuary; and Other Poems (Hemans, 1825, 1828)   217–18, 238
Forget Me Not   220
Fortunes of Nigel, 3v (Scott, 1822)   200
Fortunes of Perkin Warbeck, 3v (M. Shelley, 1830)   228, 240
'Fountain' (Wordsworth, 1798)   75
Fountain of Bakhchisaray (Pushkin, 1824)   215
'Four Ages of Poetry' (Peacock, 1820)   187
'Four Zoas' (Blake; abandoned)   65

Fourteen Sonnets (Bowles, 1789)   30
France, 2v (Morgan, 1817)   162
France in 1829–30, 2v (Morgan, 1830)   242
'France. An Ode' (Coleridge, 1798)   72
Frankenstein (M. Shelley, 1818)   154–5, 160–1, 165, **168**, 205, 221, 223, 235, 238, 245, 248, 252–3
   rejected by publishers (1817)   162
   revised edition (1831)   169, 247
   second edition (1823)   208
Frankenstein, ou le Prométhée moderne (Saladin translation, 1821)   195
Fraser's Magazine   244
Free Enquirer   233, 237
'French Revolution' (Blake, 1791)   39
Friedrich Prinz von Homburg (Kleist, 1809–10; fp Vienna, 1821; fp Berlin, 1828)   196
Friend: Literary, Moral and Political Weekly Paper (Coleridge, 1809–10)   116, 118
'Frost at Midnight' (Coleridge, 1798)   10, 63, 71
Frosty Morning (Turner, 1813)   137
Fudge Family in Paris (Moore, 1818)   170
Fugitive Pieces (Byron, 1806)   108
Fury of Athamas (Flaxman, 1790–3)   36

Galignani's Messenger   176
'Gallery of German Prose Classics' (De Quincey, 1826–7)   225
'Garden of Boccaccio' (Coleridge, 1828)   235
Garden of Florence and Other Poems (Reynolds, 1821)   193
'Garrick and Mrs Pritchard in Macbeth' (Fuseli, 1812)   131
Gaston de Blondeville (Radcliffe, 1826)   204–5
Gebir, Poem in Seven Books (Landor, 1798)   74

Gedichte (Heine, 1821)   197
Gem   235
General Election (Dibdin, 1796)   64
General History of Music from Earliest Ages to Present Period, v2 (C. Burney, 1782)   11
Genius of Thames (Peacock, 1810)   122
Genius of Thames, Palmyra, and Other Poems (Peacock, 1812)   131
Gentleman's Magazine   17
George IV at Banquet in Edinburgh (Turner, c.1822)   202
George the Fourth, a Poem (Dacre, 1822)   184
German Popular Stories (Grimm and Grimm; Taylor's translation, 1823–6)   135
Germany (Staël; English translation, 1813)   139
Gertrude of Wyoming (Campbell, 1809)   117
Ghost of Abel (Blake)   204
Ghost-Seer; or, Apparitionist (Schiller) Boileau translation (1795)   60
translation (1831)   247
Giaour: Fragment of Turkish Tale (Byron, 1813)   137
'Giovanni Villani' (M. Shelley, 1823)   208
Gītagovinda (Jayadéva)   40
Giulio Sabino (Cherubini, 1786)   18
Give Us Our Rights! (Cartwright, 1782)   8
Glasstown or Angria saga (B. and C. Brontë)   226, 244
Glenarvon, 3v (Lady Caroline Lamb, 1816)   153
Glenriddell Manuscript, 2v (Burns)   38
Globe and Traveller   211, 244
'Goethe' (Carlyle, 1828)   232
'Goethe's Helena' (Carlyle, 1828)   232
Goethe's Werke (1806–10)   116
Werke (Goethe, 1827–42)   250
'Goethe's Works' (Carlyle, 1832)   249
Goetz of Berlichingen (Goethe; Scott's translation, 1799)   77
Golden Violet (Landon, 1826; dated '1827')   225
Gondal saga (E. and A. Brontë)   244
'Goody Blake and Harry Gill' (Wordsworth, 1798)   71
'Government' (James Mill, 1820)   191
Graham Hamilton, 2v (Lady Caroline Lamb, 1822)   203
Grasmere Journal (D. Wordsworth)   82, 256
Grave (Blair, 1808)   103
Greece on Ruins of Missolonghi (Delacroix, 1826)   222
'Green grow rashes' (Burns, c.1784)   12–13
Guardian of Education   91
Guide to Lakes (Wordsworth, 1810)   104
Guillaume Tell (Rossini, 1829)   237
Guilt and Sorrow (Wordsworth, 1842)   59
Guy Mannering, 3v (Scott, 1815)   146
Gypsy Prince (Moore and Kelly, 1801)   88

'Hall of Statues' (Landon, 1831)   245
Hambletonian, Rubbing Down (Stubbs, 1800)   82
'Hamburgh' Journal (D. Wordsworth, 1798)   74
Hamlet   14, 134, 140, 228
Han d'Islande (Hugo, 1823)   205
Harlequin Freemason (pantomime, 1780)   5
Harlequin and Mother Goose (T. Dibdin, 1806)   108
Harper's Daughter; or, Love and Ambition (Schiller; Lewis version, 1803)   15
Harrington, a Tale (Edgeworth, 1817)   163
'Hart-Leap Well' (Wordsworth, 1800)   81

Hay-Wain (Constable, 1821)   193, 214
'Haymakers and Reapers' (Stubbs, 1786)   21
He's Much to Blame (Holcroft, 1798)   71
Headlong Hall (Peacock, 1815; dated '1816')   150, 160, 174, 199, 236
Heart of Midlothian, 4v (Scott, 1818)   172
Heaven and Earth (Byron, 1823)   196, 204
Hebrew (1820)   184
Hebrew Melodies (Byron and Nathan, 1815)   144, 147
Hebrides overture (Mendelssohn, fp 1832)   236, 250
Helena. Klassisch-romantische Phantasmagorie (Goethe, 1827)   250
Hellas: Lyrical Drama (P.B. Shelley, 1821)   196
Helvoetsluys (Turner, 1832)   250
Henri III et sa cour (Dumas, 1829)   236
'Here Stewarts once in triumph reign'd' (Burns, 1787)   26
Hermann and Dorothea (Goethe; Holcroft translation, 1801)   68
'Hermit: Oriental Tale' (Hays, 1786)   21
Hermsprong (Bage, 1796)   65
Hernani (Hugo, fp 1830)   239
Hesperus (Richter, 1795)   227
Hints from Horace (Byron, 1811/1831)   125
Hints Towards Forming Character of Young Princess, 2v (More, 1805)   101
Histoire de la Peinture en Italie (Stendhal, 1817)   163
Historic Survey of German Poetry, 3v (Taylor, 1828–30)   235
Historical Illustrations of Fourth Canto of Childe Harold (Hobhouse, 1818)   170
'Historical Lectures' (Southey, 1795)   56
Historical and Moral View of French Revolution (Wollstonecraft, 1794)   53
Historical View of Literature of South of Europe (Sismondi; Roscoe translation, 1823)   139
History of Brazil (Southey, 1810–19)   121
History of British India (James Mill, 1817)   168
History of Christopher Columbus, 4v (Irving, 1826)   221
History of Commonwealth of England, 4v (Godwin, 1824–8)   211
History of Decline and Fall of Roman Empire (Gibbon, 1776–88)   6, 26, 29, 154
History of England (Macaulay), vols. 6–7 (1781) and 8 (1783)   5
'History of England' (Austen, 1791)   40
History of English Poetry, v3 (T. Warton, 1781)   6
History of Java (Raffles, 1817)   161
History of New York (Irving, 1809)   120
History of Richmondshire (Whitaker, 1818–22)   175
History of Sandford and Merton, 3v (Day, 1783–9)   15
History of Six Weeks' Tour (M. Shelley, 1817)   166
'Holy Willie's Prayer' (Burns, 1785)   18
Home at Grasmere (Wordsworth, 1800)   82
'Homes of England' (Hemans, 1827)   226
Horae Ionicae (Wright, 1809)   118
Hours of Idleness (Byron, 1807)   111
Hours of Solitude (Dacre, 1805)   84
Household Furniture and Interior Decoration (Hope, 1807)   80

Title Index 291

Huit scènes de Faust (Berlioz, 1829)   230
Human Life: A Poem (Rogers, 1818)   176
'Humble Petition of Bruar Water to Noble Duke of Athole' (Burns, 1789)   26
Hygeia: or Essays Moral and Medical, 11v (Beddoes, 1802)   93
'Hymn Before Sun-rise, in Vale of Chamouny' (Coleridge, 1802)   92
'Hymn to Camdeo' (Jones, 1784)   14
'Hymn to Intellectual Beauty' (P.B. Shelley, 1817)   154, 156, **159**
Hymns in Prose for Children (Barbauld, 1781)   7
Hyperion (Keats, 1818–19)   174, 179, 193
Hyperion, oder der Eremit in Griechenland, 2v (Hölderlin, 1797, 1799)   70

I Capuleti e i Montecchi (Bellini, 1830)   240
I promessi sposi, 3v (Manzoni, 1827)   208, 227
'I stood tip-toe upon little hill' (Keats, 1816)   158
'I Wandered Lonely as Cloud' (Wordsworth, 1804)   98
Ideen zur Philosophie der Geschichte der Menschheit (Herder, 1784–91)   17
'Idiot Boy' (Wordsworth, 1798)   71, 91
Idomeneo (Mozart, 1781)   5
Il Barbiere di Siviglia, ovvero La precauzione inutile (Paisiello, 1782)   10
Il dissoluto punito, ossia Il Don Giovanni (Mozart, 1787)   27 UK fp (1817)   161, 162
Il pianto delle muse in morte di Lord Byron (Rossini, 1824)   211

Il pirata (Bellini, 1827)   229
Iliad (Flaxman's illustrations, 1793)   45
Iliad and Odyssey of Homer (Cowper, 1791)   38
I'll Tell You What (Inchbald, 1785)   19
'Illuminated City' (Hemans, 1826)   225
'Illustration of Principles of Poetry' (Coleridge lectures, 1811)   128
Illustrations of Lying in All its Branches (Opie, 1825)   219
Illustrations of Political Economy (Martineau, 1832)   249
'Image in Lava' (Hemans, 1827)   229
Imaginary Conversations of Literary Men and Statesmen, 4v (Landor, 1824–9)   211
Impartial Reflections on Queen of France (Robinson, 1791)   48
Importance of Religious Opinions (Necker; Wollstonecraft translation, 1788)   29
Improvisatore, in Three Fyttes, with Other Poems (Beddoes, 1821)   192
Improvisatrice and Other Poems (Landon, 1824)   213–14
Incondita (Browning, c.1826)   225
'Indian Serenade' (P.B. Shelley, 1823)   182, 204
Indiana (Sand, 1832)   250
Indicator   177, 181
Inferno (Dante; Cary's translation, 1805–6)   165
'Informers' (Hunt, 1817)   163
Inheritance, 3v (Ferrier, 1824)   212
Inkle and Yarico (Colman, 1787)   26
Inquiry into Authenticity of Miscellaneous Papers Attributed to Shakspeare (Malone, 1796)   62
Inquiry into Authenticity of Poems Attributed to Thomas Rowley (T. Warton, 1782)   11

Inquiry into Variolae Vaccinae (Jenner, 1798) 62
Institutes of Hindu Law (Jones 1794) 50
Intercepted Letters, or, Twopenny Post-Bag (Moore, 1813) 136
Interesting Narrative of Life of Olaudah Equiano (Equiano, 1789) 28
Introduction to Comparative Anatomy and Physiology (Lawrence, 1816) 152
Introduction to Principles of Morals and Legislation (Bentham, 1789) 33
'Introduction to Tale of Dark Ladie' (Coleridge, 1799) 80
Invariable Principles of Poetry (Bowles, 1819) 192
'Invention' (Fuseli, 1801) 86
'Invisible Girl' (M. Shelley, 1832) 253
Iphigenia (Goethe; Taylor translation, 1793) 36
Iphigenie auf Tauris (Goethe, 1787) 36
Iron Chest (Colman the Younger, 1796) 61
Isabella; or, Fatal Marriage (Southerne, 1782) 11
'Isabella; or, The Pot of Basil' (Keats, 1818) 169
Island in Moon (Blake, c.1784–5) 17
Island, or Christian and Comrades (Byron, 1823) 207
Ismael; Oriental Tale (Bulwer, 1820) 186
'It is beauteous Evening' (Wordsworth, 1802) 91
Italian, or Confessional of Black Penitents, 3v (Radcliffe, 1796, dated '1797') 65
Italy (Morgan, 1821) 194
Italy (Rogers, 1822–3, 1828, 1830) 144, **198**
Itinéraire de Paris à Jérusalem (Chateaubriand, 1811) 107
Ivanhoe, 3v (Scott, 1819; dated '1820') 183

Ivanhoe; or, Jew's Daughter (1820) 184
Ivanhoe; or, Knight-Templar (1820) 184
Ivanhoe; or, Saxon Chief (1820) 184

Jacqueline (Rogers, 1814) 143
Jane Eyre 214
'January 22nd 1824. Messalonghi' (Byron, 1824) 210
'Jean-Paul Friedrich Richter' (Carlyle, 1827) 227
'Jean-Paul Friedrich Richter Again' (Carlyle, 1830) 227
Jerusalem (Blake, 1820) 100
Jessonda (Spohr, 1823) 208
Jew (Cumberland, 1794) 51
Joan of Arc (Southey, 1795; dated '1796') 47, 60
'Jolly Beggars; or Tattermallions' (Burns, 1785) 20
'Journal in Cephalonia' (Byron, 1823–4) 208
Journal of Conversations of Byron (Medwin, 1824) 214
Journal of Conversations with Byron (Blessington, 1832–3) 251
Journal of Mission to Interior of Africa (Park, 1815) 101
Journal of Natural Philosophy, Chemistry and Arts 83
'Journal of Tour on Continent, 1820' (D. Wordsworth) 188
Journal of Tour to Hebrides, with Samuel Johnson (Boswell, 1785) 20
Journey Through Albania (Hobhouse, 1813) 137
Journey Through Holland and Western Frontier of Germany (Radcliffe, 1795) 51
'Journey to Rome' (A. Flaxman, 1787) 27
Julian (Mitford, 1823) 205
Julian and Maddalo (P.B. Shelley, 1818–19) 172

Jupiter and Thetis (Ingres, 1811)   107
Justine ou les Malheurs de la vertu (Sade, 1791)   38
'Juvenilia' (Austen, 1787–93)   27, 46
Juvenilia; or, Collection of Poems (Hunt, 1801)   10

Kabale und Liebe: Ein bürgerliches Trauerspiel (Schiller, 1784)   15
Keepsake   220, 230, 235, 239, 243, 248, 252–3
'Keepsake' (Coleridge, 1802)   92
Kelso Mail   71
Kendal Chronicle   170
Kenilworth, 3v (Scott, 1821)   189, 191, 231
Kinder- und Hausmärchen, 2v (Grimm and Grimm, 1812)   135
King Lear   168, 229
King Lear overture (Berlioz, 1831)   248
Klosterheim, or, the Masque (De Quincey, 1832)   250
Konrad Wallenrod (Mickiewicz, 1828)   235
Kritik der praktischen Vernunft (Kant, 1788)   30
Kritik der reinen Vernunft (Kant, 1781)   8
Kubla Khan (Coleridge, 1816)   68, 152, 153

L'Anglais mangeur d'opium (Musset, 1829)   238
L'elisir d'amore (Donizetti, fp 1832)   250
L'Histoire des républiques italiennes du Moyen Âge (Sismondi, 1809–18)   120
L'italiana in Algeri (Rossini, fp 1813)   135–6
  UK fp (1818)   175
'La Belle Dame Sans Merci' (Keats, 1820)   177
La Cenerentola, ossia La bontà in trionfo (Rossini, fp 1817)   159
  UK fp (1820)   183
La clemenza di Tito (Mozart, 1791)   39, 105
La Description de l'Égypte (1809–29)   120
La finta principessa (Cherubini, 1785)   18
La Folle journée, ou Le Mariage de Figaro (Beaumarchais, 1784)   17
La Grande Odalisque (Ingres, 1814)   107
La Nuit vénitienne (Musset, 1830)   243
La Peau de chagrin (Balzac, 1831)   246
La sonnambula (Bellini, 1831)   244
La Tour de Nesle (Dumas, 1831)   248
Lady of Lake; A Poem (Scott, 1810)   122
'Lady of Shalott' (Tennyson, 1832)   251
'Lady Susan' (Austen, 1793–5)   49
Lady's Diary (Jameson, 1826)   224
Lalla Rookh (Moore, 1817)   162, 197
  Dublin performance (1818)   171
  French translation (1820)   186
'Lament for James, Earl of Glencairn' (Burns, 1793)   40
'Lament of Mary Queen of Scots' (Burns, 1790)   35
Lament of Tasso (Byron, 1817)   161, 163
Lamia (Keats, 1820)   179
Lamia, Isabella, Eve of St Agnes, and other Poems (Keats, 1820)   187
Lancet   209
Landscape: Noon (Constable, 1821)   193
Laokoon (Lessing; De Quincey translation, 1826–7)   225
Laon and Cythna (P.B. Shelley, 1817)   160, 167
Laou-Seng-Urh, or, 'An Heir in his Old Age' (Wu; Davis translation, 1817)   159
Lara (Byron, 1814)   143

294 Title Index

Last Canto of Childe Harold's Pilgrimage (Lamartine; English translation, 1827) 217
Last Days of Byron (Parry, 1825) 217
Last Man, 3v (M. Shelley, 1826) 221, 222
Last of Mohicans (Cooper, 1826) 221
Late John Wilkes's Catechism of Ministerial Member (Hone, 1817) 167
Lawrie Todd, 3v (Galt, 1830) 239
Laws of Moral and Physical World (Mirabaud; Kearsley translation, 1797) 70
Lay of Last Minstrel; A Poem (Scott, 1805) 100
Lay Sermon, Addressed to Higher and Middle Classes, on Existing Distresses (Coleridge, 1817) 161
Lays of Leisure Hours, 2v (Jewsbury, 1829) 236
Le Comte Ory (Rossini, 1828) 234
Le Dernier Chant du pèlerinage d'Harold (Lamartine, 1825) 217
Le Dernier Chouan (Balzac, 1829) 236
Le Dernier jour d'un condamné (Hugo, 1829) 236
Le Génie du Christianisme (Chateaubriand, 1802) 86, 90
Le mie prigioni (Pellico, 1832) 190
Le More de Venise (Vigny, 1829) 238
Le nozze di Figaro (Mozart, 1786) 21 UK fp (1812) 133
Le Roi s'amuse (Hugo, fp 1832) 252
Le Rouge et le noir (Stendhal, 1830; dated '1831') 242
Leaping Horse (Constable, 1825) 217
Lear of Private Life! (Moncrieff, 1820) 186
'Lecture on Two Bills' (Coleridge, 1795) 59
'Lectures on *Belles Lettres*' (Coleridge, 1812) 134
'Lectures on Dramatic Literature of Age of Elizabeth' (Hazlitt, 1819) 182

Lectures on English Poets (Hazlitt, 1818) 171
'Lectures on Principles of Judgement, Culture, and European Literature' (Coleridge, 1818) **168–9**
Lectures on Rhetoric and Belles Lettres, 2v (Blair, 1783) 13
'Leech Gatherer' (Wordsworth, 1802) 91
Legend of Montrose (Scott, 1819) 178
'Legend of Sleepy Hollow' (Irving, 1819) 178
Legislative Rights (Cartwright, 1780) 3
Lenora: Ballad from Bürger (Taylor, 1796) 62
'Lenore' (Bürger, 1773) 62
Lenore: Ein Gedicht (Bürger) 62
Leonora (Bürger; Spencer's translation, 1796) 62
Leonora, 2v (Edgeworth, 1806) 105
Leonora. A Tale (Bürger; Stanley's translation, 1796) 62
Les Chouans (Balzac) 236
Les Danaïdes (Salieri, 1784) 16
Les Liaisons dangereuses (Laclos, 1782) 9
Les Orientales (Hugo, 1829) 235
Les Ruines, ou Méditations sur les révolutions des empires (Volney, 1791) 39
Les Voleurs (Friedel and de Bonneville, 1785) 8
'Letter of Elia to Southey' (Charles Lamb, 1823) 208–9
Letter on Abolition of Slave Trade (Wilberforce, 1807) 109
Letter on Education (Macaulay, 1790) 35
'Letter on Present Character of French Nation' (Wollstonecraft, 1793/1798) 71
'Letter on W.L. Bowles' Strictures' (Byron, 1821) 192
'Letter to -' (Coleridge, 1802) 90

Title Index

Letter to Abbé Raynal, on Affairs of North America (Paine, 1782) 6
Letter to Maria Gisborne (P.B. Shelley, 1824) 187
Letter to Member of National Assembly (Burke, 1791) 37
Letter to William Gifford (Hazlitt, 1818) 176
Letter to Women of England (Robinson) 77
Letter to Wyndham (Holcroft, 1795) 54
Letters from England by Espriella (Southey, 1807) 111
Letters from France (Williams, 1790–6) 40
Letters from Italy (Starke, 1800) 85
Letters and Journals of Lord Byron (Moore, 1830) 213, 239
Letters of Late Ignatius Sancho, an African (1782) 5
Letters to and from Late Samuel Johnson (Piozzi, 1788) 21
Letters Written During Short Residence in Sweden, Norway and Denmark (Wollstonecraft, 1796) 57
Letters Written During Short Residence in Spain and Portugal (Southey, 1797) 59
Letters to Young (Jewsbury, 1828) 235
Lettre à M Dacier (Champollion, 1822) 202
Lettre de Cachet (Gore, 1827) 227
'Lewti' (Coleridge, 1798) 72
Liber Studiorum, 14v (Turner, 1807–19) 112
Liberal: Verse and Prose from South
  v1 (1822) 203
  v2 (1823) 204
  v3 (1823) 206
  v4 (1823) 181, 208
Libertine, 4v (Dacre, 1807) 110
Liberty Hall (C. Dibdin, 1785) 18
Liberty Leading People (Delacroix, 1830) 241
Libor Amoris (Hazlitt, 1823) 206

Library (Crabbe, 1781) 6
Life of William Blake (Gilchrist, 1863) 4
Life of Buonaparte, 4v (Hazlitt, 1828–30) 223, 231
Life of Buonaparte, 9v (Scott, 1827–8) 227, 252
Life of Byron (Galt, 1830) 242
Life of Byron (Moore, 1830) 139, 191
Life of Fitzgerald, 2v (Moore, 1831) 245
Life of Haydn (Stendhal; English translation, 1817) 145
Life of Johnson (Hawkins, 1787) 24
Life of Johnson, 2v (Boswell, 1791) 22, 38, 57
Life of Medici (Roscoe, 1796) 65
Life of Nelson, 2v (Southey, 1813) 137
'Lines on Death of Sheridan' (Moore, 1816) 155
'Lines on Maria Beckford' (Austen, 1811) 125
'Lines supposed to have been sent to uncivil Dress maker' (Austen, 1805) 101
'Lines to Critic' (P.B. Shelley, 1823) 206
'Lines to Lady Weeping' (Byron, 1814) 130, 140
'Lines to Martha Lloyd' (Austen, 1806) 106
'Lines Written a Few Miles above Tintern Abbey' (Wordsworth, 1798) 74
'Lines Written Among the Euganean Hills, October 1818' (P.B. Shelley) 173
'Lines Written at Norwich on First News of Peace' (Opie, 1802) 90
'Lines Written at Shurton Bars' (Coleridge, 1795) 58
'Lines Written at Small Distance from my House' (Wordsworth, 1798) 71

Title Index

'Lines Written in Bay of Lerici' (P.B. Shelley)   201
'Lines Written in Early Spring' (Wordsworth, 1798)   72
Literary Chronicle   193, 228
Literary Gazette   185, 203, 204, 224, 228, 245
Literary Magnet   222
'Literary Sketches No. 1: Felicia Hemans' (Jewsbury, 1831)   244
'Literary Women No. 2: Jane Austen' (Jewsbury, 1831)   244
Little House in Kolomna (Pushkin, 1830)   242
Lives of Most Eminent English Poets, 4v (Johnson, 1781)   7
Loaves and Fishes (Blake, 1800)   82
Lodore (M. Shelley, 1835)   252
London Gazette   137
London Magazine   vii, 184, 189, **191–2**, 196, 198, 201–2, 205, 207–8, 210–11, 216, 224
Lord Byron and Contemporaries (Hunt, 1828)   231
'Lord Byron in Greece' (Bowring, 1824)   211
'Lord Byron's Poems on his Own Domestic Circumstances' (Byron, 1816)   152
Lord of Isles (Scott, 1815)   145
Lords and Commons (Gore, 1831)   248
Los Desastres de la Guerra (Goya, 1810–20)   80
'Loss of Breath' (Poe, 1832)   252
'Lost Pleiad' (Hemans, 1823, 1829)   209
Lounger (1785–7)   18, 23
Lousiad (Wolcot, 1786)   9
'Love' (Coleridge, 1800)   80
'Love and Freindship' (Austen, 1790)   35
'Love and Liberty' (Burns, c.1785)   20
Love Laughs at Locksmiths (Colman)   115
'Love Letters Book' (Hays)   7
Lovers' Vows (Inchbald, 1798)   75–6

Love's Frailties (Holcroft, 1794)   49
Loves of Angels (Moore, 1822; dated '1823')   204
Loves of Plants (Darwin, 1789)   31, 72
'Loves of Triangles' (Frere, Canning, Ellis, 1798)   72
'Lucy poems' (Wordsworth, 1798)   75
Lyric Odes to Royal Academicians, for MDCCLXXXII (Wolcot, 1782)   9
Lyrical Ballads (Coleridge/ Wordsworth, 1798)   75
  second edition, 2v (Wordsworth, 1801, dated '1800')   80, 84, **85**, 91
'Lyrical Poem on Death of Byron' (Solomos)   211
Lyrical Tales (Robinson, 1800)   84

M.P., or, Blue-Stocking (Moore and Horn, 1811)   127
Macbeth   50, 119, 131, 133, 229
'Madame d'Houtetot' (M. Shelley, 1823)   206
Madeline, a Tale, 2v (Opie, 1822)   198
Madoc (Southey, 1805)   102
Maeviad (Gifford, 1795)   20
Magic Lantern (Blessington, 1822)   198
Maid Marian (Peacock, 1822)   199
'Maid of Athens, ere we part' (Byron, 1812)   120
Man As He Is (Bage, 1792)   65
Manchester Guardian   193
Mandeville: Tale of Seventeenth Century in England, 3v (Godwin, 1817)   167
Manfred (Byron, 1817)   156, 161, 162
Manon Lescaut (Prévost, 1753; C. Smith translation, 1786)   21
Mansfield Park, 3v (Austen, 1814)   vi, 76, 125, 137, **142**, 150
  second edition   150, 151

Title Index

Manuel (Maturin, 1817)   153
'March to Moscow' (Southey, 1814)   142
Maria Stuart: Ein Trauerspiel (Schiller, 1800)   83
'Mariana in South' (Tennyson, 1832)   241
'Marie Antoinette's Lamentation' (Robinson, 1793)   48
Marino Faliero, Doge of Venice (Byron, 1821)   178, 186, 192
'Maritime Observations' (Franklin, 1785)   19
Marmion: Tale of Flodden Field (Scott, 1808)   113
Marriage, 3v (Ferrier, 1818)   170
Marriage of Heaven and Hell (Blake, 1790)   31
Mary (Wollstonecraft, 1788)   23, 29
Mask of Anarchy (P.B. Shelley, 1819)   180
Mass in D (Beethoven)   206, 253
Massacres of Chios (Delacroix, 1824)   214
Match Girl (Edgeworth, 1808)   115
Mathilda (M. Shelley, 1819–20)   180
May-Day with Muses (Bloomfield, 1822)   200
Mazeppa (Byron, 1819)   154, 161, 179
Mechanism of Heavens (Somerville, 1831)   221
Medallion Wafers (Landon, 1823)   204
Médée (Cherubini, 1797)   66
Méditations poétiques (Lamartine, 1820)   185
'Meeting of Bards' (Hemans, 1822)   200
Melincourt, 3v (Peacock, 1817)   160
Member: an Autobiography (Galt, 1832)   249
Melmoth the Wanderer (Maturin, 1820)   190
Melmoth the Wanderer (West, 1823)   207
'Memoir of Life and Writings of Mrs Radcliffe' (Talfourd, 1826)   205
'Memoir of Mr James Henry Leigh Hunt' (1810)   122
Memoir of Thomas Hardy (1832)   252
'Memoir of William Godwin' (M. Shelley, 1831)   244
Mémoires de la Vie Privée de Benjamin Franklin (1791)   34
Memoirs (Byron)   181
Memoirs (Robinson, 1801)   79, 83
Memoirs of Author of Vindication of Rights of Woman (Godwin, 1798)   71
Memoirs of Captain Rock (Moore, 1824)   211
Memoirs of Emma Courtney (Hays, 1796)   42, 64
Memoirs of Harriette Wilson (1825)   216
Memoirs of Late Mrs. Robinson (Robinson, 1801)   84
Memoirs of Late Thomas Holcroft (ed. Hazlitt, 1816)   117
Memoirs of Life of Sheridan, 2v (Moore, 1825)   219
Memoirs of Life and Writings of Benjamin Franklin (1817–18)   34
Memoirs of Queens (Hays, 1821)   188
Memoirs of R.L. Edgeworth, 2v (1820)   187
Memoirs of Rossini (Stendhal, 1824)   212
Memorials of Tour on Continent, 1820 (Wordsworth, 1822)   199
Merchant of Venice   229
Metaphysical Works, 2v (Kant; Richardson's translation, 1819)   183
Metrical Legends of Exalted Characters (Baillie, 1821)   192
Metrical Tales and Other Poems (Southey, 1805)   101
'Metzengerstein' (Poe, 1832)   249
'Michael' (Wordsworth, 1800)   84

Title Index

Midas (M. Shelley, 1820/1922)   186
Midsummer Night's Dream (Mendelssohn, fp 1827)   224
Military Register   189
Milton (Blake, 1810–11)   100
'Milton' (Macaulay, 1825)   219
Minister (Schiller; Lewis translation, 1797)   15
Minor Morals, 2v (C. Smith, 1798)   73
Minor Poems (Southey, 1815)   148
Minstrelsy of Scottish Border, 2v (Scott, 1802)   89
Mirandola (Procter, 1821)   191
Mirra (Alfieri, 1789)   180
Mirror of Parliament   249
Miscellaneous Papers of William Shakespeare (Ireland, 1795–6)   60
Miscellaneous Plays (Baillie, 1804)   100
Miscellaneous Poems (P.B. Shelley, 1826)   225
Miscellaneous Poems, 4v (Wordsworth, 1820)   188
Miscellaneous Works (Gibbon, 1796)   65
Misfortunes of Elphin (Peacock, 1829)   236
Missa Solemnis (Beethoven, UK fp 1832)   253
Missionary: Indian Tale, 3v (Owenson, 1811)   125
Moallakát (Jones, 1782)   11
Modern Greece, A Poem (Hemans, 1817)   163
Modern Griselda (Edgeworth, 1804)   100
Mogul Tale (Inchbald)   16
Monastery, 3v (Scott, 1820)   185
Monk (Lewis, 1794)   51, 69
Monk: Romance (Lewis, 1796)   61–2
'Monody' (for Princess Charlotte) (Thelwall, 1817)   166
'Monody on Death of Queen of France' (Robinson, 1793)   48

'Monody on Death of Sheridan' (Byron, 1816)   155
'Monody on Death of Sir John Moore' (Lewis, 1809)   116
'Monody on Rt Hon Charles James Fox' (Thelwall, 1806)   107
Monstre et magicien (Merle and Béread, 1826)   223
'Mont Blanc' (P.B Shelley, 1817)   155, 156, 166
Monthly Magazine   62, 64, 66, 68, 70, 71, 74 83, 224–6
Monthly Mirror   122
'Moral and Political Lectures' (Coleridge, 1795)   55
Moral Tales for Young People, 5v (Edgeworth, 1801)   88
Morgante Maggiore di Messer Luigi Pulci (Byron's translation, 1823)   181, **208**
Morning Chronicle   48, 51, 54, 130, 134, 137, 140, 142, 152, 155, 163, 189, 202, 210, 216
Morning Post   72, 79, 80, 81, 88, 92–3, 106, 130, 179
Mountain Landscape with Rainbow (Friedrich, 1810)   124
'Mourner' (M. Shelley, 1829)   238
Mouth of Nile (T. Dibdin, 1798)   74
Mr H (Charles Lamb, 1806)   108
'Mrs Charlotte Smith' (Hays, 1807)   108
'Mrs Jordan in Character of Comic Muse' (Hoppner, 1786)   16
Mrs Leicester's School (Mary and Charles Lamb, 1808)   116
'Mrs Robinson to Poet Coleridge' (Robinson, 1800)   83
Mummy! Tale of Twenty-Second Century, 3v (Webb, 1827)   229
Murder of Bishop of Liège (Delacroix, 1829)   206, 240
'My First Acquaintance with Poets' (Hazlitt, 1823)   206
'My First Play' (Charles Lamb, 1821)   197

'My Peggy's Face' (Burns, 1787)   27
Mysteries of Castle (Andrews, 1795)   55
Mysteries of Udolpho (Radcliffe, 1794; French translation, 1797)   51, 55
Nachträge zu den Reisebildern (Heine, 1831)   226
Naiad: a Tale, with Other Poems (Reynolds, 1816)   157
Naked Maja (Goya, 1797–1805)   70
Narrative of Facts, Relating to Prosecution for High Treason (Holcroft, 1795)   54
Narrative of Recent Discoveries in Egypt and Nubia (Belzoni, 1820)   190–1
Narrative, of Revolted Natives of Surinam (Stedman, 1796)   39
Natural Daughter, 2v (Robinson, 1799)   79
Natural History of Selborne (White, 1788; dated '1789')   30
Natural Theology (Paley, 1802)   93
Nature and Art, 2v (Inchbald, 1796; revised edition, 1797)   60
Necessity of Atheism (P.B. Shelley)   126
'Nelson's Victory' (Taylor, 1798)   74
New Canto (Lady Caroline Lamb, 1819)   182
New Harmony Gazette   224
New Monthly Magazine   176, 191, 205, 209, 218, 226, 229, 233, 239, 247, 249, 251, 253
New System of Chemical Philosophy (Dalton, 1808–27)   97
New Tales, 4v (Opie, 1818)   172
New Way to Pay Old Debts (Massinger)   151
Newry Telegraph   116
'Night Scene' (M. Shelley, 1830)   243
Night Thoughts (Young)   63
'Nightingale; Conversational Poem' (Coleridge, 1798)   63, 72
Nightmare (Fuseli, 1781)   9
Nightmare Abbey (Peacock, 1818)   174
Nina, o sia La pazza per amore (Paisiello, 1789)   31
No Song, No Supper (Storace, 1790)   34
Nobody (Robinson, 1794)   54
Noctes Ambrosianae (first part, 1822)   **199**
Nocturnes 1–3 (Field, 1812)   134
Non Mi Ricordo! (Hone, 1820)   188
Norma (Bellini, fp 1831)   248
North American   234
North Wales Gazette   140
Northanger Abbey (Austen, 1817)   76, 151, **168**
Notes of Journey Through France and Italy (Hunt, 1826)   216
Notions of Americans, 2v (Cooper, 1828)   223
Notre-Dame de Paris. 1482 (Hugo, 1831)   244
Nouvelle Justine (Sade, 1797)   38
Nouvelles Méditations poétiques (Lamartine, 1823)   185
Novice of Saint Dominick, 4v (Owenson, 1805)   103
Nurhamal, oder der Rosenfest von Caschmir (Spontini, 1822)   197
'Nutting' (Wordsworth, 1798)   75

'O My Luve's Like a Red, Red Rose' (Burns, 1794)   51
'O Solitude, if I must with thee dwell' (Keats, 1816)   153
O'Briens and O'Flahertys, 4v (Morgan, 1827)   229
Oath of Horatii (David, 1785)   17
Oberon (Weber, fp 1826)   221
Oberon: Ein Gedicht in vierzehn Gesängen (Wieland, 1780)   72, 221
Oberon: Poem from German (Wieland; Sotheby's translation, 1798)   72
Observations on Poetical Character of Pope (Bowles, 1821)   192
Observations on River Wye (Gilpin, 1782)   11

Observations and Reflections made in Course of Journey through France, Italy, Germany (Piozzi, 1784)   16
Observer (Sunday newspaper)   40
Oceanides (Jewsbury, 1832–3)   252
Oddities, or Dame Nature in Frolic (C. Dibdin, 1789)   33
'Ode: Autumn' (Hood, 1823)   205
'Ode. – 1817' (Wordsworth)   161
'Ode. Intimations of Immortality from Recollections of Early Childhood' (Wordsworth, 1802)   90
'Ode. Liberty' (Pushkin, 1817)   186
'Ode (From the French)' (Byron, 1816)   151
Ode on Departing Year (Coleridge, 1796)   64
'Ode on Destruction of Bastille' (Thelwall, 1789)   32
'Ode on Grecian Urn' (Keats, 1820)   178
'Ode on Melancholy' (Keats, 1820)   178
'Ode to Departed Regency-Bill' (Burns, 1789)   30
'Ode to Duty' (Wordsworth; first version, 1804)   98
'Ode to Framers of Frame Bill' (Byron, 1812)   130
'Ode to Liberty' (P.B. Shelley, 1820)   187, 188
'Ode to Naples' (P.B. Shelley, 1820)   189
Ode to Napoleon Buonaparte (Byron, 1814)   141
'Ode to Nightingale' (Keats, 1820)   178
'Ode to Psyche' (Keats, 1819)   177
'Ode to West Wind' (P.B. Shelley, 1820)   181, 187
Odes and Addresses to Great People (Hood and Reynolds, 1825)   216
Odes of Anacreon translated into English Verse (Moore, 1800)   83
'Odes to Nea' (Moore, 1803)   96

Odes Upon Cash, Corn, Catholics (Moore, 1828)   235
Odyssey (Flaxman's illustrations, 1793)   45
Odyssey (Homer)   38, 236
Oedipus Tyrannus; or, Swellfoot the Tyrant (P.B. Shelley, 1820)   188
Oeuvres complètes de Lord Byron, 10v (1819–21)   181
Of Population (Godwin, 1820)   190
'Oh Breathe not his name' (Moore, 1808)   96
'Old Cumberland Beggar' (Wordsworth, 1798)   71
'Old Familiar Faces' (Charles Lamb, 1798)   73
'Old Man Travelling' (Wordsworth, 1800)   65
Old Manor House: a Novel (C. Smith, 1793)   43
Ollier's Literary Miscellany   187
Omen (Galt, 1826)   221
Omniana, or Horae otiosiores (Coleridge and Southey, 1812)   134
'On Ancient and Modern Influence of Poetry' (Landon, 1832)   253
'On Cockney School of Poetry' (Lockhart, 1817)   165
On Constitution of Church and State (Coleridge, 1829; dated '1830')   239
'On Effects of War and Taxes' (Hazlitt, 1817)   164
'On Extinction of Venetian Republic' (Wordsworth, 1802)   67
'On Feeling of Immortality in Youth' (Hazlitt, 1827)   226
'On First Looking into Chapman's Homer' (Keats, 1816)   158
'On Garrick, and Acting' (Charles Lamb, 1811)   128
'On Ghosts' (M. Shelley, 1824)   211
'On Gods of Greece, Italy and India' (Jones, 1785)   18
'On Knocking at Gate in Macbeth' (De Quincey, 1823)   208

'On Magnetizing Power of More Refrangible Solar Rays' (Somerville, 1826) 221
'On Murder Considered as One of Fine Arts' (De Quincey, 1827) 225
'On Mystical Poetry of Persians and Indians' (Jones, 1791, 1792) 40
'On Poetry, and Relish for Beauties of Nature' (Wollstonecraft, 1797) 66
On Principles of Political Economy and Taxation (Ricardo, 1817) 168
'On Punishment of Death' (Hazlitt, 1831) 244
'On Receiving Branch of Mezereon' (Tighe, 1809) 120
'On Revisiting the Seashore' (Coleridge, 1801) 88
'On Robert Emmet's Tomb' (P.B. Shelley, 1812) 96
'On Seeing Elgin Marbles' (Keats, 1817) 160
'On Sitting Down to Read *King Lear* Once Again' (Keats, 1818/1838) 168
'On Slave Trade' (Coleridge, 1795) 57
'On Some of Old Actors' (Charles Lamb, 1822) 198
'On Spy-System' (Hazlitt, 1817) 163
'On Supernatural in Poetry' (Radcliffe, 1826) 205
'On Visiting Tomb of Burns' (Keats, 1818) 172
Ondine (Motte-Fouqué, 1811) 193
One O'Clock! Or, Knight and Wood Daemon (Lewis, 1807) 110
'One Thousand Lashes!!' (Hunt, 1810) 123
One, Two, Three, Four, Five; by Advertisement (J.H. Reynolds, 1819) 179
Opening of Waterloo Bridge (Constable) 250
Oracle 48

Original Poetry by Victor and Cazire (E. and P.B. Shelley, 1810) 124
Original Stories from Real Life (Wollstonecraft, 1788) 29, 39
Ormond; or Secret Witness (Brown, 1799) 76
Ormond, a Tale (Edgeworth, 1817) 163
'Osorio' (Coleridge, 1797) 65, 68
see also *Remorse* (Coleridge, 1813)
Otello (Rossini, 1816) 158
UK fp (1822) 200
Othello 140, 198, 229, 238, 252
Otho the Great (Keats, 1819) 179
Our Village, 5v (Mitford, 1824–32) 212
Outlines of Historical View of Progress of Human Mind (Condorcet; English translation, 1795) 50
Outlines of Philosophy of History of Man (Herder; Churchill translation, 1800) 17
'Outward Bound Ship' (Jewsbury, 1832) 252
'Ozymandias' (P.B. Shelley, 1818) 168

Pains of Sleep (Coleridge, 1816) 153
Palace of Art (Tennyson, c. 1831–2), 248
Palmyra, and Other Poems (Peacock, 1805; dated '1806') 105
Papillons (Schumann, 1831) 247
Paradise Lost (Fuseli, 1790 onwards) 34
Paris Monthly Review 203
'Parish Register' (Crabbe, 1807) 111
Parisina (Byron, 1816) 151
'Parody of Celebrated Letter' (Moore, 1812) 130
Pastorals of Virgil (Blake woodcuts, 1821) 197
Patronage, 4v (Edgeworth, 1813–14) 139
Paul Clifford, 3v (Bulwer, 1830) 240

302 Title Index

Paul and Mary (Bernardin de St Pierre; English translation, 1789) 27
Paul and Virginia (Bernardin de St Pierre; Williams' translation, 1796) 27
Paul et Virginie (Bernardin de St Pierre, 1787) 27
Paul's Letters to Kinsfolk (Scott, 1816) 148
Pauline (Browning, 1833) 252
Peace and Union Recommended (Frend, 1793) 46
Pedlar (Wordsworth) 66
Pelham, 3v (Bulwer, 1828) 232
Peripatetic (Thelwall, 1793) 46
Persuasion (Austen, 1817) 149, 155, **168**
'Pestilence' (Barrett, 1832) 248
Peter Bell. Tale in Verse (Wordsworth, 1819) 72, 177
Peter Bell; Lyrical Ballad (Reynolds, 1819) 177
Peter Bell the Third (P.B. Shelley, 1819) 177
Peveril of Peak, 4v (Scott, 1823) 204
Phantasmagoria, or, Sketches of Life and Literature (Jewsbury, 1825) 217
Philadelphia Saturday Courier 249, 251, 253
Philosophical and Miscellaneous Papers (Franklin, 1787) 19
Philosophical Transactions of Royal Society of London 84, 114, 221
Philosophical View of Reform (P.B. Shelley, 1819–20) 183
Philosophy of Melancholy (Peacock, 1812) 130
Phöbus – Ein Journal für die Kunst (1808) 113
Phytologia; or, Philosophy of Agriculture and Gardening (Darwin, 1800) 82
Piano Concerto No. 5, 'Emperor' (Beethoven, fp 1811) 128

Piano Concerto in E Minor (Chopin, fp 1830) 240
Piano Concerto in F Minor (Chopin, fp 1830) 240
Piano Concerto No 1 (Field, 1799) 50
Piano Concerto No 26 in D, 'Coronation' (Mozart, 1788) 28
'Picture, or Lover's Resolution' (Coleridge, 1802) 92
Picturesque Tour in Italy (Hakewill, 1818–20) 175
Picturesque Views of England and Wales (Turner, 1824–38) 215
Picturesque Views on Southern Coast of England (1814–26) 145
'Pine Forest of Cascine, near Pisa' (P.B. Shelley, 1824) 198
Pioneers; or, Sources of Susquehanna (Cooper, 1823) 204
Pirate, 3v (Scott, 1821) 193, 196
'Pitt' (Coleridge, 1800) 81
Pizarro (Sheridan, 1799) 78, 192
Plain Speaker, 2v (Hazlitt, 1826) 222
Plain and Succinct Narrative (Holcroft, 1780) 4
Plan for Conduct of Female Education (Darwin, 1797) 70
Plays and Poems of Shakespeare (Malone's edition, 10v, 1790) 36
Plays of Philip Massinger, 4v (1805; rev. edn., 1813) 101
Pleasures of Hope (Campbell, 1799) 78
Pleasures of Memory, a Poem (Rogers, 1792; 15th edn, 1806) 42
Plot Discovered: or Address to People, Against Ministerial Treason (Coleridge, 1795) 59
Poems, 2v (Bloomfield, 1809) 118
Poems (Browne/Hemans, 1808) 116
Poems (Burns)
 (1786) 20
 (1787) 23
 (1793) 40

Poems (Coleridge, third edition, 1803) 95
Poetical Works of Coleridge, 3v (1828) 233
Poetical Works of Coleridge, Shelley, and Keats (Paris, 1829) 239
Poems (Coleridge, Lamb, Lloyd, 1797) 68
Poems (Crabbe, 1807) 111
Poems (Keats, 1817) 160, 162, 165
Poems (Lovell and Southey, 1794) 54
Poems (Opie, 1802) 93
Poems (Poe, 1831) 244
Poems, 2v (Robinson, 1791, 1794) 41
Poems, 3v (Seward, ed. Scott, 1810) 117
Poems (Southey, 1796; dated '1797') 65
Poems (Tennyson, 1832; dated '1833') 253
Poems, 2v (Williams, 1786) 22
Poems, 2v (Wordsworth, 1807) 110, 112
  Poems (1815) 146
  Poetical Works, 4v (US edition, 1824) 215
  Poetical Works, 5v (1827) 227
  Poetical Works (pirated Paris edition, 1828) 235
Poems, Chiefly Lyrical (Tennyson, 1830) 241, 246
Poems, Chiefly in Scottish Dialect (Burns, 1786, 1793, 1801) 22, 35
Poems, on Several Occasions (Yearsley, 1785) 19
Poems, on Various Subjects (Yearsley, 1787) 19
Poems by Two Brothers (A. and C. Tennyson, 1827) 226
Poems by William Cowper (1782) 9
Poems on Various Occasions (Byron, 1806–7) 108, 111
Poems on Various Subjects (Coleridge, 1796) 62

Poems upon Several Occasions (Milton, 1785, 1791 editions) 18
Poems Descriptive of Rural Life and Scenery (Clare, 1820) 184
Poems Original and Translated (Byron, 1808) 113
Poems Written in Close Confinement (Thelwall, 1795) 51
Poésies (Gautier, 1830) 241
Poet's Pilgrimage to Waterloo (Southey, 1816) 148
Poetical Album (Watts, 1828–9) 219
Poetical Sketches (Blake, 1783) 14
Poetical Works (Scott) 245
Poetical Works of Late Thomas Little, Esq. (Moore, 1801) 87
Poetical Works of Late Thomas Warton (1802) 93
Polar Star of Entertainment (1830) 238
Political Essays, with Sketches of Public Characters (Hazlitt, 1819) 180
Political House That Jack Built (Hone, 1819) 180
Political Register 188, 203
Political Register (twopenny version, 1816) 157
'Poor Relations' (Charles Lamb, 1823) 207
Porcupine 84
Portland Gazette 190
Portrait of M. Bertin (Ingres, 1832) 253
Portrait of Nobleman [Byron] *in Dress of Albanian* (Phillips, 1814) 141
Posthumous Poems (P.B. Shelley, 1824) 187, 198, 208, 212–13
  with a preface by M. Shelley 212
Posthumous Works (Wollstonecraft, 1798) 70
Practical Education, 2v (Edgeworth and Edgeworth, 1798) 73
Practical View of Prevailing Religious System (Wilberforce, 1797) 66
Prairie (Cooper, 1826–7) 223
Precaution, 2v (Cooper, 1820) 190

Précis du système hiéroglyphique (Champollion, 1824) 202
Préface de Cromwell (Hugo, 1827) 230
Prelude (Wordsworth) 109
 Book III 89
 Book VI 35
 Two-Part *Prelude* (1799) 75
 Five-Book *Prelude* (1804) 98
 Thirteen-Book *Prelude*, Books I–V (1805) 98
 revisions (1831–2) 248
Present State of Manners of Metropolis of England (Robinson, 1800) 83
Presumption; or, Fate of Frankenstein (Peake, 1823) 207, 223
Pride and Prejudice, 3v (Austen, 1813) 64, 128, 134, **135**
 second (1813) and third (1817) editions 138
'Prince on St Patrick's Day' (Hunt, 1812) 130
Principles of Geology, 2v (Lyell, 1830, 1832) 241
Principles of Moral and Political Philosophy (Paley, 1785) 20
'Principles of Poetry' (Coleridge, 1808) 113
Prison Amusements (Montgomery, 1797) 61
Prisoner in Caucasus (Pushkin, 1821) 197
Prisoner of Chillon and Other Poems (Byron, 1816) 155, 156, 158
Private Memoirs and Confessions of Justified Sinner (Hogg, 1824) 213
Professional Education (R.L. Edgeworth, 1808) 73
Professional Volunteers (C. Dibdin, 1808) 113
Progress of Romance Through Times, Countries, and Manners (Reeve, 1785) 19
Prolegomena to Every Future Metaphysic (Kant; Richardson translation, 1819) 14

Prolegomena zu einer jeden künftigen Metaphysik (Kant, 1783) 14
Promenades dans Rome (Stendhal, 1829) 238
'Prometheus' (Byron, 1816) 155
'Prometheus' (Coleridge lecture, 1825) 217
Prometheus Unbound (P.B. Shelley, 1820) 172, 176, 180, 187, **188**
Prophecy of Dante (Byron, 1821) 178, 192
Proposal for Putting Reform to Vote (P.B. Shelley, 1817) 160
Proserpine (M. Shelley, 1832) 186, 248
Prospectus and Specimen of intended National Work by W. and R. Whistlecraft (Frere, 1817) 163
Provincial Antiquities of Scotland (Scott, 1826) 173
Provost (Galt, 1822) 201
Psyche; or, Legend of Love (Tighe, 1805) 102
Psyche, with Other Poems (Tighe, 1811) 121
Public Advertiser 11
Public Characters of 1800–1801 (1807) 108
'Push the Grog About' (C. Dibdin, 1789) 33

Quarterly Review 115, 117, 173, 176, 190, 192, 209, 219
Queen Mab (Shelley, 1813) 139
'Queen of Prussia's Tomb' (Hemans, 1826) 225
Queen's Matrimonial Ladder (Hone, 1820) 188
Quentin Durward, 3v (Scott, 1823) 204, 206
Quentin Durward at Liège (Bonington, 1828) 206

Racine et Shakespeare (Stendhal, 1823, 1825) 203
Radical (Galt, 1832) 249

Title Index 305

Raft of Medusa (Géricault, 1819)   180
Rambles Farther (C. Smith, 1796)   55
'Ravenna Journal' (Byron, 1821)   191
Rationale of Judicial Evidence (Bentham, 1827)   215
Rationale of Punishment (Bentham, 1830)   215
Rationale of Reward (Bentham, 1825)   215
'Recantation, An Ode' (Coleridge, 1798)   72
Recess, or, Tale of Other Times, 3v (Lee, 1783–5)   15
Recluse (Wordsworth)   82
'Recollections of Christ's Hospital' (Charles Lamb, 1813)   10
'Recollections of Italy' (M. Shelley, 1824)   210
'Recollections of South-Sea House' (Charles Lamb, 1820)   189
'Recollections of Tour Made in Scotland, A.D. 1803' (D. Wordsworth, revised 1822)   95–6, 202
Records of Woman (Hemans, 1825–7)   218, 238
Records of Woman: With Other Poems (Hemans, 1828)   232–3, 238
Red Books (Repton)   29
Red-Cross Knights (Holman, 1799)   8
Redgauntlet. Tale of Eighteenth Century, 3v (Scott, 1824)   212
'Reflections on Death of Louis XVI' (Yearsley, 1793)   45
'Reflections on Entering into Active Life' (Coleridge, 1796)   64
'Reflections on Having Left Place of Retirement' (Coleridge, 1795)   59, 64
Reflections on Revolution in France (Burke, 1790)   36
Reflector   128, 140
Reformists' Register (Hone, 1817)   159
Regulus (Turner, 1828)   233

Rejected Addresses: or New Theatrum Poetarum (J. and H. Smith, 1812)   134
'Religious Musings' (Coleridge, 1794, 1796)   54
Reliques of Robert Burns (Cromek, 1808)   116
Reliquiae Diluvianae (Buckland, 1823)   204
Remarks (on New Forest) (Gilpin, 1791)   11
Remarks on Antiquities, Arts, and Letters, During an Excursion to Italy (Forsyth, 1813)   90
Remorse (Coleridge, 1813)   68, **135**, 143, 161
René ou les effets de la passion (Chateaubriand, 1805)   86
Reply to Answer to Cursory Strictures (Godwin, 1794)   54
Reply to Bishop of Llandaff's Address (Wakefield, 1799)   76
Reply to Essay on Population, by Malthus (Hazlitt, 1807)   109
Requiem (Mozart, unfinished)   40, 223
Researches, Chemical and Philosophical (Davy, 1800)   75
'Resolution and Independence' (Wordsworth, 1802)   91
Restoration of Works of Art to Italy (Hemans, 1816)   154
Retrospection, 2v (Piozzi, 1801)   85
Revolt of Greeks (Buckstone, 1824)   213
Revolt of Islam (P.B. Shelley, 1818)   167
Rhodadaphne (Peacock, 1818)   169
Richard III (Shakespeare)   88, 140, 182, 229, 252
Rights of Man, 2v (Paine, 1791, 1792)   37, 41, 44
'Rip van Winkle' (Irving, 1819)   178
Rivals (Sheridan, 1775)   115
River Duddon (Wordsworth, 1820)   186

Title Index

Rivers of England (Turner, 1823–7) 210
Road to Ruin (Holcroft, 1792) 41
Rob Roy, 3v (Scott, 1817; dated '1818') 167
dramatization (1819) 17
Rob Roy overture (Berlioz, 1831) 248
Robbers (Schiller, 1782) 73
Robert le Diable (Meyerbeer, fp 1831) 247
Roderick, Last of Goths (Southey, 1814) 144
Rokeby (Scott, 1813) 135
Romance and Reality (Landon, 1831) 248
Romance of Forest, 3v (Radcliffe, 1791) 40–1
Romances of Real Life, 3v (Gore, 1829) 236
'Rome' (Landon, 1820) 185
Rome, Naples et Florence en 1817 (Stendhal, 1817; English translation, 1818) 165
Romeo and Juliet 228, 238
Rosalind and Helen (P.B.Shelley, 1819) 177
Round Table: Collection of Essays on Literature, Men, and Manners, 2v (Hazlitt, 1817) 159
Rovers (1798) 73
Rugantino (Lewis, 1805) 103
Ruined Cottage (Wordsworth) 66
Rural Rides (Cobbett, 1830) 203
Rural Tales, Ballads and Songs (Bloomfield, 1802) 89
Rural Walks (C. Smith, 1795) 55
Ruslan and Lyudmila (Pushkin, 1820) 186
'Rustic's Pastime in Leisure Hours: Helpston 1814' (Clare) 145

Sabine Women (David, 1795–8) 60
Sacontalá, or, fatal ring (Jones, 1789) 32
St Alban's Abbey (Radcliffe, 1826) 205
St Irvyne; or Rosicrucian (P.B. Shelley, 1810; dated '1811') 124
St Leon, Tale of Sixteenth Century, 4v (Godwin, 1799) 80
St Patrick's Day (Sheridan, 1775) 195
St Ronan's Well, 3v (Scott, 1823; dated '1824') 206, **210**
St Valentine's Day (Scott, 1828) 232
Safie: Eastern Tale (J.H. Reynolds, 1814) 145
Saggi de' Novellieri Italiani d'ogni secolo (Longfellow, 1832) 251
Salisbury Plain (Wordsworth, 1793) 46
Sanditon (Austen, unfinished) 159, 160
Sappho and Phaon (Robinson, 1796) 64
Sardanapalus (Byron, 1821) 191, 196
Sartor Resartus (Carlyle, 1833–4) 242
Saturday Evening Post 245
'Savage of Aveyron' (Robinson, 1801) 79
Scene on French Coast (Bonington, 1827) 226
Scene on Navigable River (Constable, 1817) 161
Scene on River Stour (Constable, 1819) 177
Sceptic. A Poem (Hemans, 1820) 183
School for Coquettes (Gore, 1831) 245
School for Widows, 3v (Reeve, 1791) 38
Schriften (Goethe, 7v, 1787–90) 36
Schwanengesang (Schubert, 1828) 234
'Scorn not Sonnet' (Wordsworth, 1827) 225
Scots Magazine 23
Scots Musical Museum (James Johnson, 1787) 25, 30, 40, 51
'Scots, wha hae' (Burns, 1794) 51
Scotsman, or Edinburgh Political and Literary Journal **159**
Seasons (Haydn, 1801) 87

Title Index   307

Secresy; or, Ruin on Rock, 3v (Fenwick, 1795)   56
Seduction: a Comedy (Holcroft, 1787)   24
Select Collection of Original Scottish Airs for Voice (Thomson, 1793–1818)   46, 51
Select Views in Cumberland, Westmorland, and Lancashire (Wilkinson, 1810)   118
Selection of Irish Melodies (Moore and Stevenson, 1808–34)   113–14, 115, 128, 139, 147, 173, 193, 215
Selection of Popular National Airs, 6v (1818–27)   170
Selection of Scots Songs (Urbani, 1794)   51
Selection of Welsh Melodies (Hemans/Parry, 1822)   200
Selena (Tighe, 1803/2012)   97
Self-Control, 2v (Brunton, 1811)   125
Sense and Sensibility, 3v (Austen, 1811)   60, 70, 118, **128**, 135, 150
  publication at author's expense   125
  second edition (1813)   138
'Sensitive-Plant' (P.B. Shelley, 1820)   185, 188
Seren Gomer (newspaper)   140
Series of Etchings Illustrative of Architectural Antiquities of Norfolk (Cotman, 1818)   9
Series of Plays, 3v (Baillie, 1798, 1802, 1812)   75
'She dwelt among th'untrodden ways' (Wordsworth, 1798)   75
Sheffield Iris   52, 55, 60–1
Shepherd's Calendar (Clare, 1827)   226
Sibylline Leaves (Coleridge, 1817)   109, 164
Sicilian Romance (Radcliffe, 1790)   35, 55
Sicilian Story, with Diego de Montilla, and Other Poems (Procter, 1819)   183
Siege of Corinth (Byron, 1816)   151

Siege of Valencia (Hemans, 1823)   207
'Signs of Times' (Carlyle, 1829)   237
'Simon Lee, Old Huntsman' (Wordsworth, 1798)   72
Simple Story, 4v (Inchbald, 1791)   37
Simple Tales, 4v (Opie, 1806)   106
'Sir Charles Grandison' (Austen, 1796–1800)   65
Sir Hornbook; or, Childe Launcelot's Expedition (Peacock, 1813; dated '1814')   139
Sir Proteus: Satirical Ballad (Peacock, 1814)   141
'Sisters of Albano' (M. Shelley, 1828)   235
'Six Lectures on Revealed Religion' (Coleridge, 1795)   57
Sketch Book of Geoffrey Crayon, Gent., 7v (Irving, 1819–20)   178, 250
'Sketch from Private Life' (Byron, 1816)   152
Sketches and Hints on Landscape Gardening (Repton, 1795)   29
'Sketches in Life of John Clare Written by himself'   192
Slavery: Poem (More, 1788)   28
Sleep and Poetry (Keats, 1817)   158
'Slumber did my spirit seal' (Wordsworth, 1798)   75
Smiles and Tears; or, Widow's Stratagem (M.T. Kemble, 1815)   150
Snob   237
Snowstorm: Hannibal Crossing Alps (Turner, 1812)   131
'So We'll Go No More A Roving' (Byron, 1817/1830)   160
'Solitary Reaper' (Wordsworth, 1805)   104
Some Account of English Stage 1660 to 1830, 10v (Genest, 1832)   253
'Song' (Byron, 1812)   120
'Song' (Wordsworth, 1798)   75
'Song of Battle of Nile' (Bowles, 1798)   74
Song of Bell (Schiller; Leveson-Gower's translation, 1823)   210

Song of Los (Blake, 1795)   60
'Song, Written for Indian Air' (P.B. Shelley, 1823)   204
Songs of Affections, with Other Poems (Hemans, 1830)   239
Songs of Experience (Blake, 1794)   55
Songs of Innocence (Blake, 1789)   33
Songs of Innocence and Experience: Shewing Two Contrary States of Human Soul (Blake, 1794)   55, 169
'Sonnet - To Science' (Poe, 1830)   242
Sonnets by Various Authors [Coleridge, Lamb, Lloyd, Southey] (1796)   64
Specimens of British Poets, 7v (Campbell, 1818)   176
Specimens of English Poets About Time of Shakspeare (Charles Lamb, 1808)   115
Specimens of German Romance (1827)   212
Specimens of Norman and Gothic Architecture, in County of Norfolk (Cotman, 1817)   9
'Spirit of Age' (J.S. Mill, 1831)   243
Spirit of Age; or, Contemporary Portraits (Hazlitt, 1825)   215
Spirit of Annuals   243
Spy: Tale of Neutral Ground (Cooper) 2v (New York, 1821)   197 3v (London, 1822)   197
Staffa. Fingal's Cave (Turner, 1832)   250
'Stanzas' (M. Shelley, 1832)   252–3
'Stanzas on Death of Byron' (Barrett, 1824)   211
'Stanzas on Death of Princess Charlotte' (Hemans, 1817)   166
'Stanzas to Memory of Late King [George III]' (Hemans, 1820)   184
Star (newspaper)   29, 30
Statesman's Manual (Coleridge, 1816)   158
Story of Rimini (Hunt, 1816)   151

'Strange fits of passion I have known' (Wordsworth, 1798)   75
Strictures on Modern System of Female Education, 2v (More, 1799)   77
String Quartet in E flat major, op. 127 (Beethoven, fp 1825)   216
Such Things Are (Inchbald, 1787)   24
'Superannuated Man' (Charles Lamb, 1825)   216
'Supplement: to Memory of Lord Charles Murray' (Hemans, 1827)   230
'Susan' (Austen, 1798–9)   76, 151 *see also Northanger Abbey*
'Swiss Peasant' (M. Shelley, 1830)   243
'Sylphid' essays (Robinson, 1799–1800)   80
'Sympathetic Address to Young Lady' (Byron, 1812)   130
Symphony No 3, 'Eroica' (Beethoven, 1805)   102
Symphonies Nos. 5–6 (Beethoven, fp 1808)   116
Symphony No. 9 (Beethoven, fp 1823)   206
Symphonie fantastique (Berlioz, fp 1830)   228, 243
Symphony No. 92, 'Oxford' (Haydn, 1789)   36
Symphonies Nos. 93–98 (Haydn, 1791–2)   36
Symphony No 101, 'Clock' (Haydn, 1794)   49
Symphony, No. 104, 'London' (Haydn, 1795)   49
Symphony No 1 (Mendelssohn, UK fp 1829)   236
Symphony No 38, 'Prague' (Mozart, 1786)   23
Symphony No 40 (Mozart, 1788)   29
Symphony No 41, 'Jupiter' (Mozart, 1788)   29
Symphony 'Unfinished' (Schubert)   203

Title Index 309

'Tables Turned' (Wordsworth, 1798) 73
Table-Talk, 2v (Hazlitt, 1821, 1822, 1824) 192
Take Your Choice! (Cartwright, 1778) 3
'Tale of Jerusalem' (Poe, 1832) 251
Tale of Mystery, a Melo-Drama (Holcroft, 1802) 93
Tale of Old Mortality, 3v (Scott, 1816) 158
'Tale of Passions, or, Death of Despina' (M. Shelley, 1823) 204
Tales (Crabbe, 1812) 133
Tales from Shakespear, 2v (Charles Lamb, 1807) 109
Tales of Alhambra (Irving, 1832) 250
Tales of Belkin (Pushkin, 1831) 242
Tales of Crusaders, 4v (Scott, 1825) 218
Tales of Fashionable Life, 6v (M.Edgeworth, 1809–12) 118
Tales of Grandfather (Scott, 1828–30) 230
Tales of Hall (Crabbe, 1819) 179
Tales of Heart, 4v (Opie, 1820) 187
Tales of My Landlord (Scott)
  First Series, 4v (1816) 158
  Second Series (1818) 172
  Third Series (1819) 178
  Fourth Series (1831; dated '1832') 248
Tales of Real Life, 3v (Opie, 1813) 137
Tales of Terror (Anonymous, 1800) 84, 124
Tales of Traveller, 2v (Irving, 1825) 219
Tales of Wonder (ed. Lewis, 1800; dated '1801') 84
Tales, and Historic Scenes, in Verse (Hemans, 1819) 178
Talisman (Scott, 1825) 218
'Tam o' Shanter' (Burns, 1791) 37
Tancredi (Rossini, fp 1813) 135; UK fp (1820) 186

Taschenbuch für 1798: Hermann und Dorothea (Goethe, 1797) 68
Task: Poem in Six Books (Cowper, 1785) 11, 19
Tatler (Hunt, 1830–2) 242
Teacher's Assistant (Trimmer, 1800) 91
Temper, or Domestic Scenes, 3v (Opie, 1812) 130
Temple of Nature; or, Origin of Society (Darwin, 1803) 91
Tennis Court Oath (David, 1791) 31
Thalaba the Destroyer (Southey, 1801, 1809) 79, 87, 92
Theatrical Recorder (Holcroft, 1805–6) 101
Theory of Moral Sentiments (A. Smith, 1759, 1790) 35
There is No Natural Religion (Blake, 1788) 30
'There was once a little girl' (C. Brontë, 1827) 226
'There was young lordling' (Tighe, 1799) 83
Theresa Marchmont; or, Maid of Honour (Gore, 1824) 213
Theseus and Minotaur (Canova, 1781–3) 8
Things as They Are; or Adventures of Caleb Williams, 3v (Godwin, 1794) 52
  see also Caleb Williams
'Third Anniversary Discourse, on Hindus' (Jones, 1786) 21
Third of May 1808 (Goya, 1814) 114
Thirty-Six Views of Mount Fuji (Hokusai, 1826–33) 225
'This Lime-Tree Bower my Prison' (Coleridge, 1800) 67
Thoughts on Education of Daughters (Wollstonecraft, 1786) 23
Thoughts on Importance of Manners of Great to General Society (More, 1788) 25
Thraliana (Piozzi diary, 1776–1809) 117

Title Index

Three Essays (Gilpin, 1792)   45
Three Histories (Jewsbury, 1840)   240
Three Trials of William Hone (Hone, 1818)   167
'Thyrza' poems (Byron, 1811–12)   128
'Timbuctoo' (Tennyson, 1829)   237
'Timbuctoo' (Thackeray, 1829)   237
Times   18, 116, 216, 248
'Times Newspaper. On Connexion Between Toad-Eaters and Tyrants' (Hazlitt, 1817)   159
Timour the Tartar (Lewis, 1811)   126
Tiriel (Blake, 1789)   33
Titan (Richter, 1800–3)   227
'To Author of *Excursion*' (Hemans, 1826)   222
'To Autumn' (Keats, 1819)   181
'To B.R. Haydon, on Seeing his Picture of Buonaparte on St. Helena' (Wordsworth, 1831)   244
'To B.R. Haydon, with Sonnet Written on Seeing Elgin Marbles' (Keats, 1817)   160
'To Charles Cowden Clarke' (Keats, 1816)   96
'To Fortune' (Coleridge, 1793)   48
'To Gentleman' (Coleridge, 1817)   109
'To Haggis' (Burns, 1786)   23
'To H.C. [Hartley Coleridge] Six Years Old' (Wordsworth, 1807)   63
'To J.H. Reynolds, Esq.' (Keats, 1818)   170
'To Jane. Invitation' (P.B. Shelley, 1822)   198
'To Jane. Recollection' (P.B. Shelley, 1822)   198
'To Kosciusko' (Hunt, 1815)   150
'To Louse' (Burns, 1785)   20
To Marry, or not to Marry (Inchbald, 1805)   101
'To Memory of Mrs. Lefroy' (Austen, 1808)   115
'To Mouse' (Burns, 1785)   20
'To Mr Fox' (Coleridge, 1802)   93
'To My Sister' (Wordsworth)   71

'To nation at large (LCS, 1792)   42
'To Shade of Mary Robinson' (Dacre, 1805)   84
'To Sky-Lark' (P.B. Shelley, 1820)   187
'To Sky-Lark' (Wordsworth, 1802)   90
'To Wordsworth' (Coleridge, 1807)   109
'To Wordsworth' (Hemans, 1826)   222
'Tom Bowling' (C. Dibdin, 1789)   33
'Tombs' (P.B. Shelley, 1812)   96
Torquato Tasso (Goethe, 1790)   36
Tour in England, Ireland and France 1828–9 (Pückler-Muskau; Austin translation, 1832)   253
Tour in Germany, Holland and England 1826–8 (Pückler-Muskau; Austin translation, 1832)   253
Tragedie, 5v (Alfieri, 1783–9)   15
'Tragic Muse' (Reynolds, 1784)   16
Traité Élémentaire de Chimie (Lavoisier, 1789)   30
Traités de legislation civile et pénale (Bentham; Dumont's translation, 1802)   93
'Transformation' (M. Shelley, 1830)   243
Translations from Camoens (Hemans, 1818)   171
Travels during the years 1787, 1788 and 1789 (Young, 1792)   25
Travels from Hamburg, 2v (Holcroft, 1804)   78
Travels in Arabia (Burckhardt, 1829)   165
Travels in Greece, Palestine, Egypt and Barbary (Chateaubriand; Shoberl's translation, 1812)   107
Travels in Interior Districts of Africa (Park, 1799)   57
Travels in Nubia (Burckhardt, 1819)   165
Travels in Syria and Holy Land (Burckhardt, 1822)   165

Treatise on Ancient and Modern
    Literature (Staël; English
    translation, 1803) 82
'Treatise on Method' (Coleridge,
    1818) 169
Trial at large of Thelwall (Thelwall,
    1795) 54
'Trident of Albion' (Thelwall,
    1805) 103–4
Trident of Albion: Epic Effusion
    (Thelwall, 1805) 104
Trifling Mistake in Erskine's recent
    Preface (Hobhouse, 1819) 183
Triumph of Liberty, or Destruction of
    Bastille (Dent, 1789) 32
Triumph of Life (P.B. Shelley,
    unfinished) 200
'Triumph of Whale' (Lamb,
    1812) 130
Troubadour (Landon, 1825) 328
'Trout' Quintet (Schubert,
    1819) 182
True Sun 249
Two Addresses to Freeholders of
    Westmorland (Wordsworth,
    1818) 170
Two First Cantos of Richardetto
    (Merivale, 1820) 184
Two Foscari (Byron, 1821)
    193, 196
'Two Founts: Stanzas Addressed to
    Lady' (Coleridge, 1827) 223
Two Letters on Prospect of Regicide
    Peace (Burke, 1796) 64

Über das Marionettentheater (Kleist,
    1810) 124
Über dramatische Kunst und Litteratur:
    Vorlesungen (A.W. Schlegel,
    1809–11) 120
Ultime lettere di Jacopo Ortis (Foscolo,
    1802, 1817) 156
Ulysses Deriding Polyphemus (Turner,
    1829) 236
United States Saturday Post 242
Universal Magazine 21

'Vala' (Blake; abandoned) 65
Valentine's Eve, 3v (Opie, 1816) 152
Valperga (M. Shelley, 1823) 185, 205
Vampyre (Polidori, 1818) 176
Vancenza; or, Dangers of Credulity
    (Robinson, 1792) 41
Vathek: Arabian Tale (Beckford) 8
    'Episodes' (1785–) 22
    Henley translation from French
        (1786 June) 22
    published in French in Lausanne
        (1786 December) 22
    written in French (1782) 22
Venetian Bracelet (Landon, 1829) 238
'Venice. An Ode' (Byron, 1819) 179
Venice Preserved (Otway) 16
'Venus de Milo' 186
'Vernal Ode' (Wordsworth, 1817) 161
'Verses Written in Solitude'
    (Blachford, 1792) 42
Versi (Leopardi, 1826) 215
Vespers of Palermo (Hemans,
    1823) 209
Victim of Prejudice (Hays, 1799) 69
Vie de Rossini (Stendhal, 1824) 212
Vies de Haydn, Mozart et Métastase
    (Stendhal, 1815) 145
View of English Stage (Hazlitt,
    1818) 170
View of Evidences of Christianity
    (Paley, 1794) 54
View of Orvieto (Turner, 1828) 233
View of State of Europe during Middle
    Ages, 2v (Hallam, 1818) 172
Views of Society in America (Wright,
    1821) 173
Village (Crabbe, 1783) 13
Village Minstrel (Clare, 1821) 195
Vindication of Rights of Men
    (Wollstonecraft, 1790) 36
Vindication of Rights of Women
    (Wollstonecraft, 1792) 41, 44
Vindiciae Gallicae (Mackintosh,
    1791) 37
Violin Concerto in D (Beethoven,
    1806) 108

Violin Concertos (Paganini, 1816–30) 124
Virginius (Bidlake, fp 1820) 186
Virginius (Knowles, fp 1820) 186
Vision of Don Roderick (Scott, 1811) 127
Vision of Medea (Turner, 1828) 233
Vision, A, of Judgement (Southey, 1821) 184, 193
Vision, The, of Judgement (Byron, 1822) 184, 193, 195, 203, 213
'Visionary Heads' (Blake) 182
Visions of Daughters of Albion (Blake, 1793) 49
'Visit to Brighton' (M. Shelley, 1826) 224
Vivian Grey, 5v (Disraeli, 1826–7) 222
Vortigern (Ireland, 1796) 62
Voyage dans la Basse et la Haute Égypte (Denon, 1802) 93

Waggoner (Wordsworth, 1819) 178
Wallenstein (Schiller, 1800) 82
Wallensteins Tod (Schiller; Coleridge's translation, 1800) 82
Wanderer; or, Female Difficulties, 4v (Burney D'Arblay, 1814) 140
Wanderer Above Sea of Mist (Friedrich, 1818) 175
'Wanderings of Cain' (Wordsworth and Coleridge, 1797) 69
Wanderings of Warwick (C. Smith, 1794) 49
'War Song of Suliotes' (Byron, 1824) 210
Wasp 224
Wat Tyler (Southey, 1794/1817) 53, 160
Watchman (Coleridge, 1796) 61
Waverley, 3v (Scott, 1814) 142, 146, 183, 226
'Waverley' novels or 'Magnum Opus' (Scott's edition, 1829–33) 237
Waverley overture (Berlioz, 1827–8) 230

Wealth of Nations (A. Smith, 1776, 1785) 35
Weekly Political Register (Cobbett) 89, 109
Werner (Byron, 1822) 203
West-östlicher Divan (Goethe, 1819) 180
Westminster Review 210, 211, 224, 232
Westmorland Gazette 172
'What is the People?' (Hazlitt, 1817) 165
What is She? (C. Smith, 1799) 77
Wheel of Fortune (Cumberland, 1795) 56
'When Freedom nursed her native fire' (T. Warton, 1786) 22
'When Winchester races' (Austen, 1817) 163
'Where braving angry Winter's storms' (Burns, 1787) 27
'White Doe of Rylstone' (Wordsworth, 1807–15) 112
White Doe of Rylstone (Wordsworth, 1815) 148
White Horse (Constable, 1819) 177
Whitehall Stairs, June 18th, 1817 (Constable, 1832) 162
Widow: Picture of Modern Times, 2v (Robinson, 1794) 50
Wieland; or Transformation. American Tale (Brown, 1798) 74
Wife; or, Model for Women, 3v (Edgeworth, 1810) 121
Wild Flowers; or, Pastoral and Local Poetry (Bloomfield, 1806) 105
Wild Irish Girl, 3v (Owenson, 1806) 107
Wild Oats (O'Keeffe, 1791) 37, 115
Wilhelm Meister's Apprenticeship, 3v (Carlyle's translation, 1824) 212
Wilhelm Meisters Lehrjahre (Goethe, 1795–6) 212
Wilhelm Meister's Travels (Carlyle's translation, 1827) 212

Title Index

Wilhelm Meisters Wanderjahre (Goethe, 1821) 212
Wilhelm Tell (Schiller, 1804; English translation, 1829) 98
William and Helen (Scott, 1796) 62
Winter Landscape with Church (Friedrich, 1811) 129
Winterreise (Schubert, 1828) 226
Winter's Tale 3
Winter's Wreath 248
Witch of Atlas (P.B. Shelley, 1820) 188
'Witches and other Night-Fears' (Charles Lamb, 1821) 196
'With a Guitar. To Jane' (P.B. Shelley, 1822) 198
Wives as they Were and Maids as they Are (Inchbald, 1797) 66
Woman; Or, Ida of Athens, 4v (Owenson, 1808; dated '1809') 116
'Woman and Fame' (Hemans, 1828) 235
'Woman on Field of Battle' (Hemans, 1827) 230
Wood Daemon (Lewis, 1807) 110
Woodstock; or, Cavalier, 3v (Scott, 1826) 219, 222
'Work Without Hope' (Coleridge, 1827) 216
Works, 2v (Barbauld, 1825) 216
Works, 9v (Jonson, 1816) 101
Works of Alexander Pope, 10v (1806) 108

'Written at Athens. January 16th, 1810' (Byron) 119
'Written at Cwm Elan' (P.B. Shelley, 1811) 131
'Written at West-Aston. June, 1808' (Tighe) 114
'Written on Day Hunt Left Prison' (Keats, 1815) 145
Wrongs of Woman (Wollstonecraft, 1798) 63, 70

'Yarrow Revisited' (Wordsworth, 1831) 246
'Yarrow Unvisited' (Wordsworth, 1803) 96
'Yarrow Visited' (Wordsworth, 1814) 144
Year's Residence in United States of America (Cobbett, 1818) 162
Yellow Dwarf 165
'Young Poets' (Hunt, 1816) **157–8**

Zapolya (Coleridge, 1817) 146, 151, 152, **167**, 169
Zastrozzi, a Romance (P.B. Shelley, 1810) 122
Zelmira (Rossini, 1822) 209
Zofloya; or, The Moor, 3v (Dacre, 1806) 106
Zoonomia; or, Laws of Organic Life (Darwin, 1794, 1796) 51
Zur Farbenlehre (Goethe, 1810) 124

Subject Index

Abbotsford see Galashiels
Aberdeen   26, 28
Aberfeldy   26
Abolition of Slave Trade Act
    (1807)   109
Abolition of Slavery Act (1833)   251
Abu Qir (Aboukir) Bay   74
Abu Simbel: Great Temple of
    Rameses II   164
Acre   77
Act of Union (Great Britain and
    Ireland, 1800)   83
Adlestrop   106
Afghanistan   178
agriculture   47, 82, 133, 241
Albania   119, 137, 240
Albaro: Casa Saluzzo   203
Aldeburgh   8
Alexandria   155, 233, 240
Alfoxden (Alfoxton) House   67, 69, 73
Alnwick   25
Alps   35, 131, 156, 233
Alresford (Hampshire)   27
Ambleside   96, 114, 241
American Revolution   3
Amherst (Massachusetts)   243
Amicable Society for Perpetual
    Assurance   123
Amiens   201
Amsterdam   56
Anglicanism and Anglicans   46, 68, 221, 233
Anglo-Maratha war   166
Anglo-Mysore war   78
Anglo-Nepalese war   152
Annan   25, 143
annuities   67, 70, 147
antiquities   33–4, 37
Anti-Slavery Society   204

Antwerp   153
apothecaries   123, 155
Appleby   117
Arcola (1796)   61
Armagh   58
Armée de l'Intérieur (France)   58
Army of England (Bonaparte, 1797)   68
Army of Italy (French)   61
arrests   48, 51, 73, 76, 90, 94, 132, 158, 160, 180–1, 183–4, 189
Arrochar   25
Arundel   228, 229
Ashbourne: Mayfield Cottage   132
Asiatick Society of Bengal   18, 21, 40
Aspern-Essling (1809)   118
assassinations   86, 131, 184, 190, 234, 247
Association for Preservation of
    Liberty and Property   44
Association of Friends of
    Poland   243
Astley's company   32
Astronomical Society of
    London   185
atheism   126, 214
Athens   33–4, 83, 119–21, 123, 126, 222
atomic weights   97
Auchinleck   57
Austerlitz (1805)   104
Australia   85
Austria   42, 58, 61, 68, 76, 83, 86, 103–4, 118, 120, 138, 140–1, 143, 189, 243, 245
Austrian Netherlands
    (Belgium)   58
Autun   35
Aviemore   26
Ayr   172

314

Bachygraig: Brynbella (house)   58
Badajoz (1812)   129
Baden   98
Bagnacavallo convent   199
Bagni di Lucca   171, 173
Bagni di San Giuliano   193, 195
Bakerian lectures   108, 111
ballads   62, 64, 89, 139, 141, 177
Ballinanmuck (County Longford)   74
Baltimore   93, 98, 190, 234
Bank of England   65
Bank of North America   21
banking crisis (1797)   65
Bannockburn   26, 51
Baptist Missionary Society   44
Basel   35, 153
Bassae: Temple of Apollo Epicurius   127
Bastille (1789)   31–2, 35, 39
Batavian Republic   56, 57
Bath   5, 7, 30, 54, 58, 74, 102, 106, 139, 158–9, 253
Bath: Abbey Churchyard   156
Bath: Ashley   144
Bath: Gay Street   100–1
Bath: Grand Pump Room   80
Bath: Green Park Buildings East   99
Bath: Lansdown Terrace   202
Bath: Paragon Buildings   69
Bath: Sydney Place   87
Bath: Trim Street   105
Battle of Nile (1798)   74
Battle of Pyramids (1798)   74
Bay of Baiae   174, 206
Beaconsfield   67
Beaufort Buildings   61
Bedhampton   175
Begums of Oudh   24
Belfast   40, 57, 100, 172, 318
Belgium   58, 242
Bell Rock lighthouse   143
Ben Nevis   172
Bencoolen (Sumatra)   175
Bengal   14, 24
Bergamo   69

Berkeley Castle   134
Berkshire   16
Berlin   68, 73, 107, 135, 194, 197, 247
Berlin Decrees (1806)   108
Bermuda   96, 98, 181, 196
Berrywell   25
Berwick-on-Tweed   25
Besançon   89
Bessarabia   186
Bexhill (Sussex)   136
biography and autobiography   26, 32, 93, 168, 249, 254
Birmingham   5, 39, 147
Birmingham Canal   61
Birmingham Town Hall   250
Bishop's Middleham   87–8
Blair Atholl   26, 142
Blair Castle   26
'Blanketeers' March (1817)   160
Blasphemous and Seditious Libels Act   182
blasphemy   61, 167
Blenheim   74, 94
Blois   42
'Bluestocking' circle   13
Board of Control (East India)   16
Bogotá   180
Bohemia   245
Boldino   242
Bolivia   218
Bologna   161, 174, 178, 180–1, 183, 196
Bonn   13, 233, 251
Bordeaux   232, 241
Borders (Scottish)   25, 39, 66
Borodino (1812)   133
Boston (Massachusetts)   3, 86, 90, 116, 190, 215, 227, 234, 255
Boston: Second Church   253
Bosworth Field   111
Botany Bay   47, 49
Boulton & Watt company   61
Boulton–Watt engines   165
Bourg-la-Reine   50
Bracknell   138

316 Subject Index

Bradford: Thornton   153, 163, 172
Brandesbury (Brondesbury)   29
Brazil   112, 202, 249
Brecon: Llyswen Farm   68, 80
Bremhill (Wiltshire)   146
bridges   5, 91, 139, 154, 221, 250
Bridgwater   67
Brientz   156
Brighton (Brighthelmstone)   14, 40, 114, 224, 232
Brighton: Marine Pavilion (constructed 1815–23)   14, 146
Bristol   16, 23, 25, 32, 45, 53, 56–60, 63, 66, 68–9, 71–4, 79, 82, 94, 110, 113, 139, 143–4, 247
Bristol: Broad Street (White Lion)   138
Bristol: Castle Green   55
Bristol: College Green   55
Bristol: Corn Market   55
Bristol: Oxford Street (Kingsdown)   62
Bristol: Pelican Inn   59
Bristol: Pneumatic Institute   75
Bristol: Theatre Royal   72
Bristol: Wellington Street   151
Bristol: White Lion   141
Britain *see* United Kingdom
British Army   53
British Association   246
British and Foreign Bible Society   98
British Institute   231
British Museum   91
  Elgin Room (1817–31)   159
  Elgin Room, new (1832–)   159
  frieze of Temple of Apollo Epicurius   127
  Townley collection   105
  'Younger Memnon'   155
Brittany   224
Broughty Ferry   132
Bruges   153
Brunswick   75
Brussels   146, 148, 153, 220
Buffalo (New York)   98
Bukhara   178

burials   17, 116, 163, 204, 208, 215, 217, 219, 222–3, 228, 245, 249, 252
  see also 'Paris: *Panthéon*'
Burlington (New Jersey)   32
Bury St Edmunds   107, 122

Cabinet   184
Cadiz   118
Cairo   165
Calabria   149
Calais   16, 35, 91, 92, 153, 179, 187
Calcutta   32, 50, 51, 127
Caledonia (steamer)   165
Caledonian Canal Commission   95
Callander   142
Calne (Wiltshire)   145, 167
Camberwell   131
Camborne (Cornwall)   88
Cambridge   49, 53, 122, 128, 142, 144, 243
Cambridge Conversazione Society, 'Apostles'   234
Cambridge University   20, 54, 114, 221, 246
Cambridge University: Chancellor's Medal   237
Cambridge University: Christ's College   231
Cambridge University: Jesus College   40
Cambridge University: Members' Prize   22
Cambridge University: Senate House   46
Cambridge University: St John's College   27
Cambridge University: Trinity College   104, 198, 230, 233, 236
Cambridge University: Trinity Hall   198
Camperdown (1797)   68
Campton   208
Canada   98, 173, 190
canals   95, 104
Canterbury (Kent)   127, 161

Canton 47
Cape St Vincent (1797) 65
Cape Verde Islands 249
Capuchins 123
Caracas 123
Carbonari uprising 189–90, 191
Carlisle 25, 28, 69, 149
Carrara 195
Caserta 31
Catania 99, 103
Catechism 32
Catholic Association 206
Catholic Relief Act (1778) 3;
   (1793) 55
Catholic Relief Bill (1825) 217
Catholicism and Catholics 58, 85,
   91, 231–2, 236
Cato Street Conspiracy 184
Caucasus 186
Ceiriog River 104
census (1801–) 86
Cephalonia 208, 210, 218
Ceremony of Supreme Being 43
Chalk Farm 107
Chambéry 182, 207
Chamonix 35, 92, 155, 156
Charenton asylum 145
Charleston 3
Chatsworth 222
Chawton 118, 162
Cheddar 32, 72
Cheltenham 133, 134
chemical affinity (electrical
   nature) 108
chemistry 89, 96–7, 218, 230
Chester 82
Chichester 175
Chichester Guildhall 95
children and childhood 7, 74, 81, 90
Chillon 156
Chios massacres (1822) 199, 214
Chirk aqueduct 104
cholera 242, **247**, 252
Christianity and Christians 66,
   86, 163
Christies 78

Church of England 15
Church Missionary Society 77
Cincinnati 246
Ciudad Rodrigo (1812) 129
Civitavecchia 243
Clapham Sect 45
class 66, 94
classical history and culture 61,
   62–3, 105, 120
Clermont (steamboat) 111
Clevedon 58
Clifton 95, 106, 116, 138, 193
Clonmel 32
Coalbrookdale: Iron Bridge 5
'Cockney' school 192
Code civil des français 98
Colchester 17, 19
Coldbath Fields 130
Coldstream 25
Coleorton (Leicestershire) 108,
   110, 122, 225, 234
Cologne 35, 152, 247, 251
Cologny 154
colonies 37, 39, 109
Combination Act 79
Commission on Administration of
   Justice in Scotland 115
Commissioners for Northern
   Lighthouse Service 143
Committee for Abolition of Slave
   Trade 25
Committee of General Security
   (France, 1792–3) 44
Committee of Public Instruction
   (France, 1792) 43
Committee of Public Safety (France,
   1793–94) 44, 46, 47
Como 142
concerts 50, 91, 124, 246, 250
Concordat (1802) 91
Congress of Vienna 144
Conseil d'État (France) 163
Constantinople (Istanbul) 83, 121,
   192, 240
Constitutional Society of
   Birmingham 39

Subject Index

Consulate (France, 1799–1804)   80
Continental System (1806)   108, 124
Convention of Cintra   115
Conwy suspension bridge   221
Copenhagen   55, 57, 111
Copenhagen (1801)   86
Coppet   155, 163
copyright   10, 51, 65, 134, 150–1, 160, 162, 192, 200, 214, 219, 229, 240, 245
  see also payments
Corn Law   146
Cornwall   88–9
Corunna (1809)   116
County Clare   239
County Donegal   76
County Durham   105, 144
County Kilkenny   121
County Longford   74
County Mayo   74
coup d'état (attempted)   94
Court of King's Bench   125
Court of Requests   245
Coventry   33
Cowan Bridge (Lancashire)   214
Cowes Regatta   228
Coxhoe (County Durham)   105
Craigenputtoch   224
Crieff   26
'crimp houses' (taverns)   53
Cromarty   172
Croxton-Kerrial   140
Culloden   26
Cumberland   11, 136
Cuxhaven   78

Darlington: Halnaby   145
Dartmouth   201
Datchet   6
Daventry   133
Deal   114
death penalty   4, 129
  see also executions
debt/s   49, 131, 156, 181, 198
Decembrists   220
Dee, River   104

'Defenders' (Catholic)   58
Della Cruscans   19
Denbighshire   37
Denmark   86, 111
Derby   6, 18, 60, 63, 68, 91, 166, 247
Derby Philosophical Society   12
Devon   63, 87, 132, 171
Devonport   248
Dieppe   214
'difference engine' (Babbage)   200, 253
Directory (France, 1795–9)   59, 80
divorce   43, 187, 188, 197, 201
Doctors' Commons   235
Don Juan (boat)   201
Dorset   20, 94
Dorset: Racedown Lodge   58, 67
Dover   57, 88, 153, 181, 233
drawings   19, 39, 79, 90, 131, 145, 189
Dresden   116, 123, 223
Dresden: Exhibition of Patriotic Art   141
Dresden (1813)   138
Drumlanrig   163
Dryburgh   25
Dryburgh Abbey   96, 222, 252
Dublin   22, 23, 40, 52, 57, 76, 95, 107, 113, 130, 195–6, 215, 218, 241, 244
Dublin: Newgate prison   73
Dublin: St Peter's Church   215
Dublin: Theatre Royal   109, 171
Dublin: Trinity College   55, 218
duels   107, 191–2, 236
Dumbarton   25
Dumfries   29, 32, 46, 54, 172
Dumfries: Burns' mausoleum   63
Dumfries: St Michael's churchyard   63
Dumfries: Wee Vennel   39
Dumfriesshire   60, 120
Dunbar   25
Dundee   26, 132
Dunkeld   26
Dunmow   97

Duns   25
Durham   80, 87, 229
Durham University Act   251

Eartham (Sussex)   43
East Bergholt (Suffolk)   77
East Cowes Castle   228
East Dereham (Norfolk)   82
East India Act (1784)   16
East India Bill (1783)   14
East India Company   15, 16, 42, 78, 152, 161, 166, 175, 177, 189, 216
East India Company: Examiner's Office   207
Ecclefechan (Dumfriesshire)   60
Ecuador   180
Edgeworthstown   218
Edinburgh   13, 16, 22–3, 25, 27–8, 30, 35, 40–1, 47–9, 64, 78, 87, 95–6, 100–1, 104, 110, 113, 125, 135–6, 139, 142, 145–6, 151, 153, 158–9, 167, 170, 173, 178, 183, 185, 189–91, 193–4, 200–3, 206–7, 212, 214, 217–18, 221, 225, 227, 229–30, 232, 235, 243, 248, 250
Edinburgh: British reform convention   48, 51
Edinburgh: Castle Street   69
Edinburgh: Comely Bank   224
Edinburgh: Court of Session   106, 119
Edinburgh: Frederick Street   138
Edinburgh: George Street   69, 127
Edinburgh: Lasswade cottage   69, 99
Edinburgh: Renton Inn   197
Edinburgh: Theatre Royal   176
Edinburgh: Theatrical Fund dinner (1827)   226
Edinburgh Coal Gas Company   209
Edinburgh Gas Light Company   209
Edinburgh High School   14
Edinburgh New Town: Assembly Rooms   24
Edinburgh Oil Gas Light Company   209

Edinburgh Theatre   121
Edinburgh University   14, 120, 226
education   81, 113, 138, 246
Egypt   74, 79, 91, 102, 120, 122, 189, 191, 229, 240
Elba   vi, 141, 146
electromagnetic induction (Faraday)   245
electromagnetic rotation (Faraday)   195
Elgin   26
'Elgin marbles'   83, **111**, 150–2, 159, **160**
Elleray   120
Ellesmere (Llangollen) Canal   104
Ellisland   29
elocution   **88**
elopements   127, **142–3**
emigration   22, 50
Emmet rising (Dublin, 1803)   95, 96
Enfield   96, 208
England   8, 9, 25, 34, 44, 46, 48, 52, 78, 83, 87, 90, 106, 112, 123, 126–7, 135, 139, 144, 245, 253
   eastern   11
   north-eastern   247
   northern   28, 60, 66
   western   11
England and Wales   215
   censuses (1801, 1831)   86
Englefield Green   84
English Channel   18, 165
engravings   24, 39, 63, 83, 103, 125, 145, 175, 198, 215, 225, 249
Ephesus   121
Epirus: Janina (Ioannina)   119, 198
essays   11, 22, 29, 45, 66, 73, 76, 102, 109, 139, 143, 146, 159, 164, 170, 181, 191, 197, 222
Estates General (France)   31
Este   166, 173, 174
Etna   99
Eton College   100, 102
Etruria factory   55
Etruria Hall   55

320 Subject Index

Europe   16, 53, 91, 118, 132, 139, 141, 223, 225
Eutin   23
Evershot   9
excisemen   32, 45, 54, 136
executions   45, 46, 48, 50, 52, 78, 94, 96, 98, 114, 131, 149–50, 166, 184, 186, 192, 220, 229, 231, 235, 241, 248
Exeter   79
exhibitions   177, 193, 222
  see also Royal Academy
exile   10, 46, 50, 78, 186, 213–14, 220, 224
Eyemouth   25
Eywood (Herefordshire)   134, 135, 136

factions   210, 218
Falmouth   118
Farnley Hall   177
Felpham (Sussex)   83, 95
fencing   56, 104
Ferney   155
Ferrara   161, 174, 178
Festival of Liberty (Paris, 1793)   48
Festival of Supreme Being (Paris, 1794)   52
feudal rights (abolition, 1789)   32
fines   122, 193
Fingal's Cave   236
fire   4, 22, 115, 117
Flight to Varennes (1791)   38
Flodden Field   113
flogging   42, 122, 123
Florence   4, 27, 106, 142–4, 161–2, 165, 179, 182, 189, 194–6, 208, 215, 230, 233, 247
Florence: Via Valfonda (Palazzo Marini)   181
Foligno   161
Fontainebleau   155
Fonthill Abbey   63–4, 79, 84, 202
Fonthill Splendens house   8
food shortages   41, 147
forgeries   60, 62

Forres   26
Fort Augustus   95
Fort de Joux   85
Fort William   95
Fox-North coalition   12, 14
'Frame Work' Act   129
France   3, 13, 23, 25, 54, 58, 93, 104, 142, 206, 216, 253
  émigré forces   52
  invades Algeria (1830)   240
  peace with Prussia, Batavian Republic, Spain (1795)   56
  republican calendar (1793–1805)   48
  restored to 1790 borders (1815)   150
  restored to 1792 boundaries (1814)   142
  royal domain   33
France: Convention (legislature, 1792)   43
Freetown (Sierra Leone)   37
French Constitution (1791)   39
French language   22, 215
French Navy   103, 229
French Republic   39, 43
French Revolution   vi, **31–59**, 141, 163, 227
  (1789)   **31–3**
  (1790)   34–6
  (1791)   37–40
  (1792)   41–5
  (1793)   45–9
  (1794)   50, 52–4
  (1795)   57–9
French Revolutionary War (1792–1802)   **42–90**
  (1792)   42
  (1793)   45, 47
  (1794)   52
  (1795)   56, 57, 58, 60
  (1796)   61–2, 64
  (1797)   65–8
  (1798)   72–4, 76
  (1799)   76–80
  (1800)   83

(1801) 85–7
(1802) 90
see also Napoleonic Wars
French Romanticism vi
  Hugo's manifesto (1827) 230
Fribourg 156
Friedland (1807) 110
Friends of Peace and Reform 50
Frome St Quintin 9
Fulham: Brandenburg House 8
funerals 68, 98, 174, 234, 239, 252

'gagging acts' 59, 61
Galashiels: Abbotsford 132, 149,
  164, 173, 181, 189–90, 207, 219,
  232, 245–6, 252
Galashiels: Abbotsford (Chiefswood
  cottage) 237
Gallow Hill (Yorkshire) 88, 89
Galloway 46
galvanism 83, 86
gardens and gardening 29, 82, 193,
  222, 235
Gas Light and Coke Company 139
gas lighting 109, 139, 164, 209
Gateshead (1812 disaster) 132
Geneva 11, 93, 181, 237
Geneva: Sécheron (Hotel
  Angleterre) 153
Genoa 181, 201, 202, 205, 207, 233
geology and geologists 101, 244, 246
German language 195, 220, 254
Germany vi, 4, 42, 51, 96, 143,
  235, 245, 253
Ghent 146, 153
Giants' Causeway 143
Gibraltar 98, 119, 126, 240
Gight 26
Girondins 48
Glasgow 87, 95, 142, 163, 185, 218
Glasgow: Andersonian Institute 200
Glasgow Philosophical Society 93
Glasgow University 225
Glencoe 95, 96, 142
Glorious First of June (1794) 52
Gloucester 52

Godmersham (Kent) 114
Gordon riots 4
Goslar 75, 76
Gosport (vessel) 106
Gothenburg 57
Göttingen 77, 78, 223
Gower peninsula 204
Gran Colombia, Republic of 180
Granada: Alhambra 221
Grand Tour 4, 127, 240
Grande Chartreuse 35
Grasmere 82, 84, 87–8, 90–1, 97,
  111–12, 117, 122
Grasmere: Allan Bank 114, 115, 118
Grasmere: Dove Cottage 80, 92,
  96, 115
Grasmere: Rectory 126
Grasmere: Rydal Mount 137, 144,
  172, 217, 237, 241
Grasmere Volunteers 96
Great Casterton 184
Great Glemham 44
Great Glen 95
Great Hampden: John Hampden's
  monument 165
Great Terror (France, 1794) 52, 53
Greece 70, 107, 119, 163, 206–7,
  210, 218, 222, 225, 230, 240, 251
Greece: National Assembly 194
Greece (ancient) 33–4
Greek language 21, 190
Greek Revolution/War of
  Independence 192, 229, 249
Greenock 143, 149
Greenock Burns Club 88
Grenoble 12
grooved rolling process (Cort) 12
Guernsey 238
guillotine 48, 52
Gwato 209

Habeas Corpus (suspensions)
  (1794–5) 52
  (1798–1800) 72
  (1817–18) 160
Haiti 39, 85, 220

Halifax 50
Halifax (Nova Scotia) 98
Hamburg 17, 26, 57, 75, 77–8, 117, 229, 247
Hampshire 11, 13, 27, 81, 87, 102, 118
Hampton Court 232
Handsworth 119
Handsworth: Soho Manufactory 33
Handsworth: St Mary's Church 180
Harris 143
Harrow School 87, 96, 102, 251
Hartz Mountains 78
Harvard University 166
Harvieston 27
Hastings 142, 233
Hawkshead Grammar School 27
Haworth Parsonage 186, 214
Hebrew 166, 234–5
Hebrides 20
Heidelberg 103, 120
Helpston (Northamptonshire) 46, 145, 212
Helvellyn 103
Helvetic Republic 72
Henley 15
Hercules (vessel) 207
Hexham 25
hieroglyphs (Egyptian) 202
Hindon 61
Hispaniola 85
history 73, 88
HMS *Barham* 247
HMS *Beagle* 248, 249
HMS *Bellerophon* 148
HMS *Bounty* 31
HMS *Northumberland* 148
HMS *Venerable* 114
HMS *Victory* 94
Holkham 29
Holy Roman Empire 42, **107**
Holyhead 218
Hondschoote (1793) 47
Horsemonger Lane 130
Horsham: Field House 43
Hotwells 75

House of Commons 9, 19, 24, 31, 79, 183, 217, 244, 246, 251–2
House of Lords 14, 117, 129, 131, 137, 188, 217, 244, 246, 250
Hoxton asylum 60
Hucknell Torkard (Nottinghamshire) 213
Hudson River 111
human life: 'large Mansion of Many Apartments' (Keats) 171
Hussars (10th) 52

Île de France 195
illuminated books 30
illustrations 35, 45, 63, 180, 195, 206, 225
Immortal Dinner (1817) 167
impeachment 24, 25
imprisonment 49, 55, 76, 78, 122, 130–1, 133, 145, 180, 189–90
  see also prisons
India 32, 252
Indiana 215
inheritance 157, 212
insanity 30, 63, 126, 145
Institute of Elocution 88
Institution for Encouragement of Fine Arts 209
Institution of Civil Engineers 168
insurrection/rebellion 31–2, 51, 114, 158, 163, 166
Inverness 26, 142
Investigator (ship) 85
Iona 123, 143, 172, 245
Ireland 23, 28, 48, 60, 64, 71, 81, 85, 125, 172, 231, 238, 245, 253
Irish Parliament 83
Irish rebellion (1798) 73–4
Irish Sea 95
iron 12, 89, 110, 154
Ironbridge (Shropshire) 5
Isle of Man 233
Isle of May 143
Isle of Wight 11, 46, 109, 161, 179

Italy 9, 25, 85, 110, 120, 124, 143–4, 170, **179–80**, 188–9, 210, **215–16**, 219, **222–4**
art transferred to Louvre 90
Ithaca 208
'ivory' (Austen) 158

Jamaica 22, 151, 171, 248
Java 161
Jedburgh 25
Jena (1806) 107
Jersey 142
Jerusalem 240
journals/diaries viii, 20, 70, 82, 101, 104, 117, 125–6, 144, 155–6, 188, 191, 196, 203, 208, 213–15, 219, 224, 233, 239, 248, 251, 254–6
July Revolution (1830) 237, 241, 252
Juvenile Library (M.J. Godwin) 102, 114
juvenilia 10, 27, 46, 226

Kashmir 178
Kassel: Hoftheater 208
Kegworth (Leicestershire) 132
Kelso 14, 25, 71
Kendal 93, 97, 107, 170
Kenilworth 231
Kent 11, 87, 102, 114, 127, 219, 241, 251
Kent's Bank (Lancashire) 217
Keswick 84, 88–9, 92–3, 97, 103, 112, 117, 122, 129, 138
Keswick: Chestnut Cottage 128
Keswick: Crosthwaite 238
Keswick: Greta Hall 83, 96, 108, 128
Keswick: Windy Brow 50
Kettering 44
Kiel 75
Kilkenny 115
Killala (County Mayo) 74
Killarney 218
King's College, London 232, 233, 236

Kingston-upon-Hull 4, 57
Kinross 26
Kirkcaldy 143
Kirkdale Cavern (Yorkshire) 204
Knole 117
Koblenz 165
Königsberg 98

La Côte-Saint-André 97
La Mira 162, 163, 166, 181
La Spezia 195, 198
Ladakh 178
Lake Como 216
Lake District 50, 51, 80, 82, 92, 95, 107, 171, 186, 199
Lake Garda 157
Lake Geneva (Léman) 153, 154, 224
Lake Windermere 218
Lanark 142
Lancashire 217
land and landowners 33, 43, 215, 220
landscape prints 253
Latin language 21, 22
Lausanne 22, 26, 65, 154, 156, 205
Le Havre 44, 51
Le Roncole 138
Leatherhead (Surrey) 37
Lechlade 149
lectures 13, 48, 55–7, 59, 61–2, 86, 88–9, 91, 97, 101, 108, 111, 113, 128–9, 131–5, 138, 141, 152, 168–9, 171, 174–5, 182, 194, 200, 217, 230, 234
legacies 55, 225–6
Leicestershire 108, 132, 234
Leipzig 19, 88, 128, 137
Leipzig (1813) 138
Lerici 199, 201
letters viii, 5, 6, 7, 21, 35, 37, 40, 54, 57, 59, 64, 71, 81, 85, 90, 93, 109, 111, 122, 130, 136, 148, 158, 173–4, 176–7, 187, 192, 202, 208–9, 213, 219, 235, 254–5
libel 125
see also seditious libel

libretti 171, 221
Lichfield 6, 110, 117
Light Dragoons (15th) 49
lighthouses 143
Ligny (1815) 148
Lille 64
Limerick 218
Lincoln Gaol 125
Lincolnshire 119
Linlithgow 144
Lisbon 20, 112, 117, 118
Literary Club 8
Literary and Philosophical Societies
  Liverpool 129
  Manchester 6, 96–7
  Newcastle 45
  Sheffield 203
Littlehampton (Sussex) 164
Liverpool 47, 82, 97, 116, 129, 147, 149, 171, 175, 241, 245
Liverpool: Lyceum 103–4
Liverpool: Wavertree 234
Liverpool and Manchester Railway 238, 242
Livorno 106, 171, 178, 185, 187, 195, 200–1, 207, 233
Llangynhafal (Denbighshire): Plas-yn-Llan 37, 47
Llanthony 113, 142
loans 209
Loch Lomond 25, 87, 163, 200
Locomotion No. 1 (Stephenson) 219
locomotives (steam-driven) 88–9, 238
Lodi (1796) 61, 62
Loire 224
London 3, 7, 9, 10, 16, 21–2, 25, 29, 33, 37, 46, 50–3, 59, 62–3, 69, 74, 76–8, 89, 93, 97, 100–1, 106–9, 112, 117, 122, 124–5, 127, 138–9, 143–7, 149, 154, 158, 160, 166–7, 170, 176, 178, 180, 183, 190, 193–4, 200, 203, 214, 218, 226–7, 229, 231, 233, 237–8, 247
London: Adelphi 184
London: Albany 141
London: Albemarle Street 77, 112, 212
London: Almack Assembly Rooms 211
London: American Legation 221
London: Argyll Rooms 213
London: Barnet 24
London: Battersea Fields 236
London: Bedford Place 88
London: Bennet Street 135
London: Berkeley Square 66
London: Berners Street 130
London: Bishopsgate 98
London: Bond Street 56
London: Bread Street (St Mildred's Church) 158
London: Broad Street 118
London: Brompton (16 Michael's Place) 114
London: Brunswick Square 208
London: Buckingham Palace 220
London: Buckingham Street 80
London: Bunhill Fields 228
London: Burlington House 111, 142
London: Carlton House 60, 129, 150, 153
London: Cato Street (1820) 184
London: Chalk Farm 191
London: Cheapside 157
London: Chelsea 123
London: Chelsea (Hans Place) 149
London: City of London 81
London: City of London Tavern 164
London: Compton Street 48
London: Cooke's Hotel 136
London: Covent Garden theatre 3, 5, 7, 12, 15, 20, 24, 37, 40–1, 49, 55, 57, 69, 75, 77, 88–9, 93–94, 100–1, 103, 108, 126, 133, 150, 152, 156, 162, 169, 179, 182, 184, 186, 191, 193, 199, 205, 209, 221–2, 230
  destroyed by fire (1808) 115
  gas lighting (1817) 164
  reopening and 'Old Price' rioting (1809) 119

Subject Index 325

London: Covent Garden, Robins's Rooms 18
London: Dorant's Hotel, Albemarle Street 112
London: Dover Street (Batt's Hotel) 134
London: Drury Lane theatre vi, 3, 11, 14, 18, 20, 24, 28, 34, 51, 54, 56, 61–2, 65, 69, 78, 82, 84, 86–7, 108–10, 116, 121, 135, 140, 142, 146, 151–3, 155, 161, 174, 179, 184, 192, 213, 217, 248, 252
  destroyed by fire (1809) 117; re-opening (1812) 134
  gas lighting (1817) 164
  management sub-committee 147
  old theatre (demolished 1791) 50; new theatre (1794–1809) 50
London: Duchess Street 80
London: East India House 177
London: 'Eisteddfod or meeting of Welsh Bards' (1822) 200
London: Exeter Street (Bell tavern) 41
London: Fleet Street 74, 123, 128
London: Fountain Court 228
London: Freemasons' Tavern 162
London: George Street 77, 230
London: Gower Place 217
London: Gray's Inn 66
London: Great Coram Street 129
London: Grosvenor Place 177
London: Guildhall 167, 251
London: Guy's Hospital 149
London: Hackney 15
London: Hammersmith 99, 124
London: Hampstead 17, 23, 132, 171, 174
London: Hampstead (Keats House) 174
London: Hampstead (Vale of Health) 159
London: Hampstead (Well Walk) 161
London: Hampstead (Wentworth Place) 174, 177, 181, 187
London: Hampstead Heath 189

London: Hampton Court 12
London: Hanover Square 213
London: Hanover Square (St George's) 204
London: Hans Place, Chelsea 92
London: Harley Street (Turner's gallery) 99
London: Harrow 229
  see also Harrow School
London: Haymarket Theatre 4, 8, 16, 17, 26, 88, 245
London: Highgate 166, 196, 209, 236
London: Highgate (Moreton House) 153
London: Holland House 138, 139
London: Holles Street 28
London: Isle of Dogs (West India Docks) 81
London: Isleworth 99
London: Islington 15, 208
London: Islington (Copenhagen Fields) 58
London: Islington (Spa Fields) 157, 158
London: Jermyn Street (Batt's Hotel) 117
London: Kensington 195
London: Kensington Palace 177
London: Kentish Town (Bartholomew Place) 213
London: Kentish Town (Wesleyan Place) 186
London: King Street 88, 132
London: King's Theatre 18, 105, 126, 161–2, 170, 175, 183, 200, 209, 243–5, 250
London: Lambeth (Hercules Buildings) 36
London: Lambeth Palace 34
London: Lancaster Place 219
London: Leicester Place: New Sans Souci Theatre 64
London: Leicester Square 5–6
London: Lewis's Hotel 133
London: Lincoln's Inn Fields 63, 88

Subject Index

London: Lyceum 110, 113, 127
   gas lighting (1817) 164
London: Lyceum (English Opera
   House) 179, 207, 213
London: Marylebone 117
London: Mortimer Terrace 187
London: Newgate 4, 53, 122, 131,
   183–4
London: Old Bailey 54
London: Old St Pancras
   churchyard 68
London: Olympic Theatre 243
London: Oxford Terrace 235
London: Paddington (Park Cottage)
   233, 241
London: Paddington (St Mary's)
   219, 245
London: Pall Mall 212
   Christies 78
   Milton Gallery 34, 78
   National Gallery 212
   Schomberg House 16
   Shakespeare Gallery 23, 34
   street gas lighting 109
London: Park Lane 111
London: Pentonville (St James'
   Chapel) 234
London: Philharmonic
   Society 250
London: Piccadilly 104
London: Piccadilly (Egyptian
   Hall) 151, 180, 185, 193
London: Piccadilly Terrace 146
London: Pimlico 204
London: Poland Street 126
London: Portman Square
   230, 237
London: Pugilistic Club 56
London: Queen Anne Street
   (Turner's gallery) 99
London: Queen Square 253
London: Queen Square Place 251
London: Regent Street 135
London: Regent's Park 135, 232
London: Richmond: King's
   Theatre 252

London: Rotherhithe-Wapping
   tunnel 216
London: Royal Coburg
   Theatre 186, 207
London: Sadler's Wells 32, 108
London: St Pancras Church 179
London: Sans Souci Theatre, The
   Strand 64
London: Silver Street, off Fleet
   Street 74
London: Skinner Street 102, 133
London: Soho 34, 242
London: Somers Town 68
London: Somerset Street 241, 252
London: South Molton Street 96
London: South Sea House 189
London: Southampton
   Buildings 188
London: Southwark: St George's
   Fields 57
London: Southwark (Dean
   Street) 157
London: Southwark (St Thomas's
   Street) 149
London: Spring Gardens 92
London: St Andrew's Holborn 114
London: St James's Place 94
London: St James's Square 169
London: St James's Street 128
   Reddish's Hotel 116
London: St Katharine's Docks 222
London: St Mary Moorfields 223
London: St Pancras graveyard 225
London: St Paul's Cathedral 17,
   103–4, 110, 190, 217, 239
London: Stoke Newington (Manor
   House School) 149
London: Strand 64, 197, 201
London: Strand (Crown and Anchor
   tavern) 168, 174–5
London: Tower of London 51,
   53, 232
London: Trafalgar Square 212
London: Twickenham 112
London: Vauxhall Bridge 154
London: Wapping 216

London: Waterloo Bridge 162, 250
London: Westminster (College Street) 181
London: Westminster Abbey 61, 155, 246
London: Westminster Bridge 139
London: Westminster Hall 28
London: Wigley's Great Room 92
London: Windmill Street 17
London Corresponding Society 41, 42, 44, 48, 51, 57, 58, 79
London Greek Committee 205, 206, 209
London Institution for Promotion of Literature 105
London Philosophical Society 128, 168–9
London Society for Abolishing Slavery 204
London Stock Exchange 86
London University (University College) 216, 221, 233, 234
Loughall (Armagh) 58
Louisiana Purchase (1803) 94
Louvain 153
Low Countries 144, 164, 206, 219, 223, 233, 242
Lowood school (*Jane Eyre*) 214
Lübeck 75
Lucca 4, 188, 191, 205
Lunar Society of Birmingham 6, 256
Lyme Regis 87, 209
Lynmouth (Devon) 132
Lyon 54, 170, 179, 207

Mâcon 36, 179
Madrid 113, 114, 115, 133, 221
Maentwrog (Merionethshire) 121
Maine: Bowdoin College 223
Maldon 171
Malta 73, 98–100, 103, 119, 126, 189, 220, 240, 247
Mamelukes 74
Manchester 6, 19, 96–7, 217, 234, 241
Manchester: St Peter's Field 160, 180

Manchester: Theatre Royal 213
Manchester Constitutional Society 44
Manchester Mechanics' Institute 211
Maniots 247
manned flight 14
Mannheim 8, 15
Marathon 121
Marengo (1800) 83
Margate 156, 161
Market Harborough 27
Marlow 156, 164
Marlow: West Street (Albion House) 160–2, 166
marriage 15, 112, 170
marriage proposals 93, 134, 144
Marseille 251
Marylebone Fields 58
'Masi affair' 199
mass meetings 48, 50, 57, 58, 59, 157, 180, 182, 231
Massa (Italy) 195
Massachusetts 243
Mauchline 15, 22, 28
Mauritius 85
Measham 84
Mecca 11, 165
medicine (profession) 75, 246
Medway River 4
melodrama 93
Melos 186
Melrose 25, 96, 132, 211
Members of Parliament 4, 16, 43, 61, 185, 239
Menai suspension bridge 221
Mendip schools (More) 32
mental breakdown 49, 60, 199, 201, 222, 224
Merionethshire 121
Merthyr Rising (1831) 245
Messina 103
Methodists 15
Metropolitan Police Improvement Act (1829) 237
Meuse 214

328 Subject Index

Mickleham (Surrey) 47, 166
Middle Ages 120
Middle East 107, 122, 165, 251
Middleton Park 134
Midlands 60, 122, 163, 166
Mikhailovskoe 214
Milan 18, 27, 65, 143, 170, 181, 216, 227
  La Scala 157, 229, 248
  Teatro Cannobiana 250
  Teatro Carcano 243, 244
militia 122, 180
miners' safety lamp (Davy) 149, 150
Minerva Press 36, 76
mints (steam-powered) 33
Mirfield 244
Missolonghi 194, 208, **210–11**, 217, 222
Mitchelstown Castle (County Cork) 23
monarchy 32, 43, 159, 211
Mont Blanc: Mer de Glace 155
Mont Cenis 182
Montalègre: Maison Chappuis 154, 155
Montauban 4
Montenero: Villa Valsovano 178
Montevideo 249
Montgolfier hot-air balloon 14
Monticello 215, 223
Montreal 98
Montrose 26
Moravia 190
Morocco 248
Moscow 78, 142, 144, 196
Moscow (1812) 133
Moscow University 247
Moseley 63
Moselle 214
Mossgiel 25
Mount Parnassus 218
Mount Tambora (Sumbawa) 147
Mull 123, 143, 172, 245, 246
Munich 5, 247, 253
murder 7, 46, 235

music 88, 91, 113–14, 144, 169, 171, 197, 206, 243
Muston (Leicestershire) 9, 104
Mysore 15

Nantes 224
Naples 3, 4, 9, 21, 23, 27, 47, 76, 78, 103, 140, 143, 150, 162, 165, 176, 179, 247
  Albergo della Villa di Londra 189
  Riviera di Chiaia 174
  Teatro del Fondo 158
  Teatro San Carlo 149
Naples Revolution (1820–1) 187
Napoleonic Wars (1803–15) vi, **94–150**
  (1803) 94, 96
  (1804) 98–100
  (1805) 101, **103–4**
  (1806) 105–8
  (1807) 110–12
  (1808) 113–16
  (1809) 116–20
  (1810) 123
  (1811) 125
  (1812) 129, 132–5
  (1813) 136–8
  (1814) 140–2, 144
  (1815) 146, **148**, 149–50
Nashoba (Tennessee) 220, 229, 246
National Assembly (France) 31
National Constituent Assembly (France, 1789) 31–4
National Convention (France, 1792–5) 43, 44, 52, 59
'National Convention' (UK, 1794) 51
National Guard (France) 32
Nauplion 225, 246
Navarino (1827) 229
Navarre 27
'Negative Capability' 167
Nepal 133, 152
Nether Stowey (Somerset) 53, 62, 64, 66–8, 71, 73, 78–9, 82, 89, 110

Netherlands 4, 51, 45, 79, 242, 253
  see also Low Countries
Neuilly-sur-Seine 44
New Forest 11, 109
New Harmony (Indiana) 215
New Jersey 32
New Lanark 81
New Shoreham 43
New York 12, 22, 50, 74, 76, 98,
  118, 149, 162, 190, 197, 204,
  223, 232, 237, 244, 246, 250
Newark 108, 111
Newcastle 25, 45, 149
Newington Butts (Surrey) 39
Newington Green 15, 21
Newmarket: Six Mile Bottom 137,
  141, 142, 144, 145, 146, 149
newspapers/press 16, 29, 30, 40, 84,
  116, 130, 140, 159, 182, 216, 248
Newstead Abbey 73, 97, 114, 115,
  117, 127–8, 132, 140, 143–4, **167**
Niagara Falls 98, 246
Nice 233
Nicopolis 119
Niger River 57, 101, 209
Nijmegen 247
Nile 169
Nordhausen 76
Nore mutiny (1797) 66
Norfolk 62, 82
Norfolk (Virginia) 96
Normandy 163, 195, 224, 238
North Sea 95
Northamptonshire 46
Northern Department 8
Northumberland 39, 135, 229
Northumberland
  (Pennsylvania) 50, 97
Norwich 9, 29, 36, 52, 90, 110
Nottingham 92, 247
Nottinghamshire 129, 213
Nubia 191
Nuneaton 182

Oban 172
Odense 102
odes 9, 22, 30, 32, 64, 72, 74, 83,
  90, 92, 96, 98, 106–7, 130, 141,
  151, 161, 177–9, 181, 186–9,
  205, 216, 235
Odessa 186
oil paintings 62, 78, 222, 228, 245
'Old Price' rioting 119
Old Windsor 84
Oneida Nation 98
opium 100, 144, 153
Oporto (1809) 117
Orange Order 58
Orange Society 58
Orkney 143
Orléans 40, 42, 44, 224
Ostend 35, 144, 146, 153
Ottery St Mary 72
Ottoman Empire 76, 102, 114, 192,
  198–9, 222, 229
Oxford 13, 52, 74, 93, 94, 149, 154,
  192, 227
  University Church of St Mary 231
Oxford Canal (to Coventry, 1790) 33
Oxford University 18, 38, 43,
  221, 235
  Balliol College 42
  Christ Church 34
  Magdalen Hall 164
  Merton College 147
  Oriel College 182, 199, 227
  Trinity College 35
  University College 126
  Worcester College 99
oxygen 36

Paddington 8
Padua 9, 157, 173
Paestum 3, 174, 247
Paisley 25
Palermo 76
Palgrave (Suffolk) 7
Palmyra 122, 131
pamphlets 54, 130, 167
Panama 180
Panopticon (Bentham) 47
'Pantisocracy' 52, 53, 59

Subject Index

pantomime 108
Papal States 190, 194
parallel motion mechanism (Watt, 1784) 16
Parham (Suffolk) 44
Paris vi, 4, 6, 7, 9, 12, 19, 25, 27, 30–4, 39–41, 44, 48, 51, 60, 78–9, 82, 86, 88, 92–3, 107, 110, 114, 124, 127, 139, 142–3, 146, 148–50, 153–4, 163, 177, 181, 183–5, 188–90, 195, 201–2, 207, 210–15, 224, 232–5, 239, 241, 245–6
  royalist rising (1795) 58
  September massacres (1792) 43
  surrender to allied forces (1814) 141
Paris: *Champ de Mars* 35
Paris: *Comédie Française* 252
Paris: *Fête de la Fédération* (1790) 35
Paris: *Galerie Le Brun* 222
Paris: Legislative Assembly 40, 43
Paris: *Louvre* 90, 186, 230
Paris: *Notre Dame* cathedral 100
Paris: *Opéra* 16, 234, 237, 247
Paris: *Panthéon* 37, 38, 53
Paris: *Salle Pleyel* 249
Paris: *Salon* 31, 100, 180, 214, 229, 240–1
Paris: *Théâtre de la Porte Saint-Martin* 248
Paris: *Théâtre de l'Odéon* 17, 228, 231, 243
Paris: *Théâtre Feydeau* 66
Paris: *Théâtre Italien* 211
Paris: *Théâtre Porte Saint-Martin* 223
Paris: *Théâtre-Français* 236, 239
Paris: Tuileries palace 32
Paris *Conservatoire (École Royale de Musique et de Déclamation)* 199, 243
parliamentary reporters 134
parliaments 34, 58, 85, 94, 137
  see also House of Lords
parody 71, 110, 130, 134, 182, 237

Particular Baptist Society 44
Pas-de-Calais 43
patents 16, 19
patrons and patronage 6, 13, 23, 83, 106, 136, 139, 172, 228
Peace of Amiens (1802) 45, 90
Peace of Versailles (1783) 13
Peak District 63
Peele Castle 106
Peking 47
Peloponnese 119, 123, 229
pen-names/pseudonyms 30, 40, 61, 70–2, 92–3, 104, 124, 141, 145–6, 158, 163, 165–6, 168, 170, 172, 178, 183, 189, 191, 193, 196–202, 206–9, 216, 219, 227
Pen-y-Darren ironworks 89
Pennsylvania 20, 52, 117
Penrith 84, 93, 117
Pentrich 166
Penzance 75
periodic table 97
Perth 26, 47, 142, 207
Peru 180
Pesaro 41
'Peterloo' massacre (1819) vii, 180
petitions 137, 160, 252
Petworth 95
Petworth House 228, 253
Philadelphia 19, 22, 34, 50, 98, 121, 190, 215, 219, 221, 223, 245–6, 250
  Chestnut Street Theatre (first to use gas lighting, 1816) 164
Physical Society of Guy's Hospital 45
piano music 28, 50, 128, 194, 240
Pickering manuscript poems 112
pirated editions 125, 235
Pisa 106, 142, 171, 181, 188–203, 227, 233
  Bagni di San Giuliano (Casa Prinni) 188
  Casa Aulla 192
  Casa Frassi 184

Palazzi di Chiesa 196
Palazzo Galetti 189
Palazzo Lanfranchi 196, 201
Pizzo (Calabria) 149
plagiarism 124
Plesiosaurus fossil 209
Plymouth 98, 148
poetry 138
  definition (Wordsworth, 1800) 85
poets laureate 18, 138
Poland 150, 245
policing 197, 237, 245
Polish Uprising (1830–1) 243
politics and politicians 88, 94, 130
Pompeii 3, 174, 179, 247
Pontcysyllte aqueduct 104
Portland (Maine) 109
Portland Vase 34
Portpatrick 172
portraits 95, 99, 103, 141, 147, 185, 193, 253
Portsmouth 98, 129, 155, 189, 247
Portugal 24, 59, 82, 112, 116, 202
poverty 89, 93, 164
power loom (Cartwright) 19
Prague: National Theatre 27, 39
press-gangs 53, 63
Prevesa 119
printers 30, 101
prisoners and prisons 47, 53, 85, 90
  see also imprisonment
private printings 102, 139
Privy Council 31
Protestants 58
Provence 233
Prussia 22, 43, 106, 111, 136, 138, 141, 148, 197
Pterodactyl fossil 209
publication at author's expense 4, 56, 125, 190, 234
  see also sales and sales figures
publication by subscription 116
puddling furnace (Cort) 12
pyramid of Khefren (Khafre) 169
Pyrenees 241

Quakers 219
Quatre-Bras (1815) 148
Quebec 98
Quiberon Bay 52

radicals 51, 79, 89, 185, 210, 246
Radnorshire 131
railways 219, 238, 242
Rainhill 238
Ramesseum 155
Ramsgate 180, 196
Ratzeburg 75
Ravenna 176, 178, 180, 183, 189, 190–1, 195–6
Reading 19, 149
reform (parliamentary/constitutional) 19, 89, 158, 180, 244
Reform Act (1832) vi, 251
Reform Bill
  First (1831) 244
  Second (1831) 246
  Third (1831–2) 248, 250–1
Regency 30, **125**, 126
relief engraving 24
religion 29, 164, 167, 209
republicanism and republicans 44, 78, 120, 159
Retreat from Moscow (1812) 134, 135
reviews 111, 112, 134, 144, 162, 169, 173, 176–7, 185, 187, 190, 192, 224, 231–2, 238, 246, 252
Revolutionary Tribunal (Paris, 1793–5) 45
Rhayader (Radnorshire): Nantgwyllt 131
Rhayader: Cwm Elan estate 131
Rhine 143–4, 153, 165, 214, 219
Rhineland 164, 233, 251
Riga 14, 17, 30
riots and rioting 4, 39, 53, 119, 146, 158, 241, 245, 247
Rivoli (1796) 61
Rob Roy's Cave 163
Rocket (Stephenson) 238
Rochdale 127

Rochefort 148
Rokeby (Northumberland) 135
Romagna 194
Roman Catholic Claims Bill (1812) 131
Roman Catholic Relief Act (1829) 236
Romanticism vi, 120, 175
Rome 3, 4, 9, 17, 23, 27, 28, 36, 105, 107, 143–4, 162, 165, 173–4, 178–9, 185, 215, 247
   Accademia Veneziana 182
   Corso (Palazzo Verospi) 176
   Eastlake's house (Turner's studio, 1828) 233
   Palazzo Trulli 233
   Piazza di Spagna 161, 190
   Protestant Cemetery 178, 191, 201
   Teatro Argentina 151
   Via Sistina 176
Rosetta Stone 91
Rotherham: Aston Hall 138
Rotterdam 143, 165
Rouen 39, 155, 196
Royal Academy vi, 5, 9, 16, 19, 21, 34, 40–1, 56, 62, 66, 72, 78, 82, 87, 89, 103, 110, 112, 125–6, 129, 131, 137, 147–8, 161–2, 177, 185, 193–4, 200–1, 206, 212, 217, 226, 228, 232, 236, 239–40, 245, 250
Royal Academy Schools 33, 77
Royal Amphitheatre 32
Royal Astronomical Society 185
Royal Circus 32
Royal College of Surgeons 152, 157
Royal Danish Academy 55
Royal Edinburgh Volunteer Light Dragoons 65
Royal Institution of Great Britain 77, 86, 89, 101, 113, 131, 139, 194, 230
Royal Manchester Institution 209
Royal Navy 53, 65, 68, 86, 103–4, 111–12, 116, 229
   mutinies (1797) 66

Royal Society 84, 109, 150, 187, 221, 230
Royal Society of Edinburgh 14, 190
Royal Society of Literature 194, 211, 217
Rugby School 175, 233
Rügen (island) 87
Russell Institution 129
Russia 58, 64, 76, 79, 86, 91, 103, 106, 111, 131, 138, 141, 197, 243, 247
   Napoleonic invasion (1812) 133, 134, 135
Russian Empire 220

St Asaph: Bronwlfa 120, 133
St Asaph: Rhyllon 234
St Helena 148, 193
St Petersburg 10, 91, 134, 186, 220, 247
Saint-Domingue (Haiti) 39, 85
Saints (Clapham Sect) 45
Salamanca (1812) 133
Salem (Massachusetts) 99
sales and sales figures 100, 113, 122, 140, 142, 151, 153, 165, 167, 183, 200, 212
   see also copyright
Salford: Marple aqueduct 52
Salisbury 127, 187
Salisbury Plain 46, 59
Salona (Amphissa) 120
salons 14, 169
San Lazzaro degli Armeni (island) 157
Sandgate (Kent) 251
Sandleford Priory (Berkshire) 17
Sanskrit 21
Santa Marta 243
Santo Domingo 85
Saragossa (Zaragoza) 80
Sardinia 119
satire 54, 69, 107, 117, 141, 151, 249
Savona 118
Saxe-Coburg-Saalfeld 153, 242
scandal 20, 199, 222

Subject Index

Scandinavia 57
Scarborough: Brompton 92
schools 5, 13, 15, 19, 27, 32, 34, 42, 81, 87, 96, 102, 149, 214, 233, 244
science 105, 246
Scotland 17, 28, 87, **95-6**, 107, 171, 185-6, 197, 211, 230, 241, 245-6
   censuses (1801, 1831) 86
   rising of 1745-6 202
Scottish Highlands 11, 25-6, 44, 95, 142, 164, 202
'Scottish Martyrs' (1794) 49
Scottish Society of Friends of People 48
sculpture 80, 105, 125
Seaham (County Durham) 144, 145
sedition 47, 48, 51, 76, 79, 95, 160, 193
   see also treason
seditious libel 45, 55, 123, 130, 167, 182, 245
Seditious Meetings Act (1795) 59
seditious writings (royal proclamation, 1792) 42
Selkirk 25
Selkirk: Ashestiel 99, 102, 115
Selkirkshire 80, 132
sermons 67, 70
Seville 221
Shaftesbury 68
Shanklin 179, 180
Sheffield 52, 55, 60-1, 88, 203
Sheffield Constitutional Society 50
Shefford (Bedfordshire) 208
Shetland 143
Shoreham (Kent) 219
Shrewsbury 53, 70, 117
Siberia 220
Sicily 23, 34, 99, 119
sieges 151, 194, 207
Sierra Leone Company 37
Simplon Pass 35, 143, 181, 188
Singapore **175**
Sintra 24, 82, 116, 118

Six Acts (1819) 182
Skye 143
slave revolts 39, 248
slavery and slave trade 7, 22, 28, 30-1, 34, 37-8, 57, 175, 204, 220, 251
   France and French colonies 39, 49, 109
smallpox 62, 232
Smethwick: Soho Foundry 61
Smyrna (Izmir) 121, 240
Society for Constitutional Information 3, 33, 44, 51
Society for Missions to Africa and the East 77
Society of Apothecaries 155
Society of Friends 219
Society of United Irishmen 40, 57, 79
Sockburn Farm (County Durham) 78, 79-80
soldiers 60-1, 160
solicitors 43, 167, 226
Somersby (Lincolnshire) 119
Somerset 32, 53, 94
Sompting (Sussex) 224, 228
songs 25, 33, 46, 51, 55, 74, 77, 89, 95, 113-15, 144, 200, 254
sonnets 30, 54, 64, 71, 91, 145, 169, 178, 183, 186, 199, 225, 242
Sounion (Cape Colonna) 121, 124
Southampton 19, 46, 115, 108, 161
Southend 241
Southwell 99, 108
Spain 45, 56, 59, 83, 107, 119, 221, 223
   constitution (1812) 183
   declares war on UK (1796) 64
Spanish Constitutionalists 241
Spanish Empire 180
Spanish fleet 103
Spanish Revolution (1820) 183
Speedwell (ship) 98
Spielberg (fortress) 190
spies 4, 67, 95
Spithead mutiny (1797) 66

334 Subject Index

Srirangapatna 78
Staffa 123, 143, 172, 236, 245
Stafford 4
Staffordshire 106
Stathern 9
statues 100, 186, 245
Stettin 224
Steventon (Hampshire) 13, 87
Stirling 26, 27, 185
Stockholm 42
Stockport 63
Stockton–Darlington railway 219
Stoke Newington 216
Stoke-on-Trent 55
Stonehaven 26
Stratford-upon-Avon 164, 231
Strawberry Hill 13
Stuttgart 180, 250, 253
Suffolk 44, 77
sugar 38, 219
suicide 56, 58, 71, 128, 156, 201
Suliotes 210
Sumatra 175
Sumburgh Head 143
Supreme Being cult (France) 52
surgeons 152, 157, 171, 177
Surinam 39
Surrey 37, 39, 47, 107, 166
Surrey Institution 134, 168, 174, 182
Surrey Theatre 169, 184
Sussex 11, 43, 83, 96, 102, 136, 161, 164, 228
Swansea 140, 156
Swedenborgian New Jerusalem Church 31
Sweffling 44
Swing riots 241, 245
Switzerland 35, 72, 90, 142–3, 155, 157, 187, 222–4
Sydney Cove 28
syllabuses 20, 54
symphonies 23, 29, 36, 38, 49, 102, 116, 203, 206, 228, 236, 243
Syracuse (Sicily) 99, 103
Syracuse (USA) 98
Syria 122, 191

Tagenrog 220
Tahiti 31
Talavera (1809) 119
Tarbes 127
Tarbolton: St David's Lodge 7
Tarbolton Bachelors' Club 5
Teignmouth (Devon) 169
tempera paintings 118
Temple prison 43
Tennessee 220
Tennis Court Oath 31
Tepelene 119
Terni 161
Test and Corporation Acts (repealed, 1828) 232
Thames 131, 149, 154, 183
Thames-Severn Canal 33
The Hague 51, 57
Third Estate 31
Thuringia 10
Tibet 133
Tierra del Fuego 249
Tilford (Surrey) 107
Timbuctoo 209, 237
Timor 31
Tintern Abbey 47, 74
Tolentino 149–50
Tønsberg 57
Tories 117, 131, 170, 172
Torres Vedras (1810) 123
Tory press 130
Toulon 47
Tours (France) 78, 142
Trafalgar (1805) **103–4**
translations 8, 11, 13, 15, 17, 21–2, 26–7, 29–30, 34, 36, 38–40, 43, 50–1, 60, 62, 65–6, 68, 70–1, 75–6, 82, 86, 90, 93, 95, 98, 107, 110, 116, 120, 135, 139, 143, 145, 154, 162, 165–6, 171, 181, 184, 186, 194–5, 198, 203, 205, 210, 212, 217, 220, 225, 227, 239, 247, 253
transportation 4, 47, 49, 186, 241
treason and high treason 4, 53–4, 79, 94, 158, 184
see also sedition

Treasonable Practices Act (1795) 59
Treaties of Tilsit (1807) 111
Treaty of Alexandria (1801) 91
Treaty of Campo-Formio (1797) 68
Treaty of Fontainebleau (1814) 141
Treaty of Ghent (1814) 145
Treaty of Mangalore (1784) 15
Treaty of Paris (1814) 142
Treaty of Paris (1815) 150
Treaty of Pressburg (1805) 104
Treaty of The Hague (1795) 57
Tremadoc: Tanyrallt 136
Tremeirchion 193
Trier 171
Trieste 242–3
Trossachs 95, 200
Trowbridge 140, 249
Troy 121
Troyes 142
tuberculosis 121, 169, 184, 234
Tübingen 70, 116, 120, 124, 250
Tunbridge Wells 117
Turin 207
Turkey 137, 139
'Two Bills' (1795) 58–9
typhus 13, 199, 214

Ullswater 104
Unitarianism and Unitarians 5, 67, 70, 101, 219, 242
United Britons 94
United Irishmen 94
United Kingdom vi, 11, 23, 58, 64, 76, 79, 85, 96, 103, 106, 108, 111, 198, 223, 236, 250
 cholera (1831–3) 247
 French declaration of war (1793) 45
 war with USA (1812–14) 132, 144, 145
United Kingdom: Board of Agriculture 47, 133
United States 11, 17, 19, 31, 49–50, 66, 86, 94, 117, 135, 144–5, 160, 171, 173, 178, 190, 200, 214–16, 236, 255
 declares war on UK (1812) 132

US Army 227
US Bill of Rights (ratified, 1791) 26
US Congress 30
US Constitution 26
US Navy 112
University of Göttingen 76, 218
University of Jena 92
University of Virginia 216, 221
University of Würzburg 218, 246
Uranus 6

vaccination 62
Valence (France) 77
Valenciennes 39
Valley of Kings (Egypt) 165
Valmy (1792) 43
Vendéen rebels 48
Venetian Republic 67
Venezuela 180
Venice 4, 34, 67, 143, 158, 161–4, 166, 168, 170–3, 181, 189, 215, 222, 247
 Grand Canal 172
 Palazzo Mocenigo 171, 172
 Piazza San Marco 157
 Teatro La Fenice 135, 240
 Teatro San Benedetto 135–6
Venus (goddess) 100
Verona 157
Versailles 14, 31, 32, 155, 201, 207
Vesuvius 139, 179
Vevey 154, 156, 216
Vicenza 157
Vienna 23, 28, 29, 72, 87, 118, 128, 185, 194, 217, 226, 234, 240
 Kärntnertortheater 206
 Theater an der Burg 10, 21, 33, 86, 196
 Theater an der Wien 102, 104, 108, 121
 Theater auf der Wieden 40
Villa Diodati 155–6
Vimeiro (1808) 115
Vinegar Hill (1798) 73
violin concertos 108, 124
Virginia 98

visions 24, 49, 127, 182, 184, 193, 195, 203, 213, 233
Vitoria (1813) 137
Vostitza 120

Wagram (1809) 118
Walcheren Expedition (1809) 125
Wales 34, 58, 93, 122, 137, 195, 215, 247
Wales: North 11, 214, 246
walks and walking tours 52, 69, 80, 92, 107, 120, 132, **171–2**, 188, 198, 200
War of American Independence (1775–83) 3, 6, 11, 13, 14
War Office 101
Warkworth 25
Warsaw 240
Warwick 193
Warwick Castle 231
Washington DC (1814) 98, 144, 215, 246
Watchet 69
watercolours 78, 118, 225
Waterloo (1815) vii, **148**, 187, 200
Weimar 23, 26, 43, 72, 83, 92, 97, 98, 113, 246, 249
Wellington House Academy 210
Welsh language 140
West Allington (Lincolnshire) 9
West Indies 38
West Point 227
Westbury-on-Trym 70
Westminster School 34, 42
Westmorland 11, 136, 170
Whigs 117, 129, 130
White Terror (France, 1794–5) 54
Whitehaven 49, 50
Whitton Park 154

Whitwick (Leicestershire) 234
Wickham (Hampshire) 81
Wiltshire 114, 145, 146
Winchester 162, 180
Winchester: College Street 163
Winchester Cathedral 81, 163
Winchester College 81
Winchilsea: George Finch-Hatton, Earl of 236
Windsor 149, 213, 219, 224
Winterslow (Wiltshire) 114, 119
women 19, 41, 44, 60, 63, 70–1, 76, 81, 97, 108, 116, 121–2, 140, 191, 218, 221, 230, 235, 238, 244, 251, 254
  enfranchisement 252
woodcuts 197
Woodstock (County Kilkenny) 121
workers 163, 166
Worthing 228
Wrington (Somerset) 32
Wye Valley 32

Yale College 94
Yarmouth 63, 74, 77
Yasnaya Polyana 234
'Year Without Summer' (1816) 147, 155
York 55, 60, 127, 246
Yorkshire 16, 88, 95, 177, 204
Yorktown (1781) 7, 8
young people 55, 230, 235

Zante (Zakynthos) 210
Zea (Keos) 123
Zitsa 119
Zong (British ship) 7
Zoological Society of London 232
Zwickau 122

Printed and bound by CPI Group (UK) Ltd, Croydon, CR0 4YY